Henry Ostrander

The Life of Henry Ostrander

With selected sermons

Henry Ostrander

The Life of Henry Ostrander
With selected sermons

ISBN/EAN: 9783337087173

Printed in Europe, USA, Canada, Australia, Japan

Cover: Foto ©Raphael Reischuk / pixelio.de

More available books at **www.hansebooks.com**

THE LIFE

OF

HENRY OSTRANDER, D. D.

WITH

SELECTED SERMONS.

EDITED BY

W. R. GORDON, S. T. D.

PASTOR OF THE REFORMED CHURCH OF SCHRAALENBERG, N. J.

New York:
BOARD OF PUBLICATION OF THE REFORMED CHURCH
IN AMERICA.
1875.

PRINTED BY

DE BAUN & MORGENTHALER,

64 & 66 JOHN ST., N. Y.

TO

THE CLASSIS OF ULSTER:

AND TO THE

CHURCHES OF CAATSBAN AND SAUGERTIES,

THIS VOLUME,

IN MEMORY

OF A PASTOR WHOSE SERVICES WERE RENDERED AMONG THEM
FOR THE PERIOD OF FIFTY YEARS, IS
RESPECTFULLY DEDICATED.

INTRODUCTION.

"History is the essence of innumerable biographies." Biography is the history of individual experiences, agencies and influences. Aggregations of these, setting forth the gain and loss of human purposes, the success and failure of human projects in skilful arrangement, with circumstantial connections, make up history.

The narrative of any man's life, distinguished for mental vigor, practical efficiency and impressiveness of influence, within the circuit of its expenditure, is always and justly deemed worthy of preservation by every generous thinker, and a matter of interest especially profitable to those engaged in pursuits similar to that which absorbed it. Although it be true that individual experience be idiocratic because the result of experiments in which individual self plays the prominent part, yet there are general principles, historical threads, upon which all experiences are strung, bringing human life to the realization of its happiest issues. Biographical illustrations of these are worthy of faithful record that they may be better understood by all who are disposed to make the most of their own existence.

Many persons of all professions and pursuits, who have been pushed by combining circumstances to the front, in the march of humanity with the lapse of time to higher attainments, have been thought most worthy of honorable mention upon the roll of fame; but without injustice to them, others of less circumstantial prominence may be classed as equally worthy with themselves, who, unmade by circumstances, and devoid of all external incident such as the world admires, in a quiet way have unfolded, wholly from within, resources of intellect, force of reason, brilliancy of talent, influence of opinion, refinement of culture, strength of character and patient perseverance in doing good, throughout the rolling years of a long life spent in the service of God and man.

Biographies of such persons can only be fairly formed out of materials furnished by themselves without intention of becoming known to fame. They rarely leave records of themselves, beyond the mere facts and events of a laborious life, and hardly ever give a clue to the successive states of mind and heart by which their own progress in the formation of character may be clearly traced. In those few instances of exception to this rule, which modest worth prescribes to itself, and where minuteness is most needed by the interested inquirer, such records generally fail, because they grow weak with the advance of the story from early manhood to old age. This evidently is on account of reluctance to record short-comings which might be magnified into positive failures, and experiences liable to be perverted by honest incompetency, into whose hands the luckless manuscripts might fall. Nevertheless these briefs, defective as they may be, are valuable to narrators; for they at least form banks to the channels through which their narratives must flow.

The subject of the following sketch happily left a few notes he deemed worthy of writing, for the information and interest of his immediate family. Among them are some sufficiently copious for the purpose of the present narrator, who, though having no claim upon the partiality that selected him for this service, yielded to the request that he would record, as best he could, the life of one whose excellencies of mind and heart were out-wrought by the Spirit of God into a character that challenges admiration and praise, and to which his pen cannot do adequate justice. These at once came to the surface in the writer's first interview with him, for which he was indebted to the worthy pastor of the Reformed Church at Flatbush, the Rev. Wm. B. Merritt, whose ministry he attended during the last few years of his life. Dr. OSTRANDER, in this and subsequent interviews, unintentionally revealed himself as possessed of all that greatness of mind and goodness of heart spoken of in the various " Resolutions " recited in the sequel and in no instance overwrought.

He left a large number of well digested sermons, fully written, with the exception of verbal brevities, contractions, elisions and ellipses, which it is hardly possible to fail in correctly filling out. From these a selection has been made, as samples of his various lines of thought and of method in presenting the gospel to the hearts and consciences of his auditors. He also left a full series of expository Lectures upon the Heidelburgh Catechism, which exceeds anything that has fallen under the writer's notice on that admirable summary of divine truth. Some of them might have been advantageously presented in this volume, as showing the rare dialectic power of their author; but it was thought best not to break in upon the series, which if properly prepared for the press would make a profitable publication for *the purchasers*.

The exuberance of feeling upon the part of those bearing witness to him in the resolutions aforesaid and in other documents subsequently introduced, with expressions from various quarters that a *memorial* volume of this sort might be furnished, have induced the preparation of this one. It is hoped that it may prove acceptable to the public, especially where Dr. OSTRANDER was best known, and profitable to many souls often stirred by the living voice, now no more heard, of one who was "an old disciple," and "an Israelite indeed, in whom there was no guile."

It becomes the writer to express his thanks to those brethren whose names are mentioned in connection with papers kindly furnished him, and which he found essential to the execution of his task. He regrets the delay of the appearance of this volume, and can only plead the common excuse of "circumstances beyond our control."

LIFE

OF

HENRY OSTRANDER, D. D.

This excellent minister of the gospel was the son of many prayers. He was born at New Marlborough, now the town of Plattekill, March 11, 1781. His great-grandfather was Jan Ostrander, the most distant ancestor of whom any thing definite is known. He probably lived between the years 1664 and 1724. During this period many of the Huguenots of France and Holland, oppressed by the cruel persecutions which followed the revocation of the Edict of Nantes, fled from those countries and settled in America. Among them, it is believed, was Jan Ostrander, who with his family settled in the town of Kingston, N. Y. He had several children, some of whom at various periods removed into the counties of Albany, Rensselaer and Saratoga.

Henry, the grandfather of the late Dr. Ostrander, was born and reared at Kingston, N. Y. In the marriage record of the old Kingston Church, however, he is set down as an inhabitant of Hurley, who married Elizabeth Wambomy of Kingston. This lady, brought up a French Catholic, appears to have accompanied her family and friends of the Huguenot emigration, in the early settlement of this country. She had a brother, Christopher, who lived to a great age in the city of New York, and died in the faith and communion of the Reformed Dutch Church during the collegiate pastorate of Drs. Livingston, Linn, Abeel and Kuypers. She too became a Protestant, and tradition says she was very much noted for her exemplary christian life, and intellectual attainments; that she was familiar with Romish theology, and well educated in other respects. Her conversion was attended with certain remarkable occurrences and experiences, in consequence of which she became exceedingly zealous as a Protestant, and somewhat celebrated in her neighborhood for a profound knowledge of the Scriptures, strong faith, and ardent piety.

Soon after his marriage, Henry Ostrander purchased a farm at Esopus, just at the foot of Hussey's Hill, where the rocks and forest afforded shelter for deer, and not far from Kallicoon Hook, a place noted for wild turkeys, where, in their season, they gathered in great numbers. This game afforded rare sport for the sons of the family, now increased to so respectable a number that their father, having lived on this farm for many years, judged it expedient to enlarge his domain. He accordingly sold out, and soon after, about 1760, purchased the principal part of a patent, known as Marschalm, at Plattekill. This tract, consisting of two thousand acres of excellent land, was afterwards so divided as to make farms of two hundred acres apiece for his sons.

On one of these farms Willhelmus, the father of the subject of this memoir, was settled. He married Sarah, the daughter of Dene Relyea, a French Protestant, who came to this country at an early period. Miss Relyea had been well trained by a mother of Holland extraction, who proved her influence to have been all-controlling over her family of nine sons and one daughter; for they all became obedient to the faith, having been carefully brought up "in the nurture and admonition of the Lord." It is remarkable that so many children in a single family should have reached, the most of them, four score years; and that all of them should have died in the assurance of christian peace and hope. Such is believed to have been the fact, and is so recorded by Henry, who was the sixth son.

This is one out of many instances, illustrative of the faithfulness of God to the holy industry of pious parents uniting prayer, precept and practice in ruling their households. The promises of God are sure, and reliance may be placed upon them to any extent; for this is his command with promise, "Thou shalt keep his statutes and his commandments, that it may go well with thee, and with thy children after thee." "I will pour my spirit upon thy seed, and my blessing upon thine offspring; and they shall spring up as among the grass, as willows by the water courses. One shall say, I am the Lord's; and another shall call himself by the name of Jacob; and another shall subscribe with his hand unto the Lord, and surname himself by the name of Israel."

Unto obedient children God has promised the best of temporal blessings. "Honor thy father and thy mother that it may be well with thee, and that thou mayest live *long upon* the earth." There are indeed many exceptions to this general rule, the causes of which are various, and not easily understood; but they are not numerous enough to invalidate the rule which is amplified into one of the most eloquent Psalms that ever resounded in the Temple service, the last few verses of which declare the purpose of God toward his faithful servant. "Because he hath set his love upon me, therefore will I deliver him; I will set him on high because he hath known my name He shall call upon me, and I will answer him: I will be with him in trouble; I will deliver him, and honor him. With LONG LIFE will I satisfy him, and show him my salvation."

It is quite evident that long life upon the earth, when accompanied with the favor of God, as indicated in this Psalm is, next to eternal life, the best boon of heaven; and this appears to have been the allotment of the members of this numerous family, whose prosperity must be associated with their principles, and whose principles were early implanted by a pious mother's care, which made her nursery the seed-bed of truth for the young soul, no less than the repository of comforts for the bodily wants of infantile years.—O how many can repeat, only with broken utterance, the exclamatory sentences of reflecting filial love, as they issued from the heart of Henry, one of these tenderly and piously reared sons, long after such mothers have been laid beneath their little mounds of earth!

"When I think of my mother, O how many tender and interesting recollections throng my memory! How many associations beset me of a most impressive character! How long the time that would be required to detail the incidents that render the remembrance of her unutterably solemn and tender! *If I forget*—let memory forget its power; let annihilation overtake the remembrance of every scene and every object! What on earth will so vigorously gather up all the affections into an intensity of emotion as the thought of Mother! What look more engaging, what bosom more tender, what hand so soft as hers! Whatever I may omit, let me not fail to mention with melted affection her painful anxieties in regard to her children; her care over me in the infancy of life; her tender forbearance to my guilt and disobedience; her protecting arm in time of danger; her assiduity in providing for me food and raiment; her agony when I was sent away from her embrace to pursue my literary toils. How many wearisome nights and days she spent to make me comfortable during my absence at study; with what exuberant joy she witnessed my return; who could number the prayers she uttered in my behalf! O how ungrateful was I, when her benedictions descended upon my head! O that I could expiate the guilt of my base ingratitude! How now can I be sufficiently penitent for undervaluing her care, her labor, her unfailing kindness? Ought such a son to live, who has been so ungrateful to such a fond and faithful and affectionate mother? One thing consoles me. Her pious tears streaming from her face in time of prayer, her agonizing desires for her own and her family's salvation; and most of all, her utterances in the extremity of her last suffering, when she said to sympathizing friends aching almost with her pain, 'My sufferings are nothing compared to those which Christ endured for the salvation of my soul.'—O what relief and hope and gratitude must not she have felt, when the sorrows of Christ crucified so filled her contemplation and expanded her powers of thought! I trust she died in Jesus, and pray that I may see her clothed in a white robe, having a palm in her hand."

What considerate son is there who, having lost a worthy mother, can withhold his tears upon the perusal of these sentences so well expressing the mournful feelings of a grateful child, as he thinks upon the dear absentee who yet lives and moves before the fond gaze of faithful memory? How seemingly in harmony with the admirable economy of nature, by which not a leaf falls from a tree until its little nursling, the tender bud, is perfected and so protected that it shall be able to withstand the severities of cold and storm, and then, "when the winter is over and gone" shall reproduce the beauty of its mother that had seemed to perish forever! Thus it was with this appreciative son. His young heart, in the *camera obscura* of a holy home, received the image of his future piety and life from the object of a praying mother. Happy the mother who thus leaves early impressions upon her children to ripen into genuine principles of piety, after she has fallen like a leaf from the tree of this mortal life!

Henry was sent to a school in the neighborhood of his home, at the early age of three years. He was an active child, and instinctively alive to a variety of things; and withal only got the credit of being a busy-body inconveniently interested in everything nearest at hand. Perhaps this forms an explanatory reason for his early acquaintance with the school-house; for on the very day of his entrance he was not very agreeably surprised by the application of the rod for thrusting his hands into the water-pail. He ever after kept clear of that indulgence, but his early youthful life was like an overflowing cup receiving more than it can hold, and discharging the surplus all around. His mind being no less active than his body, he made satisfactory improvement in all the branches, then usually taught in the common school where he continued until he had attained his twelfth year, under the tuition of several teachers, all of whose names were remembered, at least by one, long after they were dead.

These teachers followed each other in rapid succession, averaging a little more than a year apiece in that school where Henry was first introduced to the mysteries of the alphabet. Notwithstanding this unhappy frequency of change, he continued to make steady progress. Soon after his entrance, his precocity of intellect was made manifest by efforts to spell before he knew his alphabet. He took to his primer with unusual interest, and became a favorite with one of his teachers, whom he remembered with great affection, as having deepened the early impressions made by his mother. Of him the record is found:

"Anthony Turk was a pious and benevolent man, and became a useful Methodist preacher. He prayed at the opening of his school, and made me repeat a printed prayer, thus beginning: 'Almighty God and merciful Father.' One day he took me out into an adjoining grove, after a refreshing shower. The sun shone with delightful brilliance, and a robin poured forth its notes from the top of a tall oak. The whole world seemed to be embellished with variegated beauty. He pointed out the remarkable bird that seemed to express by its warblings its gratitude in ecstasy of praise to the Almighty, who had chased away the dark tempestuous clouds, and spread his bow in the atmosphere, unfolding unutterable splendor. The design of my teacher seems to have been to enforce upon me the wholesome inference, that if the melodious songsters of the woods seemed to have so much intelligence as to praise the glorious Deity, how much more should we, endowed with reason, realize the sweetest obligation to love and worship Him."

The remembrance of this incident, occurring at so early an age, shows that the lesson was not lost upon the unfolding mind of Henry. Such instructors in our common schools of the present day, would be incalculable blessings to parents and children, and upon Church and State. The schoolmaster's true vocation is not merely to instruct the intellect, and make experts in the mysteries of numbers or in ornate penmanship. If he have no higher view, he is a huge mistake. We do not want accomplished intellects under the control of unimproved hearts, but such as are obedient to the dictations of a conscience enlightened, disciplined and sanctified by Divine truth early instilled. He who graduates a lad thus smitten with the love of truth, with a reverence for God and religious principles, confers upon his country a permanent benefit. That man has not lived in vain who, from the humblest school-house in the land, has sent forth a young soul inflamed with a passion to *do right.* And on the other hand, how awful the responsibility of the instructor who fails to educate the heart into a love for that which is good; into a reverence for justice, virtue, and the authority of God, as the controlling sentiment and all-pervading feeling that should early occupy the youth under his care! All honor to Anthony Turk, and every such man as appreciates his high vocation. No Senator in Congress, no dignitary on earth is his superior in the possession of influence and advantage for the service of his country.

Henry, though young, was unquestionably a remarkable boy. He had "a sound mind in a sound body," but was of a nervous and highly impressible temperament. Just here, the writer prefers to let him tell his own story written for no eyes but those of his children, suppressing only such things as should be reserved for them alone.

"When I was perhaps eight or ten years old, an affair occurred producing more powerful, though less agreeable effects, and perhaps of more permanent and useful consequence than others of the same kind. A disease broke out among the children in our neighborhood, carrying to the grave successively a number of my youthful comrades. The frequency of the funerals I was called to attend, the ministrations by which they were accompanied, and the tidings of new cases of disease gave me an overwhelming shock, which I could not overcome without securing religious comfort to my astonished and intimidated soul. The world appeared to me a region of gloomy mortality and wretchedness. While I persevered in playful amusements, the awful thoughts of death and eternity often assailed and disconcerted my mind, and drove me to secret and stated devotion. My native proclivity to amusement and pleasantry was exceedingly strong. I was not inclined, nor did I think it absolutely necessary, to abandon entirely my playfulness and mirth; yet in the midst of my frolicsome career, I did not forget, nor could I conveniently to my conscience omit the duty of private supplication."

" There were a few places near my father's house to which I ordinarily resorted for prayer. I remember well some corners in the fence, some spots among the bushes, and some recesses in the woods where I could.

as I thought, safely secrete myself from the observation of my friends, while I sought to commune with God and Christ. I do not recollect any special exhortation from the pulpit, or by my parents on the subject of personal religion; but I well remember their manifested attachment to fundamental doctrine, and high appreciation of what they deemed essential in christian experience. Their religious sentiments, well known to me, had much influence over my modes and habits of thought; while the pathetic exhortations of the Methodist preachers awakened within me many solemn emotions. I do not recollect that at any time I had very alarming views of sin. I knew but little of my heart, its depravity, weakness, or deceitfulness; nor do I recollect that the question occurred to me whether God was beginning or improving a work of grace in my heart; or preparing me in his secret counsels for any future entire dedication of myself to God; neither dare I assert with confidence that at that time there was any true spirituality or evangelical sincerity in my exercises. I leave all this to the judgment of God, in whose sight I always was an utterly base and unworthy being. I only say what were the feelings, whether right or wrong, that then seemed to possess my wicked soul. One thing I remember, that in my secret seeming conversation with God, though I knew then little of the evil of sin, I had sometimes wonderful views of the glory and benevolence of my Maker, and the infinite love of a dying Saviour who seemed to stretch out his arms for my salvation."

"Such views sometimes transported my mind to such a degree that I seemed to myself to be absolutely willing and ready to commit my all into the Saviour's hands. One morning, after prayer in a concealed place, where I was consoled with sweet and elevated apprehension of his dying love, having left it with great comfort and satisfaction, it occurred to me that I ought to have made a more solemn and formal confession of my faith before God. Immediately I returned to the place of my seclusion, and there uttered my confession in the words of "the Apostles' creed," which seemed to me very beautiful and appropriate. I think I cordially adopted it in the presence of God as the formulary of my faith, and the instrument of my confession. Had I not been so young and ignorant—being about ten years of age—I would probably have acted differently. God only knows what he intended by suffering me to form such solemn vows in the period of youthful ignorance and instability; God knows that I always was, and still am but dust and ashes, weakness and corruption."

"One thing I must declare in this account of myself, though it operate to my shame. I must not hide it lest I seem to myself to have written the above with unpardonable selfishness and hypocrisy. Notwithstanding my habits of secret devotion and my occasional transportation of thought to the scenes of the heavenly world, very soon this solemnity of mind and these transports of fervor would give way to a frivolity of spirit which I recollect with shame and loathing. I dared not indeed mingle with the grossest acts of impiety, but often I so slackened the reins of restraint and so resisted the monitions of conscience, that I must own I was one of the vilest creatures of God. I forgot not entirely the Saviour whom I once seemed to love and adore, but I could not lay a decided claim to christian character. I viewed my case as entirely uncertain, having only occasional and probably delusive apprehensions of the Saviour's love."

"On one occasion, having been employed at play on Sunday with the boys of my neighborhood, by whom my spirits were aroused into the greatest glee and merriment, I was suddenly constrained to abandon their fellowship; and abruptly retired to a secluded spot for religious meditation. Often, indeed, on my bed my recollections threw me into misery; but who knows whether it were more than the sorrow of the world that worketh death? Who can tell how often and how the Spirit of God moves the conscience of the half-awakened sinner? Whether saving grace had or had not laid a foundation of hope, the boy who had so long tempted God could not conveniently omit wholly the work of prayer, or stifle the impressions of reverence and affectionate regard for God and Christ."

"I have mentioned these things that no one of you might think more highly of me than he ought, and that I might not condemn myself for omitting reminiscences under the influence of criminal selfishness or vile self-exaltation. On what foundation can such a sinner rely but that of unmerited mercy uninfluenced by personal recommendation? More especially as his own religious exercises appear to himself so superficial, so inadequate, so mingled with corruption and vanity, if anything in his youthful experience be salutary, let grace have all the praise."

Such a record of the first dozen years of childhood is very remarkable. It proves two things: first, that the prayers and pains bestowed upon the early cultivation of their children by faithful parents are honored with God's blessing; and second, that the exuberance of joyous hilarity in the early spring of life is not incompatible with the work of the Spirit upon the soul. That which is often branded as youthful folly, is but the welling up of natural, instinctive emotion, whose regulation may be safely entrusted to the control of grace, when it has early lodged in the heart reverence for God and the love of divine things. Religion belongs to the soul, not to the body. It has to do with the nobler feelings of our moral nature, and not with animal impulse. Its province is not to cure strabismus, or a wry neck; but to root the principles of divine truth in the soul. And then, when advancing years have somewhat cooled the fervor of young blood, we shall find, as in the instance before us, that early manhood is richly adorned with all that gives excellency to character.

The subject of these exercises was far in advance of his years. His temperament had a natural love for sport. Humorous, joyful and happy, he could always make an easy transition from gayety to gravity; and, no doubt, often presented both in such close proximity, as to be amusing; yet withal, there was in him developed a power of thought, a scope of comprehension, and a piety of inclination unusual for his years. It seems evident that the sanctifying influence of the Holy Spirit was the dew of his youth, so that like a vigorous rosebud, there was a moral beauty and loveliness apparent in the first unfoldings of his intellectual perception. Hence the interest awakened in his behalf was naturally enough intensified upon the part of his parents and friends, and high hopes clustered around a life so auspiciously begun. Let us have the rest of his own account of himself.

"At twelve years of age, I was considered a good

proficient in the branches which were then taught in the common schools of the town.   In the year 1793, I was sent to the Latin school of Rev. Stephen Goetschius, New Paltz. The Latin grammar called Ruddiman's Rudiments, was first put into my hands, with the design that every essential part of it might be committed to memory; and truly this grammar became so familiar that I could repeat almost any part of it without mistake or hesitation. *Hic labor! Hoc opus!* Other methods more convenient have been since adopted, but my experience is, that no method is so effectual to secure a competent knowledge of grammatical construction, as to commit to memory the fundamentals of the grammar in the outset, and learn by careful study their correct application. With this beginning my progress was easy, and I became greatly encouraged.   In about a month, Ruddiman was my own, although I understood not one particle of the language: but when I came to apply my key, the bolts flew back; and I walked into the most difficult of the Latin classics with comparative ease.   In process of time the grammar and interpretation of the Greek language, in like manner, opened up to me the wealth of Socrates, Zenophon, Lucian and other authors; pursuing at the same time Geography, Logic, Philosophy and kindred branches."

"During my preparatory studies, the great question was constantly before me—shall I proceed with a view to the holy ministry?—I thought of that profession when very young. There was in it a sublimity, a solemnity, an everlasting importance that attracted my regard supremely; and a coincidence of circumstances favored the enterprise. The ardent wishes of my parents, the approbation of other relatives, the nobleness of the ministerial work, my own salvation, the glory of a beloved Redeemer, with the hope of a competency of earthly things to sustain my efforts in this holy vocation, animated the wishes of my heart into intense desire, and determined me to persevere in the great pursuit."

"When about fifteen years of age, I was prepared to enter Union College, and did enter the Sophomore class on an advanced standing. But here I studied under great disadvantages arising from an obstinate attack and long continuance of tertian fever, which at that period of the year often prevailed near marshy districts, and along the margins of streams, and coasts of lakes and rivers. It suddenly prostrated my strength, and remorselessly returned every other day with unabated violence. Still I continued to keep up with my class, but a boy's courage, under such circumstances, in a strange place away from the sympathies and comforts of home, will soon ooze out. I felt like a sick stranger in a strange land, bereft of consolation; and the smallest share of kindly notice was more highly appreciated by a sense of want. I cannot forget, however, the kind consideration of the President of the Institution, Dr. John Blair Smith, who, meeting me one day on my disconsolate way to recitation, bestowed the sweetly sympathetic exclamation, 'poor young fellow!' Nor can I fail to remember the soothing advice of Dr. Dirk Romeyn, the Pastor of the Dutch Congregation of Schenectady, who interested himself so kindly in my convenience and proficiency, exhorting me to remember that *by much tribulation only great objects were to be obtained.*"

"The preaching of President Smith interested me

much. O what a plain, animated and fearless preacher of the cross! The Rev. Jacob Sickles at that time was a colleague of Dr. Romeyn. The chaste simplicity and evangelical tone of Mr. Sickles' discourses made him a most acceptable and useful minister of the Word. I cannot forget how, at that early period of my life, I gave my cordial preference to the simple truth of the gospel; while I viewed with cold indifference the displays of splendor and picturesque verbiage of self-aggrandizement."

"My malady continued, and at the ensuing vacation I returned to my father's house at Plattekill, where I met the love of family and friends which a long absence teaches one to appreciate. But my mind became disconcerted, and discouragement so settled down upon me that I partially gave up my hitherto dearly cherished project. Recovering again my spirits, I resumed my studies with the hope of ultimate success. I then went to the Academy of Kingston, under the direction of Timothy T. Smith, who was an excellent teacher and well qualified to guide me through the whole course of study then customary in our colleges. Fully understanding the bent of my mind, he wisely advised and satisfactorily aided me in those studies which were most intimately connected with the profession to which I had devoted my life. Nothing of special interest occurred during my residence at Kingston. My extravagant pleasantry drove me into frivolity which, while I remember with shame, I recall with amazement on account of its alternations with opposite states of feeling. Diffidence and ambition, seriousness and hilarity, alike possessed me; yet, most astonishing to myself, was the prevailing sense of obligation which led me to frequent and earnest supplication for divine guidance. It is to me a wonder that such should be the experience of a boy, for in all my frivolity and worldly-mindedness I ever felt a profound regard for Christianity around which my affections, so often moved by it, seemed to gather. How strange, that I still sought the ministerial calling, and hardly for a moment relaxed my wishes to expend my life in the service of the Sanctuary."

Mr. OSTRANDER did not return to college, probably for two reasons. The periodical appearance of the tertian fever in its neighborhood impressed him with the belief that should he return, he would again fall a victim to its ferocity; and since he was able to secure at Kingston all the advantages nearly that Union College could then furnish, he was content to be considered an alumnus of the institution, without graduating with his class. Having finished his preparatory studies, and become fully persuaded as to his duty, he devoted his life without reservation thenceforth to the work of the ministry; and in 1798 spent some months under the care of Rev. S. Goetschius at Marbletown, with a view to such general reading as might be immediately useful.

There were at this time three Professors of Theology, acting under appointment by the General Synod of the Reformed Protestant Dutch Church in North America; viz.: Dr. John H. Livingston, Dr. Dirk Romeyn, and Dr. Solomon Froeligh. Under the direction of the last named, young OSTRANDER commenced his Theological course.

His text-book was MARKII MEDULLA. Of this he writes in his "notes." "The language employed in it was ancient and difficult Latin, interspersed with Hebrew and Greek phrases of difficult interpretation, but which when analyzed and understood seemed to express the intended idea with inimitable force, precision and perspicuity. Many of these compendious sentences were taken from the controversial writings of primitive divines who thereby expressed their precise views of controverted points, and were introduced into the Symbolic formularies whereby the different denominations expressed their theological peculiarities."

This testimony is true. The text-book in question was the text-book of the Seminary of our Reformed Church down to the close of the professorship of good old Dr. Milledoller, who in the use of the same, made good work in his department. The General Synod of 1847, made this strange utterance, "A text-book, we apprehend, is not so much a book from which the student is to learn, as it is a general guide to the professor in teaching!" There never was a greater *mis*apprehension on the subject, and the Church, whether she knows it or not, feels the effects of it until this day.

The fellow-students of HENRY OSTRANDER were Jacob Schoonmaker, to whom he became greatly attached, and with whom he held a life-long intimacy; Ralph Westervelt, John Christie, P. D. Froeligh and Charles Hardenberg. "All these," to use his own words not long since penned, "have gone the way of all flesh, and I alone survive to pursue my solitary way."

This class studied with Dr. Froeligh at Schraalenberg, N. J., where he was settled, and were pleased with the mode of instruction adopted by their teacher. Just here it will be pertinent to introduce an extract from the memoranda furnished us, relative to a "Revival of Religion" at Schraalenberg. Mr. OSTRANDER says:

"It was to my advantage, too, to reside with Dr.

Froeligh at the time I was with him for study. It was at or near the close of an astonishing revival of religion, during which about two hundred souls were received into the communion of the Church, when I saw some of the marvellous effects of the operations of the Spirit. How many illiterate brethren became eloquent in prayer! What large numbers attended prayer-meetings! I will mention the case of a young negro who, while Dr. Froeligh was preaching, began to sigh aloud, and cried out so boisterously that he was taken away out of the assembly. Once or twice I attended the prayer-meeting of colored communicants, and how singular was it, that so many low, ignorant, depraved wretches called upon God with so many signs of zeal, sincerity, and heavenly-mindedness!

"It was not singular that the spirit of persecution, and opposition should arise; but one thing was incomprehensible. While the principal converts were eloquent in prayer, exemplary in conversation, and unreserved in their acknowledgment and lamentation of their deep corruption, THEY failed not to express malignity and bitter hatred of their adversaries. It seemed to me that these converts were really taught of God, and renewed by the grace of the Spirit. I admired their zeal, piety and devotion; and yet on many occasions they appeared malignant and extremely uncharitable and unforgiving. They were indeed unjustly accused and injured by the malicious conduct of opposers, and no wonder they were sometimes deeply exasperated. But *why* were they so grossly inimical, and apparently malicious? At their prayer-meetings they constantly poured forth bitter resentments! No one could exceed them in contemptuous allegations, and provoking insinuations! It seemed to me, also, that no one could be popular or acceptable among the praying brethren who would not join them in denouncing the Cooper and Romeyn party as utterly graceless and reprobate! Indeed in order to win the approbation of the praying brethren, it seemed imperatively necessary not only to condemn indiscriminately every advocate of the opposite church of Rev. Jas. V. C. Romeyn, but also to speak in the strongest terms of reproach and condemnation against Toryism from which their forefathers, as they alleged, suffered much cruelty and outrage!"

"It was remarkable that almost universally the members of Dr. Froeligh's church were anti-federal Republicans, as their immediate ancestors were Revolutionary Whigs and Democrats. It was remarkable also that the members of Mr. Romeyn's church were almost universally Federalists, and anti-Jeffersonians. So contentious was the spirit of the times that those who belonged to the church of Dr. Froeligh and happened occasionally to go to the place where Rev. Mr. Romeyn officiated, were immediately denounced, if not as unworthy, yet as suspicious characters. I recollect that having occasionally attended Mr. Romeyn's church when I had no convenient opportunity of attending the ministrations of Dr. Froeligh, I became the subject of unfavorable animadversion. My friends, Jacob Schoonmaker, Westervelt and others became involved in similar reproach."

"The Froeligh party, it seemed, considered themselves the evangelical followers of Christ, while they considered their enemies, as they called the members of the other church, *hypocritical formalists*, who regarded merely the external organization and exhibition of

Christianity. Notwithstanding the unpleasant aspect of things in these two churches I always regarded it as an advantage which a merciful Providence conferred on me, that I had resided in a place where the mighty operations of the Spirit were conspicuous in making some at least so evangelically fervent for God." (!)

"During my term of study at Schraalenberg, an event occurred which produced universal excitement in the land. Washington, 'the father of his country,' died in 1799. The intelligence diffused universal mourning throughout the United States, where the scenes of the Revolutionary War were still fresh in the remembrance of the people. My own youthful mind, having no recollection of the war, which terminated about the period of my birth, was much less affected than those of the thousands older than myself, who had been familiar with the disasters of the revolutionary struggle. Indeed, the calamities of the war were peculiarly felt in New Jersey, where so many battles had been fought, so many cruelties endured, and so many of her sons fell victims to the scourger. General Washington had been the military chief by whose skill and courage the American Army had been conducted, amid many reverses and successes to that final victory which was celebrated with universal joy, and diffused unwonted prosperity through the country. 'He was great in war, great in peace, and great in the hearts of his countrymen.'"

"On February the twenty-second, occurred the anniversary of his birth; and then with unanimous consent his name was to be celebrated and his death lamented by elegiac orations and ceremonies of mourning throughout the land. By what means in the vicinity of Schraalenberg, attention was directed to me as one who might officiate as speaker on the noble subject, I do not plainly recollect; but I endeavored to compose an oration for the occasion, and I intended to deliver it in the church. It was an oration in which I afterwards discovered innumerable marks of childish extravagance and weakness in oratorical pomp and bombast of expression. I began with a quotation of Horace on the death of Mecænas: "*Quis.*"

"Washington himself was not the most popular politician at that time, in some parts of that county (Bergen). The correctness of his policy in his signing and defending 'Jay's Treaty' with England, had been a subject of angry animadversion among the anti-Federalists of that day. By what motive the Consistory of Schraalenberg were influenced, I cannot positively say; but a suspicion arose that their opposition to any apotheosis, in which the commander-in-chief might be celebrated in the spirit of extravagant laudation, was their real motive for apparent indifference to the commemoration of his virtues."

"The idea of a public oration on Washington was consequently abandoned. This being settled, myself and others, on the twenty-second of February, (his birth-day being chosen as the proper one for the demonstration of the country's sorrow) repaired to New York to hear the discourses of the most celebrated Orators and Divines of that age; Dr. John M. Mason, and Dr. Wm. Linn. The fame of these talented speakers commanded the attention of large auditories. I clearly remember the animated description Dr. Linn gave us of the renowned hero followed by his armed hosts, brandishing his sword, and uttering his commands on his prancing steed. I remember his mournful ejaculations accompanied with uncommon earnestness in gesticulation on account of the death of Dr. Mercer, who fell at Bunker Hill, and whose bloody mantle the orator seemed to lift from the mangled body, to spread it before the world as proof of sincerest and noblest patriotism. The pathos and animation which the doctor sometimes manifested in his public addresses were often very affecting, as they seemed to raise the hearer from his seat forgetful of his location."

"Dr. Mason, on the other hand, was more uniform in his delivery, calm in his gesticulation, very solemn in his reasoning as well as polished in his diction; and through every part of his performance exhibited a pleasing portrait of the admirable hero, calculated to win the sympathy and approbation of the audience. Exhorting us to weep for Washington, he introduced an expression of grief from a song suggested by inspiration. It was the song of David on the death of Saul and Jonathan: 'How are the mighty fallen, and the weapons of war perished!' He added another sentence so peculiarly pathetic, I could never forget it. 'Daughters of America who have just prepared the festive bower, and the laurel wreath, plant now the cypress grove, and water it with your tears.' Would to God the church might recognize in all her ministry such men of might and power for the inculcation of pure, unadulterated, and vital Christianity."

Mr. OSTRANDER was very much attached to Dr. Froeligh as "a learned Divine, and an excellent instructor." No man more sincerely deplored the state of things, above referred to, which so severely reflected upon Dr. Froeligh as a leader of the adverse belligerent party in the Dutch Church, which though small, continued the needless and absurd agitation until the overt acts of its leader led to his formal deposition from the ministry. Yet Mr. OSTRANDER was ready, from this personal attachment, to extenuate the crime of Dr. Froeligh; though, however much solicited, he could not unite with him in ecclesiastical rebellion for which there was not the shadow of a plea, yet he says:

"Without justifying Dr. Froeligh in his views of secession, we may partially, at least account for his errors." "Unhappily there were strange animosities, and extreme partisanship in his congregations when he accepted their call. He was more than once the instrument of compromise and reconciliation; but finally overwhelmed by the turmoil of strife and persecution,(?) he yielded too far to the temptations that assailed him, connected himself with a party in the Church, and exposed himself to slanders and animadversions till his Master released him from sin and suffering in death." Such were the apologetic words which in the writing, betrayed a conflict between the head and the heart of their author.

In the Fall of 1800, Mr. OSTRANDER obtained his Professorial Certificate which entitled him to an examination before the Classis of Paramus for Licensure. He was their first candidate. The record is as follows:

"Tappan, September 3, 1800, 3 o'clock, P. M. The Classis met according to appointment. The Rev. Nicholas Lansing appeared and took his seat.

"Mr. HENRY OSTRANDER, a student of Theology under the care of Professor Froeligh, applied to be admitted to examination. After having produced his credentials and explained 2 Corinthians 4:5, he was examined on the Original Languages of the Sacred Scriptures, Didactic and Polemic Theology, and also on Ecclesiastical

History; he having discovered sufficient knowledge in these several branches, and having given evidence of vital and experimental piety, as also that his views in desiring to become a candidate in the ministry are pure, is authorized to preach the Gospel."

"Wednesday, Oct. 6, 1801. The Rev. HENRY OSTRANDER requested a dismission from this Classis in order to join the Classis of Albany. Resolved, that Mr. OSTRANDER's request be granted, and the clerk hereby ordered to furnish him with a proper dismission."— *Records of Classis of Paramus, Vol. I. pp.* 3, 18.

After his licensure, he preached in various churches for a while, and received two "calls," one from the church at Minisink, and the other from the church of Coxsackie. The latter he chose to accept. It was dated May 26, 1801, and signed by the Elders Thomas Houghtaling, Philip Canine Jr., Jacob Cuyler Jr., Abraham Hallenbeck; and by the Deacons Peter C. Bronck, Tunis P. Van Slyck; and attested by the Rev. Jacob Sickles, Moderator. This Call was laid before a Committee on Calls, appointed by the Classis of Albany, for their sanction; and after an examination by said Classis convened at the Boght, Mr. OSTRANDER was ordained and installed the pastor of said church, Oct. 21, 1801.

Previously, however, he had made provision for himself in another way. Jane Nottingham, born in the same neighborhood where he spent his early years, was a descendant of Capt. William Nottingham, who came from England with Col. Nicolls at the time of the surrender of the Colony of New Netherlands to the British Crown, 1664. Her ancestors were settled in the southern part of the county, to which they gave the name of Ulster. Henry and Jane, in callow youth, became school-mates and playmates, and in riper years, at the time now spoken of, May 7, 1801, they became mated for life. Attachments of this kind rarely ever wear out for the most obvious reason. After he had left school to pursue his studies at Union College, she left also, to pursue hers at Kingston, and subsequently at a private school of some note in the city of New York. Five children were in the course of time the fruit of this marriage, only two of whom now survive. The oldest was a son who attained the age of thirty-seven. He became a physician, was possessed of fine talents, gained success and high respect in his profession; but his promising career was cut short at the age of thirty-seven. Mary Eliza, the oldest daughter, and wife of Dr. Dumont, followed him within a year, and some fifteen years after, Laura died; leaving Ann Catharine and Jane to mourn her loss.

Mr. OSTRANDER commenced his labors in the ministry with vigor, and continued them with much pleasure to himself and profit to his people; faithfully executing the duties of his office which at that early date were both numerous and onerous by reason of the great extent of territory over which he had to travel. The beneficial influence emanating from his pulpit performances and pastoral work soon became manifest throughout the community. Possessed of qualities that made him at once a good pastor, an agreeable companion, sincere, sociable and kind, he naturally rose in the esteem of all men because of his natural adaptedness to make for himself friends without appearing to intend it.

Not content with the educational facilities afforded in the town he put forth his energies to found an Academy at Coxsackie. From various causes he partially failed in this enterprise, but not altogether. Retaining a fondness for classical studies, he was easily persuaded by parents to undertake the tuition of their youth. He proved a fine instructor; and as such he is still remembered by some with grateful regard. He had a class of about twenty at this place, engaged in classical studies, of whom two are yet living; Abraham Spoor, M.D., age 83; and W. Van Bergen Hermance, age about 77. These gentlemen, with many others who attained to some eminence in their respective spheres, received all their classical education from Mr. OSTRANDER.

More than fifty years after, Dr. Spoor chanced to be on a visit at the house of his old instructor for the enjoyment of the Christmas festivities. In allusion to the effects of frost, the former repeated the first couplet of an Epistle of Horace he had studied when a boy under the tuition of the latter, but hesitating at the third line, Dr. OSTRANDER immediately took up the words where Dr. Spoor halted, and repeated the whole Epistle. This recital, after the lapse of so many years, showed that he had an unusually retentive memory, and that he kept it in such good repair that nothing filtered through. His students without exception nourished a high regard for him, which they transmitted to their posterity to be shown to their fathers' venerated friend and pastor.

As to the results of his ministry at Coxsackie, no very definite information can be gleaned at this late date; but of this we are assured, a uniform and steady growth was observable in his churches. He generally memorized carefully prepared sermons which he always delivered with uncommon vigor of diction, and earnestness of manner. Their uniform design was to *instruct* his people in the great doctrines of grace, and to show their necessity to the symmetry and solidness of Christian character "according to the faith of God's elect, and the acknowledging of the truth which is after godliness;" so that the avowed believer in Jesus might be able to render a reason for the hope that was in him. Loved as a man, revered as a pastor, popular as a preacher he lived among an appreciative people, wisely dividing to them all the bread of life, and having the satisfaction of seeing many of the young as well as the old turn to the Lord. Dr. Spoor attributed his conversion at the age of twelve years, to a sermon on the text: "The harvest is passed, the summer is ended, and we are not saved;" and many others at an early age experienced the power of his ministry, during which at Coxsackie, Mr. OSTRANDER gave evidence of various gifts which attracted the attention of the older and prominent members of the Classis of Albany. Drs. Sickles, Dirk Romeyn and Bassett; Rev. Messrs. Vedder, Jansen, and Labagh, with others of less note regarded him as a minister whose opening career was full of promise to the Church at large. Hence he was chosen as a commissioner with Dr. Sickles by "The Standing Committee of Missions for the Reformed Dutch Church in America," to visit Canada for the period of three months to assist in serving the churches established there in connection with the Reformed Dutch Church by Rev. Robert McDowall who had been sent thither in 1798. He had organized several churches in the Upper Province, and had applied to the aforesaid committee for aid in sustaining the enterprise. It had been agreed upon by the Classis of Albany (as the most feasible plan) that two of their number should perform this service for three months, to be succeeded by other two for the same length of time, and so on, until some permanent provision might be made for the success of this mission. Accordingly these two brethren spent the period allotted them with some degree of success. During their three months of labor they preached eighty sermons, administered the Lord's supper thrice, received thirty persons into the church, and baptized thirteen children. Subsequently however, circumstances proved adverse to the prosecution of this mission by the Classis of Albany; and it was, contrary to his advice, finally given up. These churches formed and fostered for awhile, were resigned to the care of other agencies; and the Classis directed their attention to, and expended their efforts upon more promising fields.

The church of Catskill, now called Leeds, becoming vacant, a call was made upon the Rev. HENRY OSTRANDER which he thought it his duty to accept, to the great grief of the people of his first love. It was approved by the Classis of Ulster, May 24, 1810, who appointed the Rev. John Gosman to install him in his new charge. With this Classis he then united for life, as events proved; and in this charge he formed new and lasting friends, among whom were the children of Rev. Johannes Schuneman, who had spent all the years of an active ministerial life, greatly beloved, as his predecessor. Mrs. Elizabeth Schuneman, now of Brooklyn, dates her conversion to one of those arousing sermons by which Mr. OSTRANDER occasionally exerted an unusual power; and many others had reason to bless God for his faithfulness in hard pressure upon the sinner's conscience.

He remained however in this charge but two years. There was a strong and growing attachment between pastor and people, but, unsought by the former and unwelcomed by the latter, a pressing call was made upon him by the church of Caatsban and Saugerties. He considered it well, and made up his mind to the acceptance of it as his duty. The people regretted, and so did he; but he always set duty before inclination. Thus impressed, he sought and obtained release from this his second charge, and entered upon his third on September 27, 1812; on which day he was installed by Rev. Stephen Goetchius appointed by Classis for that purpose.

The church of Caatsban and Saugerties, as then known, has a history of some interest in connection with the settlement of our country. The following traditionary facts gathered by Mr. OSTRANDER have all the appearance of verisimilitude:

"In the year 1710, a colony of Germans who had been employed in the military service of Queen Ann, the Sovereign of Great Britain, were dismissed from said service, and furnished with vessels, provisions, agricultural implements and other necessary facilities, by which they might safely emigrate from the scene of their former military toils and bloody labors, and settle in this distant part of the queen's dominion.

"The colony thus organized and prepared under the direction of her Majesty, commenced their dangerous enterprise at an inauspicious season. The company consisted partly of such as were educated in the old Lutheran Church of Germany, and partly of such as belonged to the German Reformed Association. Accordingly the two denominations at that time living in commendable harmony, and yet tenacious of their respective creeds and peculiarities, chose, each of them, a minister, and worshiped the God of their fathers promiscuously and unitedly in the exercise of brotherly love.

"West Camp, but a few miles north of Saugerties, was the place of destination. Prospered in their voyage, they landed, as tradition says, on the twenty-fourth of December in the year above mentioned. They enjoyed the occasion of their landing with more than ordinary satisfaction, not only because they had successfully accomplished their long and dangerous voyage on the tempestuous main, but more especially because it was a day of extraordinary calmness, tranquillity and beauty, the sun filling the whole atmosphere with warmth and brilliancy. They regarded the propitious day as an omen of a period of long tranquillity, plenty, prosperity and peace in the region which the kindness of their queen had allotted to their fruition.

"In the stillness of the evening they constructed habitations only for temporary use, which appeared to be of no great necessity even in winter, the season being so moderate and beautiful. These tents were probably built without much regard to present convenience or durability. Quietly they laid themselves down therein to the composure of sleep, committing themselves to the protection of that God whose care for them up to that moment had been constant and inspiring; and trusting to invigorating repose for the strength needed for the promised mildness of the ensuing day when they hoped to expend it to the best advantage. But just then, they had thrust upon them the most unwelcome kind of proof that appearances are deceptive; for on the early approach of morn, they were awoke by the noise of a tempest and the rigor of the cold. In dismay they beheld their habitations torn asunder, and parts of them driven to a distance by the violence of the storm. How different were their ideas then from the pleasant ones which had soothed them into the solid comfort of profound repose! Instead of safety, they were surrounded by unlooked for danger, having no shelter save the walls of snow that had been made around their beds by the howling wind. Trained, however, to trust in God, to labor, and patient endurance, what could they not accomplish with His blessing? With unbroken courage they met the difficulties of their situation. In due time they built among the bushes more substantial houses. No sooner done, than they directed attention to the erection of a sanctuary. They built their house of worship upon the very spot where the Lutheran church now stands at **West Camp**. It is a small but interesting monument of ancestral piety.

"The two ministers served alternately and harmoniously the same congregation, composed of their respective adherents; but it was not long before the minister of the Reformed Church was called away to his heavenly heritage. The Reformed, tenacious of their peculiarities, and unwilling to merge themselves entirely into the communion of the Lutheran Church, sought the alliance of some Hollanders and Germans in the vicinity. The consequence was a coalition with the latter in the neighborhood of Caatsban and Saugerties. They built the church at present standing at Caatsban, and denominated themselves 'THE CHURCH OF CAATSBAN AND SAUGERTIES,' both places being considered as entitled to ministerial services."

The building at Caatsban was finished in 1732 and the congregation organized about the same period. For a great while they were supplied with the occasional services of an old minister of Catskill, now Leeds, whose name is not remembered; (Weiss?) also by Rev. Messrs. Mancius, Rysdyck, Rubel, Quitman, Ritzema, Fryenmoet and others. Sometime after the union between the *Coetus* and *Conferentie*, a violent controversy being thus happily composed, they prosecuted successfully a call on Rev. Lambertus DeRonde. After his departure they called Rev. Petrus Van Vlierden, 1792, a learned and venerable minister from Holland who ended his services about 1806. Afterwards they settled Rev. James Demarest, who remained but two years. In 1812 they called the Rev. HENRY OSTRANDER, who removed to, and remained at Caatsban for twenty-two years, at the end of which time, he removed his family to the village of Saugerties, where they remained for six years. In 1840, he moved upon his own farm at Glasco, where all things went well with him until 1846, when his wife was called away by death, on the twenty-second of May of that year.

This was the severest stroke he had been called to endure. Mrs. Ostrander was a lady well informed, and possessed of excellent qualities. In person, she is said to have been graceful and prepossessing. Her natural temperament was delicate and sensitive. Her decision of character, inflexible. Her affection constant. Her mental endowments natural and acquired, considerable. Her energy unwearied. Grave and reserved in her manners. Her spirit so impressible, that at times she bordered on melancholy. Possessed of qualifications suitable to her condition as the wife of a clergyman, she assumed to herself almost all the cares, anxieties and responsibilities of the family. She was a con-

stant reader of the Bible, and much attached to the
Episcopal Book of Common Prayer, as was her husband,
for the reason that it was an excellent aid to devotion,
much of its contents having originated with the Conti-
nental Reformers.   Her influence was therefore commanding, and when she bid adieu to her disconsolate
partner, and her affectionate children, they felt as none
can feel but those who pass through the furnace
of affliction, heated to the same degree.   Yet God sustained his servant, and he continued more earnestly
than ever to proclaim the gospel of the Kingdom, and
the unsearchable riches of Christ.

The adaptations observable in the world of mind, are
no less marks of design than those seen in the world of
matter, and they are accepted as proof of the continuous agency of the great Arbiter of human destiny,
operating among and controlling the affairs of the
world.   Men are prepared for positions and positions for
men, in the execution of God's providence; and local
histories furnish abundant illustrations of the fact.   Mr.
OSTRANDER had assigned him the work of his life in
connection with the Classis of Ulster, and in the charge
last mentioned, by the Head of the Church, who sends
laborers to sow the good seed of the Word, and to
gather the fruits of his harvest.   The labors were
arduous and exacting, but our young athlete was now
possessed of a robust constitution.   In person he was
about five feet ten, well proportioned, with a benevolent
sun-lit countenance the flash of whose eyes revealed a
mind of no ordinary mould.   His kindly cheerful disposition had a magnet's attraction, and like the beloved
disciple among the twelve, he was regarded with high
esteem for his manly qualities among his brethren.

Owing to the absolute dearth of ministers in this region at the time spoken of, his services were numerous and arduous; and he proved himself equal to the great demand. His was a ministry of instruction, whose aim was to make the doctrines of grace familiar to the ears and comprehension of all to whom he ministered the word of life, and his efforts were blessed to the salvavation of many souls; how many will not be known until the day when the secrets of all hearts shall be revealed. His charge proper was a large one embracing two hundred families, and of twelve hundred persons, of whom one hundred and seventeen were members in what is called "full communion." Besides, there were outposts which he statedly visited, and where he forcibly preached to assemblies gathered from many miles around, both in Dutch and English, as occasion required. His extended field of labor was bounded on the east by the Hudson River, on the west, by the "Round Top" of the Catskill mountains; on the north, by Catskill, as now known; and on the South, by Kingston. Within this large district of country there was but one church edifice at the time of his settlement (save an old Lutheran church, no services,) belonging to the Consistory of Caatsban and Saugerties. For the sake of regularity in service, it was divided into six parts, in each of which there was a location for stated service. Besides preaching, Mr. OSTRANDER gave catechetical instruction once a week, and many of the congregation would travel from eight to ten miles to attend these exercises, the importance of which he inculcated as necessary to the spiritual health and growth of the church.

He recognized the wisdom of our constitutional requirements, touching the special pulpit services devoted

to the explanation of the catechism, as well as the duty
of instructing the young in divine truth, by means of
their committing it to memory. In the school of Christ
it should be the class-manual by which the disciples of the
Lord should be conducted into a *systematic* acquaintance with divine truth. In all other departments of
truth, physical or mental, the student learns by means
of text-books. No teacher would send forth a child
into the fields to study botany, without having first
informed his mind upon that subject by means of a well-
digested book of first principles; nor would he expect
him to make any advance in mathematical truth, without familiarity with the first principles of arithmetic.
The knowledge of moral truth depends for its accuracy
upon the same process, and why should it be thought
that a competent knowledge of revealed truth can be
gained by a different process, or by no process at all?
Shall the children of this world be wiser than the
children of light in the matter of acquiring the knowledge they respectively deem the best? Is growth in
grace, and in the knowledge of our Lord Jesus Christ
promoted by spiritual starvation, and ignorance of the
leading and distinctive doctrines of the Cross? Is it to
be gained by the miraculous agency of the Spirit of
God, setting aside the necessity of studying the Word
Himself inspired for instruction, the entrance of which
giveth light? Ah, the hard *experience* gained of late
years by the absurd *experiment of neglect* in this matter,
proves that ignorant professors led by numerous expedients into the church, are very different from intelligent
possessors won "through sanctification of the Spirit,
and belief of the truth," the acquisition of which is
necessary to make them "wise unto salvation." Christ

prayed that his disciples might be sanctified by the *means of* the truth, and this implies that they should be made first to understand it and value it by such continuous efforts as parents pledge themselves to put forth in the baptismal obligation designed to secure to the young the benefit of a religious education.

Mr. OSTRANDER well understood the advantage of this method of instruction which was conscientiously adhered to in his day. "We feel," said he in a report made by his church to the Classis, "we feel that too much praise cannot be bestowed on that part of our ecclesiastical system, which requires the catechising and instruction of the youth whereby orthodox, intelligent, and useful professors, it is to be hoped, will in due time compose a good portion of the Church of Christ." He was faithful in the use of the Heidelberg Catechism as prescribed by the Constitution of the Reformed Dutch Church. By it he led the people of his charge to perceive the logical connections of revealed truth, and so they became qualified to read the Word of God with an appreciative mind and heart.

The Church of Christ, though not of the world, must be in the world, and hence hers has always been a militant state; and will be, until He come again. Not infrequently however many of her conflicts arise from disturbing elements within her own bosom. Such was the case for a time in the Classis of Ulster with which Mr. OSTRANDER was connected. He was a man of peace which he would purchase at any cost, except the price of purity and principle. When the interests of the Church required it, he was just as ready and as well qualified to contend for the right in the arena of debate, as he was prepared to plead for the truth in the ordinary proclamations of the gospel. A view of his happy agency in this particular is necessary to a fair estimate of his character, and of the essential service he rendered to the interests of his beloved church.

Mr. OSTRANDER began his ministry in troublous times, when the circumstances of the country, and of the church first established here were all adverse to the spiritual welfare of the people. Without making reference to secular and other difficulties, it is pertinent here to mention that two parties had originated in the Church, known respectively as *Coetus* and *Conferentie*, whose conflict over the matter of procuring an entire ecclesiastical independency of the Mother Church in Holland, was of long continuance, and at times, of an exasperating nature. By the wisely directed influence of Dr. J. H. Livingstone, first exerted in Holland and subsequently here, articles of union were at length agreed to for the purpose of composing this strife, and so uniting the churches in Classes and Synods that as a consolidated body, the Reformed Church of this land might be more successful in prosecuting the common work of the gospel. But it was a long time before all the churches could be induced to adopt them, and fall in with the measures proposed.

To retard progress and complicate troubles, another difficulty arose in the adverse efforts of Dr. Solomon Froeligh, who had been chosen one of the Professors of Theology some years before the location of the Seminary at New Brunswick was fixed. By Synodical action Dr. Livingstone was unanimously chosen as the then only recognized Professor of Theology in that institution. This gave mortal offence to the first named Rev. gentleman, who was not disposed to think the General Synod acted wisely in their choice; and he soon became convinced that there was "something rotten in Denmark." At length, he became so far alienated as to imbibe, indulge, and promote the spirit of schism. It appeared from his letters to different parties, by them made known subsequent to his open revolt in 1822, that he early meditated, if not formed a project of heading a secession upon the plea of corruption prevalent in the church, which plan he matured and carried into effect at the last named date, by uniting with himself while under the process of discipline, four other ministers also *suspended* and finally *deposed*, with four other persons who had previously served, two as elders and two as deacons, in small and obscure churches from which the aforesaid ministers had been separated. This was the sorry outgrowth of the evil influence originating at first a line of sympathy with Froeligh, variously extending from the Classis of Paramus of which he was a member, to the Classis of Ulster which he hoped to enlist in his effort within whose bounds his former pupil, the subject of this Memoir, was settled. Mr. OSTRANDER had become already conspicuous for his talents, when, about eight years after his settlement, an occurrence took place of which it has often been said: " Behold how great a matter a little fire kindleth ! " And had it not been for his well-directed agency, the aforesaid purpose of Dr. Solomon Froeligh might have been greatly subserved in the Classis of Ulster.

In the year 1808, the Rev. John Gosman was called to the then vacant pulpit of the Church of Kingston. He had been trained under the tuition of the celebrated Dr. John M. Mason of the Associate Reformed Church. He was a man of great natural gifts, and like Apollos, eloquent and mighty in the Scriptures. When he first appeared in the Kingston pulpit, he made such an impression upon the people, that they prosecuted at once a call upon him to become their pastor. But there was a respectable minority of the congregation opposed to this movement, composed mainly of the older people, on the ground that the pastor elect could not officiate in the Dutch language, and themselves unable to understand the English tongue would consequently be debarred all opportunity for instruction. They therefore, naturally enough, united in a protest against the Classical approbation of this call, only for the reason just stated. To meet this difficulty Classis " resolved, that it be earnestly recommended to the Consistory of Kingston, in case of Mr. Gosman's acceptance, to obviate the objection of the Memorialists to obtain as much Dutch preaching as the interests of the congregation should from time to time require." This was satisfactory to both parties. An instrument or contract was drawn up between the Memorialists and the Consistory to the effect that this resolution should be faithfully carried out, and the call was approved in Nov. 1808, at the same session at which the Church of Kingston, after an independent existence for some twenty-five years, united with the Classis of Ulster which had been constituted in the year 1800.

Matters being thus adjusted, it was hoped that all difficulty was harmoniously settled; but subsequent events proved far otherwise. For some cause the Consistory was either unable or unwilling to comply with the terms of the contract. Misunderstanding and dissatisfaction took place, and the judgment of the Classis was again invoked. Their advice and adjudication were in favor of the Memorialists. Yet the difficulties increased, and the matter was brought before them at several times. During the contest, the validity of the "contract" signed by the representatives of both parties was called in question. At length the Classis came to a formal decision that the "instrument" securing Dutch preaching to the aforesaid Memorialists in the Church of Kingston was valid, recommending the Consistory to fulfil their part of the contract. From this decision the Consistory appealed to the Particular Synod of Albany, giving certain reasons for their course of action, among which were certain "allegations," "charges," and "accusations" against the Classis. This appeal was not only sustained, but all the offensive allegations embodied in the reasons, were admitted as true, and the Synod passed a severe censure upon the Classis. Feeling themselves much aggrieved by this procedure, the Classis confidently appealed the case to the General Synod. But the General Synod sustained the action of the court below in every particular, with some exceptional remarks as to the want of "clearness in the testimony, and the confused state of the minutes," upon which the decision was rendered.

This proceeding of the General Synod in 1812, very naturally called forth from the Classis an indignant remonstrance petitioning for redress; and feeling their honor assailed, and their integrity to have been unwarrantably and cruelly impeached, they determined to have redress, or in case of failure, to part company with the Synods who had visited them so severely for the adjudged error of giving wrong advice to the Consistory of Kingston. Matters now were hopeful to those sympathizing with the Froeligh party, and deemed perilous by those who regarded that party as treasonable to the Church of their fathers. The Classis were prompt in their action and appointed a committee to draft a suitable Memorial expressive of the wrong done them. This paper, put together by Mr. OSTRANDER, was considered a vigorous document, showing its author to have been eminently fitted for the defence of the Classis. Clear in its statements, discriminating in its logic, and pungent in its arguments, yet respectful to the General Synod, it sought from that body a solution of various absurdities into which they had been led.

An inability or a disinclination to meet this request, with a sense of a superior dignity to be respected, may have led the Synod of 1813 to renew their censure, which they did, with some appeasing expressions. A "circular letter" was addressed to the clergy and churches of the Classis of Ulster which while it was less condemnatory in its statements, and more conciliatory in its tone, did not expressly exonerate the Classis from the odious charges made against them, and of which they had shown themselves innocent by the aforesaid document. Besides, Synod appointed a committee to visit the churches of the Classis, to distribute their minutes among them, and to do what they could to allay the storm themselves had raised. The proceedings of this committee only made matters worse, as they endeavored to get the Consistories to convene, offering to preach in their congregations, reading the proceedings of Synod, and making such comments as they thought proper; and all this in the absence of the the ministers of Classis who were known to be at the time convened in special session upon this very business. A resolution was passed at this session of the Classis of

Ulster, declaring "that the Consistories and Congregations under the jurisdiction of this Classis ought not to be summoned together at the request of the two Rev. gentlemen composing the Committee of Synod, because in making such request, they exceeded the bounds of their commission." The Classis had said in the close of their Memorial sent to the General Synod of 1813: "If you grant them that redress which their case imperiously demands, they will honestly seek to erase those hard and unpleasant impressions which a sense of injury has unavoidably produced. If you reject their application, they have only to appeal to the impartial tribunal of Heaven, and await the decision of the Judge of all the earth who will do right." The Synod did not grant the redress asked for, but sent a circular letter to the churches of the Classis with commissioners as aforesaid; and the Classis with their Consistories refused to allow them the use of their churches for the agitation of this subject.

Thus it became perfectly evident that unless the Synod could be actuated by wiser measures, the Classis would feel themselves justified in withdrawing from the Reformed Dutch Church by the force of circumstances, and against their own preference. None felt this more keenly than Mr. OSTRANDER, and he labored to gain the consent of his brethren to continue their efforts, if perchance they might gain the reversal of a Synodical action which had been unfortunately precipitated without a thorough and intelligent investigation. He succeeded, and once more he found himself the chairman of a committee whose business was now to investigate the minutes of the General Synod of 1813, in relation to their proceedings on the aforesaid memorial. He produced another well-argued paper, in which the mistakes of the Synod were illumined with sunlight, and the Classis ordered it to be sent to the next General Synod as representing the unanimous opinion and feeling of the Classis in regard to their grievances; and earnestly asking for a reconsideration of the odious Synodical action. This was sent as a second memorial.

Had it not been for the persistent exertions of Mr. OSTRANDER, the Classis of Ulster probably would have made no further effort to obtain from the General Synod that just consideration to which the members of it considered themselves fairly entitled, and which alone could have retained them in happy relations with the Synod.

Anxious to know the end of the matter, and yet reluctant to attend the Synod of 1814, he was persuaded to go as a Commissioner of Classis, and was well received by many of the members of Synod. After the presentation of the second Memorial, and the reading of the resolutions embodied therein, it was not without some wrangling that a formal action of Synod was had, allowing Mr. OSTRANDER to state the grievances of the Classis of Ulster uninterrupedly, which he did, and then retired.

The consideration of the whole matter was given to a committee with instructions to report. Mr. Abraham Van Vechten was the intelligent and active chairman. He voluntarily sought, and said to Mr. OSTRANDER: "I never understood the case before. *Ostrander, you write the resolution just as you wish to have it, and I will see it passed.*" Probably Mr. Van Vechten had not understood that the difficulty *causative* of the quarrel between the Classis of Ulster and the General Synod was the ratification of the action of the Particular Synod of Albany by which the Church of Kingston was transferred from it to the Classis of Poughkeepsie for reasons based upon grounds inculpating the former, and held by them to be false, and injurious to their honor and christian integrity. When this was made plain, by the speech of Mr. OSTRANDER, his agency was sought as aforesaid, to get the Synod out of the difficulty. He wrote the exonerating resolutions which were accepted by the committee with a single unimportant change in the verbiage, and they were unanimously passed. In this, the Synod was indebted to him for this pacific action, which averted a calamity dreaded by the Classis.

Thus terminated this unhappy contest. He had written both memorials, and had kept his hand hard upon the tiller, while he piloted the Classis of Ulster successfully through the storm. Had it not been for his wise counsels, and incessant watchfulness and care, the probability is that a secession of some importance and commanding influence would have taken place, some years before the discreditable and abortive action of Froeligh in 1822, and on a basis of principle and truth. But this was averted by that combination of generous denominational love, superior talent, and intelligently pious zeal which culminated together in the character of Mr. OSTRANDER. While he was noted for liberal sentiments and brotherly affection for all who love the Lord Jesus Christ in sincerity, the Dutch Church was the home of his heart; an enlightened view of her doctrines, mode of worship and form of government, moulded his natural preference into an intelligent choice; and he loved her more intensely with the lapse of years out of a pure heart fervently. His success, therefore, in the contest just related, was to him a matter of unspeakable joy.

In 1813, the Church of Caatsban was repaired and much improved in appearance, the old walls having been left standing. The spiritual interests of the congregation however continued to engross the heart of the Pastor. When relieved from the anxieties and troubles incident to the controversy above mentioned, he applied himself with renewed energy to his ardently loved work, nor were his efforts unattended with signal tokens of the Divine favor. His style of preaching attracted a crowd, and the procession of carriages returning from his morning services was usually larger than is now seen on any occasion in that part of the country. The annual reports to the Classis from his charge show an almost continuously gradual increase of membership. Prayer-meetings were statedly held in all the neighborhoods within his large circuit, and he frequently attended them, but was always present at the one held at Caatsban. The result was a stirring interest, more or less kept up, in the matter of religion; and although no publicity was given to the fruits of his labors, what would now be called "a revival" would be an accurate statement of the condition of things during many years of his long pastorate. He did not, however, regard his work worthy of special remark, yet the whole aspect of it from one year to another, exhibited the blessed agency of Him whose province it is to take of the things of Christ and show them unto the people. The word preached was accompanied with an influence which mere moral suasion can never command.

Services were now held in the Dutch language once a

fortnight, but the use of this tongue for the preaching of the gospel was wholly abolished in 1825. Thenceforward all services were conducted in English.

In 1821, efforts were begun for carrying out resolutions of the Caatsban consistory to build a new church edifice in the village of Saugerties. Mr. OSTRANDER took the subscription paper and himself mainly raised the requisite amount. The building committee, of which Mr. Jeremiah Russel, a noble-minded man, was Chairman, always consulted him in carrying out his own plans, and brought their accounts for his adjustment. Although he had many and efficient helpers, yet they all relied on him as the manager; and when the work was done, the Consistory passed a series of resolutions expressing their high appreciation of his services, and their thanks for the same in loving and laudatory terms. A beautiful and a large church was erected, and a fine congregation statedly met within its walls to listen to sacred themes as they were expounded by their much revered minister. Throughout this large charge Bible, Tract, Missionary and Temperance Societies were formed, and thus the interest of the people, by the activity of their pastor in every good work, was kept alive in having something to do for the common good of society. Years rolled on, leaving successive records of prosperity and peace.

In 1839, the congregations of Caatsban and Saugerties resolved to separate, as each was now competent to support a minister. The number of communicants had now arisen to over three hundred, and the duties began to wear upon the pastor. There were more than seven communities to each of which he ministered for many years. He therefore resigned his call in October, and in accordance with his desire the consistory united with him in an application for a dissolution of the pastoral connection. This was a great trial for the older people of Saugerties, nor did the consistory let the occasion pass without a suitable record of generous sentiments and feelings.

"We, the Elders and Deacons, do hereby with reluctance consent to his request, and recommend him to the world as a Minister of the Reformed Protestant Dutch Church in good and regular standing. He has labored with us in the gospel ministry, more than twenty-seven years; and during that whole period, his deportment and labor, his faithfulness and zeal have borne decided testimony to his character as an evangelical steward of the mysteries of Christ. The period having arrived when we are required to subscribe his dismission, the vivid recollection of his manner and doctrine as a public expositor of Divine Truth, brings to us emotions peculiarly solemn and tender. While the moment of separation occasions sensibilities of regret and sympathy, it also excites the tenderest solicitude for his future welfare. May the great Head of the Church who seperated him for the ministerial work, and conferred on him his peculiar endowments, still longer protract the period of his usefulness, kindly protect, in his declining age, and finally crown him with the benediction of 'Well done, good and faithful servant.'"

Agreeably to a previous understanding, the old church at Caatsban recalled Dr. OSTRANDER. This Church is the mother of many daughters, and the number of families now adhering to the old organization were about a hundred, while the communicants numbered fifty-four. With unimpaired ambition for the work of

his Master, he devoted the remnant of his time to this
people, and the annual reports of the church exhibit
gratifying results which seemed to increase with the
age of the pastor.

At the Commencement exercises of Rutgers College
in 1844, the honorary degree of Doctor of Divinity was
conferred upon Mr. OSTRANDER by the unanimous vote
of the Trustees of that Institution. It was worthily
bestowed, but more valued by his friends than by himself; though he was not insensible to the honor, nor
ungrateful for the compliment.

The Classis of Ulster had now become so extended,
that it was thought expedient to divide, setting off half
their number to be formed into a new body to be called
the Classis of Kingston. It was proposed to consummate this division at the regular Spring session of 1856.
The occasion was made especially interesting by an
address of Dr. OSTRANDER in response to an address by
Dr. Stitt on behalf of those who were now to separate
from their brethren. We are indebted to the Rev. A.
Dubois, D.D., who was a member of that Classis at the
time, for a full report of the proceedings. From it the
following remarks of Dr. OSTRANDER are extracted for
their worth as a recorded portion of his ripe experience.

'Brethren: For more than fifty years, I have been a
minister of the Reformed Dutch Church; and for four
and forty years I have stood connected with the Classis
of Ulster. I shall not remain in it much longer, for I
am near the end of my pilgrimage; and the burden of
years and increasing infirmities grows heavy upon me.
I thought I would come at least this once more, as your
meeting was so near my own habitation; perhaps it
might be the very last opportunity. When I part from

you now, brethren, it will be to leave you to work with a longer portion of life before you than remains to myself. You will not be far off; and my brethren will meet you; but I can not expect it. I shall not see your new Classis; others may: but as for me the grave is my doom.

'I said that for four and forty years I have stood connected with this Classis. You will believe that in that time I have seen many changes, and have acquired some knowledge and experience. And you will allow me —it may be my last opportunity—to speak to you of some things I wish to impress upon the minds of my younger brethren. And especially would I speak of the change which your observation and experience will work upon the character of your preaching and ministry. When I began to preach, I confess that I sought to adorn my discourses with the beauties of human literature, and the acquisitions of human learning. My God, forgive me this my sin! And now, as for the last time I address my young brethren, I must speak plainly to them. I hear sermons sometimes that have too much of mere ornamentation, too much attention to style and adornment, too much that amuses the imagination, rather than convicts the conscience, and strikes home upon the heart. You will see more and more the importance of preaching the great doctrines of the gospel. This conviction is deepened by the experience of my whole life and ministry. Preach especially the depravity of our nature, the awful depths of corruption, misery and sin into which man is plunged; our entire loss of all that is good, and of all ability for it; the derangement, perversity, wretchedness, and awful wickedness of the human heart; the *total depravity of our nature*. And preach

Christ for salvation, only Christ. Oh! my brethren, determine to know nothing among your people but *Christ crucified.* We must have life by the gospel, we must have our salvation from Christ.

'Brethren, now we are to constitute two Classes, but we part from you with the warmest feelings. I bid you God speed, in your undertaking. I hope to hear of your great prosperity, but I shall never see you more. We part now, not to meet again in this world; but now, and when I am gone, may God's richest blessings attend upon all you do. May the love, the protecting providence and blessings of God the Father, and the grace of God the Son, may the enlightening influence, and guiding, and sanctifying power of God the Holy Spirit ever be yours. Brother, farewell!'

"Dr. Ostrander appeared feeble, and supported himself on a cane. His whole frame seemed languid, and his white hair told of a long sojourn in a world of decay. His countenance however was full of emotion, and his eye seemed as bright as when half a century ago, he first declared his Master's message. His remarks were delivered in a solemn and impressive manner. We felt that the scene, the actors, and the whole occasion were unusual, and it would be only true to say that many hearts throbbed hard, and many eyes saw only through their tears."

In 1857 an unusual degree of interest sprang up in Dr. Ostrander's congregation. Prayer-meetings were multiplied, and were numerously attended. At one communion forty-seven united with the church upon confession of their faith. All the time and strength of the pastor were severely taxed, but willingly and joyfully given up to the work. A few advanced in years became subjects of grace, but the greater number were from the ranks of the young and middle aged. A large proportion of these new members were found quite limited in the knowledge of scriptural truth, and for their benefit the pastor established a Catechetical Class, and a conference for the general improvement of the congregation in doctrinal and practical christianity. The effort was blessed in largely accomplishing the end for which it was intended.

In 1860, the pastor made a record in the church book, which shows that the state of religion continued very encouraging; so that what would have been emblazoned as a *revival*, by many at the present day, had been a work of grace in silent progress for years; but quietly, solemnly and effectually accomplishing the great end of the gospel. In relating this state of things to the Classis, the pastor said: "The rage of fanaticism does not seem to constitute the element of religious action among our people; but a deep solemnity of mind. Our devotional meetings are quiet, sometimes solemn and impressive."

The advanced age of Dr. OSTRANDER now compelled him to notify his people, that he was fast becoming unequal to the work upon his hands; and that especially on account of the growing interest of religion among them, he thought it their duty to seek for a successor. The consistory "resolved, that it was their wish and the wish of the congregation that he should continue as their pastor as long as his age and health would permit." The pastor consented to retain his relations to them until January 1, 1862.

The last entry made by this venerable man of God, in the church book by his own hand, is as follows: "During the ministry of HENRY OSTRANDER in this town,

Marriages about 552; Baptisms, 1133; Members received, 627." O, how few are the Pastors who can show such a record of members received by their own individual instrumentality into the Church of Christ! With what exultation might he have rejoiced over the noble work so long continued by the permission and gracious direction of the Lord of the harvest! Yet Dr. OSTRANDER was not the man to boast. Modesty and humility ever dictated his descriptive language when relating his own efforts and varied experience, laying all his laurels, with a loving heart, at the feet of his Master.

When the period arrived which had been designated for the severance of the pastoral relation, continued for so long a time, the deepest emotions naturally subdued both pastor and people, the sacredness of which forbid any thing beyond a mere mention. The Rev. Dr. Gosman, his old friend and co-laborer of the Classis of Ulster, was invited to superintend the formalities of the dissolution; and having so done, he annexed his name to a report that "the whole transaction of the dismission was harmonious, amicable and pleasant." This was signed and dated April 7, 1862.

The Classis of Ulster met on the 15th of that month, when Dr. Gosman rendered the report upon which the Classis proceeded to act. It was not to be expected that he could refrain from the following statement:

"The duration of this relation is unusual, and rarely can such a record be made of the continuance of ministerial labor in *one field*, contrasting strongly with the present, in which the incumbent may be said to be '*a wayfaring man, that turneth aside to tarry for the night.*' The church of Caatsban is one of the most ancient churches of the Reformed Dutch Church of our State (founded in 1732.) The original territory was large, but in the revolutions of time, new organizations have circumscribed its limits.

"The Heavenly Husbandman seems to have regarded it as a vine of his own planting, and amidst all the shakings and changes, the aged pastor was surrounded by those on whom in infancy he had sprinkled the symbol of consecration to God, and were enrolled among the professed followers of the Lamb; and, as becoming their descent from a generation who had themselves been trained to esteem him very highly for his work's sake, they cherished with filial love their pastor, and yielded with a struggle to the closing of his labors.

"The deeply solemn and tender address of the retiring pastor awakened profound emotions, and formed a fitting close to his able and instructive ministry; while my own thoughts were carried forward to that day when pastor and people shall stand before the Chief Shepherd, realizing the conception of the poet,

> "And when the last stupendous morning springs
>   Big with the fate of all terrestrial things,
> Then, holy, happy shepherd, thou shalt stand
> With all thy ransomed sheep, at Christ's right hand.
> Receive thy great reward! To glory rise,
> And like a star, illume the upper skies!"

Released from the beloved charge in which he had so faithfully served for half a century, Dr. OSTRANDER retired upon his own farm, where his time was extended to the period of ninety-one years and eight months. The end of this long web of life unfolded the usual thrums of exhaustion incident to old age; yet while his tabernacle was a-taking down, his active mind remained unimpaired; and upon all occasions admitting the effort, he ceased not to preach "the unsearchable riches of Christ." His presence in the sanctuary was always a matter of interest to pastor and people, and his voice in prayer and brief addresses, always heard with affectionate attention. By the Classis of Ulster he was beloved as their own honored patriarch, and by the people composing its churches, he was held to be an impersonation of greatness as a preacher, and of goodness as a man; whose long and well directed influence, like the light of day, had given hue and color to many plants of renown in the garden of the Lord.

But, at length, he was confined to the precincts of his own home: yet, like him to whom an angel said, " O man greatly beloved, fear not: peace be unto thee; be strong, yea, be strong;" he was comforted by the increase of faith, and the infusion of spiritual energy. His soul, like a retired merchant having withdrawn from worldly cares, lived upon her wealth of piety and peace, waiting with "earnest expectation" to hear the call: "Come."

The last prayer he uttered in family worship was unutterably tender. With pathos and unusual energy, he prayed for a blessing on those he had to leave; he prayed for the church, for the coming of the Lord; for the millennial glory. On the morning of the day on which he died, he arose and partook of some breakfast, but soon after assistance was called to replace him in an elevated position in bed. The call from above then came, and dropping his head, his hand clasping that of his daughter near him, the last words he uttered—O how beautiful! — were responsive: "My heavenly Father!" And so he fell asleep, November 22, 1872.

When a noble vessel, long completing, is finally

launched, she glides along her ways in stately movement amid the shouts of an admiring throng. So, our aged brother moved out of time into eternity, and ministering angels, we have reason to believe, hailed the movement of his passage into the joys of his Lord.   Now

> "See where he walks on yonder mount that lifts
>   Its summit high, on the right hand of bliss.
>   Sublime in glory, talking with his peers
> Of the incarnate Saviour's love, and passed
> Affliction lost in present joy! See how
> His hands, enraptured, strike the golden lyre!
> As now, conversing of the Lamb, once slain,
> He speaks; and now, from vines that never hear
> Of winter, but in monthly harvest yield
> Their fruit abundantly, he plucks the grapes
> · Of life!"

The funeral procession, with measured tread, bore his body to the Church of Saugerties. O what tender associations clustered around that place of worship, and crowded within that hour of service! He who had so often addressed assemblies gathered on similar occasions, himself was now the coffined dead. Other voices must now be heard in doing for him what he had done for hundreds. How solemn the reflection that these voices, with all others of our brethren thus expended, shall soon be hushed in silence! O, what is life? "It is even a vapor that appeareth for a little time, and then vanisheth away." Time is the Niagara of eternity, ceasing never, day nor night, to pour its constant flood over the awful precipice ; while human tears, like its widened spray, and human wailings like its incessant roar, cease not for a moment. O sin, mother of woe! No thought can reach the depths of anguish due to thee, no language has a fitting phrase to tell the meaning of thy horrid name!

But there is a bow upon that spray: "Death is the wages of sin, but the gift of God is eternal life through Jesus Christ our Lord." Hence, in spite of death, it is a great gain to die. From a state of sin and sorrow where pleasure interlocks with pain, the christian passes through a short dark tunnel into the blaze of heavenly glory; for "to be absent from the body, is to be present with the Lord." We therefore can enter the sanctuary for a funeral service with tears of joy, when a trophy of reclaiming grace is transferred from the battle ground of sin and death, to the glorious place prepared for it by the Captain of our salvation.

FUNERAL SERVICES.

The services held within the Church of Saugerties upon the occasion of carrying him to his burial, were very impressive. The building was thronged by those whose fathers had been the parishioners and warm friends of the deceased, whom they had been taught to revere; and they came to commingle their sympathies as participants in a common sorrow.

These services were opened with Invocation, and the reading of the ninetieth Psalm by the pastor of the church, the Rev. O. H. Cobb.

The 727th Hymn, "Hear what the voice from Heaven proclaims," etc., was then sung, with an evident feeling of impressiveness pervading the congregation.

Prayer was then offered by the Rev. N. F. Chapman, who was the pastor of Dr. OSTRANDER's old congregation at Caatsban. After which the following address was delivered by the Rev. Dr. J. C. F. Hoes, the subject of which, by request of the family, was "Dr. OSTRANDER's relation to the Classis of Ulster."

"Help, Lord; for the godly man ceaseth: for the faithful fail from among the children of men."

"Another standard-bearer has fallen. He, whom the most of us have been accustomed to regard as a very aged man, (for nearly thirty years since, when the speaker first became acquainted with him, he was then older than the speaker now is, himself,) is no more. Yes, the aged and venerable Dr. HENRY OSTRANDER, full of honors and of years, having attained more than four-score and ten, (Job 5: 26) 'has come to his grave, in a full age, like as a shock of corn cometh in his season.'

"The period of Dr. OSTRANDER'S ministry is contemporaneous with the history of the present century. Having finished his theological studies, he was licensed by the Classis of Paramus to preach the gospel, in the year A.D. 1800. He very soon received a call from the Reformed Dutch Church of Coxsackie, to become its pastor, which he accepted, and appeared before the Classis of Albany to be examined for ordination and installation. His trial sermon was preached before that Classis (convened in the Church of the Boght) on the 29th of September, 1801, from Deut. 6: 4, as the text— 'Hear, O Israel, the Lord our God is one God.' By the appointment of Classis, he was inducted into the ministerial and pastoral office, in connection with the Church of Coxsackie, by the Rev. Hermanus Van Stuysen, pastor of the Churches of Heldenberg, Salem and Jerusalem; Dr. Dirk Romeyn of Schenectady, and John B. Johnson of Albany, on the 21st day of October, 1801. Among the people of his first love, he labored faithfully and successfully for a period of nearly ten years, when he was called to the pastorate of the Church of Catskill, at that time connected with the Classis of Ulster. On the 24th May, 1810, a call was extended to him by the Church of Catskill and was approved by the Classis of Ulster, and soon thereafter, he was, by the appointment of Classis, installed as its pastor by the Rev. Dr. John Gosman. His ministry at Catskill was of brief continuance, for on the 5th November, 1811, the Classis approved a call extended to him by the Church of Caatsban; and, by the appointment of Classis, he was installed at Caatsban on the 27th September, 1812, by the Rev. Stephen Goetschius of Marbletown. Dr. OSTRANDER remained pastor of the Church of Caatsban for fifty years. Here he spent the prime and vigor of his life in close application to study, and in labors abundant for the spiritual welfare of the people committed to his charge. Here, also, he spent his declining years, and when, in the providence of God, in consequence of the increasing infirmities of age, he resigned his pastoral charge, the Rev. Dr. Gosman, who had fifty-one years before installed him as pastor of the Church of Catskill, presided in the Consistory of Caatsban, at his dismission from that church.

"Dr. OSTRANDER was the connecting link between the past and present generation of ministers of our Church, residing on the west bank of the Hudson River. In early life, contemporary in this Classis with Peter and Moses Froeligh, Jesse Forda, Stephen Goetschius, Peter S. Wynkoop, Peter Overbach, Jacob Brodhead, John Gosman and Isaac N. Wyckoff, (*venerabilia nomina*,) he has survived them all, only to be regarded by his *present* contemporaries as the venerable father—nay, patriarch of our Classis.

"In 1810, when Dr. OSTRANDER became a member of the Classis of Ulster, within its boundaries were included all Churches on the west side of the Hudson River above the Highlands as far north as, and including Catskill, embracing the territory at present composing the Classes of Orange, Kingston, Ulster and a part of Greene.

"For a period of sixty-two years, the deceased has been more or less closely identified with the history of these Churches. During this protracted period of time, extending through more than two generations, he has witnessed seasons of adversity and prosperity—religious declension and revival—strife and peace; and with them all has been closely allied; and in them, was a prominent actor.

"At the time of his connection with the Classis, the Church of Esopus was in painful state of dissension. This was followed by a protracted controversy in the Church of Kingston, arising from the introduction of the English language in conducting the public services of the sanctuary. The older members of the Church and congregation could not tolerate this innovation, and were tenacious to have preaching in their vernacular tongue—the younger portion of the congregation could not understand the Dutch, and they demanded preaching in English; and thus the controversy waxed warmer and warmer—hotter and hotter; affecting not only the Church of Kingston and the Classis of Ulster, but involving both the Particular and General Synods. So fiercely was this controversy carried on that the Classis of Ulster was on the point of seceding from the jurisdiction of the Particular and General Synods; and it was only allayed by the pacific action of the latter, and by transferring the Church of Kingston from the Classis of Ulster to the Classis of Poughkeepsie, on the east side of the Hudson River.* Some ten or twelve years sub-

---

* Since the delivery of this address, its author has been informed, and led to believe, that Dr. OSTRANDER was the originator of the "pacific action" referred to.

sequently to the adjustment of these difficulties, the large and influential Church of Rochester was agitated by internal dissensions, which seriously retarded its prosperity, and at one time threatened its perpetuity.

" Other serious ecclesiastical difficulties subsequently arose in other churches, to which time will not allow me even to allude.

"The prominent and active part which the deceased took in the adjustment of these complicated and embarrassing difficulties illustrated several of the more prominent traits of his character, and it is for this purpose alone that I allude to them.

"Many of the papers, connected with these controversies, found on the records of our Classis, are the productions of his vigorous pen. For perspicuity and vigor of style—for potency of logic, they stand unrivalled. His mighty mind, vigorous and active, was fruitful in devices to adjust ecclesiastical strifes. In crises like these, he rose to the dignity of a lofty manhood, in firmness of purpose, and in determination not to yield in matters of principle, while at the same time he was kindly yielding in matters of expediency. He was a bold, fearless and formidable advocate, and few men, either of the laity or clergy, were able or prepared to meet him on the field of controversy, or in the arena of extemporaneous debate. I have often listened, with admiration, to his process of reasoning; although at the same time he swayed and controlled my feelings, he failed to convince my judgment. It was difficult to detect the fallacy of the logic, for it was faultless;—it was so consecutive, that conceding his premises, his conclusions were irresistible.

"But while he was decided, and at times imperious,

he was also equally magnanimous, kind and conciliatory, ever ready for the adjustment of difficulties by mutual concessions and compromises, of which his mind was fruitful. So that while he was regarded as the great polemic, he was equally distinguished as the great pacificator of the Classis.

"His advanced age, large experience, and varied attainments in learning, led us all to regard him not so much in the light of a brother, as of a father. Even the most aged of us were willing to sit at his feet, and to receive with docility the lessons of counsel, admonition, and even of reproof, which might drop from his paternal lips. We often repaired to him for counsel in matters of moment affecting ourselves, and the churches committed to our care; and we have generally found it safe to carry his advice into execution.

"It was his delight to dive into the abstract questions of Philosophy and Theology, and to explore their mysteries. In these departments of learning he became an adept; and was, therefore, for many years honored as being the standing examiner of the Classis on these subjects.

"His intercourse with his ministerial brethren was marked with the dignity and courtesy of a christian gentleman of the olden school.

"Warm and strong in his affections, he wound his way into our hearts, and securing in return our confidence and love—yes, we loved him as a brother in Christ, and as a father in the common ministry of the gospel. We have already deplored the absence of his venerable form, his whitened locks, and his sage counsels, in our ecclesiastical assemblages. Who shall arise to fill his place? On whom shall the mantle of Elijah fall?

"But I fear I may have already trespassed upon the fifteen minutes of time assigned me for this address.

"Instead of saying any thing more myself, I prefer that the venerable and venerated dead shall speak for himself, and utter his own words of parting counsel and affection.

"Among the papers in the archives of the Classis of Ulster, will be found a letter, of recent date, addressed by our departed father himself, to his brethren in the ministry composing the Classis. As it contains his views on varied interesting and important subjects, as well as an expression of his feelings towards each individual member of the Classis, we deem it appropriate to this funeral occasion, and a fitting close to what we have to say, to read this letter."

"SAUGERTIES, April 16, 1871.

"Dear Brethren:—I must first of all apologize for my non-attendance at some of the previous meetings of your reverend body, by alleging indisposition and the painful infirmities of extreme age. I feel constrained to report to you that my decrepitude and diseases are constantly increasing, so that I am compelled, every moment, solemnly to anticipate the near completion of my earthly career. May the precious Redeemer, on whom I rely, gently loosen the cords of life, and in his own time, permit the old unworthy sinner 'to enter into the rest that remaineth for the people of God.'

"I congratulate all my brethren on the events which predict the gradual dethronement of the 'Man of Sin.' The tenth part of the old empire of Rome is rapidly falling. The eldest son of the church is marvelously stricken. 'The time, times and half a time—the forty-two months—the three years and a-half,' so prominent in prophecy, are about to be gloriously and luminously accomplished.   Now is the time for faith to become more clear, more animated, more operative and laborious, and the ministers of Christ to arise from their apathy and inglorious remissness, in which all of us have so long ignominiously slumbered.   Amidst the triumphs of divine truth, are there not palpable indications of increasing audacity, violence, corruption and false alarm on the part of the enemy?

"But amidst all this degeneracy, how little is the amount of my ability to co-operate!   I am seldom free from pain — mournful inconvenience, distressful disquietude, and agitations of unbelief.   Occasionally, only, can I attend the devotions of the sanctuary. Sometimes indeed I gladly assist by short exhortations. How melancholy the condition of one who has preached so long, and now can preach no more!   How sad the bereavement of so precious a privilege.   With many emotions of sadness and grief do I recollect my former unfaithfulness and deplorable omissions!   Irrevocable errors!   In the mean time when I look abroad, I see much to regret.   How frequent and deplorable the removal of ministers!   What agitations and strife in some congregations, — what disregard of some vital doctrines of Christianity!   What contempt of heart-religion, what languor in devotion!   What guilty remissness in myself and others!   Be persuaded, dear brethren, that I am comforted by the thought that your ministrations are in some degree successful.   Permit me also to say, without consciousness of flattery or falsehood, that my secret supplications to heaven are made not only for the Classis in general, but also, every day,

I present your *names individually* before the Throne; and I pray that you will not cease to be faithful in duty in the midst of labor, fatigue and trouble; that you inculcate gospel truth in all simplicity, never failing to feed the lambs of the flock; that you may edify the spiritually hungry. While I am going to the place prepared for me to glorify the blood of the Lamb, may you be long continued in your places to 'note the passing tidings of the times,' to rejoice in the dealings of God's providence, 'valiant for the truth,' until the period of your labor has expired, and you join me among the throng who shall sing forever the song of 'Moses and the Lamb,'

> 'The God of mercy from above
> Give light, and life, and power of love!'

"Finally, will you not pray for an aged departing brother who would fain commune with you on earth; hopes soon to pass over 'Jordan,' and at the appointed time would, around the throne of God, grasp you in his embrace, and bestow upon you all a thousand blessings with feelings of endless love ?

HENRY OSTRANDER."

"N. B.—My age is 90—eyes dim—natural force abated—consequently I say of this paper *Hic labor, hoc opus est.*"

"What more can we say ? Nothing more.

> 'Servant of Christ, well done.
> Rest from thy loved employ.
> The battle fought, the vict'ry won,
> Enter thy Master's joy.'"

This was succeeded by an address by Dr. C. Van Santvoord, which is as follows:

"Three years ago I was present in Chicago, at the first meeting of the graduates of Union College, having their homes in the Northwest. All graduates of the College living in that region, whose addresses could be learned, had received invitations to the re-union. Among the answers received of those not able to attend, was one of singular interest, the reading of which at the table, produced a deep impression on the company. It was a letter written with tremulous hand, but vigorous in expression and graphic in reminiscence and detail, by the Rev. Hubbell Loomis,* of Upper Alton, Illinois, then ninety-four years old, and who had graduated from Union College in 1799, one year before the opening of the present century.

"The circumstance got into the newspapers, and it was widely published, that this patriarchal man was the oldest graduate then living in the United States. This statement I knew to be erroneous, and made the correction publicly. I knew two men, at least, then living, who had graduated from the same College, in the same year, 1799, and who thus were as old, in point of graduation, as Mr. Loomis. One of these is the Rev. Herman Vedder of the Reformed Church, still living at the age of ninety-four. The other is the venerable man whose remains are lying before us, and who, having 'served his generation by the will of God,' has, at length, 'an old man and full of years,' fallen asleep, to be awakened only when the graves shall open at the trump of God!

"Ninety years! It is a long time to live. To the child looking into the future, it seems an indefinitely remote if not unreachable boundary. To one, even with

* Since deceased.

the dew of his youth upon him, the interval looks vast indeed, between life's dawn and four-score years and ten. Looking backward, however, over the steps trodden, changes everything. Years shrivel, illusions are dispelled, and life stands forth to view in its real brevity. 'Few and evil have the days of the years of my life been,' said Jacob, as he surveyed the span which separated his one hundred and thirty years from his childhood in his father's tent. It is the uniform experience of the aged. To the hoary-headed traveller, 'leaning on the top of his staff' as the evening closes in, the comparison of the life-journey to 'a dream,' 'an hand-breadth,' 'a weaver's shuttle,' is clear as a sunbeam in its fitness and force.

"But a very long life, whether it seem short or not, is, after all, only an incident in a man's career. To say of a man, that he died full of years, if nothing more can be said of him, is not to say much. He is an exception, it is true, to the general rule. He began life with millions of infants who never got beyond the time of infancy, with millions of children who never got beyond the period of childhood, with other millions of youth and middle-aged people who never got beyond these periods respectively. This man has outlived the countless millions who have fallen, at various stages of life, strewed like autumnal leaves over all the face of the world. We point to such aged survivor as something exceptional, something out of the ordinary course of events. It is a noticeable thing, this extreme age. But if there has been nothing positive or marked about the person's character, either good or bad, the circumstance of age, itself is not of much account. If all these years have been merely a blank, how great is that blankness! The person might have died at one time as well as another and society been neither worse nor better for his removal. But if the aged person had been strongly marked in life and character by moral obliquities, a lover and doer of evil, continually, then, the more the years, the greater the infamy. No crown of honor, wrought of the good deeds and christian charities of a long life would adorn his hoar hairs. Old as he might be, none would be found so poor as to do him reverence in life or bless his memory in death. Extreme age would be just as remarkable in his case as in that of other men as old as he. But with the wonder occasioned by this, would be mingled another wonder expressed by the question of Job: 'Wherefore do the wicked live, become old, yea, are mighty in power?' Of all the inscrutable things beneath the sun, one of the chiefest is, the lengthening out to extreme old age of the life of a man whose whole career has been a defiance of God, and a continuous blow struck at the highest interests and well-being of man.

"On the other hand 'the hoary head is a crown of glory, if it be found in the way of righteousness.' This is the engaging picture divinely painted, of an aged servant of the Lord. He wears a crown even before his translation, and his honored white hairs are that crown; a crown, too, the lustre of which increases with increasing years. This is God's fiat, and human laws, opinions, fashions, cannot set it aside. The man who does what he can as beneath God's eye, to advance the cause of truth and righteousness, of morals and religion, who brings good tidings to the poor, who comforts the sorrowing and forlorn, warns against snares and dangers, and 'points the strayed to the Good Shepherd's fold' for safety, who instills wholesome lessons into youthful minds to form them for usefulness and honor, and who, in his sphere, is prompt and constant to benefit and bless man and society—such a man, wherever found, is a power for good in community, whose work is beneficent, and whose memory, when he passes away, is fragrant. If he maintain this character, and continue these labors for well-nigh a century, his power strengthens, and his influence brightens; for, 'the path of the just is as the shining light which shines more and more unto the perfect day.' May we not fitly say, that the white hairs which press the lifeless brow of him who lies before us, form such a crown as this?

"Our departed father's life-work is known to you all. His ministry began almost with the century. He was licensed to preach in 1800, and in 1801 he entered on his chosen work at Coxsackie, as pastor of the Reformed Dutch Church there, then a large and influential body. He continued to serve this church till 1812, rendering additional services for two of the last years of this period to the Reformed Dutch Church, in the town of Catskill.

"In 1812, sixty years ago, he accepted a call to the Reformed Dutch Church of Caatsban. This congregation, at that time, spread over a wide territory, embracing within its compass Saugerties, Malden, Plattekill and Blue Mountain, in all of which places, self-sustaining churches have since arisen. The Church of Saugerties was built in 1825, to accommodate the wants of a fast-growing village, and Dr. OSTRANDER continued to minister to the people who erected it, performing, also, regular services at Caatsban till 1840, when it was found desirable to have the two churches maintain separate organizations, each supporting its own pastor. His services were thereafter confined to Caatsban, whose limits had grown gradually narrower in consequence of the erection of other churches around it. In this quiet and pleasant field, surrounded by loving parishioners, he continued laboring faithfully and acceptably till 1862, when he had passed his eightieth year, and fulfilled the fiftieth of his pastoral connection with the people. Then, admonished by the infirmities of advancing years, he retired from the active work of the pastorate, rendering however, when requested, occasional services, till within a year or two of his death. Thus, it may almost be said, that the bow of his strength was hardly unbent, till the summons came for him to put the weapons of his warfare aside, and enjoy the rest, so sweet exceedingly to the warrior after his long and wearisome toils.

"If the ministry of our father and friend was long, it was also fruitful. He was a skillful expounder of the Word. He was an adroit dialectician. He was learned in the Scripture lore. He was a thorough theologian, and loved to explore and expound the great doctrines of christianity, resting upon the atoning sacrifice, the true foundation laid in Zion. In this his great strength lay. He was rich and powerful and cogent here. Few could hear him without stronger impressions of the guilt and peril of sin, or clearer apprehensions of the majesty and holiness of God, and the amazing condescension and love of Him who 'though He was rich, yet for our sakes became poor.'

"His mind was keen, analytical and discriminating, as well as fertile and comprehensive; and his presentation of a subject was felt by the thoughtful listener to be at once convincing and complete. He was thus 'apt to teach,' and instructive to those seeking instruction. Perhaps there was less of the popular element about his preaching than some might have desired. There was certainly nothing of the sensational about it, which not a few of those who run to and fro at the present day for Sabbath stimulus seem to crave. The flowers of fancy and of rhetoric he appeared to regard but slightly, rarely setting any before his hearers, agreeing with Robert Hall, that 'men cannot live on flowers.' But the strong and nourishing meat of the Word he knew how to provide, and did provide with liberal hand, and the fruit of this was seen in the spiritual health and growth and comeliness of those who enjoyed these stated repasts.

"On occasions which did not seem to require the precision or formality of a set discourse, he was often wonderfully happy and effective in his addresses. His language then was more familiar, direct and practical, while an unction pervaded it, springing fresh, as it seemed, from a heart alive with sympathy toward the sorrowful and grief-stricken before him. He had great facility of extemporary speech, and I have heard him in the house of mourning, when called upon unexpectedly to speak, arise and, from the impulse of the moment, as it appeared, pour forth a flood of adapted and eloquent remarks which produced the liveliest impressions. His gift of prayer, too, was remarkable, his petitions being not merely copious and varied, but clothed in the fittest words, appropriate as well to the subject in hand, as to the situation and needs of the worshiping assembly, the church at large and the whole family of man. Beside the couch of languor and suffering, this faculty assumed its tenderest form, and in strengthening the feeble and soothing the last hours of the many who, during his protracted ministry, called for their kindly offices, its value, as a benign agency and on a wide scale, is greater far than words of ours may fittingly portray.

"Our venerable friend wore the robes of the ministerial office with dignity and decorum. He did not spare himself in the labors manifold which his weighty charge imposed, but was earnest and unwearied, during the years of his active pastorate in bringing the influence of his sacred calling to bear upon the hearts and lives of men. While he was brave and fearless in proclaiming the truth, he was a son of consolation in the homes of the grief-burdened and afflicted. Infants, whom he baptized when he began his ministry in this town, are now, if living, among the old men and women in the community. The ties, ramified through all ages and classes, which have so long bound him to these are among the strongest that link society together and hallow the relations between man and man. And when an endeared pastor, around whose name and ministry such tender associations cluster, who for so many years has 'allured to brighter worlds and led the way,' is called from earth to heaven, it seems to survivors a translation like that which Elisha saw, and they are impelled almost, to hail the sight as he hailed it, by exclaiming, more in joy than in sorrow, 'My father, my father, the chariots of Israel and the horsemen thereof.'

"With this sketch of the character and work of our venerated father, I release your attention, having already, I fear, gone beyond the limits marked out for me. I will only add, that the seeds of this long ministry have been scattered broadcast over this community, to spring up and yield fruitage, under the eye of God, and in His good time. They are sown, like the body, in weakness; they are raised, like it, in power. Some of these seeds have already come to light, and borne fruit to the glory of God. Others still lie beneath the dry hard soil, where they have lain for years, without apparent vitality or strength to germinate and pierce the stubborn ground, and rise into a promising growth. Some of them may yet appear, and yield their thirty and their sixty fold. God, whose is the soil and the sunlight and the fertilizing rains, alone knoweth. He hath spoken the words to each of us—O friends and brethren in the ministry—'In the morning sow thy seed, and in the evening withhold not thy hand, for thou knowest not whether shall prosper, this or that.' We cannot tell—no, we cannot tell which shall prosper, but we yet sow at His command. And so did our dear departed father sow the seed in the morning of his life and in its evening did not withhold his hand, trusting to the God of nature and of grace for rich returns. Nor has he been nor will he be disappointed. He toiled well and now he rests, dying, I was just about to say, in the faith in which he lived. But *dying*, as denoting struggle and pain, is too hard a word to use here. For so gently did the aged hand relax its hold on life, so softly were all mortal burdens laid down, that the words 'sleep,' 'he sleepeth,'—an expressive euphemism that the sacred writers love to use—would seem, in this case, literally descriptive of his sinking to rest. And, if there be those who cannot but grieve and be in bitterness as they look upon the placid face of this honored 'lover and friend' whom death has put far from them, let them find calm and courage in imagining his own voice speaking, just on the verge of his going hence, a parting word of solace and good cheer, bearing a burden such as this:

> "And friends, dear friends, when it shall be,
>   That this low breath is gone from me,
>   And round my bier ye come to weep—
>   Let one most loving of you all
>   Say, 'Not a tear must o'er him fall:
> 'He giveth his beloved sleep.'"

After the singing of the 773d Hymn, thus beginning—"What have I in this barren land," the Rev. M. L. Schenck made another address which is here given but in part, for the reason that its lamented author was suddenly summoned to follow his old friend; and amid the confusion and distress occasioned by this affliction, the whole of it could not be found.

"Rev. HENRY OSTRANDER was ordained to the gospel ministry in September 1800, in the twentieth year of his age, and was in the active pastorate sixty-two years, *i. e.*, up to the eighty-second year of his age. After which he rendered occasional service as opportunity offered or his infirmities permitted, up to the time of his death.

"He belonged to a former generation. Labagh, Cannon, Brodhead, Gosman, Westbrook, Overbaugh were his contemporaries. Long has he survived them all; not one remains to tell of his youth, his early manhood and the activities of life's meridian. The very elders in this audience were children or not yet born when he settled as pastor over this flock. In the Classis of Ulster he has been the lone patriarch for years, having been continuously a member of the Classis since 1809, over thirty years longer than any of us. So that none of us can claim personal acquaintance with Dr. OSTRANDER previous to the sixtieth year of his age.

"He has stayed so long behind his time that he now waits for burial by the hands of the second—nay, fourth generation of his successors. 'While he yet stood,' to use the figure of an ancient poet, 'he was as the oak that stands solitary after the surrounding forest has been hewn down, stretching out its stiffened arms as if to implore mercy from the wind and the storm.'

"Yet, there is a sense in which this figure that so strikingly depicts old age, fails to set forth the lengthened days of Dr. OSTRANDER. There were features of mind and heart that yielded not to the frosts of time, he had a social side that never grew old. He could forget his age and lead his friend to forget it too. His was the happy art of forgetting himself in promoting the gratification of others. Such was his cheerfulness and vivacity, his sympathy in the welfare of others, or readiness to yield to the current of another's thoughts, even while he was drawing them out and guiding them, that all felt, in his company, at home; and in more youthful, if congenial society, he was himself rejuvenated. For the past thirty years, in all my intercourse with him, it never occurred to me that he was almost forty years my senior. Not that I would fail in respect to his gray hairs; he was ever venerable to me as a father, a counselor and teacher; his learning and experience made him sage. But it is not his age that impresses me now; my heart regards that form as though fallen in his full strength. I loved him as a brother, an associate, as a companion and a friend. Why he thus condescended to regard me I cannot say, but I hold it no small honor to know that he counted me his friend, and under this sense of bereavement I mourn his loss. He has fallen. But to me the mighty oak, though prostrate, is clothed with the rich exuberance of summer foliage. His physical frame weakened by the way, his infirmities retired him from the world, or what they saw of him was indeed as 'the aged oak stretching out its stiffened arms.' Not so to those who enjoyed his intimacy; to such, after the first salutation, he seldom spoke of himself, never of his personal affairs, but poured a stream of thought upon some topic then of interest in the social, literary or theological world, until all thought of infirmity or disparity of years was forgotten.

"But the end has come, and this whole community have an interest in these solemnities as closing the history of a marked, protracted and useful life.

"The words of David at the grave of Abner befit the occasion, 2 Sam. 3 : 38, 'Know ye not that there is a prince and a great man fallen this day in Israel?'

"There are those who can admire *external greatness* alone. They ask for pomp, glitter and display, where captive trophies must be brought to grace the triumph. But few among the followers of David could appreciate the greatness of Abner as connected with the failing house of Saul. So here we meet devoutly to carry to the grave the remains of one who filled, during a long life, a quiet country pastorate. We have no record of calls to higher fields of labor as accepted or rejected. He occupied no professional chair from which students graduated to spread his praise. His labors were not in Gothic churches nor upon streets of concourse where learning and wealth sat under his ministry, and multitudes blazoned his name into widest popularity. He left no printed works as a heritage to those who come after, or as monuments of his worth. Wonderful is the century in which he lived, in its external greatness, its progress in population and the arts, his age almost coeval with our national existence. Yet, amid all these changes of growth and advancement, this man has stood in his lot employing his great talents, learning and piety, as a servant of God and the church, in enforcing every public and private duty upon the hearts and consciences of his generation; that in the midst of external advancement and prosperity, they might not lose sight of moral obligation : to impress upon all hearts the life and immortality brought to light in the gospel. Thus, by motives drawn from God and eternity calculated to influence all the faculties and powers of their souls, he sought to promote their civil as well as religious interests.

II. "To those who admire intellectual or mental greatness, we say, 'Know you not that a prince and a great man has fallen this day in Israel?'

"One man differs from another in the original frame and strength of his mind, as truly as one star differeth from another star in glory. Some are distinguished from the mass of mankind with bright and glowing genius, which is the essence of mental greatness, the peculiar gift of heaven. And even to such there are degrees, some marked in one form and some in another. The personal of the mind is as marked and individual as that of the body. These are real and distinctive faculties of which we become cognizant as existing in others by our intercourse and observation. Sometimes the opportunity of exercising their power and peculiar gifts is given by extraordinary concurrence of circumstances, as in the cases of Moses and David, a Paul and a Luther, a Washington and a Lincoln. In such cases we cannot say the circumstances made the men. For circumstances do not create, they only develope character. So on the other hand we must not judge of men by their achievements alone, or by the fact of their becoming historic. It is only now and then that scenes open to draw forth the latent energies of great minds, or if given, it may be the arena was not such as lifted the actor to the public gaze. The glory of Jesus upon the Mount of Transfiguration was revealed to but few competent witnesses, while his helplessness as a suffering victim, enduring the taunt 'If thou be the Son of God, cast thyself down from the cross,' was in the sight of assembled Jerusalem. True, we now see his moral greatness as 'enduring the cross, despising the shame.' Yet even his disciples saw it not then, for in the suffering and death of Jesus, the hope that he would redeem Israel yielded to despair.

"We speak not of Dr. OSTRANDER, in view of work accomplished, as though he had done what no other man did. He presents no such claims to greatness. But we do speak of him as endowed with mental powers of a wider compass, combining properties that are seldom found in a single person.

"There were few whose perceptions were so quick as his. He seemed to take in the main features, the strong points of a given case at a glance, to touch the key-note of truth, or to strike the tap-root of a heresy as by intuition. Yet, with this attribute of genius, he was capable of the plodding patience of investigating toil.

"Thus he became, with the glow and fire of genius, the deep and accurate scholar; and, with piety and zeal, a laborious and efficient minister of the gospel, whose long service was no less successful than remarkable."

Prayer was offered by the Rev. W. B. Merritt, and the solemn service was closed with the Benediction.

The remains were reverently borne to their appointed resting-place, and "the mourners go about the streets." Soon after the funeral solemnities, the Rev. N. F. Chapman preached an appropriate sermon in memory of the deceased, from Prov. 10 : 7, "The memory of the just is blessed." The auditors were numerous, and the services of an unusual interest. Thus ended all demonstration. It was enough.

> "What is this world?
> What but a spacious burial field unwalled,
> Strewed with death's spoils?
> The very turf on which we tread, once lived;
> And we that live, must lend our carcasses
> To cover our own offspring!"

The following was the action of the Consistory of the Church of Caatsban:

"*Whereas*, God in his allwise providence has been pleased to remove from this life our former pastor, the Rev. HENRY OSTRANDER, D. D., who, for the period of half a century, served this church and congregation in the ministrations of the gospel of the blessed God, therefore

"*Resolved*, That while in this event we recognize the hand of God, who does all things well, yet we feel constrained personally to give expression to the emotions of sorrow which fill our hearts, because of the departure of him who was to us 'lovely and pleasant' in his life, and who is still precious to us in his death.

"*Resolved*, That we will be ever thankful to the great Head of the Church, for sparing to us for so long a time, one whom he had so fully endowed with the gifts of his Spirit, and qualified to come to us 'in the fulness of the blessings of the gospel of Christ;' and whose pleasure it was to be ever diligent in leading us in the way of truth and the knowledge of Christ, until the infirmities of four-score years admonished him that the time had come when he must cease from the labors of his long pastorate.

"*Resolved*, That in behalf of ourselves whom he served in the gospel, from the days of our earliest recollection, and also in the behalf of our fathers who sleep, with whom he commenced his work in this church, we desire, even more than we can express, to bear our affectionate testimony to his earnest fidelity in all the duties of the pastoral work, wherein he manifested his hearty work for the Master, and proved himself to be a man chosen of God, thoroughly furnished as an ambassador of Christ.

"*Resolved*, That while we are sensible that his death is to us a great bereavement, inasmuch as we know, that, to the last moment of his life, his love for his dear church and people did not grow less, that our welfare lay near his heart, that we ever had a large place in his warmest sympathies, and daily prayers; and while our hearts are filled with sorrow that we shall 'see his face,' and hear his familiar voice 'no more;' yet considering his gain, we cannot say to the Master that he has called his aged servant too soon, nor would we 'recall him, if we could, from his present higher joys to the happiest lot this world can give.'

"*Resolved*, That we tender to the bereaved family of

our beloved pastor our warmest sympathies, assuring them that with them we can weep, because of the taking away of their father from them, and with them can rejoice, because he has gone to be with Christ whom he loved and served.

"*Resolved*, That we will place on the inside wall of the church at the right hand of the pulpit, an appropriate memorial tablet ; and that we affectionately ask the members of the church and congregation to aid us in erecting this testimony to his memory.

"*Resolved*, That a copy of these resolutions be sent to the family of the deceased."

The following resolutions were adopted by the Classis of Ulster, April 15, 1873:

"*Whereas* it has pleased our Heavenly Father during the past year to remove our venerable father in the ministry, the Rev. HENRY OSTRANDER, D. D., from the scene of his labors here, to the inheritance of his reward above, therefore

"*Resolved*, That while we recognize in this event the supreme will of God, who must ever have the right to say to his servants, when it pleases him—'Come up higher'—we do also recognize our bereavement in the loss of one, who, for the long period of more than sixty years, was a member of this Classis, whose ripe judgment we regarded as a safe rule, and whose counsels were wise and pacific.

"*Resolved*, That we will ever cherish a lively remembrance of his many social and Christian virtues, his magnanimity, his profound scholarship, and of his superior excellencies as a preacher of the gospel of Christ.

"*Resolved*, That we are thankful to God, that he was so long spared to us, and to the church, and that he was enabled to fill up his protracted life with usefulness, and at last was brought 'to the grave in a full age, like as a shock of corn cometh in his season.'

"*Resolved*, That as an expression of our sympathy, a certified copy of these resolutions be sent to his bereaved family.   A. M. ARCULARIUS, *Prest. p. t.*

I. N. VOORHES, *Clerk p. t.*"

At a regular meeting of the Ministerial Association of the Town of Saugerties held on December 20th, 1873, the following minute was unanimously adopted, and the Secretary was directed to send it to the bereaved family with an expression of the most cordial sympathy, and with the earnest prayers of all the brethren in their behalf.

"The undersigned, a committee appointed by the Ministerial Association of the Town of Saugerties to prepare a notice of the death of the Rev. HENRY OSTRANDER, D. D., for sixty years an honored minister of the Reformed Dutch Church in this town, offer the following:

"That having had the pleasure of the company of our deceased father in the gospel, and having been profoundly impressed by his wisdom, his extensive learning, his deep spirituality, and his meetness for heaven, we place this tribute to his memory on record; and most devoutly pray the Head of the Church to raise up others who shall as worthily represent the Master in their christian character and serve him as faithfully in the Christian Ministry.   A. H. FERGERSON,

M. L. SCHENCK,

N. F. CHAPMAN."

At an extra session of the Classis of Paramus, held November 26th, 1872, the following resolutions were unanimously adopted:

"*Whereas*, The Rev. HENRY OSTRANDER, D. D., (the first licentiate of the Classis of Paramus, licensed in September, 1800,) has been called from earthly toil to heavenly rest, leaving behind him the record of a faithful ministry, and of a life hid with Christ in God; therefore,

"*Resolved*, That while we rejoice in the thought that our brother is to-day with Christ, we desire, as representatives of the Classis in which he received licensure seventy-two years ago, to express our sense of the great loss which the church has sustained in the death of this venerable man of God; a preacher of righteousness. who by his life, no less than by his pulpit utterances, proclaimed the power of the gospel of Christ.

"*Resolved*, That our warmest sympathy is extended to those more immediately bereaved by this dispensation. We commend them to God and to the word of His grace.

"*Resolved*, That these resolutions be published in *The Christian Intelligencer*, and that a copy of the same be transmitted to the family of the deceased. Attest,

"MARSHALL B. SMITH, Stated Clerk."

The following letter, coming from a distinguished physician in the City of New York, will be read with interest:

"Rev. and Dear Sir:—In answer to your note of the first inst. making some inquiry respecting my acquaintance with the late Rev. Dr. OSTRANDER, permit me to say that I became acquainted with him when I was about ten years of age (fifty years ago), at which time my father and family moved to Saugerties, Ulster Co., N. Y. Dr. OSTRANDER was then preaching in the Stone Church at Caatsban, and at Saugerties on alternate Sundays I think, or during the forenoon at one place, and in the afternoon at the other. At the former, he preached every other Sabbath in Dutch. His hair was, at that time, as white as snow; and he was revered during my childhood, as the 'Old Domine.' During my youth, he was my friend: and when I arrived at manhood, and commenced the practice of my profession, I had the honor of being his family physician, and of enjoying his kind social qualities, with the benefit of his wise counsels.

"Dr. OSTRANDER was most truly an extraordinary man; one of rare ability; a profound scholar, reaching great depths of thought; an accurate reasoner, and powerful in argument; and while I feel that it is but a simple act of justice and duty to say this, I believe him to have been most truly a meek follower and disciple of his Blessed Master: yet he was not the man to brook an insult, come from what source it might; nor would he, by remaining silent, ever yield a tacit acquiescence in pernicious opinions; being ever ready to vindicate the truths of the Bible, and to stand up in the defence of the right, and of the oppressed.

"He was very happy in argument, always having a large reserve fund to draw upon. For his readiness in this line, I was inclined to think him rather given to controversy. I remember visiting, years ago, his little grandson, who was in a critical state from malignant scarlet fever. During the fore part of an evening, I casually made some remark connected with my profession as founded on *fact*, when the doctor at once corrected me by saying, that his profession was founded on *fact*, but mine was founded upon *observation*. An argument at once ensued, which lasted until broad daylight of the following morning. That night will ever be remembered by me, but not from any argument that I advanced; for I knew the impregnability of the fortress too well to harbor the idea of controverting successfully a single argument of his. His premises were not assumed, but were historical facts; and his deductions were volumes of beauties.

"I loved him most dearly, and to know him was to love him. Did I possess the power, how gladly would I be a modern Plutarch to write his history. The feeble utterance of mortal man can hardly do him justice, much less eulogize his life and character; and when language proves inadequate to a full expression, silence may convey more than words can indicate.

" His name was a tower of strength. The wide-spread philanthropy of his boundless heart, will be remembered by all who know him; and his precepts will remain like spots of verdure to gladden the hearts of those who are making the pilgrimage of life, after we have passed away.

"I had the pleasure of seeing him but a short time previous to his death, when he was bowed under the weight of years, and far advanced in the winter of his earthly existence. Even then, his sparkling eye kept pace with the unimpaired brilliancy of his intellect, and at that very late period of his life, he was still the Rev. Dr. OSTRANDER. And as his life's sands were fast descending, they bore unmistakable evidence of those of the righteous, for they *glittered* as they ran.

"Thanking you for the extreme privilege of adding the above mite of testimony to the memory of that great and good man,

"I am very truly yours,

"M. FRELIGH,

"31 West 24th St., *July 9th*, 1873.

"Dr. W. R. GORDON."

To the foregoing testimony, honorable alike to a generous mind and heart, it is proper to add the impressions of another, brought up under his ministry. The Rev. A. Dubois, D. D., has kindly furnished the following:

"My recollections of Dr. OSTRANDER are among my earliest of any person in the ministry. My parents residing at Kiskatom, attended divine service at Leeds; and many a tedious ride of six miles have I had in childhood over the rough, broken country, and through the 'five mile woods' to Leeds, to hear the dear good domine who preached there with so much youthful vigor. In all the country, for many miles around, Domine OSTRANDER exercised his long ministry.

"His habit was to maintain regular preaching services at different points along the Catskill Mountains, and across the country to the Hudson River. His nearest point in such regular appointments was at the School House in 'Yankee Town,' where afterwards a small church was built. I well remember my anxiety to see him there when I was a small boy, now more than forty years ago. Even then he seemed to me an old man. His head was nearly white, but his eye was so intensely black and sparkling, his action so impressive and singular, his words so strangely expressed, and full of fire, and his sermons so instructive and eloquent, that while the older people hung with profit on his preaching, it was not strange that he should be a wonder to a child. Once at Yankee Town I heard him preach from the words: 'And Gallio cared for none of these things.' His first words were, '*And wasn't that strange?*' Then he showed what Gallio was, and had; and what was within his reach by the preaching of the apostle, and this to show us, as his sermon advanced, what trifles we pursue while the riches of God are urged on our acceptance in the gospel. Then taking a fixed position and lifting one hand high above his head, and pointing downward with the other, he contrasted earth and heaven in a series of sentences occupying a good many minutes, with a beauty and power of language which I have never heard surpassed.

"His manner was often abrupt, and sometimes seemingly harsh as if in anger. Coming once to a school house near us, which was crowded with people on a hot summer afternoon, he looked in at the door and exclaimed, 'This place is *too hot to preach in*, come out under the trees,' when a regular stampede took place, and the service was conducted in the cool grove.

"Dr. OSTRANDER's manners among his people were affectionate and fatherly. They loved him dearly and consulted him with utmost confidence even on matters of a delicate and trying nature. His habit was to study thoroughly for himself new questions as they presented themselves, and then take an open stand upon them. Very early there had come to be some agitation at Leeds about new measures, and the nature and effects of special seasons of revival. To quiet matters, Domine OSTRANDER was asked to preach on the subject, which he did, and showed, in a full discussion of the whole subject, that revivals had occurred as blessed visitations of God's mercy from the earliest times of the church, and should be encouraged and wisely and prayerfully used for the upbuilding of religion. When Millerism began to attract attention he deemed the subject worthy of careful study, which he gave it, and then publicly stated his reasons, the results of his own original investigations, why the church need not expect immediate translation to glory. So, too, did he thoroughly study the subject of assurance of faith, and the claim of entire sanctification.

"There are few men to whom it has been my good fortune to listen who have instructed and moved me more thoroughly than Dr. OSTRANDER. His command of words in extemporaneous address was always remarkable, often wonderful, and his fancy exuberant and admirably well sustained. He loved the more profound themes of pulpit discourse, and caused his sermons some way always to revolve around the cross, and so close as to receive love and life and power from it. If one were asked, What did Dr. OSTRANDER most preach? he would reply without hesitation, The ATONEMENT. His sermons constantly brought into highest prominence the doctrines of human salvation, by the person and work of Jesus Christ. We can have no better subject for the pulpit, and it would be for the safety and true advancement of the church if this kind of preaching could displace the important, and elegant *nonsense* so frequently paraded in high places as the gospel. 'No man having drunk old wine, straightway desireth new; for he saith, The old is better.'"

It is proper in this connection to add the hearty expression of those who succeeded Dr. Ostrander in the pastoral charge at Saugerties. In unison with the testimony of Dr. C. Van Santvoord at the funeral solemnities of our departed father, Dr. J. Elmendorf writes:

"His reputation as a preacher, theologian, controlling member of church judicatories, added definite attractions to the invitation to a settlement which would make me his neighbor. And it was peculiarly gratifying to have Classis appoint him to preach the sermon on the occasion of my installation. This discourse, which was from Matt. 11:21—an unusual text for the occasion—fully sustained his fame. It was a clear and exhaustive presentation of the truth under consideration, and applied with impressive originality and force. Although at the time he was several years passed threescore and ten, yet his delivery was energetic and commanding, and in impassioned passages, his voice was thrilling, and his eye flashed with the fire of youth. The few other public efforts by him, which it was my privilege to hear, were equally characterized by perspicuity, thoroughness and originality of treatment.

"It was in the meetings of Classis that Dr. Ostrander's varied and surpassing abilities especially impressed me. He was the 'standing' examiner in Theology, and was quite the dread of candidates, because of the searching manner in which he did his work. He was accustomed to lead them out in the direction of every doctrine, as far as they knew the way, and then by a question or two, to show them that it went on far beyond the point they had reached. None who noted the intimations of his profound reflections thus given, can fail to hope that they have been fully elaborated and preserved, so that they can be given to the church. His unsurpassed familiarity with the letter of the Constitution of the Church not only, but also with the principles and practice of ecclesiastical law, made him very prominent and influential in trying and deciding cases of discipline. Only they who witnessed his efforts could have any adequate idea of his resources. A genius and taste for jurisprudence that would have made him a leader in the front rank of the legal profession, were shown in his management of ecclesiastical lawsuits. Having observed his efforts in two important trials, I am prepared to credit any representations of his success, consistent with legitimate possibility. His relative standing and power in ecclesiastical assemblies resembled those of the contemporaneous giants in our national councils who, with himself, have passed away. Alas! when, in church or state, shall we see their like again?"

Rev. Dr. J. Gaston says: "I was frequently in Dr. Ostrander's company during the seven years that I lived at Saugerties, heard him preach a number of times; was present upon several occasions when he conducted the examination of candidates for the ministry upon natural religion and systematic theology; besides enjoying the privilege of frequently attending his discussions of the various current questions of church polity, which from time to time claimed the attention of Classis. Having had these opportunities of forming a judgment of his abilities, I do not hesitate to say that he possessed in a very unusual degree a large, quick, and comprehensive mind. His perception of things was prompt, clear, and discriminating. It always seemed to me that he excelled most other men in the gift to discern at the same glance the centre and the circumference of a proposition."

Rev. S. H. Cobb says: "The clearness of his mind was remarkable to the very last. The breadth of view and sharp analysis of the accomplished theologian never failed him. Amid all the physical weakness incident to extreme old age, his intellectual sight and vigor were in all their prime. A striking instance of this I remember in the examination of a candidate for licensure in the May preceding his death. Being present at the meeting of Classis, he was invited to conduct the examination in Theology. I think that every one who listened to that exercise, must have been astonished at the masterly skill the examiner evinced. Those that had, by a long acquaintance, been more conversant with his powers, were surprised at this exhibition of them. The accurate discriminations, the fine points of definition, slight divergencies in doctrine which require the keenest of logical acumen, were as sharply and definitely handled as they could be by any theological professor. He showed that, despite his years and infirmities, he retained the full vigor of a first-rate mind."

Left to our own reflections upon the long experience and completed character of the departed, how natural that a crowd of thoughts should clamor for utterance! An age of ninety years at any time, in any country, clothes a man of ordinary mould with unusual interest in the eyes of those around him who never expect to see it; but how greatly is the interest increased when such a life as here fills our attention, presents associations of time, place, and circumstance now rarely met with! He shook hands with the heroes of the Revolution, and with ourselves. He was personally interested in the various questions which arose in the infancy of our Republic, and in those of the present day. He was born when a journey from Saugerties to Albany, or to New York, occupied a long time; was difficult, if not dangerous; and when weeping friends often bedewed each other with their tears, over the gunwale of a sloop. He died when steamboats plow our rivers, when the electric telegraph encircles the globe, and when the reception of a message from Europe *antedates* the hour of its composition, by our time. The first census of the United States included him, amounting to 3,929,328; and so did the last, amounting to 38,558,371. In his boyhood, the thirteen original colonies bordering on the Atlantic, composed the States of the Union; while three-fourths of his own State of New York was an unbroken wilderness; in his old age, he could count forty-two States and Territories lying between the two great oceans of the world. When he was a youth, the population of the City of New York was 33,000, speaking the Hollandish and English languages; when he was an old man, the population of that city was 910,000, speaking some eighty languages and dialects, the English of course largely predominating. With all questions of politics, of internal and external prosperity and adversity; with all religious questions, and denominational interests, incipient and progressive, from the beginning of our national existence to the present day, he was more or less familiar; and the interest he took in passing events, and the associations he formed with prominent men, made his a comprehensive experience, more varied than that which any of the present generation can ever attain, and a character moulded by a greater variety of influences, and processes of thought, than those impressing the men of our day.

That character is not easily delineated, because marked by qualities seemingly incompatible among themselves. He was proud, without being pretentious; and humble, without being obsequious. By turns, he was cheerful and melancholy, gay and grave, quick and slow; and, in short, variable in feeling, but firm in principle. It was not great talent, nor learning, nor spirituality alone that made him a marked man; but a fertile genius, a sound judgment, a fiery courage, a child-like simplicity, a noble charity, honesty of purpose, and generosity of action united in forming him what he was; so that while we mean to do him justice, we may fail in the attempt.

Dr. OSTRANDER was constitutionally of a mirthful spirit, and his quick perception of the ridiculous often led him into expressions of it, that often caused him to reflect more upon himself severely than others would ever think of doing. His overflowing good nature would sometimes intrude itself at times and in places where it was not expected; but somehow never to his disadvantage. An instance of such intrusion will let in some light upon this side of him.

The Rev. Martin L. Schenck was a man after his own heart, to whom he was greatly attached. Mr. Schenck had been settled at Plattekill, for a number of years, and then left for another field of labor; but after a while he was recalled to be their minister, and was installed on June 22d, 1869. On this occasion Dr. OSTRANDER delivered the charge to the pastor. Knowing the proclivities of the pastor-elect to be in some respects like his own, he felt himself, in view of previous relations, impelled to the expression of what came uppermost, and thus he began:

"First of all let me repeat, as well as I can, a Latin verse of an ancient poet,

> "'Difficilis, facilis, jucundus, acerbus es idem,
>   Nec possum tecum vivere, nec sine te.'

"Mark the translation made by an ancient philosopher:

> "'In all thy humors, whether grave or mellow,
>   Thou art such a touchy, testy, pleasant fellow,
>   Thou hast so much of wit and mirth about thee,
>   There is no living with thee, nor without thee.'

"I do not introduce this quotation as entirely appropriate, or containing any charge against you of immoderate indulgence in cheerfulness of disposition, for now we are all cheerful and happy in the consideration that one who was comparatively dead to us, is alive again among us; yet there is danger of immoderation in this respect, from the fact that you live in near contiguity to an old example (you know whom I mean) of occasional frivolity who penitently deplores his excesses while gradually returning to the dust. Correct, if you please, this error, and by simplicity, solemnity, and sobriety of thought, honor and glorify your Master who has given us a solemn and holy call from above.

"But there is another part of this verse to which I would more particularly refer. 'There is no living with you, nor without you.' Once indeed this people and their ancestors seemed to acquiesce in your departure; they thought they could live without you, but they found themselves mistaken. Let congregations who are so ready and stupid to give up their ministers without necessity, and send them away in disrepute and obloquy, consider that they may, at the same time, send away the favor of God. While they seek to remove their candle, they may furnish occasion for removing the candlestick, and expose themselves to regret, disappointment, disadvantage and ruin. In the present case, however, and in this congregation, there seems to be a return to reason and reflection, so far indeed, that they now see that they 'cannot live without you.' Their liberality, and multiplied inducements constrained the far West to yield to their demands."

This was followed by a series of remarks upon the importance of the ministerial relation to a congregation, which went to show the responsibility and danger of those seeking its infraction for a trivial cause. The whole address was a pencil of rays directed upon this subject. His buoyancy of spirit contributed much to his efficiency in the prosecution of his work.

Dr. OSTRANDER, it is hardly necessary to say, was not free from faults. He was sensitive, and at times impulsive; and this often rendered him liable to be misunderstood. When he felt sure that he was right in any line of action, he was ready to give his reasons for it, and as ready to bear down upon any opposition which he thought was unreasonable; yet he was ever magnanimous to an opponent. He had his share of those failings of which all men partake; but what of it? The sun has spots, yet in spite of them he shines with undimmed glory. No man was less self-asserting than he, and no man apparently knew himself better than he. Whatever an unfriendly criticism might find to discount from his character as here imperfectly depicted, one thing is certain, and it is enough, "He was a good man, and full of the Holy Ghost and of faith, and much people were added unto the Lord."

As a preacher, he was powerful in diction, and impressive in appeal. His imagination, well poised on pinions of strength, while attempting no gyrations for the entertainment of his auditors, did its duty in tastefully adorning those webs of argument his reason wrought out. It was a good illustration of Akenside's poem:

> "Lo! she appeals to nature, to the winds,
>   And rolling waves, the sun's unwearied course,
>   The elements and seasons; all declare
>   For what the eternal Maker has ordained
>   The powers of man; we feel within ourselves
>   His energy divine: he tells the heart,
>   He meant, he made us to behold and love
>   What he beholds and loves, the general orb
>   Of life and being; to be great like him,
>   Beneficent and active. Thus the men
>   Whom nature's works can charm, with God himself
>   Hold converse; grow familiar, day by day,
>   With his conceptions; act upon his plan;
>   And form to his, the relish of their souls."

While yet a young man, he was invited to accept a chaplaincy, in the war of 1812; but he chose a more laborious field of labor, and one to the cultivation of which he was eminently adapted. Here he labored with unflagging ardor. Of commanding personal appearance, the dignity and reverence of his manner in the pulpit, the earnestness of his address, the fire of his eloquence were exceedingly impressive. All this, however, is lost to the reader of the following sermons; but one can imagine the power with which they must have fallen upon the ear, when driven with the force of such propulsion. To illustrate. On one occasion an auditor was drawn up from his seat, and, as if entranced, stood unconsciously bent over, like an interrogation mark, with his eyes fixed upon the preacher. On another, a hearer unconsciously became an actor, vigorously gesticulating responsively to the sentiments which fell from the lips of the doctor. On another, a gentleman was so carried away, as to keep up an audible muttering, not knowing that he was disturbing others around him. The Rev. M. L. Schenck was accustomed to relate the following anecdote. "At a certain Classical meeting Dr. OSTRANDER was to preach. A minister of some note was present, not a member of the body; and when the 'Old Domine' ascended the pulpit, this minister settled himself in the corner of a pew, in such a manner as to convey the idea of *endurance* on his part. But as the discourse proceeded, the interest increased. He was captivated, and half rising from his seat, with opened eyes and moving lips, unconsciously attracted observation. This continued until the end; when his mind was released from its tension he sank back in his seat, and with a long breath exclaimed aloud, 'that's a rouser!'" Many other instances of a similar nature might be given, but these are related only to justify a previous remark.

In the preparation of his sermons, he studied them well before writing, and being thus filled with a subject, when aroused, he would leave his notes and pour out a volume of thought and intonation inspired by the occasion; so that his written discourses were by no means faithful representations of his most effective efforts.

In the arena of debate, he was a master of the situation, and often would accept the position of an adversary, and adroitly beat him in the use of his own arguments.   On such occasions, when wrought up to a high pitch of excitement, he would storm his opponents with shot and shell, and after the battle, repair all damages.   His wonderful power in this and other respects, as a controlling mind in the Classis of Ulster, is attested by those who have borne witness to his usefulness in settling ecclesiastical difficulties, and composing matters of strife.

He was a profound thinker and student until the last. His interest in the prophetical Scriptures was always great, and no amount of laborious research could deter him in grappling with a difficulty.   His anxiety was to comprehend the mind of the Spirit as set forth in prophecy. By the evidence of the last sermon, in the following selection from his pen, it is quite clear that his mind was laboring unsatisfied with the ordinary method of treatment in the exposition of the prophetical Scriptures. Like the man in the gospel whose eyes were touched by the Great Physician, for a while he saw "men like trees walking ;" but like him when subjected to a second touch, he saw clearly and correctly the great truths of Eschatology and its stupendous facts in their chronological relations.   He had a firm conviction that what is called pre-millennarianism is the only sure method by which the Scriptures, as a whole, can be intelligently and consistently expounded.   He esteemed it as the only key adapted to unlock numerous Scripture difficulties that had long lain in his way; and at the last, it was a source of comfort to his mind and heart, altogether above and beyond the prevailing sentiment of the church, which he came to regard as inadequate and unsatisfactory, owing to a method of interpretation, unphilosophical in theory, very fallacious and mischievous in practice. Such were his sentiments as expressed to the present writer, and always accompanied with delight gleaming from his animated face, as he expatiated upon the expansiveness and consistency of view he enjoyed as to the coming of the Lord, and his glorious personal reign upon the reclaimed earth.

The following extract from a letter to the writer by Rev. Wm. B. Merritt, whose ministry at Flatbush Dr. OSTRANDER often attended, and to whom he was greatly attached, bears decisive testimony on this point:

"In catechising me one day, he discovered that my mind had been somewhat exercised on the personal reign of our Lord on earth. He at once desired that I should read 'Faber,' and to this end loaned me his own copy; calling my attention to many passages he had marked. After this, he frequently alluded to the subject and expressed himself decidedly on the side of Pre-millennarianism, frequently adding: 'It is by far the surer method of interpreting prophecy.'—'In interpretation of prophecy, therefore, I hold strongly to the ground which Millennarians have so nobly fought.' In speaking of the second coming of our Lord, his face would shine as he exclaimed, 'O how I should love to be here, when He comes to renovate the earth wherein shall dwell righteousness!' This was a favorite saying of his. It was my pleasure to present him with a copy of 'Christocracy,' which he fairly devoured. He not only read the book through at least three times, but carefully studied those parts of it which were of the greatest interest to himself in respect to his previous difficulties. He exclaimed, 'O that our ministers would read this book!' The day before translation to his heavenly home he was reading it, and repeatedly said,

'I thank the authors of Christocracy for so clearly setting forth views which must yet be adopted by the whole church militant.'"

"The state of his mind on this subject was most beautifully disclosed in a prayer he offered some little time before his departure, at the close of a meeting of the Classis of Ulster held in the Church of Flatbush, which was not very far from his own dwelling. He moreover thought that the spirit of religious bodies toward harmony in co-operative union, intimated preparation for the coming of the King who is to sit on the throne of his father David, unto whom shall the gathering of the people be."

A letter from the daughter upon whom he most relied, contains evidence of his sentiments and feelings on this subject. "He always regarded the common view as unsatisfactory, and for years while unable to decide in his own mind fully that the Pre-millennarians were right, he never believed with the opponents in their spiritualizing process. He always said there was 'great inconsistency' in that method of interpretation, and gradually came to feel more and more confirmed in this conviction. When Rev. Mr. Merritt brought him the 'Christocracy,' it was like a new revelation to him. The time of the 'Judgment' had always perplexed him before. He could not reconcile the different parts of prophecy in regard to it. But now he was clear. 'Why, Ann, the Judgment will go on all through;' meaning the Millennium. It was a new delight to him, as a solace, a joy to find the mystery unravelled, the harmony of prophecy respecting 'the Coming One.' His countenance would be all lit up, his thoughts and words being beyond my comprehension."

"A few mornings before his death—the third—upon inquiry as to sleep during the night, he said that he 'had not slept at all.' 'Why did you not call for company, as usual?' He replied, 'O, I had such a pleasant night, such transporting, heavenly views.'"

"Occasionally, only, he could see to read. These moments were occupied in reading Christocracy and the Bible; and towards his end, these two books were the only ones he called for; and he always had them within reach. For years, he said to many persons that he could better interpret prophecy by taking the 'Pre-millennarian view;' and as his days advanced he became more inclined to that opinion; and as life drew to a close, he did not doubt."

Dr. OSTRANDER was a remarkable man for his executive abilities. Of this the testimony of the members of the Classis of Ulster is unanimous and copious. Nothing can or need be said in corroboration of their statements as to the *tout ensemble* of the man they loved. These records exhibit how much we have *lost* in the departure of this eminent servant of God. Nay, that is not the word. Spared to a ripe old age, and having made full proof of his ministry, an honored instrument of long use in the Master's service, we have lost nothing in his departure, but have gained much to enlighten, encourage, and cheer us in our earthly pilgrimage. "He being dead yet speaketh."

The following selection out of four hundred and fifty-five sermons written out, will serve to show his method of thought and discussion, whilst the saving truths of the gospel presented may yet protract that blessed influence which he so long and so happily exerted for the salvation of them that heard him.   Gifted with uncommon mental and physical energy which, unspared, was gladly devoted to his profession, he was foremost upon the field in "bearing the heat and burden of the day."   He went forth weeping, bearing precious seed; and when Christ comes, he shall return bringing his sheaves with him.   Thanks be unto God for such gifts to his church as the Rev. Dr. OSTRANDER.   With a noble character, and an untarnished reputation, he left nothing to mar the work of a long and a laborious life of usefulness.   Blessed is his memory, and glorious is his destiny among the stars that shine forever and ever.

SERMONS.

THE EXISTENCE OF GOD.

Rom. 1 : 20. "For the invisible things of him from the creation of the world are clearly seen, being understood by the things that are made, even his eternal power and Godhead."

There are many moral truths which, however obvious to the human mind, require to be frequently enforced upon reason and conscience. Though the idea in each be clear to our perception, as natural in itself, and important to us, it may eventually become faint to our mental vision, and fail to impress us as at first, by reason of our occupancy with the inferior crowd of other ideas that arise from the variety and claims of our daily concerns.

It is, moreover, quite possible, that a very simple truth may be shorn of its power over the heart, because it is seen to be unfriendly to our peace derived from carnal pleasures which we are prone to pursue, and therefore may be thrust away from our consideration. In such case, it is quite customary to treat it with contempt as unworthy of our attention; but that is not the real reason which, say what we will, lies in the dislike for it of which we are all the while conscious. The consequence of all this is deplorable enough. That moral truth which at first was so plain and simple, and so well calculated to prompt to duty becomes inoperative by this process, and lies dormant in the soul. Hence the conduct of men often is such, as if that truth had never been known or felt by them at all. We all believe, for example, that there is a God, but alas, how few act as if they felt the force of their own admission!

These considerations will justify me in taking for my subject, at this time, the great moral truth of the Existence of God. The text affirms it is a truth exceedingly plain: "For the invisible things of him from the creation of the world are clearly seen, being understood by the things that are made, even his eternal power and Godhead."

I. I propose to adduce a few arguments in support of this truth which ought to have the most commanding influence over our lives and conduct. We begin with general thoughts.

1. When we speak of GOD, we refer to the self-existing, ever-living, and infinitely perfect Being who is the only independent and almighty cause of all things; who holds all things in absolute and perpetual dependence on Himself; and governs all things in subserviency to His own purposes. His natural perfections are independence, simplicity, immutability, eternity and immensity. His moral perfections are holiness, power, wisdom, justice, goodness and truth. It is not our object, at present, to show that these perfections essentially belong to God; for, admitting his Being, we must admit them as its qualifying terms; but we mean to show that His existence is a *fact*, that should be to us an omnipresent and controlling truth.

While we contend that such an awfully great and holy Being exists, essentially possessing these perfections, let it not be supposed that we assert our adequacy to comprehend His mode of being, or his ineffable glory. No created intellect can possess this power. "Who by searching shall find out God? Who shall find out the Almighty to perfection?" Such knowledge is too wonderful for us, we cannot attain to it. There are, indeed, various names given Him in the Scriptures, to assist our conceptions of His Being and attributes; yet there is no one name of an import so comprehensive as adequately to describe the Almighty Maker of heaven and earth. Because he is incomprehensible, he is not nameable by any single appellative. "Wherefore dost thou ask concerning my name, seeing it is hidden?" "What is his name, or his Son's name, if thou canst tell?" As all our knowledge of invisible objects is derived from analogy that is, from the resemblances which they have, or bear in their properties to visible objects, and as there is no object in existence that has the exact and full resemblance of the Deity, it is evident that His awful nature must be infinitely more exalted than we are capable of conceiving; and every attempt to adequately describe him must be futile and presumptuous in the extreme. Hence the second command of the decalogue forbids the formation of any likeness of God, because it would be a caricature, and an objective blasphemy.

2. Yet, while it may be difficult for us to speak with sufficient and satisfactory precision on this mighty subject, we can most assuredly affirm, that there is such a glorious Being; the original and self-existent cause of all things. This is a truth so plain and obvious, that it is passing strange how any such sentiment as Atheism expresses could ever have existed. Strange, indeed, that any one should be able to strip himself of the

principles of his own nature, and so pervert the powers of his own understanding, as to deny in sincerity the existence of a God! Great allowances are indeed to be made for the thoughtlessness of many, who take up any sentiment without examination, and are guided more by the opinions of others than by conclusions of their own; and for that wildness and eccentricity of some persons, whose conduct can hardly be viewed as consistent with any principles at all; allowances also must be for the habits and manners of people, which have a great influence on their belief; and for the wishes of others, whose interest it would be that there should be no God. But after all, it seems impossible that any person whose wish it is, that there were no God, should so far succeed in forming their principles agreeably to their practices, as to settle themselves down into a uniform and fixed belief that there *is no God*. This is no less amazing than absurd.

3. Of one thing however we may be confident. Practical Atheism largely abounds. That such sentiments are entertained, and such practices are pursued as seem compatible only with the disbelief of His existence is too apparent, for otherwise a clear conviction of the truth in question should naturally operate as checks to the freedom which licentiousness assumes. Some men have speculative knowledge of His existence. They barely believe it possible or probable, but not with that settled conviction which influences to circumspection in the pursuits of life. But though it might be useless to argue the matter for the purpose of bringing speculative opinion up to the character of a reasonable and controlling faith, it surely must be of consequence to illustrate the fact, for the purpose of enforcing its

power, exciting your reverence, and prompting your obedience.

II.   Let us then attend to some points in the general argument which establishes the fact in question beyond all reasonable doubt, and shows Atheism to be incompatible with all principles that regulate human opinion, and control the mind in coming to a fixedness of faith on any subject whatever.

1.   In the first place we direct attention to that general impression of a Deity resting upon the universal mind of mankind, as a fact beyond dispute; and therefore a fact beyond explanation, if the human understanding were not naturally endowed with an intuition easily accounting for the universal belief in the existence of God.   It has indeed been observed that there is no such thing as an innate idea of God, and that this impression of His existence is derived altogether from sensation which comes only from reflection upon the visible world.   But this is an assumption not easily justified, and certainly not in agreement with the inspired account of the matter; for speaking of the Gentiles, Paul says that "The works of the law are written upon their hearts,"—an assertion seemingly supported by the general impression just spoken of.

The multiplicity of deities of contrary character in the heathen world, has also been urged as an objection against the idea of God as natural to man; but this, we hold, proves directly the reverse; on the contrary, it is an argument in favor of it; for how otherwise can we account for any object of worship?   In consequence of a general impression variably distinct, but all-pervading, we find every nation acknowledging a deity of some kind; and history shows that this has always been the fact. If there have been individuals, at times, declaring that they were never conscious of any such impression, we are not bound to believe them, while they claim to have their rational powers unimpaired, since this universal impression is common to universal mind; and if any heathen have been found who have discovered no symptoms of the knowledge of God, it is fair to believe that they have been misrepresented through the inadequacy of those making the assertion, since the most stupid Hottentots, Greenlanders, Kamscatkians and American savages have discovered a belief in, and a regard to Deity.

In consequence of this general impression of a God, we find that the most wicked and abandoned are often disturbed by a dread of His anger. There have been those who may have *labored* to persuade themselves that there is no God, but they have been unable to conceal their fears; for the stories of ghosts and apparitions have frozen them with horror! This general impression thus asserts itself even in those who deny it. Moreover the stupidest heathen discover a willingness and readiness to acknowledge a Supreme Power. Missionaries have often found great difficulty in the inculcation of Christianity upon the heathen, but no difficulty at all in procuring from them an acknowledgment of the Almighty. Amidst all their ignorance they know there is a God; it is a doctrine written on their hearts, and engraven on their consciences. And now we ask, whence could their universal impression come, but from the power of a fact omnipresent to and omnipotent over the world of mind? What priest could have branded it into the universal conscience of our race? What prince, or power of mortal, would or could have imposed it upon the successive generations of the world? Since all nations have their own peculiar customs and habits, how could the same custom and the same habit exclusively and universally prevail, when no intercourse obtained among them? Amid the variations of manners and customs in every generation of every kind of people, how happens it, that this alone remains the one only universal moral characteristic of all mankind from age to age? There is only one explanation. The impression of Godhead is instinctive in manhood, or it is the unobliterated result of revelation flooding the world from the beginning with the evidence that there is a God, and that He reigns supreme over the affairs of men.

III. Let us advance a step further. The original production of all things clearly demonstrates the existence of God, and of these nothing more powerfully than man himself. We turn our eyes upon ourselves, and we know intuitively that we exist. We are possessed of bodies wonderfully fashioned, all whose parts are so disposed as precisely to answer the exigencies of our condition. We are possessed of an intellectual power which thinks, reflects, remembers, ponders, reasons, and conducts the affairs of men. We also perceive ourselves surrounded by a system of immense magnitude, of endless variety, of perpetual motion, and of wonderful adaptation of parts, for a vast variety of effects. As it is natural to trace effects to their causes, we inquire what is the origin of beings with their properties of being? As to ourselves, we have not always existed. How then came we into being? The universe around us also must have had some great moving and almighty cause. Shall we say that matter is eternal, and that the universe in substance has existed from eternity? Though even that should be admitted, there must have been some mighty moving cause to make such a marvellous disposition of inert matter, giving it such admirable forms, such regular varieties, such exact proportions, such numerous adaptations as we witness, showing all the ingenuity of contrivance, and all the wisdom of benevolent design. Shall we say that nature is the efficient author of the whole? What then is nature but another name for God?—a *name* which, even the pretended Atheist must acknowledge, designates a Supreme Power. Shall we say that Fate controls the universe, and gave it forms and motions that excite the astonishment of the mind with every discovery made, and every subject studied? Then we ascribe to Fate the perfections of Deity. Shall we persevere in our endeavors to get rid of the idea of a personal God, ascribing all things to the fortuitous concourse of atoms, or to the "agency of chance"? This is the worst and maddest subterfuge of all. Could ever such a work as creation, consisting of an innumerable variety of parts, and a wonderful disposition of the whole operating to so grand an end as we see, have been the work of chance? "Much more easily," says an author, "might we conceive one able to throw the letters of the alphabet out of a bag at random into the exact form of a poem; more easily, that a painter, by spinking colors at random, should form the exact picture of a man; more easily, that a general might procure an army by waiting till chance should bring them, without his orders, into the arrangement of rank and file; more easily, that the materials of a magnificent building—stone, mortar, timber, iron, lead, and glass—might come together by chance, in complete arrangement and perfect order than that the wonderful machinery of the universe might come forth as the production of chance. The longer we think of it, the denser does this absurdity become.".

Furthermore, the preservation and government of nature declare the existence of God. Who or what supports the world without pillar or foundation? Whence that projectile force by which the vast heavenly bodies take a course that is constant, and invariable, with a propensity to move on therein forever? Whence that principle of gravitation which keeps together the immense machine, or that centripetal force by which all bodies are inclined to the centre of the system; or that centrifugal force by which all bodies are inclined to fly off from it; or the mutual counteraction of each, by which they must take regular curved orbits around the centre of gravity? What power has fixed the sun in the centre of his system of planets, the dispenser of light and heat to them all, in variable proportions; and commanded them to perform their courses around him in regular revolutions; or who has given orders to the moon, that in her circuit around the earth, she should confer her share of benefit upon its inhabitants?

In the language of Scripture we may exclaim: "Who hath laid the measure of the universe, or who hath stretched the line upon it? Whereupon are the foundations fastened, or who laid the chief corner-stone? Whence the morning stars, and shut up the sea with doors, made the clouds the servants thereof, commanded the morning to appear, and the dayspring to know his place? Who hath divided a water course for the overflowing of rivers, or a way for the lightning of thunder? Hath rain a father, and who has begotten the drops of dew? Out of whose womb came the ice, and the hoary frost, who hath generated it? Who bindeth the sweet influence of Pleiades, and looseth the bands of Orion? Who bringeth forth Mazzaroth in his season, and guideth Arcturus and his sons?"

Turn to the vegetable world, and let the oak of the forest, the flower of the field, and every leaf and every blade of grass proclaim to the soul, the existence and power of God. Who hath inwrought that incomprehensible principle of vegetation by which an insignificant seed cast into the earth, separates, germinates, grows, blossoms, and bears fruit, and seed after its kind? And the healing herb, who hath planted it in the very countries where those diseases most prevail which require its application? The fruits of the field, who hath appointed them to supply the wants and preserve the life of the animal creation? Who hath taught the vegetation of Spring to clothe itself with beauty, and again in Autumn to resign all its glory? "Marvellous are thy works, O Lord Almighty; in wisdom hast thou made them all."

Turn again to animated nature, in which every worm and reptile, consisting of numerous members wonderfully adjusted, is a living proof of the Divinity that produced it. Who hath given them all that instinctive sagacity by which they prepare their lodgings, promote their health, and protect and nourish their young? Who hath given them clothing precisely suited to their necessities, and armed them with weapons of warfare and defence? Who hath directed the marvellous peregrinations or wanderings of the fishes of the sea, and the fowls of the air, at such seasons, and with such plans as best promote their own preservation, and subserve the benefit of mankind? Well is it said: "Ask now the beasts, and they shall teach thee; and the fowls of the air, and they shall tell thee; or speak to the earth, and it shall teach thee; and the fishes of the sea shall declare unto thee."

Especially let man contemplate his own nature, and examine the mechanism of his own frame, and the powers of his own sensation. Who has adapted the ear to the reception of sounds, and the eye to the discernment of colors, and the taste to the discriminations of articles of food? Examine the powers of thine own mind, O man, made in the image of God. Whence that reach of understanding denied to the lower creation, enabling thee to make thyself a subject of investigation; or that memory, by which thou retainest thine own ideas; or that conscience, which approves or condemns thee? Whence that soul with a nature and a capacity for immortality? Well might the poet say of it—

> "Warms in the sun, refreshes in the breeze,
> Glows in the stars, and blossoms in the trees,
> Lives through all life, extends through all extent,
> Spreads undivided, operates unspent."

IV. Finally the power of a controlling governmental providence, as it is displayed in the preservation of the righteous, and in the punishment of the wicked, declares the existence of God, whose intelligence directs it to specific ends. How comes it to pass, that a society, denominated the Church, established among men almost from the beginning of time, has so long been preserved, notwithstanding all the persecutions and slaughters she has encountered; while those ungodly nations, once so powerful and so cruel, who persecuted her with relentless fury, have in continual succession been consigned to desolation and ruin? Where now are the Canaanites, who so long vexed the people of God? Where the proud Assyrian monarch, who boasted of his strength? Where the mighty Empire of Rome, whose Emperors raised numerous bloody persecutions, and afterwards cherished the man of sin and son of perdition? How comes it that those nations of the Eastern World who still exist, do, in their present form and appearance, prove that God has rewarded or scourged them according as they have promoted or persecuted the Church of God? The fact is too plain for denial; there must be a God, that ruleth in the earth.

If we refer to the fates of individuals, the same truth will be illustrated, that the Deity is known by the judgments which he executes. Under the impression that there is a God who executeth vengeance in the earth, Cain exclaimed—"My punishment is greater than I can bear!" Is Pharaoh guilty of blood, in destroying the children of the Israelites in the waters of the Nile? God gave him blood to drink by changing its waters into blood. Is David guilty of blood and adultery? By blood and adultery is he punished; for the sword departed not from his house; and his wives were taken by his sons. Had Ahab and Jezebel committed the most atrocious cruelty? Their blood is marvellously shed.

Not only sacred, but profane history records many awful retributions, by which the impression is fixed on the mind, that there is a God. Who was it that so comforted and supported the Martyrs, that they manifested great cheerfulness and tranquillity amidst the most dreadful tortures and lingering deaths? What power inflicted upon Herod that signal punishment which history records, the stench of his bodily infection becoming intolerable to all, and his mind tortured by horrible anticipations? And what power inflicted upon Nero that mental torment which induced him to solicit another to dispatch him? The death of Julian the Apostate—that most cruel persecutor—is too loathsome for description. He died an awful witness of the existence and power of an avenging God. "If," says an author, "a collection should be made of all those persecuting tyrants who have not been visited after the common visitation of man, and have not died the common death of all men, but whose plagues were horrible and strange, the hardest skeptic would be moved by the evidence, and compelled to admit that there is a God who judgeth in the earth."

The inferences from our subject are quite natural, and ought to be impressive.

1. We see the folly of atheism, not merely that form of it which asserts itself in open blasphemy, but that *practical* atheism which induces many to wish in their hearts that there were no God. If any such be here, a few questions are worthy of their consideration. Would you regard yourselves more happy, could you be convinced that no Deity exists? Would not licentiousness and vice have the same tendency they now have to obscure the understanding, and to fill the breast with tormenting passions? What pleasure can be derived from the idea of annihilation,—an idea accompanied with horror and producing melancholy for life? Or, would the idea of impunity from all punishment relieve you? If we were to admit that there is no God, would our admission alleviate the miseries of life? Whether there be a God or not, there is misery on earth, and the

tendency of sin is ever to misery; and would not the same tendency operate to the same issue hereafter? You may suggest that there will be no hereafter, but if it be mere chance or fortune that makes men miserable in this life, how know you but that the same chance or fortune will perpetuate your existence after death, and perpetually inflict far greater misery as the consequence of sin? So that whether there be a God or not, it seems that the wicked must be miserable. For aught they know, the same cause that operates so woefully now and here, will work a far more intensified misery hereafter, when all the comforts of an animal existence shall be no more for alleviation. Would you not be more miserable now, if there were no God? Suppose that there is no God, under what government do we live? What demon then has possession of the world? What malignity and cruelty constitute his character? What malicious pleasure may he not take in our ruin? Is there no horror in having our existence in a world without a God to manage its concerns in righteousness, to provide rewards for the good, and punishments for the bad? Does not that supposable state of things blot out all moral distinctions, and annihilate all hope of our ever having the disorders of our nature removed, and the blessedness of harmony and happiness conferred upon our souls? If then we wish that there were no God to punish, we wish also that there were no God to bless, and the existence of such a wish in any heart is to it an evidence of present misery, and a sure indication of exclusion from future happiness.

2. We know that there is a God by the evidence set forth in our text, "The invisible things of him from the creation of the world are clearly seen, being understood

by the things that are made, even his eternal power and Godhead." This is the argument for faith in and worship of him ever acknowledged by the world of mind. There is such an intimate connection between a sense of the Divine existence, and a sense of human obligation to worship and adore him, that all nations have acknowledged the former and confessed the latter; and have actually adopted some mode or other of religious worship. This is a fact that cannot be the result of accident. It is as much a fact as the belief of the existence of the human soul. Now a universal impression is a truth, and can only be made by an irresistible cause universally operating. We assert, that cause is God. Man is a religious being, and that fact proves the existence of God, since all religion is in reference to him; and the sense of our obligation to worship is perceived to be a natural result from this impression upon our rational nature. If God be the author of our being, why should he not have made this impression to be the consequence of an adaptation of mind to receive it from reflection upon "the things that are made," that "his eternal power and Godhead" should excite our adoration, and prompt us to render the homage due his ineffable Majesty? Thus we have a perfectly satisfactory explanation of a wonderful fact, otherwise inexplicable. The worship of God is a duty which necessarily flows from a sense of his existence, and they who refuse to render it are fairly taxable with a practical denial of his authority, and a moral wrong done to their own souls. Are they not practical atheists, and that by a course of thought and feeling no less absurd, than the brutalizing sentiment of him who denies the being of God altogether? What must we say of those who, regardless of his authority, contend that their judgment is a law unto themselves in all matters of right and wrong? Can their opinion claim coeval authority with, or in anywise modify for themselves that invariable standard of rectitude that necessarily must emanate from the divine Mind? What shall we say of those whose practical neglect of God, is incompatible with their admission of His being and attributes? Does not the spirit of unbelief show its contempt by the rejection of the gospel, impeaching the veracity of the Almighty? Are not all such persons atheistical in disposition and practice, just as much, though not so offensively, as the openly avowed atheist? Is it not likely that God will judge them so, when He shall judge all men "according to the deeds done in the body"?

Beloved, it is for the purpose of exciting your adoration that God has impressed upon your souls a sense of his eternal power and Godhead. For this, He causes the sun to rise upon the earth in dazzling splendor; for this, the moon to traverse the vast expanse in silvery brightness; for this, the twinkling stars to bespangle the sky of night; for this, the regular successions of the seasons, summer and winter, seed-time and harvest; for this too, He has spread out the beautiful landscape with flowers among the waving grass, and flocks and herds feeding out of his hand, upon the verdant fields, and singing birds pouring out their varied melodies from bush and tree. O, shall we resist these invitations from the inferior creation to adore the great Parent of the universe?

3. The time shall come when the most unreasonable and persistent skeptic shall be made to realize the exist-

ence and power of God. He may indeed manage to keep his courage up in the promulgation of sentiments abhorrent to every generous heart, while health and strength shall last; but when these give way, and his mind be forced to dwell upon probabilities which may possibly be certainties, he shall, in spite of himself, become a little nervous as an exasperated conscience gains strength with his approaches to the gates of death. "What, after all, if there be a God!" Such an exclamation will usher in an unwelcome train of thoughts that shall prepare the fuel for the fires of remorse never to go out.

O what misery, what agony, what depths of wretchedness shall be uncovered, as the unhappy godless soul makes its entrance upon its future state! O shall we never devoutly acknowledge God, until we come to experience the power of his anger! Shall we never awake to the fact of our unspeakable folly, until we feel its penalty cannot be avoided! O, then, be wise in time, if you would be happy in eternity. Consider the interests you imperil by the crime of neglect. There is a God whose omnipotence will vindicate his honor. He is now willing to be reconciled to the chief of sinners who cry for mercy. How he has followed us in the gospel of his Son, inviting, beseeching, expostulating, persuading! He is a God of love, the unparalleled manifestation of which is the gift of his own Son, to procure redemption for us. Truly you have no reason to be offended in such a God. His mercy and lovingkindness ought to melt your hearts. His wondrous plan of salvation ought to break in upon you as the light of the sun, unfolding, as it does, the resources of infinite wisdom and benevolence, such as no human intellect could ever contrive. Here is the evidence by which is understood his eternal mercy to be the culmination of his eternal goodness. And, oh! to think of Him in all His loveliness; to be consciously with Him in the solitude of night; to feel that He is near, in all our perplexities and afflictions to do us good, and to make our adversities contribute enlargement to our ultimate happiness! What a source of sweetest, purest, highest consolation! What an ineffable pleasure to pray to Him, encouraged by His most wonderful promises! What rapture, to die in his arms! "Why art thou cast down, O my soul? and why art thou disquieted within me? Hope thou in God: for I shall yet praise him, the health of my countenance, and my God."

PRINCIPLE IN RELIGION.

James 1 : 26, 27. "If any man among you seem to be religious, and bridleth not his tongue, but deceiveth his own heart, this man's religion is vain. Pure religion and undefiled before God and the Father is this: to visit the fatherless and widows in their affliction, and to keep himself unspotted from the world."

Man is the only creature on earth originally made in the image of God, and he seems to have been thus formed for the specific purpose of a religious life. Fallen from his integrity, he has indeed lost the pure principle of religion, by the influx and control of sin over his entire nature. But notwithstanding this, his mental and moral constitution still incline him to religious exercises. His mind perceives the obligation to love and worship his Maker. His heart and conscience feel the force of law, and, in the abstract, approve of the duties that clearly grow out of his relation to God, his Lawgiver and Judge. Accordingly, we find him under all circumstances, in every continent, island, and corner of the world inclined to present his devotions, in some form or other, to a Supreme Being. He is not satisfied, except he render to him some oblation of praise. He would rather practice the most abject superstition, some irrational ceremony, some absurd worship than have no religion at all.

In consequence of this universal feeling, the world is full of religion. Whatever be the moral degradation of the nations of the earth, they must have their religion, be it even composed of superstition and abominable licentiousness. The sense of guilt is universal, and hence the heathen seem anxious to propitiate their deities by various forms of worship. However blinded and perverted, they cannot be charged with willful hypocrisy in this matter, for with sincere devotion do they bow down to their false gods. With what singular self-denial, for example, does the worshiper of Juggernaut sacrifice his life under the car of that grim idol.

So Saul of Tarsus, in his religious fury, considered himself very sincere in persecuting to death all who embraced Christianity, and at the same time gave himself the credit of walking in all good conscience before God, and believing in his heart that he must do many things contrary to the name of Jesus.

We do not now expound the principle on which the sincere devotion of Jew or Pagan is to be regarded abominable and fatal, we only insist on the fact, that the vilest sentiments and pursuits, under the notion of religion, are compatible with the feeling of sincerity. The Pagan may be conscious of no delusion, while his path lies through pollution to perdition. And it is not irrelevant to inquire whether, if there be so much sincerity and zeal in such worship, we may not have reason to fear that among sincere worshipers in Christian lands, there may be amidst all their conscious sincerity, such a gross deviation, as to warrant a suspicion of evangelical integrity. Permit me then to discriminate between false and true religion in the Christian world, as indicated by the apostle James in our text.

I. As to *False Religion.* Our moral nature itself prompts to devotion in the midst of deep inherent corruption. It cannot be strange, therefore, if that corruption should originate a thousand forms of spurious and polluted worship. Where the pure light of Christianity blazes, superstition and unhallowed feeling will often arise, as a false flame in imitation of the true. The religion of holiness, it seems, must be engrafted upon the religion of nature, to constitute a service acceptable to God ; but never was there a greater or more injurious mistake. Nothing short of, and nothing beside regeneration by the Spirit of God, can implant the seed which will produce Christian life, correct experience, and consistent practice. Often there is such a resemblance between the religion of nature, under the external influences of Christianity, and the religion of the Spirit of grace, that mistakes can only be avoided by care in acquiring scriptural knowledge, and caution in observing scriptural admonition.

We need not show more clearly that which, by its simple statement, is made so plain, namely; *speculative conviction* of the truth of Christianity is only an introduction to true religion ; that even solemn and deep impressions of its importance are no infallible evidences of true piety ; that anguish and remorse, in the apprehension of " the wrath to come," may torment the mind in the absence of all sanctifying grace; that nothing less than the love which regeneration produces can be acceptable to a holy God.

Nor is the religion of *Doctrine* sufficient, for while a regard to orthodoxy is exceedingly important, it is possible to feel an uncommon zeal in its behalf, which is nothing more than a selfish aspiration to overthrow the opposite of it by a love for victory. So far from being a decisive test of humble piety, it is often characterized by sectarian pride, and rigid exclusiveness, which manifest the absence of all true holiness.

Nor will that religion which consists in the love of Form and Ceremony produce better results. How sadly has the simplicity of gospel truth, and the beauty of the christian church been buried under the pomp and show of ritual devotion! How strong the propensity of human nature to supply the deficiency of heart religion by outward, noisy demonstrations, and expensive ceremonials! How often has a spurious christianity been exhibited by an overweening fondness for splendor and extravagance! O, it would be well for those who love to herd with the fashionable, and to avoid the poor in the ecclesiastical splendor of a garnished sanctuary, to examine the nature of that zeal which relates to outward glories instead of inward graces.

There is a religion of *Sympathy*, too, or of sentiment exceedingly defective. It relates to the sublimity of christianity, as interesting by its affecting histories; doctrines; developments; and conflicts with which the natural man is inclined to sympathize. Where is the generous mind, not moved by the condescension of the Almighty shown in the great scheme of Atonement?

Who is not affected by the wonderful history of the humble Jesus, born in a manger, bred to the lot of the poor, dispensing constant benefactions in work and word; yet hated by his countrymen, insulted by the rabble, betrayed by the wicked, scourged by his persecutors, and finally declared innocent, yet condemned, and doomed to the horrid death of crucifixion! Around his cross the hero weeps, and need not be ashamed! A tear is graceful on the soldier's cheek, who witnesses his extraordinary death; yet these sensibilities are no decisive proof of piety. The philosopher may indulge his sympathy with extraordinary emotions, when he observes the wonderful career of the "Teacher come from God." We all admire the divinity of his discourses, we are amazed at his wisdom, when from ordinary subjects he adroitly turns a conversation to what is sacred and important. We are struck by the beauty of his parables, where he simplifies and enforces religious truth; our wonder is excited when, by a few words, he effectually repulses the objections of his enemies, and renders a doubtful point plain and perspicuous; we so admire the dignity, the candor, the wisdom, the condescension, the lofty eloquence of this divine teacher, that we inquire: Whence hath this man this wisdom and those mighty deeds, and how is it that he speaketh with authority, and not as the scribes?

A thousand tender sensibilities are awakened in my bosom, but I dare not refer them to a certain principle of piety. I sympathize with the sufferings, the virtues, the patience, the triumphs of his disciples in every age; especially when they encounter the rack, the scaffold, the flames; and see them expire with dignity, with composure, and inflexible adherence to their Master; yet I dare not, from this, infer indubitable piety; for I remember who has said, "Behold, ye despisers, and wonder, and perish!"   Notwithstanding the total corruption of my nature, I feel so much respect for virtue, so much approbation of what is great and good, and so much admiration for what is exalted and heroic, that my soul is moved within me by the example of Jesus, and the unearthly spirit of his followers in life and in death; yet I dare not on that account, alone, determine favorably in my own case. For how often have such sensibilities failed to reconcile the heart to the self-denials of religion! How often have they resembled the emotions produced by the affecting tales of fiction which only survived the moment that gave them birth! Nay, like the hosannahs which were once sung to the Son of David, how suddenly may they give place to the sentiments of a different description, which only lead to the cry for crucifixion and death.

There is also the religion of *Excitement*, equally spurious and suspicious. We do not deny that seasons of excitement may arise, and are sometimes glorious seasons, when truth with an almighty power reaches and subdues the heart; but then it is the truth alone that does it; it is solid instruction that does it as the instrumental cause; and not the excitement, for this is simply a bodily exercise of nervous influence always to be condemned. The best criteria by which this fact can be tested, are the fruits thereof observable by growth in knowledge, and in habitual piety. But how often are excitements succeeded by lamentable departures from truth and piety, and even by loathsome apostasy and infidelity! The human mind is wrought upon by various extraneous influences, and exercised by moral sensibilities and animal affections. Passions, such as hope and fear, joy and sorrow, love and hate, desire and aversion, dwell within us, and render us susceptible of deep emotions. Now it is easy to infer from the eccentricities, the frenzy and madness of fanatical extravagance to which human nature is liable in other matters, that in the matter of religion, from the same causes and susceptibilities, we are exposed to similar results.

That the Divine Spirit avails himself of our natural emotions to implant the principle of piety in the heart is beyond doubt, but the mode of his operation we cannot determine, beyond the fact that it is by the truth of the Word alone. But excitement, apart from this instrumentality, is no sure evidence of piety; nor is the transitory emotion of penitence ; nor the gloomy cloud of desperation ; nor the sudden rapture of the soul such evidence. None of these can prove regeneration certain. Independent of the testimony which is given by the permanent fruits of holy living, there is often so much selfishness of spirit, so much conceit and boasting, so much wild pretension, and fanatical confidence in emotional exercises as to render the whole affair suspicious. Care must be taken, indeed, that we do not discredit true revivals, when the word of truth is accompanied with powerful application to the heart and conscience ; but let no man place reliance on warmth of temperament, or the vivid excitement of imagination. The results of the Spirit, productive of evangelical piety, are thus given : "Love, joy, peace, long suffering, gentleness, goodness, faith, meekness, temperance." "They that are Christ's have crucified the flesh with the passions and lusts." This brings us to the consideration of the—

II. topic as defined in the text : " Pure religion, and undefiled before God the Father." That which is impure and defiled, clearly exists by the evidence of the text, which purposely uses the opposite terms to define that which is genuine and true. We call pure religion the result of a new principle of implanted life, that is the result of being born again, and the foundation of all holy exercises. Thus the children of God are said to be "born, not of blood, nor of the will of the flesh, nor of the will of man, but of God." That is, " not of blood," no privileged class; "not of the flesh," or not by our own efforts or works; " not by the will of man," or not by any agency or effort of man; "but of God," or by the exclusive agency of Divine power.

Some have chosen to consider true religion as consisting essentially in exercises, feelings, desires, and aspirations of mind ; but nothing can be farther from the fact, according to the text just quoted. If piety consisted altogether in feeling, where is the religion of the idiot who, though having a moral nature, seems incapable of exercising or discovering holy affections ? What becomes of those infants who, though sanctified from the womb, have faculties not yet so expanded as to evince any holy exercises at all ? Or where is the holiness of the adult Christian himself in the hours of sleep, or in the absence of all reflection, or when he is utterly unconscious of all feeling, all exercises, and all moral affections ? The better way of considering the subject is by placing true religion farther back, within the spirit where regenerate life exists ; and whence moral feeling flows as the source of spiritual affections. Now it cannot be denied that such a fountain may be opened, by divine grace, within an infant before reason has dawned upon its mind. It may be opened within the soul of an irresponsible idiot, whose imprisoned faculties are incapable of rational piety. It is surely ever living in the adult believer, while lost in the unconsciousness of sleep ; or dozing in the lethargy of inaction and of extreme old age ; or engrossed in his necessary worldly business which, for the moment, supposes the absence of all religious feeling.

These considerations, I think, will show that religion, as a thing spoken of, must be regarded a foundation of holy exercise, not the exercise itself ; a fountain of moral feeling, not the feeling itself ; a principle of holy obedience deeply planted in the heart, not the obedience itself. We do not mean that it is in its own nature a dormant, inactive, inoperative principle ; but a living, productive thing, originally set agoing by the Spirit of God, in the previously dead soul of a man " renewed in the temper and spirit of his mind." How long or how much it may lie dormant in the infant, the idiot or the declining Christian, we presume not to determine ; but where the intellect is sufficiently opened, and the beautiful objects of religion are set before it, there is an eye to see them ; and there is a life to enjoy them. And especially in revivals of religion, its influence will animate and invigorate the soul. And this is the proper idea of revival, for religion must previously exist in the soul before it can be revived. Revival means the stimulation of the inward principle of religion already implanted, to exercise and action. Religion is revived by the force of truth externally exhibited to the understanding, and operating on the inward principle of holiness susceptible to the action and influence of exciting causes. All other meaning put upon the term is an imposition.

Now as to the effects of this principle, they are characterized by a beautiful simplicity. What, for example, is more simple and intelligible than love ; not the mode of its exercise, but the principle of its operation ; a constituted habit of mind and heart, disposing one to the sacrifice of selfishness, and to the pleasure of affection, strongly working out the feelings and plans of benevolence ? The highest and noblest effect of it is delight in God. It is a sincere and cordial approbation of the Divine character, a joyful admiration of the Divine purity, justice, goodness and truth. It involves a resignation of soul to the Divine disposal, it implies an entire submission to the Divine scheme of redemption, in all its duties, self-denials, and sufferings ; and such a regard for God and Christ, and the interests of scriptural truth and holiness in the world, that the mind is, at times, swallowed up by its own lofty contemplations. Nor can the heart prefer any carnal or secular enjoyment to that noble exercise which generously prevails in it, affording a perfect fullness of satisfaction as it thinks and rests upon Christ, and Christ alone, as one with the believer.

Gratitude for redeeming mercy is shown in the disposition to promote the glory of Christ, and the success of his cause, the interest of his church, and the good of mankind. Love to God in Christ, and love to men for his sake becomes the commanding feeling of the heart, and regulates the outward life. Were all men governed by this principle, it would be impossible for wars, fraud, oppression, slander, licentiousness, malice, envy, lust and pride to exist. So simple and excellent is that principle of divine grace, that its evident tendency is the sure proof of the divinity of the religion of Jesus Christ.

As this principle is implanted in the heart by the internal work of the Spirit, so its existence and efficiency are wholly independent of external circumstances. It may be excited by means and instrumentalities, but its life and power are in no way dependent upon them. Not so is the vain religion spoken of in the text. That is the product of nature, or the result of accident, or the fruit of circumstances. True religion has resources within itself, whereby it is sustained and enlarged, should no external circumstances concur to cherish and increase it. But the vain religion, spoken of in the text, has no bridle for the tongue, while it has deception for the heart. It has no support but that which is derived from incidents, occasions and casual circumstances. Education may sway the mind into modes of thinking; selfishness, pride, and interest may govern its predilections; peculiar measures may arouse hope and joy; vociferation may have created alarm; and the prayers of those professing confidence in us may have allayed our alarm, and through them the mind be drugged into a deceitful calm. Now such a religion has no resources of its own. It cannot live apart from the circumstances that produced it. Take away the companionship, the novelty, the moving incident, the crowded audience, the enchanting grove, the cry of the anxious, loud songs of the joyful, the circumstantial variety, the mechanical mode of producing the results designed, and this religion dies. But true religion lives by and of itself, because it is a life as real as that which supports the beating pulse and the heaving lungs. So far from being dependent upon education, it often earnestly works in opposition to early habits; so far from drawing nourishment from the outward things of which we have spoken.

it often seeks retirement for this purpose. It can live alone, it can flourish in solitude, it feeds on its own resources. Secret prayer, the Bible in hand, the earnest thought of divine things in heart, prepares the pious man for the exertion of such an influence in the world as shall command its respect, as he works for its good; hence arises a stability of mind, a fixedness of purpose, an unflinching decision which secures the soul amid the changes, the tumults, the temptations and delusions of the world, the flesh, and the devil.

There is scarcely any thing, brethren, in the piety of the present age more disreputable and loathsome than its mutability. By some means or other, the public mind is taught to detest and condemn inconstancy in religion. By some instructive natural dictate of common sense, this mutability is declared to be mean and despicable. The reputation of Christianity suffers extremely by its frequent exhibitions. Apostasies are awfully prejudicial to its character, but of this we are forewarned by the Master. "Offences shall come, but woe to the man by whom the offence cometh." No man will believe that religion to be a reality where its hold upon the mind is so precarious. What prospect can cheer us in relation to the personal influence or usefulness of those who are blown about with every wind of doctrine, or tossed hither and thither by a thousand waves of commotion? Reuben-like, they are the objects of grief to the church, and of contempt to the world, occasioning the reproaches of the irreligious and the profane. Unstable as water, how can they excel? In the language of Jude: "Clouds are they without water, carried about of winds; trees whose fruit withereth, without fruit, twice dead, plucked up by the roots." Contrasted with this, how pleasing, how charming is the steady course of the honest, unwavering professor! How beautifully he shines in the brightness of a godly example, an honor to his faith, a living testimony to the world. "Rooted and grounded in love, he is able to comprehend with all saints what is the breadth, and length, and depth, and height; and to know the love of Christ which passeth knowledge, that he might be filled with all the fullness of God." His aim is, as he has received Christ Jesus the Lord, so to walk in him, rooted and built up in him, established in the faith, unbeguiled by enticing words, unspoiled with philosophy or vain deceit. He is content with the christianity of the Bible, wishing on the whole no better constitution of mercy; no easier method of attaining life; no more indulgence than the gospel allows; no exemption even from those self-denials and disasters which wisdom has appointed in subservience to his progress. Thus contented, resigned, resolved and devoted, "his path is the path of the just that shineth more and more unto the perfect day."

Finally, true religion is distinguished from all spurious imitations by its power of ascendancy over sin. It was to Christians Paul wrote, "With the mind, I myself serve the law of God, but with the flesh the law of sin;" and John says: "If we say that we have no sin, we deceive ourselves, and the truth is not in us;" and James says: "In many things we offend all." Nothing is clearer than this; whatever may be our attainments, sin dwelleth in us. And it is this which makes the christian life a warfare. It is self-conflict. And hence all the admonitions addressed to Christians, in reference to this great enemy, which is indeed subdued, but not cast out. No christian therefore can be such in reality who does not keep up this warfare, just as none could be farther from grace than they who would claim to be without sin, which no one of a sound understanding will do. The principle of love to God implies the principle of hatred of sin, and perpetual conflict; for "the flesh lusteth against the spirit and the spirit against the flesh, these are contrary one to the other, so that ye cannot do the things that ye would." True religion, therefore, maintains this conflict, and shall overcome. But, on the other hand, where religion is nothing but a temporary feeling, a spasmodic emotion, or a freak of enthusiasm, how calmly and willingly does its subject retreat from the conflict, and give up the strife! He has no warfare against corruption. Even when he is under the influence of excitement, his strife is directed more against the luke-warmness and iniquity of others than his own; his object is more to banish iniquity out of the world, than to expel it from his own bosom. With reference to others, he is censorious; with reference to himself, he is easy and indulgent; and so when excitement leaves him, it leaves his heart under the dominion of sin. Can the true soldier of the cross, think you, thus entirely abandon himself to carnal security when there is nothing special to stimulate him to piety? Never. Sometimes his resistance is weak, his zeal languid, his strength enfeebled by the long duration of the warfare, and the cunningly contrived onsets of the watchful foe; yet, never will he abandon his post entirely, nor desert the cause of holiness and God. His enmity to sin is too implacable, his love of the Redeemer is too unconquerable; his convictions of truth and duty too deep, habitual and forceful. Through innumerable perplexities, he has already passed; through many still to come he expects to toil and wade. He is reconciled to the conflict, and never expects deliverance till the hand of death releases him to pass away beyond the scenes of strife in a world of sin. Whatever occasional advantages it may gain, sin shall never have dominion over him. His career of conflict closed, he enjoys the victory where the angel describes him as having passed through great tribulation, as having washed his robes, and made them white in the blood of the Lamb.

Since, then, there is clearly the *false* and the *true*, co-existing in the all-important matter of religion, let every hearer remember that it is his own essential interest to be able wisely to discriminate between them. If true religion be an inward principle of spiritual life, it is a fatal mistake to regard it as an outward exercise of animal life involving simply sentiments, emotions and feelings? Why encounter so much expense and care for the externals of Christianity, and overlook what is primary and essential? While there is so much ado about religion, so much rush and roar in the management of its interests, why lose sight of the one thing needful, without which all other things make religion vain? Why contented with sound doctrine, if the mind must be renewed? Why be extravagantly fond of forms and modes, if true religion dwell only in the heart? Why rely on sympathies and sentimentalities which have so little effect upon the permanent habits of the soul? Why make the mode of observing sacraments, or the preferences between forms and names indicative of true religion, when these things have really nothing to do with the state or disposition of the heart? Let them not be confounded with the religion of indwelling life and principle. This lies at the bottom of all holy exercises. There is a simplicity in its nature consisting only and wholly of habitual love to God and holiness. It is independent of circumstances, and grows and thrives amid a thousand disadvantages. It is reverently modest and mild, humble and quiet in its deportment. It is stable and uniform in its operations, by which it is far more precious than the fluctuating flame which often has no other fuel to support it than wood, hay and stubble. It is eventually victorious, secretly besieging its adversaries, until its warfare ripens into victory. O that none of us might rest, until this principle of life become the center of our powers, and the source of our movements! It is the product of the incorruptible seed of the word. It is a fountain of holiness opened up within. Of other waters men may drink, yet they shall not be satisfied; but whoso drinketh of this water shall never thirst again; for this vital principle shall be in him as a well of water springing up to everlasting life.

PROCESS OF DIVINE OPERATION.

John 6 : 44. " No man can come to me, except the Father which hath sent me draw him."

The statement of the text is so clear and precise, it needs no verbal explanation. It is, however, a matter of great consequence so to examine as to perceive how the agency of the Father is exerted to secure the coming of a sinner to Christ for his own salvation. The *honor* of our Maker is deeply concerned in this point, and matters ought so to be represented that it may be clearly understood how God is free from blame in our condemnation, and at the same time the only author of salvation and glory. The interest of sinners is intimately connected with the views they cherish on this subject, for in consequence of their mistakes here, some, it is to be feared, are building their hopes of salvation on their own efforts and strength as co-operative with divine efficiency. By this they are involved in extreme danger, while others, impressed with the entire uselessness of their own exertions, are supinely and wilfully neglecting every means of deliverance, sullenly charging their Maker with their own ruin.

It must be acknowledged that there are difficulties on this subject that require caution and discrimination in presenting it in such a light as to prevent confusion and embarrassment, since it is impossible for us to comprehend perfectly how the agency of the Deity is compatible with the entire freedom of the creature. Both, however, are facts susceptible of the clearest demonstration. The most dangerous difficulty arises from the conceit which influences many minds, that every mystery of the Divine Agency must be adequately comprehended, before they can be reasonably required to yield themselves unto God. Our object is to show that such conceit is not even plausible, and that whatever importance we attach to our own agency in our salvation, the text teaches us to ascribe all the credit of it to Divine influence. In order to form clear ideas which shall be useful for comprehensive views of the plan of grace and its execution, we must inquire into the nature and necessity of Divine Agency.

I. As to the nature of it, we remark that it is indicated by the same expressive word in various addresses of the God of Israel to his chosen people. Thus, in Jerem. 31 : 3, "With loving-kindness have I *drawn* thee." And also in Hosea 9 : 4, "I *drew* thee with cords of a man, with bands of love." Cant. 1 : 4, "*Draw* me, we will run after thee." Jeremiah thus addressed the Lord: "Thou hast *enticed* me, and I was *enticed:* thou art stronger than I, and hast prevailed." This word in our text, has the same meaning as in those just quoted; it signifies the *power of persuasion,* and not the force of compulsion.

By the Agency here spoken of, we must understand that influence of the Divine Spirit through the Word on the heart of the reluctant sinner, whereby he is finally and freely induced, notwithstanding all his corruption, to forsake his iniquities, embrace the salvation of the gospel, and live to the Redeemer's praise.

By this definition, you learn that we consider the sinner who is drawn by the Spirit of God, as *reluctant* to follow the infallible guide. He indeed wishes to be happy, and revolts at pain and misery; yet he thinks it hard to abandon the practices to which he has been so long devoted, and to which he is so powerfully inclined; hard to mortify the deeds of the body; hard to submit himself to the sovereign disposal of God; hard to be indebted to uninfluenced grace, to deny himself, take up his cross, and follow the Redeemer as his Lord and Master. Divine agency however, as the power of persuasion, pursues him in all places of retreat, amid all circumstances of life, and with all appliances of expostulation, entreaty and remonstrance; until his resistance is reduced to weakness, and with feelings of agony he gives up. Then the principle of a new life is infused into his soul, and he exclaims in the words of Jeremiah, "Lord, thou art stronger than I, and hast prevailed."

The Agent and instrument employed in this work of salvation are doubtless the Spirit and Word of God. All that the latter can do by its own efficiency is comprehended by the idea of moral suasion. It attempts to persuade us by all the motives drawn from the past, present, and future of a life spent in alienation from God, to turn our hearts to Him, and bestow our affections upon Christ; but all is unsuccessful, until the

Word be accompanied by the energy of the Spirit, whose common operations even, are no more than moral suasion, until He exerts the exceeding greatness of his power in regenerating the soul. Then the sinner is effectually drawn to the Lord. He is persuaded, not driven; he is drawn by the enticement of love, but not dragged by the terrors of fear. And all the results of an altered disposition and conduct are attributable to a new life whose infusion, by the regenerative work of the Spirit, explains everything as to the matter and manner of a new nature, so strongly contrasting with the old, in its proclivities and manifestations.

At what period precisely amidst all the exercises of the drawn sinner the seed of regeneration is secretly implanted, it is impossible to tell; but this throws no suspicion upon the reality of such implantation, because in any form of life we cannot explain its nature nor detect the first movement of vitality. Perhaps it is before the understanding has those remarkable views of the Divine character, which certainly accompany the work; and that those realizing views of divine things are the natural results of the implantation admits of no question, because they fall upon eyes spiritually open to see, and this is a capability of spiritual life only; perhaps before the conscience is fully awakened, so that its activity in this matter is the effect of the new principle at work within; perhaps the understanding is first enlightened, and the conscience alarmed, before the work of regeneration is begun. Many persons are apt to date the commencement of their christian life at the period of their first conviction, others at the period of their first felt emotion of love; others at the time when they had joy in the inward persuasion of justification by faith; but it is impossible for them to demonstrate by feeling or otherwise to themselves that the new principle of spiritual life was not previously implanted as the foundation of all their exercises. No doubt many have insensibly received regenerating grace sometime before they were aware of it, while others have had their sensibilities aroused before they became new creatures in Christ. It is not a test of regeneration that we should know the precise time when the new birth takes place in the soul. So variously does the Spirit of God operate upon individuals that there are diversities of gifts and operations, but the same spirit; differences of administration, but the same Lord. As to what we feel, we know; but as to the time, and the manner in which the new principle was infused, as the foundation of what we feel, we can know nothing; and this we are taught by the Lord. "The wind bloweth where it listeth, and ye hear the sound thereof, *but canst not tell* whence it cometh, or whither it goeth; so is every one that is born of the Spirit."

But notwithstanding these diversities, there is a degree of sameness in the sensible experience of all the saints ; for in consequence of the drawing of the Father, they all come to Christ. As the Father sent the Son to seek sinners, so He sends sinners to seek the Son, by the Word and Spirit, as already shown. For when we are drawn by Him, it is in fulfilment of the promise referred to by Christ in the verse immediately succeeding our text. "It is written in the prophets; And they shall be all taught of God. Every man therefore that hath heard, and hath learned of the Father, cometh unto me." It is perfectly clear, therefore, that He draws by instruction. The understanding is certainly enlightened, but evidently in different degrees of illumination, all-sufficient, however, for securing the sinner's coming to Christ. Some have been more gradually visited, by the light of the gracious Spirit; others more suddenly. The views of one, have been more clear and extended than those of another; the perceptions of some, have been more coincident with the line of nature and the course of reason; others have been transported, as it were, into a new region by strong strange and wonderful views and impressions crowding in upon the soul. All the saints have thus been dealt with by the Spirit. There is a *variety* in the *sameness* of the work. How otherwise can it appear that God should accommodate himself, so to speak, to the nature of intelligent beings, whose peculiarities of understanding are concerned in diversifying all their movements? How could their hearts be drawn to the objects of religion, if these objects were not disclosed in agreement with the power of the understanding to distinguish and discern? And how could the understanding, which is so thickly enveloped in clouds of prejudice, ever perceive those objects without such peculiarities of an enlightening influence as are adapted to dissipate them? The agency of the Spirit is therefore to draw the attention and to fix the eye of the mind firmly and steadily on essential truth; to dissolve those prejudices which operate to conceal it; to counteract that unbelief which sustains indifference; to soften that enmity which is begotten of depravity; and by a perpetual concurrence, to keep the soul awake to her immortal interests, and the awful realities of the future, where the results of salvation and damnation shall be fully realized by the receivers and the rejectors of Christ. The Apostle prayed in this form of words, for the Ephesian christians: "That the God of our Lord Jesus Christ, the Father of glory, may give unto you the Spirit of wisdom and revelation in the knowledge of him; the eyes of your understanding being enlightened: that ye may know what is the hope of his calling, and what the riches of the glory of his inheritance in the saints; and what the exceeding greatness of his power to usward who believe."

The next effect of this Drawing, is the excitement of *Conviction* in the conscience of the awakened sinner; and this is the natural result of an enlightening influence. We all know that we must understand the truth and fact of any position in which we may be, before the convictions it ought to produce in us, can be excited. It is not otherwise in the matter of our position as sinners guilty and condemned in the sight of God. Without deep conviction of guilt, how is it possible that the heart should ever be drawn into esteem and admiration for the Lord Jesus, as our proffered guilt-bearer, whose merits may be legally transferred to us for our deliverance from guilt? How could the intensity of our love be drawn out to him, unless we were convinced of the unutterable love which he has shown to us so utterly unworthy of his generous interposition in our behalf? How could we adore his infinite condescension, unless convicted of the fact that we had not a shadow of a claim to his mediation? How could we so intensely sympathize in his sufferings, unless convinced that they were substitutionary in our behalf? How could we cast our souls upon him and his matchless mercy, unless convinced that he is as willing as he is mighty to save? How would God call out our gratitude, praise and obedience, without conviction wrought into our souls, that Christ is "the chief among ten thousand, and altogether lovely"? Without this conviction, what is there in the nature of things to awaken our songs of joy over the ineffable glory of redemption? Wherefore, though some may have more pungency of conviction than others, and various degrees of emotion be elicited according to peculiarities of temperament, all who are savingly drawn by the Father, are the subjects of this feeling, as the result of realizing their position as children of wrath by nature, who can only become children of God by a loving acceptance of His grace.

Again. At some period or other before, during, or after these convictions, the work of regeneration is effected by the immediate power of the Spirit infusing a new life into the soul, which is the principle by which "old things pass away, and all things become new." Hitherto the Holy Spirit has drawn by moral suasion only, enlisting natural faculties, and interesting minds in the discovery of truth; but now he puts forth a *creative* agency and supernaturally regenerates the soul; animating it with a new life whose pulsations are quite distinct from the feeble influences that previously issued from the understanding and the conscience. They indeed had a preparatory work to do, but they could not produce the change succeeding. There was an adaptation of seed to soil, but that of itself could not produce or sustain life. Could the powers of the mind avail to the production of spiritual life, then every soul would be induced by rationality, conviction or remorse to exercise its energies in begetting within itself this new life; whereas, thousands are convicted, but never converted; thousands are affected by the obstinacy of their wills, who never change them; thousands speak of their want of feeling and lack of interest, which they never remedy. What is the reason? Because a creature can never become a creator of life in itself. An extraneous power must do this, if it ever be done. As generation in nature, so regeneration in grace implies *activity* in the begetting power, and *passivity* in the thing begotten; and the distinction between them is the difference between cause and effect. This change is therefore quite a different thing from the slight modification of sentiment and feeling produced by moral suasion. By the considerations of the condemning power of sin, and its awful consequences, the impetuosity of worldly-mindedness may be checked for a while, but the corrupt inclinations of the heart cannot be overcome: they may be diverted into another channel, but they will never cease to flow in some direction. The new principle of which we speak is alone adequate to render the soul capable of being drawn to Christ, because there is produced a congenial quality of spirit between him and the soul drawn to him. There is a hearty approval of the motives which the gospel urges, and the attractions of the cross become resistless. This new principle is the foundation of all spiritual affection, which characterize the new man, and it is speedily called into exercise, lest the grace of God should have been received in vain. Moral suasion is now addressed to a new set of sensibilities, and is more effectual to draw into exercise and carry on to maturity the infant energies of the new life. Before the implantation of this principle, moral suasion is used to bring home light to the understanding, and some degree of conviction to the conscience, but it can never subdue the will, nor purify the affections. After the change spoken of has taken place, then moral suasion has something new to work upon. It calls up the new life into all those exercises of inward and outward piety which the gospel requires. We do not mean that the regenerate sinner is left to himself to govern his heart by motives and means urged upon him by the gospel merely, for the Spirit of the Lord still continues to draw him by clothing these motives with a more powerful energy; but we mean that the Spirit no longer puts forth any creative agency, only a sustaining one, employing means that are adapted to appropriate effects in the ordinary line of the new nature imparted, means for progress and improvement until the convert come to the full stature of a man in Christ Jesus. Never, never would the soul be effectually drawn to the Lord without being first made alive from the state of death in trespasses and sins. An unregenerate sinner would remain reluctant to eternity, and remain an enemy to God, even in heaven, were it possible for him to get there; but the new principle being imparted, he becomes morally fit, and sympathetically adapted to holiness and happiness.

Hence, faith in God's word as a directory for the information of the mind, for the ruling of the heart, and for the regulation of the life, becomes predominant, and the first and continuous effect is repentance. This is not a mere conviction of conscience which was before experienced, but a generous, godly sorrow for sin, leading the penitent to forsake it, to hate it, to get away from its controlling power, and to seek an assured interest in Jesus Christ for its entire removal. This becomes the business of his life. Repentance is reformation, and implies a continuous endeavor to do "works meet for repentance." In imitation of the Apostle, he is ever disposed to give vent to his grief by praising the law which condemns him. "The law is holy, just, and good, but I am carnal, sold under sin," and his desire is to be united with the Lord Jesus Christ who, by his life and death, "magnified the law and made it honorable."

His will is, therefore, drawn into compliance with all that God demands, however great his own short-coming. It is perfectly voluntary and free in its inclination to honor Him, by acting in conformity with his convictions. There is no compulsion here, but the greatest possible remove from it, and the reason is found in the new principle by which the will acts as freely in faith and duty, as it formerly did in unbelief and rebellion. It chooses the Lord Jesus as the greatest and the best of Saviours. It gladly abandons self-righteousness, and self altogether, submitting with all gratitude to the sovereign grace of God and the mercy of Christ as the cause of his pardon.

His affections are drawn into the service of God. He delights in prayer and praise, in the Word and works of God; in the character and instructions of Christ; in the observances of a practical piety; by all of which he exhibits his love for religious principles, practices and influences, aiming to glorify God with his body and his spirit which are God's. No more his own, he aims to be faithful in the services for the performance of which he was purchased by the blood of atonement, and "created in Christ Jesus unto good works."

His hope is drawn to Christ alone, in whom he lives and moves, and has his spiritual being. The empty hopes which looked for all happiness in this present life have sank out of mind, and are engulfed in that good hope which maketh not ashamed. No servile fear mixes with his motives, but the joy of the Lord gives character to them all. The sorrows of disappointed ambition no longer embitter his cup, but he has learned to be content with the allotments of providence. Since he was not purchased with silver and gold, these earthly riches are quite too poor to excite his cupidity. His pleasures are no longer supplied in the gratification of " the lust of the flesh, the lust of the eye, and the pride of life "; but they come from the sublime entertainment of the soul from him " whom not having seen he loves, in whom, though he sees him not, yet believing, he rejoices with a joy unspeakable and full of glory." O how sweet that heavenly influence, which so gently, lovingly, powerfully draws his soul away from vanity and misery, to objects worthy of its embrace !

II. The necessity of Divine Agency in bringing a sinner to Christ. This is strongly indicated in the text. " No man CAN come to me, except the Father which hath sent me draw him." We should be content with this assurance, even if we found ourselves unable to account for the necessity alluded to, because the word of Christ in itself being absolute truth cannot be gainsaid, and is therefore by itself a sufficient reason for faith. But yet there are various considerations from which this necessity may be easily argued.

1. From the necessary dependence of the whole universe upon its author, and by consequence of man in all that concerns him. It was a philosophical as well as a divine truth observed in the polished assembly of Athens, that it is " God in whom we live and move and have being." Not only for existence and preservation

are we perpetually indebted to a Divine co-operative agency, but for all our improvement in every art and science; for of the plowman who opens and breaks the clods of the earth, it is said: Is. 20 : 26, "His God doth instruct him to discretion, and doth teach him." And surely if the skill of the husband and the wisdom of the artificer, and all those discoveries which have been made by men for the advancement of civilization, and the advantages of the race in rendering life more agreeable and commodious, are to be attributed to a Divine influence, then it is clear that the art of living wisely, and for the enjoyments of a superior state of existence must come from God. If it be necessary that He instruct us as to the pursuits of this life, with which we are familiar, how much more that He should instruct and influence us to seek the blessings of a life to come with which we are not acquainted, and towards which we have naturally no inclination? Worldly affairs cannot be clearly understood, nor strenuously pursued, nor successfully accomplished without help; much less the reformation of a corrupt and benighted soul.

2. This necessity is argued from the formidable opposition of a perverse nature which we have no power to surmount. David exclaimed, "Lord, how are they increased that trouble me, how many are they that rise up against me?" This is the language of those exclaiming upon the malignant efforts of spiritual enemies; "the world, the flesh, and the devil;" "the lust of the flesh, the lust of the eye, and the pride of life set themselves in array against me." By these the christian is constantly assailed, and in that fact he finds the necessity of watching unto prayer; well knowing that the instrumentalities of his unseen enemy that "goeth

about as a roaring lion seeking whom he may devour," are variously combined to take the advantage of his ignorance and weakness.

3. This necessity is argued from "the law of sin waring in our members." Hence from the resistance which the new heart must continually make, the Christian's life is appropriately called a warfare. There are some constitutional sins, and many habitual infirmities which so easily beset us, that the extirpation of them is attended with great difficulty and pain. To reform the external irregularities of life is comparatively easy, but to root sin out of the soul, and to consecrate the heart to inwardly operative purity in thought and emotion, as a holy temple of the Lord—this requires supernatural agency. There is also the influence of a degenerate world, whose corrupt examples press like a torrent to persuade us to follow the multitude to do evil; and often these evil examples succeed in concealing the evil behind some seeming innocence by which we may be coaxed into compliance. Beneath the whole, is the agency of the prince of darkness, whose efficiency is in "the cunning craftiness," by which we may be ensnared. Surely then, to advance such a mighty work as our salvation, a divine interposition is necessary. Well may we say: "Had it not been for the Lord who was on our side, when our confederate enemies rose up against us, they had swallowed us up quickly; when their wrath was kindled against us, the waters had overwhelmed us, the stream had gone over our soul."

4. The excellence of the results proclaims the work Divine. Behold a character of the following description. A man of the world devoted to it in soul and body, becomes a man of the church as ardently at-

tached to Christ and his cause. The difference between these pursuits is the difference between the broad road that leads to death, and the narrow path that leads to life. Once he wallowed in the mire of sensuality, once he hated the very name of religion; but, behold now he prayeth, his aversion to his former pursuits is as strong as his previous love for them; and his love for Christ and Christians far exceeds that which he ever had for his former associates. How is this to be accounted for? Is it a mere accident, a charm, a flight of enthusiasm by which this wonderful transformation must be explained? Can it be the effect of human exertion growing out of a resolution begotten of moral suasion? No. The great change seen in the man is the effect of a superior influence; "Not by might, nor by power, but by my spirit, saith the Lord of Hosts." That is the explanation. There is a new creation, a new birth, a resurrection of dry bones; the glorious result of the exceeding greatness of Divine power, drawing the sinner out from the horrible pit and miry clay, and placing his feet upon a rock, and establishing all his goings. Was it, think you, worthy of God to command the light to shine out of darkness, when the huge chaos was spoken into being and order; to invest the sun with it so as to gild the globe, and to dress all objects around us with such a various assemblage of colors that a robe of beauty should enwrap the earth; and is it not more worthy of him to lighten up the benighted soul, and to bring its chaos into harmony and order?

5. The thing might be argued from the imbecility of the means by which it is accomplished. It is not the refinements of learning nor the charms of eloquence, by which such a work is produced; for though these may

have their influence to enlighten the understanding, to charm the attention and arouse the sensibilities of the mind, it is with the mind this influence stops; the heart all the while is unreached. It is frequently the case, that after all that eloquence and learning can do, nothing effectual is done, when afterwards the plainest addresses from a weak and trembling tongue have been the means of performing that which the superior talents of many were unable to accomplish. "The treasure is contained in earthly vessels that the excellency of the power may not be of men, but of God."

But just here, when the fact of God's grace in drawing sinners to himself is made plain, we are often confronted with this vile objection, that if such an almighty agency be indispensable, sinners are clear of the blame of that corruption by which they are retained in the bonds of their impenitence, and that all the fault of their ruin is attributable to their Maker! May God strengthen us to vindicate His character from the foul reproach! O, is it possible, that we are under this necessity? Is there any sinner so daring as thus to insult his God with a charge of blame in relation to his own doom? Yes, there are thousands who in their excuses and subterfuges, and still more in their thoughts and imaginations, are loading the Deity with guilt! Unwilling to take to themselves the blame, they ascribe it with infernal presumption to God! There is a wickedness in this absurdity, that of itself proclaims their unspeakable iniquity. Does not the very fact that sinners must be supernaturally drawn, clearly indicate their own criminal corruption, the damnableness of their sin, and the horrible nature of their depravity? Why is it necessary that you be drawn if your corruption, wholly your own, be not exceedingly strong? Is it not the aversion of your heart to God, by which you instinctively turn away from the proffers of His grace and mercy, that connects you with all the guilt and blame of your rebellion? Doubtless, it is because we are, by our own consent, so abominably wicked that nothing short of Divine influence can prevail with us to abandon our sin, and place our love upon God and his Christ. Is not this the very thing that so fatally condemns us? "Light has come into the world, and men love darkness rather than light because their deeds are evil." Never lisp another syllable of objection while it is evident that your culpable depravity renders it necessary that Divine power should interpose. Can God rest under obligations to sinners so vile, that His is the blame, unless He draw them into obedience, and make them happy by force or otherwise? Does not all blame rest upon your own souls who are unwilling to exercise that natural power of attention which you undeniably possess, and as undeniably refuse to bestow upon the instructions and the grace of the gospel—attention to the motives He urges, the condemnation He threatens, the glory he proposes? How shall the Almighty draw you? Shall it be like a stock, or a stone, by physical force? Would you then deny your rational nature, and degrade yourselves below the beasts of the forest? Have you not eyes to see? Who blinds them? Have you not ears to hear? Who stops them? Have you not the ordinary powers of mind, faculties that God employs in the matter of drawing sinners to Himself? Who withholds their exercise, who chooses not to have them employed in the line of duty and obligation? True it is, that all your attention and effort will not avail without a mighty interposition ; but is it

not evident that the moment of conviction which you
may attain, by attention to motives, by considerations
of fact, and doctrine in Divine truth is generally the
moment of this effectual drawing? To what can you
attribute "*the* condemnation" but your own unwillingness to come to the light, to be convinced of sin, and
your voluntary unbelief by which you shut your eyes,
and close your ears, and harden your heart, against the
means by which the Spirit draws? Heap the blame on
God, ye rebels against heaven, as long as you please;
eternity will disclose your blame, and hell shall meet its
terrible deserts.

Finally, let us improve our subject by using it for
examination and comfort. Teaching has for its immediate object learning, upon the part of them that are
taught. The doctrines of truth implanted within the
mind enlighten it, impressed upon the heart enlivens
it ; and thus brings us into the sweet exercises of evangelical piety.

1. As to the examination of ourselves. Are we witnesses, O Christians, of the secret, powerful drawing
influence of the Word and Spirit of God? Have our
attentions been intensely excited, our consciences powerfully impressed, our wills subdued and our affections
attracted to God and to holiness? Are we willing to
subject ourselves to Divine Sovereignty, with implicit
confidence that the Lord of the whole earth will do
right? Are we glad to be indebted to divine grace for
our rescue from sin and ruin? Shall we in consequence
be willing to mortify the deeds of the body? Do our
minds, having their spiritual senses exercised to discern
the excellence of duty and privilege, seem desirous to

regard duty as privilege, and privilege as duty, thus realizing our happiness in the pursuit of our high calling? Destitute of this frame of mind, how can we enjoy comfort, how can we have any degree of satisfaction in the relation we profess to hold to the Lord Jesus? Possessed of these evidences, we have the witness within us of the Spirit, that we are born of God. Let our souls then pant for immortality among the just, and evince the feeling by an appropriate heavenly-mindedness, discoverable to all men within our associations and influence.

2. As to comfort. What unbounded satisfaction to us is the assurance that God is a Sovereign. His plan of grace can never disappoint any confiding soul. We honor Him by so regarding Him. What consolation that He has resolved in sovereignty to draw us by his Spirit, overcoming our sinful reluctance, and moving our sluggish affections to lay hold upon those things most worthy of our love? Because of this, we entertain the hope that many stout-hearted who are far from righteousness shall yet be made willing in the day of His power, and that the whole world shall yet be filled with the knowledge of His truth, and the subjects of His grace.

To this sovereignty absolute we must submit, or remain forever fallen. If we see not that God can justly forbear to draw us, and justly leave us to a merited hell, we cannot be saved; for if we consider the Deity under such obligation to us, that at any future time when we please to exercise a little attention He must interfere in our behalf, we would postpone the period of our promised return, until the visitation of death, closing us up to an irretrievable damnation. If we are deeply convinced of His sovereignty, and that He can justly exclude us forever from the happiness of heaven, surely the conviction must awaken us to a prayerful anxiety, to ardent supplication, and to a diligent use of those prescribed means of grace which God employs to bring sinners to himself.

As our destiny is in the hands of a Sovereign God who may justly condemn, or mercifully save, let not any soul continue in a state of indifference, which we may be sure is always a state of danger. Now is the time to attend to this matter, because no future time is assured to us. "Now is the accepted time, and now the day of salvation." Why should we allow the conviction of our intelligence to be smothered by the force of our passions, clamorous for self-indulgence in that which we must know will work out our ruin? What infatuation is equal to this! O, what an awful condition is that of the sinner who "knows the right, and still the wrong pursues"! Is there anything within the power of moral suasion to overcome this dreadful stupidity? No, our experience teaches us, that no means will avail unless rendered effectual by the Holy Spirit, and therefore we cry: "Come from the four winds, O breath, and breathe upon these slain that they may live!"

Have any of us come to Christ, it is because we have been drawn of the Father. Having been drawn by His mercy, by His word, by His Spirit, by His love, let us walk in His ordinances blameless; and live upon the food which he has provided for our nourishment and growth; so shall it be well with us, when called to begin the experience of the future so awful to us now because of our ignorance and our guilt. But the former being measurably taken away by the word and spirit of Christ, and the latter being altogether removed by the blood of Christ, let us rejoice in the hope of the glory of God. If the declaration, that "death is the wages of sin," terrify us, let our alarm subside by what immediately follows : "But the gift of God is eternal life through Jesus Christ our Lord."

PROCESS OF DIVINE OPERATION.

John 12 : 32.   "AND I, IF I BE LIFTED UP FROM THE EARTH, WILL DRAW ALL MEN UNTO ME."

A company of Greeks, as we learn from the context, came to Jerusalem on a certain occasion to worship; who or whence they were, it is not stated; they may have been Gentile proselytes; or Jewish foreigners; the probability is that they came from Galilee, since it is stated that they "came *therefore*" to Philip who was of Bethsaida of Galilee, and desired him, saying, "Sir, we would see Jesus." They evidently had heard much of Him from others, but they had a great anxiety to see and hear for themselves. Not wishing to defeat their own purpose, as they might, by unceremonious intrusion, they requested an introduction. Philip mentioned the matter to Andrew, and both of them told Jesus. We have reason to think that these honest Greeks were granted an interview; and that what is recorded in the history given took place in their presence. Having been presented by these brethren, Christ spoke to them concerning His mission into the world, and the object of it. He stated that whoever loved his own life above this amazing salvation, should lose it, and he that hated his life in this world in his preference for this salvation, should keep it unto life eternal. The auditors listened to His amazing statements, and were no doubt confounded. But when He appealed to God, saying, "Father, glorify thy name:" an overpowering attestation came from heaven. Some said it thundered; others said, an angel spake to him; for it thundered out these words; "I have both glorified, and will glorify it again;" but Jesus said: "This voice came not because of me, but for your sakes;" that is, that they might learn how Jesus was approved, commissioned, and qualified by the Father to accomplish the most wonderful work the world ever saw, and which was now at hand. In this connection he uttered the words: "And I, if I be lifted up from the earth, will draw all men unto me." The Evangelist tells us, "This he said, signifying what death he should die."

We propose to speak upon two important points suggested by these words, by which Christ predicted the mode and influence of his own death.

I. The influence of the Saviour's crucifixion to draw men to himself. This mode of death was not allowed by the Jewish law, it was inflicted as a Roman punishment. The prediction, therefore, excludes the idea that Christ spoke from the mere calculations of probability. It is significantly expressed by his being "lifted up from the earth." There seems to be an allusion here made to the brazen serpent lifted up on a pole in the camp of Israel where numbers who were mortally wounded by poisonous serpents, might, by divine appointment, look upon it and live. That this was a type of Christ, we learn from Himself, in his discourse with Nicodemus. It was a beautiful emblem of the power of faith which, looking to the Redeemer on the cross, heals the sting of sin, and recovers the soul from the jaws of death. Two things are here noticeable.

1. The influence of drawing men to Christ is attributed not to His *life*, but to His *death;* and not to His death only, but to the *mode* of it. There is something in the very expression of Christ intimating that His *life* would not save the sinner, and that His *death* alone could redeem. These Greeks desired to "see Jesus." Drawn by curiosity, surprise, sympathy, and the common commotion excited by His works, they gain an interview with Him. Now notice the text, as a reply to their anxiety. I appeal to your own perception. Does He not seem to say, "What good will it do you to see me alive? It has done no good to others. I was wonderfully born, but the fact never converted a single soul. The predictions of Moses and the prophets respecting me, though evidently fulfilling before their eyes, are in vain; for they will not believe. My preaching of repentance is not more successful than that of John the Baptist, whose testimony respecting me was in vain. Anna the prophetess could make no impression. The songs of Elizabeth and of my mother had no effect; nor could the journey of the shepherds, nor the star that sprinkled his splendid rays over Bethlehem enlighten the people; nor could angels by their songs, though they might have charmed the multitude when they sang an inimitable anthem, transform one enraptured heart. I walked in my simplicity, and innocence, and benevolence, and compassion, among multitudes; and though they were often surprised, and melted, they grew no better. My addresses, my reasoning, my expostulation, my expulsion of demons, my teaching by parables, and demonstrations of truth could not disarm

depravity of its power, nor work the renovation of the sinner's heart. Even my miracles, overwhelming and astonishing as they were, left no lasting impression. Though they gave sight to the blind, they never opened the eyes of a single sinner ; though my finger, or the touch of my garments could heal the sick, the malady of a single soul was not reached. My power raised the dead to life, but none in consequence were raised from the grave of spiritual death. Well might I say—Ye have Moses and the prophets, why do you demand that the damned in hell should come forth to describe their torments for the conversion of their ungodly kindred upon earth ? Surely if they will not believe Moses and the prophets, neither would they believe though one should rise from the dead."

What, then, would these Greeks have—poor, honest Greeks—what would they have ? For what would they see Jesus ? To gratify the feeling of curiosity would be but a poor incentive for their visit. How many people in every age wish to be charmed by short and sweet discourses, that shall tingle in their ears, bewitch their attention, satisfy their love of wonder, and create a momentary enthusiasm, or a soft convulsion, or a loud lamentation ! There is no harm in all this, were it not that such emotions are taken to be the proof of piety. Herein people miserably deceive themselves. They mistake animal feelings for spiritual exercises, and think they are very religious.

These inquiring Greeks, however, were not left without the knowledge of their duty. By the spirit of the whole contextual passage, we may contemplate the Redeemer as saying, " What would they obtain by a momentary sight of me, if they see not by faith the object of my coming into the world? I have not drawn them by my *life*, as I have not drawn others; but this was not my design, for that is connected with suffering and death. Now is the judgment of this world; now shall the prince of this world be cast out. And I, if I be lifted up from the earth, will draw all men unto me."

The Redeemer predicted his own death, not by saying definitely that he would die on a cross, not by foretelling every particular form and circumstance of his crucifixion, for that might have given occasion to his enemies to exert their ingenuity so to modify the manner of his death as to make the event differ from the prediction, and thus to slander his veracity, and destroy his character. He only said that He would be lifted up from the earth; He did not say, by the cross or a gibbet. This expression, "from the earth," would be sufficient, after the event took place, to convince the world that He foresaw and foreknew the mode of His own death so extraordinarily accomplished, and yielded to it voluntarily, and was indeed that prophet that should come into the world, the Messiah of God. He only said that in the event of his being *lifted up*, He would draw all men unto Him. He did not reproach His enemies in advance, with the cruelty they would manifest, nor for the agony and shame they would inflict; but he made this prediction for subsequent proof that should demonstrate His purpose and willingness to die; and the magnanimity He felt in the approach of unparalleled suffering. Surely as He foresaw the cruelty of His enemies, and the misery that awaited Him and would not avoid the danger, it is demonstrated that He died as no man ever died before, as a substitute for sinners, a willing sacrifice to the justice of God, as one who had power to lay down his life and to take it again.

II. We propose now this question for consideration—What bearing has the crucifixion of Christ on the salvation of sinners? How is it that the death of the cross draws sinners unto Christ? In other words, what adaptation is there in it to this effect?

Some have resolved the agency of the crucifixion to draw men to the Redeemer into *moral suasion*, as though a dead sinner might be persuaded to embrace Christ merely through the operation of moral motives without the Spirit's regenerating power. This is a Socinian scheme pregnant with a thousand falsehoods and a thousand dangers. Let us consider it.

1. It is true, the spectacle of an innocent, bleeding Saviour will have effect on generous minds. The idea of the holy prophet of the Lord, and the disinterested Redeemer of sinners living in poverty, and dispensing untold blessings upon the ungrateful; and then dying, innocent of harm, in ignominy, agony and shame and scorn, will often melt the heart into sorrow and painful emotion. If we consider the extraordinary birth of Christ, His degradation in infancy, His innocence in childhood, His obedience to his parents, the wisdom of His riper years, the eloquence He displayed, when "He spake as never man spake," His activity in doing good, while suffering "the contradiction of sinners," His labors, privations, and wrong endured, His meekness and perseverance amidst prejudice and persecution, the unreasonable rage and unrelenting enmity of the people whom He came to seek and to save, the tender sensibility of His heart when weeping over their sins, His intercession for them, His forgiving love, His prayers in their behalf;

that after all this they took Him by treachery in the night, cruelly scourged Him, penetrated His sacred head in cruel mockery with a crown of thorns, tearing the flesh from His temples ; that in this mangled, bloody condition compelled His fainting body up the hill of Calvary, there to strip Him to be crucified between thieves, as though the very devil had taken entire possession of their hearts frantic with hellish hate ; see how they spiked His hands and feet to the cross, and then raising the burden, plunge it into a hole made for its reception, thus stretching and tearing every limb, by a tremendous jerk. See them smite the crown to make the thorns penetrate more deeply. See them wag their heads in scorn, adding every indignity they can think of. O ! sickening sight ! O ! cruelty infernal, be thou forever my abhorrence, and with thy sons, let not my soul partake.

This history of blood and treason, of murder foul, of cruelty intense toward innocence and virtue in a life of unsullied purity, and that contrasted with wondrous meekness, and the voice of prayer arising above the uproar ; "Father, forgive them, for they know not what they do !" O, this is enough to break a heart of stone ; yet the feeling is but moral suasion. Our blood boils as it courses through our veins, it is but moral suasion. Our sympathy becomes painful in its effects, it is but moral suasion. As the dreadful story is told the world weeps, it is but moral suasion. The gospel is preached, the doctrine of a substitutionary death in the awful death of Christ, is preached ; the feelings of nature are excited, hearts are saddened, but all is simply the barren result of moral suasion. Good indeed, so far as it goes, nay, of great value when accompanied by the common influences of the Spirit, yet it is but moral suasion; and that by itself always evaporates, and leaves the soul just where it was, not effectually drawn, but still in sin, impenitency, and unbelief.

2. The power of the cross to draw, is the purchase of the cross to subdue the rebellious sinner. That purchased power is the Holy Spirit who takes of the things of Christ and shows them unto us; and in the light of His showing, the hard heart melts like wax before the fire.

Whatever attraction arises from the Exhibition of the Cross, it cannot alone prevail. The preaching of the life of Christ in its innocence, meekness, disinterestedness, loveliness and charming beauty, cannot renew the heart. Whatever sympathy we feel, however the judgment may be convinced, whatever tumult of tender feeling the subject may occasion, it will not draw us to His bosom. We soon forget our compassion, our sympathy grows tired in its exercise, and our tender excitement gradually sinks into a dead calm. Thousands have thus been melted, yet they have hardened again; thousands have been filled with unutterable emotion, yet they have lost it all. The reason is, draw the sinner as you may without giving him a new heart, and he remains a sinner still. Wash the Ethiopian as you may, you cannot alter his skin. Treat the leopard as you please, you cannot remove his spots. How then can he do good, whose very nature accustoms him to do evil? Charm a serpent by sweet music, so that he is softened into gentleness, he remains a serpent still; ready, when the spell is broken, to discover his poisonous fangs. Moral suasion is like a wash to the Ethiopian, like means employed to change the spots of the leopard, like strains of music to charm the serpent; it may excite sympathy, and variously arouse natural affection, but it cannot effectually draw a sinner to Christ. Nor can the sinner draw himself to Christ without the Spirit of God. He has no will to change his will. He has no choice to alter his choice. A bad heart will never choose to be better. A dead soul will never exhibit the activities of life.

What remedy then is there for this deplorable evil? Only this. When Christ is seen lifted up on the cross, and regarded as our substitute, a victim, a sacrifice in our stead, and we are brought by the Holy Spirit to feel that despair in ourselves compels our look to Him as our only hope, then the merits of His death are plainly in our view available to us as the lost whom He came to save. Thus there is an adaptedness wrought in our perception to see, and a preparation in our hearts to feel the power of the attraction of the cross. Before the crucifixion, the common influences of the Spirit like drops of rain, overspread the world; but after that event, He descended copiously, as a shower, and His special influences saved millions.

3. How comes it that the sacrifice of Christ, lifted up from the earth, is so meritorious of drawing influences? His life upon the earth had no such drawing influence. How many went away, and "walked no more with Him"? He could not be such a sacrifice, except by the stipulation of his Father, by the consent of the Eternal Son, in virtue of the infinite dignity of His person, by the shedding of his blood, by his resurrection from the dead to new life and power, as the Son of Man. By a compact between the Father and the Son, His voluntary sufferings should be imputed to

the sinner ; there should be thus a vicarious commutation, or substituted satisfaction implying that Christ's death was in our law-place, in our room and stead. Leave out this idea, the phraseology of the New Testament becomes hopelessly enigmatical, and the ceremonial worship of the Jews from which it was borrowed, a senseless thing, and utterly absurd; but with this idea all becomes plain, beautiful, glorious.

In this respect the sacrifice of Christ was incomparably different from the death of Moses, David, Stephen, Paul and all other martyrs. These also died in attestation of the truth, and for the good of others, but not in their room or stead. Moses lived and suffered for the Israelites, and was willing to die for them ; but there is no idea given of literal substitution, or that his sufferings should pay for their sins. David, an eminent type of Christ, lived and died, having suffered for all Israel, but there is no hint given that his sufferings made an atonement for them. So of all the rest. They died as heroes for the faith, witnesses to Christ's sacrifice, as the hope of sinners. None of them had personal worth sufficient to cancel a single sin, but "the blood of Jesus Christ cleanseth from all sin;" they needed atonement for their own sins, but He was holy, undefiled, separate from sin and sinners. Yet Socinians say that Christ's death is in no respect different, as to atonement, from the death of prophets and martyrs, and generous soldiers who die for their country on the battle-field ; that if Christ draws sinners to Himself, it is by moral suasion. In other words, the representation of His blood to our feelings, even as the death of a martyr, affects our sympathies.

Now this matter must be clearly understood, or the doctrine of atonement is but a shadow. If the death of

Christ be atonement only in the sense in which the prophets and martyrs made atonement, then we have ten thousand saviors to divide the glory with Him. Nay, the word is a misnomer, for there is no comparison between the sinless Saviour and the guilty sons of men, either in life or in death. No. "There is but *one* mediator between God and man, the man Christ Jesus." Eternal redemption is procured for us only by the shedding of His most precious blood. By virtue of His act alone, as our atoning High Priest, the Spirit draws, convinces, persuades us to be reconciled to God.

We need not stop to prove that there is no universal salvation, though there is a universal drawing by means of the truth in the common operations of the Spirit, wherever the glad tidings of great joy are proclaimed. It is because moral suasion is not sufficient, that thousands who are drawn by common influences are still not saved. Where is there a sinner so hardened that does not sometimes relent? But what do these relentings accomplish? Nothing beyond the demonstrations of conscience writhing under a sense of guilt. These are the occasional spasms evinced by the resistance of strong depravity.

4. The insufficiency of moral suasion upon the natural heart, by exemplifications recorded in the Bible, should not be lost sight of in this discussion. The end had in view is to counteract outward delusion and self-deception to which we are exposed by falsity of reasoning and perversity of inclination. We very much fear that the religion which is now abroad in christendom, is largely of the Socinian cast; that we esteem too highly the natural powers of the soul, as though our hearts were not entirely depraved; that we look to those

exhibitions of truth which will affect our sensibilities, and excite our feelings, as alone sufficient to create religious principle and establish genuine piety within the heart, without any special influence of the Holy Spirit ; that we often mistake virtuous wishes, and certain occasional elevations of vapid sentiment, for the evidences of personal preparation for death; that consequently we pray not with due anxiety for that inward transformation of character, without which we cannot be saved; and that while we dishonor the Holy Spirit as the efficient cause of our sanctification, we likewise dishonor the Son of God ; who procured for us this Divine Agent for that inward moral renovation which must be added to legal justification, in order that those who are emancipated from condemnation, may be inwardly fitted for salvation procured by atoning blood.

The surest and the simplest way of arriving at solid hope in the matter of salvation, is to feel the fact of our entire apostasy from God ; so that we may see there is no strength in us, who are by nature "*dead* in trespasses and sins;" and to count no virtue, no groans, no bodily exercise, no convulsions of feeling as reliable for the renewal of our nature, but as they are the results of moral suasion operating upon the new life begotten of the Holy Spirit.   Now, as I have said, there are exemplifications of the utter insufficiency of everything to effect the renewal of the soul, apart from the Holy Spirit, scattered throughout the Bible ; and to these we must appeal to justify our position, which is this. All applications of truth to the conscience, all the warmth of feeling imaginable, all the commotions excitable within us, are not sufficient to draw us to holiness, without the principle of a new life implanted by the Spirit.   Attend,

I pray you, to historical facts which are recorded for our instruction and admonition.

First fact. As soon as I have opened my Bible to read the history of the human race after the apostasy, I find in CAIN a heart so hard as to be impenetrable by the moral suasion of the kind words of God Himself. He is the first-born, the eldest son of Adam; he is well instructed by weeping parents whose penitence and grief for sin made them habitual mourners, as exiles from Paradise ; and who had fled to the hope set before them in the first gospel-promise. Cain, as well as Abel, is taught to seek and pray ; and by prefigurative bloody sacrifice to look to that "seed of the woman who should bruise the serpent's head." Both of them had the same capabilities, as well as the same advantages; but it appears that Abel was a renewed man, and offered a lamb in sacrifice, fit and appropriate, as an act of worship. Why did not Cain? He offered the fruits of the ground, probably the products of his own tillage, thanking God for temporal mercies, and wholly omitting the idea of a sin-offering as necessary to an appropriate worship. Like a Socinian, Cain could see no virtue in blood, but good reason for his own acceptance by God, on account of the exhibition of the fruit of his own toil. And when his offering was rejected, on account of its intrinsic inappropriateness, and that of Abel accepted, because in conformity with the instruction both of them had received as to acceptable worship, the wrath of Cain arose against his brother ; and when kindly spoken to by the God of mercy, the moral suasion of the language had no influence over him; nor was he satisfied until his wrath was quenched by the blood of a murdered brother. The Almighty might have justly smitten him as a wretch not fit to live, but he did not. Mercy even in his case might be extended; for when he was sent only into exile as a fugitive and a vagabond, God allayed the fears of the murderer, by expedients that should have operated for the safety of his forfeited life. His lamentation, "My punishment is greater than I can bear," was met by sparing mercy. Who knows what agony convulsed him, what tears, and groanings, and howlings accompanied his remorse? But did these agitations of soul recover the transgressor? Did the sparing mercy of God move his heart to penitency for his crime? Did his knowledge of the way to be saved, as previously imparted, lead him to a penitential return to God? Why is he not drawn to cast himself upon that mercy which had already, in Divine forbearance, appeared mingling with a judgment too light for his crime? The Spirit of grace could have drawn him to repentance, reformation and salvation. Let no man ask the reason why, for Sovereignty from the throne of the universe thunders into silence the presumptuous caviler. With the awful decisions of our offended God, we have nothing to do. The fact in this instance, only concerns us. Cain sought no favor, he would not be drawn by the mercy which allowed him still to live. No emotions of shame, grief or remorse could create within him a new heart.

Second fact. Take the case of Esau. Our sympathy is excited in his behalf, because he was not destitute of natural sensibilities and affection. Indeed, he may have been possessed of more natural virtue, honest simplicity, and honorable feeling than his brother Jacob. But contrary to his instruction, and despising the benefit, he undervalued his birthright, and put contempt upon it by selling it for a mess of pottage. The sale was an offence, but the price was an additional insult to God who had by Divine arrangement established its value. But he discovered his mistake too late, and he mourned and wept. We are moved by the history. And when he heard the words of his father, he cried with an exceeding great and bitter cry: "Bless me, even me, O my father." True, he had despised his birthright, and every one so doing makes himself unworthy of forfeited advantages. Had he remained utterly impenitent and profane, we might have curtailed our sorrow for him thus bereft by his own wickedness ; but he mourned bitterly under the influence of considerations which constitute moral suasion. After his rash act, and when brought to reflection, he fully realized his loss ; for "ye know how that afterwards, when he would have inherited the blessing, he was rejected ; for he found no place of repentance though he sought it carefully with tears." Esau's tears and entreaties could not recover the temporal advantages of the birthright, but still there was a greater personal blessing within his reach, not included in that birthright. Why did not his self-condemnation and regret lead him to that which was more excellent ? He not only despised his birthright, and mourned over it, with regret for his folly, but he despised his God in undervaluing the greater blessing he might have had ; and this we learn from the fact, that God styled himself "the God of Abraham, Isaac and Jacob ;" not of Esau. Moral suasion had no effect upon him.

Third fact. There is something in the history of BALAAM peculiarly striking. How remarkably was he exercised, and how sublime were the emotions produced by what he saw in prophetic vision ! What reason can be given why they were not effectual to conduct him to holiness and happiness? The simple answer is, the new heart was not given him to correspond with the attractions of heavenly things. Long and repeatedly did religious influences overwhelm him. God himself uttered advice to the unworthy man; but notwithstanding his commission to prophesy and declare the word of the Lord, he was under stronger influences for evil. God sent an angel to meet him with a drawn sword to hinder him from his madness. He confessed that he had sinned. He owned the truth, and said: "How shall I curse whom God hath not cursed, or defy whom God hath not defied; far from the top of the rocks I see him and from the hills I behold him. Lo! the people shall dwell alone, and shall not be reckoned among the nations. Who can count the dust of Jacob, and the number of the fourth part of Israel? Let me die the death of the righteous, and let my last end be like his." "If Balak would give me his house full of silver and gold, I cannot go beyond the commandment of the Lord." See how, in language most acceptable and sublime, he speaks of Christ whom he sees at a distance, the Son of God Most High. "I shall see him, but not now; I shall behold him, but not nigh. A star shall come out of Jacob, and a sceptre rise out of Israel, who shall smite the corners of Moab, and destroy all the children of Sheth." O strange, that his mind should be so wonderfully moved by the realities of religion, his understanding so enlightened, and his sensibilities so affected, and should, after all, have no principle of reformation; that the reign of the Messiah should become apparent to him, and yet his heart not be drawn by its attractions; that he could have the enlightened spirit of a prophet, and yet destitute of the spirit of a believer; that he could so clearly see the unutterable doom of the wicked, and yet himself remain a voluntary sinner! O, is not the least spark of light in the sinner's heart of more value than all the wisdom of philosophers and prophets, more efficacious than all the intelligence of men and angels? What a wonder is the history of Balaam! What an example of the inherent weakness of moral suasion!

Fourth fact. The case of SAUL is also interesting, and discovers to us the necessity of a new principle that men may be effectually drawn into Christian obedience. He was certainly a man whose heart had been touched with religious sentiment, and so highly did he soar in the expression of religious feeling and devout utterances that the people exclaimed, "Is Saul among the prophets?" God had chosen and anointed him king of Israel, and endowed him with many excellent qualifications. But the history shows how often and grievously he sinned. O, what ailed it, that this man thus exercised in mind, the anointed captain of the Lord's inheritance, could not exercise the spirit of obedience and unsophisticated piety? It was the want of that new life which the Spirit infuses into every pious heart. He was operated on, but not regenerated by the Spirit. He had some religious feeling, but not the native principle of godliness. Strong were the attractions by which he was drawn, but nothing could draw his affections without religious principle rooted in his heart, and prompting to the obedience of faith.

Fifth fact. AHAB is another instance of the inefficacy of religious applications where religious principle is wanting. Ahab had grievously sinned when from con-

descension to Jezebel his wife, he permitted her to
execute the project of murdering Naboth in order to
seize his vineyard. He greatly trembled, however,
when Elijah expostulated with him on the subject of
his crime, and predicted the deserved punishment. God
was yet so kind as to enlighten, admonish, and warn
him, that he might seek repentance and salvation. The
effect was to disquiet his soul, and make great outward
demonstrations of humility. "He rent his clothes, and
put sackcloth upon his flesh, and fasted and lay in sackcloth, and walked softly ;" so that the Almighty said to
Elijah : "Seest thou how Ahab humbleth himself before
me? I will not bring the evil in his days, but in his
son's days, will I bring the evil upon his house." One
would think that the dreadful prospect which was
before him of personal ruin and the extermination of
his household would have led him to perpetual mourning and entire reformation. But it did not. Does Ahab
restore to the family of Naboth the vineyard of which
he had so violently robbed them? Does he put away
Jezebel who had ensnared him into the bloody crime?
Does he renounce that idolatry by which his Maker was
offended? Does he make the least effort to restore the
dishonored worship of the God of Israel? Does he
seek the reformation of his own heart? No, notwithstanding the heart-searching word from God had reached
his stupid conscience so that it trembled, and had impressed his insolent soul so that his tongue uttered grief
and lamentation, yet he remained unchanged. His
wicked nature soon returned to that course from which
it had been violently forced, discovered other channels
in which his depravity might flow, and found at least
arguments for relapsing into base indulgence. O, what

little confidence can we have in temporary convictions, impressions, and alarms! What purpose will the applications of truth, or mercy, or the discipline of providence answer, if no right principle be infused into the heart which will respond to the drawing influence of Divine grace upon the soul?

Sixth fact. Passing over the perturbations of mind which Herod felt, for ordering the head of John the Baptist in a charger; and the anguish produced by dreams in Pilate and his wife, on account of the mock trial of Christ; and the conviction of the astounded Centurion at the cross, when he exclaimed: "Truly this was the Son of God;" and the horrible case of Judas; and the thousands of Israel, greatly excited by the teachings and miracles of Christ, who wondered and perished; we cannot omit to notice the case of an amiable man whose heart was the subject of deep impressions, and seemed in earnest while inquiring into his own prospects for heaven. We feel interested in him, especially because when Jesus looked upon him, he loved him. His moral character was without reproach. His standing was high among the people for integrity, benevolence, charity, and an amiable, winning disposition. He came *running* and *kneeling* to Christ, and inquired with all demonstrations of respect and confidence: "Good Master, what must I do to inherit eternal life?" Is not this "an Israelite indeed in whom there is no guile?" Every witness of his manner would surely say so. But he was in the presence of "the Searcher of hearts," whom he did not acknowledge as such. Hence Christ said: "Why callest thou me good? there is none good but God." As if he had said, "God alone is good, and therefore if I be but a man, I am not good. You are a man, therefore talk not of goodness." Here was an instant discovery of the deception of human goodness, as a ground of reliance upon which this amiable young man depended. At the very commencement of the subject of inquiry, Christ introduced the question as of infinite importance to his hope. Like a faithful physician, he at once probes his soul, to discover to him the fact of his own corruption so deeply covered up, and to manifest the self-deception of the human heart, that he might be led to see the source of his errors, the cause of human misery, and the fatal danger of self-righteousness. He taught him the necessity of a better principle of goodness. But to instruct him more effectually, he taught him what his goodness must amount to, that it might be a reliable foundation for solid hope. He unfolded to him the comprehensiveness of the law, its spirituality and its broad demands. But the sense of goodness is so deeply rooted in his poor nature, with all self-complacency he asserted that he had obeyed every command, and triumphantly put the question : "What lack I yet?" Now what shall be done for the dear young ruler, who thus challenges Christ to discover an error in him? From youth brought up and trained in the belief of personal goodness as the meritorious and sure qualification for heaven, he persists in his self-righteous claims ; and boasts his immaculate morality. How deeply rooted is the pernicious sentiment, how interwoven with all his thoughts! To give it up, would be to abandon all dignity and self-respect ; especially, since from his youth, he had been so careful, so conscientious, so cautious as to maintain an upright character which was always considered the best title to heaven. What shall be done for the poor young man? Rich, indeed, in this world's goods, but in reality poor, and blind, and naked. What shall be done for him? The Saviour will not give him up yet to final delusion, and as argument was useless, he applies a test. "Give your all away, and come and follow me, and you shall have treasure in heaven." This will end the discussion, this will throw his soul into distress from which he will arise, if the right principle be in him, into an entire surrender of himself, and bring life and peace into his bosom. But he has not got the good principle, and so all expostulation and persuasion are spent on him in vain. He cannot give his all away, but is sorrowful that this great demand is made. He cannot, for his soul is bound up in his wealth; he cannot, for his heart will not detach itself from honor's gaudy show; O, he cannot, for his great estate has engrossed his affections. He cannot cast into contempt his accredited and exalted religious character, for on it are founded his precious hopes of heaven. What, then, shall he do, having no inlaid principle that puts a superior value upon the gospel? His soul is sorrowful within him, because he may no longer cherish vainglorious self-righteousness. He regrets most bitterly the contrariety between the religion of Christ and the spirit of the world. O, young man, what were thine honors, pleasures, and possessions all, compared to the incorruptible inheritance the Lord of Glory offered? He went away sorrowful and offended, and so millions in every age fail, from the want of a proper principle that will respond to the drawing power of moral suasion in the gospel. Such are samples of all upon whom moral suasion tries its power in vain. It moves them, like the breeze producing ripples on the lake, while all below the surface is calm and still.

As galvanism may produce a violent spasm in a dead man's limb, so moral suasion may greatly excite the natural sympathies of those dead in sin ; but soon it exhausts itself, and leaves the subject less susceptible of religious emotion than he was before.

Our doctrine is that Christ's death is a real sacrifice, purchasing the Spirit for our renovation ; that moral suasion operates conviction ; that generally in the hour of conviction, a new life is infused necessary to our being effectually drawn by moral suasion ; because a sinner cannot be drawn unwillingly, or by compulsion. Naturally he has no relish for the doctrines of the cross, however he may be affected by the contemplation of Christ. There must be a correspondence between the state of the mind, and the doctrine of the cross, that the former may willingly respond to the drawing power of the latter. There must be an affinity between objects before they can attract each other ; there must be a moral adjustment, adaptation, congeniality, before the drawing of the cross will produce a movement of the soul towards it. Naturalists have employed their skill to ascertain affinities in the natural world. They bring materials together that they may discover results, and they find that where there is no previous affinity, the drawing influence of one, will be resisted by the repulsion in another against it. Even so in the moral world. If a mind has no taste for a principle, it cannot approve or adopt it, it cannot be drawn by it. So spirits of darkness are never reformed by their miseries. The skin of the Ethiopian will not change, whatever climate he is subjected to ; the spots of the leopard will remain, no matter what be the circumstances of his situation ; the serpent, however domesticated by the art of man, or soothed by charms, remains just as ferocious in his nature, and just as poisonous in his bite.

We therefore say that Socinianism is a fatal heresy, subversive of the gospel. It tells us that Christ is a mere creature, though of the most exalted nature ; that he came into the world as a prophet, a great teacher for our instruction, and to show us how to escape our woe ; that he died by a concourse of circumstances, which arose from the adverse opposition of unreasonable men ; he died as a martyr to exemplify the sublimity and dis-interestedness of true virtue, and in attestation of truth ; not as a sacrifice in the room of the guilty, not to make satisfaction for the guilt of the sinner, not as a substi-tute in our law-room to pay our debt ; but only for our benefit, as an example, as did Peter, Paul and Stephen ; that he draws us by that moral suasion which consists in the external affecting exhibition of suffering innocence, by which our hearts are touched and melted ; and we are thus turned into the path of virtue and piety ; that a remedial law is now instituted which the sinner can easily obey ; and this obedience secures to him a pardon, without atonement, by the benevolence of God ; that all now needed for salvation, is external decorum ; some virtues ; graces ; sensibilities excited by the contempla-tion of the cross, without anything like a regeneration of the heart by the Holy Spirit, such as we assert the Saviour himself declared necessary. This scheme we again affirm is subversive of the gospel, and has no affinity to Christianity, as we have shown ; and might continue to evince by extended arguments. No, it makes the cross of Christ of none effect.

Before salvation could be achieved, though "pro-mised before the world began," it had to be made certain that "in the fullness of time Christ should come," made of a *woman*, made *under* the law that he might redeem them that are under the law, that we might receive the adoption of sons." The victim must die, and rise again in demonstration of his victorious power. He must ascend to heaven as the mighty conqueror. He must there present the "blood shed for the remission of sins" as our "High Priest," and "intercede" for us by the price paid for redemption. The language of the New Testament in reference to the nature of the death of Christ, is language borrowed from the Old Testament descriptive of atonement. He was "the Lamb of God that taketh away the sin of the world," and when he ascended on high, it was in the character of "High Priest" going within the veil, with his own precious blood to intercede for his people. These were essential parts of the work of atonement, whereby he purchased them for justification, and purchased for them the Holy Spirit for sanctification, so that their right to heaven might be laid in their external freedom from condemnation, and their internal moral fitness for heaven's enjoyments. They needed not only a new standing in the "Second Adam," but a new nature by the work of the Holy Spirit purchased for creating it, an imparting a principle of life upon which the cross of Christ should draw, and through which they should be drawn effectually into union with Him who is made unto them "wisdom, righteousness, sanctification and redemption."

III. The agency of the crucifixion of Christ operating on the new principle, in order to draw sinners to himself. "I, *if I be lifted up*, will draw all men unto me."

1. An excellent foundation for this attraction, is laid in the new principle of holy love. I might still farther demonstrate that all the attractions of the cross, and all the convictions produced, though useful, though valuable, though generally marking the period of regeneration, are ineffectual and incompetent till holy love, or spiritual life be infused into the soul. Unless you could draw a man into duty by compulsion, unless you could draw a man to heaven unwillingly, or make a man truly happy against his will, or gratify the appetite with food for which it has no relish, or make objects coalesce which have no affinity, or make the power of magnetism attract the water, as well as steel or iron, or make the needle point spontaneously to the south as well as to the north, you could not bring a depraved soul to Christ by mere moral suasion. It is impossible that an unholy heart can be attracted by a holy object. The affinity, the congruity, the congeniality must previously exist before attraction can operate to the end had in view. The tragic scene of the cross may affect our constitutional sympathy, but the holy, pure, gospel principles implicated by the cross, no unregenerate soul can relish ; and therefore has no true sympathy, no genuine feeling, however one may weep *around* the scene of Calvary.

But let holy love be infused by regeneration, and then the heart being drawn will run into the loving embrace of Jesus. The reason is, that the affinity is formed, the conformity of taste and relish is produced. How often is this exemplified in the gospel history. " And Jesus walking by the sea of Galilee saw two brethren, Simon called Peter, and Andrew his brother, casting a net into the sea, for they were fishers. And he said unto them, '*follow me*, and I will make you fishers of men.' And they *straightway* left their nets, and followed him.   And going on from thence he saw other two brethren, James the son of Zebedee, and John his brother, in a ship with Zebedee their father, mending their nets, and he called them.   And they *immediately* left the ship and their father, and followed him."   How can this be rationally accounted for, but upon the fact of a secret infusion of spiritual life that prompted them to abandon their all at the voice of a stranger whom they had probably never before seen?   Was this natural?   Before the inward change is made to renew the soul, you sympathize with Christ as an ordinary person who seems to have no other claim to special attention than that which a common humanity exacts, in any case of extreme suffering. Not so, the feeling we experience toward a friend we love.   To see such an one in the abyss of agony, racks the power of sympathy with pain.   It makes us weep tears of blood, as it were, and fain would we endure a part of his torment, could we alleviate his sorrows. Well then, think how a good man is drawn by the crucifixion of the friend he dearly loves.   Christ is our friend, above all others beloved.   *Because we love him,* are we pierced by the nails that entered his hands and his feet.   We feel the crown of thorns that pierced his sacred temples.   We feel the scourge that lacerated his beloved body, and the scorn and the shame that covered him, because it was our *friend* who was the victim of horrid cruelty.   The daughters of Jerusalem wept, but much more the daughters of love.   The former soon forgot the bloody scene when the victim was dead. The latter never can forget to feel.   With the former it was merely constitutional sympathy ; with the latter it was a holy principle that lasts forever.   Hence, while others retired, his believing loving female friends found their affections gathering around the tomb of Christ, whence he was taken from the cross. No wonder Mary stood at the sepulchre weeping and stooping down to see the place where her Lord had lain. "Woman, why weepest thou?" said one whom she supposed the gardener. Mark the answer, "Because they have taken away my Lord, and I know not where they have laid him." And when her quick ear recognized the tone of that dear voice that had often said "Mary," her soul was poured out upon a word, "Rabboni," and O how she flew to embrace him!

Mourners who take no special interest in their dying friends, mourn over the scenes of dying humanity, and afterwards weep no more. But real friends whose souls are knit to the departed, love their memory after death, and can never cease to love. So while others may be in a measure affected by the story of the cross, the lovers of Christ delight to "show forth the Lord's death until he come."

2. The cross of Christ draws very powerfully on our faith. But what is faith? It is the activity of the new life imparted by the Spirit laying hold of Christ with a grasp that nothing can relax. How differently did his crucifixion operate upon our minds when we had no other feeling for him than that of sympathy mourning over the tragedy of his death, from the attractions of his cross first felt when we first believed. O, they drew us then with resistless power, because we found in the suffering Saviour a substitute, who delivers us poor sinners from the wrath to come.

Go to the theatre, and you may be interested in a matter which is the mere fiction of an inventive imagination. The play opens. A scene is before you. Some tragical event is about to transpire, the death of Cato, or of Caesar; or the murder of Cicero; of Socrates; or some other bloody drama, clothed with all the seeming realities of other days. Lost now to the realities around, you are absorbed amid circumstances belonging to a by-gone age and people. As the plot thickens, your interest increases; as the various parts succeed, your tears fall, your emotions intensify; the fountains of sympathy open, and your whole soul is put into a tumult of feeling over fictitious events; yet all the while you *know it is fiction*. Therefore however interesting the scene which has transpired, when it is over, your sympathy soon subsides because of the influence of unbelief, as well as because you have no personal interest in the whole transaction. So an avowed skeptic, or any unbeliever, may be brought to mourn a little around the cross, but there is no lasting attraction there. When his momentary attention is released, his heart is still the same, obdurate and unbelieving. It is all for him only a fiction. On the other hand, if the history of Christ's death be received as a reality, and faith bends her eyes upon him as "lifted up" in the endurance of agony in our stead; if faith sees that our hoped-for salvation is in his precious hands, and our deliverance is effected by his dying groans from the horrors of the second death, what then is the power of the attraction by which we are drawn? O it is omnipotent! O, how the weeping soul is drawn into amazement and wonder, and loving submission to Christ! Thence nothing can draw her. That which fastens one to the cross and to the cause of Christ, is a riveted adhesion which never can be loosened.

His person and His glory become the absorbents of never-dying love.

3. This sight of the Cross draws upon our penitence. Such is the next natural result. The penitence of the pious is different from the sorrows of the unregenerate. These are but the sorrows of the world. They are selfish, they are malignant ; they are torment ; they produce no real reformation ; and so they have no true affinity for the cross, which consequently cannot attract the selfish soul. But a generous true penitence is poured out at the foot of the cross. It cries for pardon and reconciliation with God. Under its influence we cannot rest without obtaining the soothing influence of hope. And where shall we go for pardon except to Christ alone, the one "lifted up," who, in virtue of his death, is exalted at the right hand of God to give pardon and remission of sins? With a just view of the cross and its significance, it is exceedingly natural to go to Christ ; for the pardon proclaimed as a free gift to the unworthy, is so free, so full, so desirable, that the penitent can see nothing to equal it, and for that reason, will not neglect it. He is drawn by its sweetness, its generosity, its absolute certainty. Reconciliation with a justly offended God, is that for which he sues, and that without which all his comfort dies. It cuts him to the heart when he thinks of his baseness, and his dreadful deserts, but then when he understands the cross, he is drawn to it by a power which exists in nothing else. It is true, all this is but moral suasion, but it is moral suasion operating upon a new heart. There is a correspondence between the adaptation to be drawn, and the adaptation of the drawing power. The magnet will not draw stone, but let steel be put in its place, you will instantly

see motion in the one, produced by the influence of the other. So the cross will not draw the natural heart, for "the natural man receiveth not the things of the Spirit of God, they are foolishness unto him, neither can he know them, because they are spiritually discerned." But let that heart be qualified by an adapting new nature, and the attraction of cohesion will soon unite it to Christ.

4. It is remarkable how the believer is drawn by the generous action of his own free will. The sinner who is subjected to the drawing influence of the cross, may be partly persuaded of the importance of religion, but he is constantly embarrassed, and entirely prevented by a refractory rebellious will. His will is free for those pursuits which his heart naturally likes in self-indulgence and worldly pursuits. It cannot dislike what it likes, and therefore rejects compliance with duties that thwart its own inclinations. His reason, his conscience, his education and other things, may draw him to the house of God; but he feels no heart-felt sympathy with the exercises of prayer and praise. He may be attracted by the charms of music and of eloquence, but as to the subject matter of either, he has no interest whatever. But why is it that his christian neighbor enters into these things with all his soul? He may be his inferior in mental powers, how is it that he is his superior in acts of devotion? Ah, it is because his will is bent in its inclination to the cross. He has an instinctive liking for the holy employment which is the natural feeling of a new life operating within him. The same moral suasion in both cases comes in contact with different qualities of spirit. In the former, it is powerless with an opposing will; with the latter, it is

powerful with a yielding will delighting in the cross of Christ.

Hence the necessity of a principle of grace, to render moral suasion effectual to draw men to the Saviour. Now the result of all this reasoning is to show, that the regeneration of the soul is essentially necessary in our effectual calling. If we get not this, we remain corrupt reluctant sinners, who resist the influences that would bind us, and cast away the cords that would entwine us ; and as far as we go in apparent reformation, we are only dragged unwillingly, propelled by the force of conscience and of sympathy. We do not deny that this moral suasion which cannot regenerate, but makes the heart somewhat tender and susceptible, is exceedingly useful ; reason is useful ; convulsions of the conscience are useful ; the word of exhortation is useful ; our emotions, excitement of sympathy, and lamentations are useful. They prepare the mind for renovation by the Spirit, they generally precede that work ; they imply deep attention, and, it may be, earnest longings ; they repress our resistance, they restrain our natural enmity ; they greatly disarm opposition ; but they are not themselves renovation, or the effects of it. They imply no holy predisposition, for that does not exist ; no moral preparation, for that would imply holiness. But these excitements of conscience, and pungency of feeling, I call preparatory, because they generally precede renewal in the order of time. This connection they have by the appointment of God and by the nature of man with the renovation of the soul, but not by their own tendency. And God be thanked, that when the sinner feels thus wretched, thus forlorn, God imparts a regenerating virtue by which he is susceptible of being drawn to the cross, as the great necessity of his soul.

In conclusion, I know not what I may hereafter say in exposing that great heresy, the subtle heresy of Socinianism. It would assure us that we are not so depraved but we may be persuaded into religion, without the necessity of a new principle of life. Therefore there was no need that Christ should be stretched on the cross to *purchase* for us the life-giving Spirit. We only need his word, and the common influence of truth and of the Spirit, without regeneration, to charm us into piety! It is the most dangerous heresy of our day. Even in orthodox churches, many ministers preach and practice as though they believed it. Our own church, as far as practice is concerned, seems to harbor it. Many of the popular sermons of the day, seem based on the doctrine that we need no regeneration. Therefore it is not discussed ; no efforts seem to be made in that direction, while moral suasion seems to be the only thing relied on for the production of christian character. The idea is, that we must be charmed into piety ; persuasion of men in the use of preaching is enough ; momentary feeling in a revival will produce it. Perhaps this is the reason why there is so little *principle* at the root of our *practical* christianity, so little stability in our professed piety ; such a call for what may excite and charm, and entertain ; and the dishonored, forgotten life-giving Spirit is offended by the usurpation of His work ; and thus the churches are forsaken by Him. I must not blame others, however, more than myself ; for I ought to have employed more energy in exposition of radical truth. O that I could make some atonement !

Let me now protest before God and the world, that religion will not grow in our hearts without a new principle which we do not possess by nature. Men may preach, angels may preach, providence may preach, Christ himself may preach, yet withal we remain in our sins. Yes, men may get up excitements, they may interest, they may agitate, they may inflame and convulse our feelings; yet they cannot make us religious; they may make hypocrites, but they cannot make believers. They cannot persuade effectually a single soul into religious life and action.

To produce this new principle is the prerogative of the Spirit who breathed life into creation, and who alone can breathe life into a dead soul. Must I explain to you the difference between religious principle and religious feelings? In a word, I would say, religious feeling is that which you have sometimes, and only when you are awake; but religious principle is that which you have at all times, whether asleep or awake; for it is this principle that makes a man a christian, and not feeling, which is transitory, evanescent, mutable. This principle we must have, by the infusion of a new life by the Spirit; for all the music of heaven, all the attractions of paradise, all the agony of the damned, while they may create feeling, cannot produce this principle, and without it we can never be saved. Well did the Saviour repeat his instructions on this vital point. Twice over, he said in the same conversation, "Ye must be born again." O let all solicitude be expended over this subject. You are encouraged by a promise made powerful by an appeal to parental affection. "If earthly parents know how to give good things to their children, how much more will your Father which is in Heaven give the Holy Spirit to them that ask him?" Obtaining this, all nature, all grace, all providence, all truth, all heaven, all earth, will combine effectual attractions by which we shall be certainly drawn up to purity of life, to the religion of holiness, to the joys of heaven, and into the very bosom of God. Without this, though wooed and awed, cherished and blessed, we remain flagrant rebels still, doomed to ruin.

The result in the world shows that the crucifixion of Christ is the ground of the Spirit's operations, by which he draws, persuades, convinces, urges, and converts sinners through the instrumentality of the word. Christ prophesied thus. "I, if I be lifted up, will draw all men unto me." This of course referred to all kinds of men. In less than forty years after that wonderful event, the gospel had pervaded all the provinces of the Roman Empire. Such was the early fulfillment. So greatly were the people enlightened by the Spirit of truth, that they abandoned their idolatry, and the temples of paganism were converted into sanctuaries of Christian doctrine. May the time speedily come when this gospel of the grace of God shall be published throughout the whole world, when all the nations of the earth shall become illuminated by the sun of righteousness, and rejoice in the glory of the Cross.

ELECTION.

2 Tim. 1 : 9. "WHO HATH SAVED US, AND CALLED US WITH A HOLY CALLING, NOT ACCORDING TO OUR WORKS, BUT ACCORDING TO HIS OWN PURPOSE AND GRACE, WHICH WAS GIVEN US IN CHRIST JESUS BEFORE THE WORLD BEGAN."

The doctrine stated in our text ought certainly to be considered by all with great humility, reverence and candor. It is one of the most difficult doctrines of Christianity. It has occasioned some of the greatest controversies which have agitated the church of Christ, and what is much to be lamented, a controversy carried on with needless bitterness, and inexcusable malignity, tending to keep at a distance from each other many honest disciples of the Blessed Master; for it is not to be denied that many pious and reputable names have ranged themselves on either side of it.

It is also a doctrine that has often proved perplexing even to honest and humble souls, who, not able to see it reconcilable with the benevolence of God, and apprehensive that it closed the door of salvation against them, and yet not daring to deny what the Scriptures record on the subject, have been reduced to a state of painful reflection and distress.

My object in introducing it is not to indulge or encourage a spirit of controversy. When shall Christians learn to bear with each other's peculiarities in the spirit of charity? The spirit of controversy, contending for contention's sake, instead of throwing light upon the doctrine, has covered it with obscurity and deformity ; and antagonists, instead of meeting each other in the spirit of brotherly kindness, have augmented the breach ; and on either side have been driven into absurdities.

Nor is my object to rail or ridicule, but to endeavor to clear the truth from some of the mistakes which the spirit of controversy has engendered. I respect the articles of the Church to which I belong. I believe them calculated to glorify God, and humble the sinner ; but they must not be interpreted according to the notions which any or every person may attach to them. They must be considered according to their intended import. The discussion of them is carried on frequently by certain metaphysical terms and expressions which have in them a nicety and precision of signification which we must be careful properly to understand, and never to pervert.

I shall merely state the doctrine, and then show its reasonableness, wisdom, and benevolence.

I. What is the doctrine of Election?

It is the statement that God from eternity determined to bring certain persons, sinners of mankind, to a state of glory through the mediation of the Lord Jesus Christ.

We concede that the word Election, as used in the Scriptures, sometimes denotes a *national election*, as that by which the Jews were chosen from all the nations of the earth to be the Lord's. Deut. 7: 6. "The Lord thy God hath *chosen* thee to be a special people unto himself, above all the people that are upon the face of the earth."

Sometimes it means a *temporary designation* of some particular persons to certain offices and stations in the church to which the Lord hath chosen them. 1 Sam. 10 : 24. "See ye him whom the Lord hath *chosen*, that there is none like him among all the people?" John 6 : 70, "Have not I *chosen* you twelve, and one of you is a devil?"

Sometimes it denotes the act of God, *effectually calling* certain sinners in time to fellowship with himself, John 15 : 19. "Because ye are not of the world, but I have *chosen* you out of the world, therefore the world hateth you."

But there are other passages innumerable which signify more, and accord with the definition of election as I have given it, and these must be adduced as proof. The statement in the text is too specific to be misunderstood. It speaks of "God, who hath saved us and called us with a holy calling, not according to our works, but according to his own purpose and grace which was given us in Christ Jesus, *before the world began.*"

Eph. 1 : 11. "In whom we have obtained an inheritance, being predestinated according to the purpose of him who worketh all things after the counsel of his own will."

Eph. 3 : 11. "According to the eternal purpose which he purposed in Christ Jesus our Lord."

Rom. 9 : 11. "For the children being not yet born, neither having done any good or evil, that the purpose of God according to Election might stand, not of works, but of him that calleth."

Is. 46 : 9, 10. "I am God, and there is none like me, declaring the end from the beginning, and from ancient times the things that are not yet done, saying : My counsel shall stand, and I will do all my pleasure."

Rom. 9 : 20. "Nay but, O man, who art thou that repliest against God? Shall the thing formed say to him that formed it : Why hast thou made me thus?"

Matt. 20 : 16. "So the last shall be first, and the first last ; for many are called but few chosen."

2 Thess. 2 : 13. "God hath from the beginning chosen you to salvation, through sanctification of the Spirit, and belief of the truth."

John 15 : 16. "Ye have not chosen me, but I have chosen you, and ordained you, that ye should go and bring forth fruit."

Eph. 1 : 4. "According as he hath chosen us in him before the foundation of the world, that we should be holy and without blame before him in love, having pre-destinated us unto the adoption of children by Jesus Christ to himself, according to the good pleasure of his will."

Rom. 11 : 7. "Israel hath not obtained that which he seeketh for ; but the Election hath obtained it, and the rest were blinded."

Tit. 1 : 1. "According to the faith of God's elect."

I have examined the modes of interpretation which are employed to prevent these passages from conveying the idea of God's predetermination to bring certain sinners to glory, but they appear to me to be too forced, and unnatural, and inconsistent with their respective contexts ; and I feel constrained, contrary to my corrupt inclination, to admit such a determination in God. How can I do otherwise, since the words of these passages seem to be picked out for expressing clearly and unmistakably the doctrine, as I have defined it?

I cannot admit that this is a conditional election of *all mankind*, for, to elect all mankind to salvation is not an election at all, since it implies some chosen out of many. I cannot admit that there is no other election but that which is formed *in time*, for the word "eternal," Eph. 3:11, forbids that idea : and such an election, formed *in time*, but before actual salvation, would be liable to the same exception, for if it be harm for God from eternity to elect sinners to salvation, it would be equally hurtful to do it in time before actual salvation ; besides, it militates against the unchangeableness of God. I cannot admit that these passages refer merely to *temporal advantages, privileges and prerogatives ;* for spiritual benefits and final salvation are stated by many of them as that to which sinners are elected ; and indeed such an election to temporal privileges which lead to salvation, and from which others are excluded, is a doctrine liable to the same exception, for on the same principle of objection it may be asked : How can an impartial God give to some persons certain revelation and other privileges which lead them to salvation, while he excludes others, no worse than they, from these advantages, by which exclusion their welfare is endangered?

It is in vain to say, that those who are destitute of those privileges may also be saved in another way ; for, though this be admitted, yet it must be allowed that there is greater probability of salvation under these advantages than without them, for otherwise these advantages are no advantages at all.

I forbear however to pursue a subject so extensive. I have no time to collect all the arguments from the wisdom, the unchangeableness, the foreknowledge of God—his prophecies, his promises, the principles of

Divine government, all of which seem to imply such a determination in God; neither have I time to attempt a refutation of all that may be said by way of objection. I intended only to illustrate the reasonableness and benevolence of God's determination.

II. To save some sinners of mankind. This method, we trust, is better calculated to teach us the import of the doctrine, which is but little understood; and to clear it from that gloomy and unseemly aspect under which it has been viewed by many, by whom hard thoughts have been entertained of a just and benevolent God.

1. In the first place, let it be considered that nothing can afford *greater consolation* to a serious, thoughtful sinner than the idea of a determination in God to save some. Without such a revelation it would have been a total uncertainty, both to God and man, whether any would be delivered from the ruin into which we are fallen; for, had not the very sinners been determined, it could not have been certain that any would be happy; and had He formed no purpose previously, His unchangeableness would have prevented Him from forming any purpose subsequently; and without a purpose to save at all, none would have been saved.

Why then had He formed creatures for glory without purposing their salvation? Why sent His Son for their Redemption? Why form a Heaven for their reception? And why crowned them with opportunities without a fixed purpose to save?

2. While the elect are thus benefited by the purpose, are the *non-elected injured* by their being passed by? Yes, if they are meritorious of salvation. Yes, if at any time they sought salvation. But they are

neither meritorious of salvation, neither do they seek it, and so they are considered in the decree respecting them. Let it be remembered, that in the decree that fixes punishment they are considered not as innocent, but as guilty; as rebels, as hardened offenders who willfully reject mercy; and even were there no decree to punish them, or to leave them to themselves, their own ungodly temper would punish them, and being left to themselves, as we daily see they are, they voluntarily plunge themselves into ruin.

3. The reasonableness of our doctrine appears if we consider in what light the decree is unconditional. If a decree of salvation ought to be termed conditional because it contemplates faith and holiness as necessary to salvation, then we say the decree is conditional; for it fixes in salvation no person without faith and holiness; but it is termed unconditional to imply the certainty of faith and holiness which shall be given to the elect, who shall certainly seek and obtain the same; and if the decree of punishment ought to be termed conditional because it contemplates unbelief and impenitence as the meritorious cause of misery, then we say that decree is conditional; but we term it unconditional, merely with respect to, the certainty, that those whom God leaves to themselves will certainly be and remain impenitent, unbelieving sinners, deserving to be damned. Inasmuch therefore as there is no decree to give salvation without faith and holiness, and as there is no decree to fix punishment upon any but the impenitent and unbelieving, what injustice is there in God? Nay, is it not benevolence in Him to tell us previously that he has decreed salvation to the person of every poor penitent, and endless condemnation to

every one who rejects the Saviour? Therefore it gives us no view of the doctrine at all to say, that the elect will be saved, be they as bad as they may—and the non-elect will be damned, be they as pious as they may ; for the decree *connects misery with disobedience only, and salvation only with Christian piety.* Neither does it illustrate the doctrine to say, that it implies one is born to be saved, and another to be damned ; for, according to the Divine decree, all men had the privileges of salvation, and whoever abuses them *is the author of his misery.* Neither is any one unconditionally damned from eternity, inasmuch as the decree is only the Divine purpose' to damn for willful disobedience and neglect of Christ.

4. The Righteousness of God further appears if we consider in what sense the decree is *efficacious.* The idea is not that the decree operates by compulsion, or produces a necessity which impairs free agency. It is denominated efficacious because the event most certainly follows, but it does not follow because the sinner is forced. Those who are saved, *freely* choose salvation through the kind operations of the Spirit of Grace, and as freely as though there were no decree at all respecting them ; and those who are damned, freely choose the lusts of their own heart, and as freely as though there were no decree respecting them. It is true the event shall come according to the decree, not by any necessity produced by the decree, but through the free choice of the sinner who voluntarily chooses life or makes choice of ruin. Does the certainty of an event or action force compulsively that action or event into the world? It was a matter of certainty, as appears from Joseph's dream, that he should be exalted, and his

brethren reduced to obeisance. Did that force compulsively the one or the other? It was said previously, the elder shall serve the younger. Did that compel the Israelites to pre-eminence and the Edomites into servitude?

A thousand things were predicted by the prophets, which should certainly take place. Did that destroy the free agency of those through whose instrumentality the things predicted were accomplished?

All things are certain with God, are therefore all things under the influence of compulsion necessarily? Even so, while the Divine decree is infallible, no necessity is imposed on free agents, for their free agency is recognized in the decree; properly speaking, it is not the purpose of election itself that saves any, but the act of God regenerating them; and not the circumstance that the non-elect are passed by that punishes them, but their own wickedness efficaciously leads them to misery, while the purpose of God only connects deserved misery with their crimes. Wherefore it is useless to talk of "irresistible decrees," for these decrees are not objects of resistance; they contemplate the sinner as a free agent, who freely chooses or refuses eternal life.

5. The unblameableness of God in his decree relating to the salvation or condemnation of sinners, must appear by considering what is the *agency which God employs* in the production of great events.

The notion of many when they think of decrees is this—that the Deity by the secret Almighty agency of His providence, creates our actions according to His purpose. No one will find fault if we say that He forms and creates His people anew in the spirit of their mind, and thus prepares them for Glory. But is it true that by a positive efficiency He creates sin in the heart of the impenitent? This we deny. We allow that God has decreed the sin and the impenitence, but how has He decreed it? Has He decreed to create it or merely to suffer it? Had He decreed to create it according to the common notion of those who dislike the doctrine, they would have reason to dislike it. If, by an irresistible agency of His providence, He became the cause of sin, and this was contemplated in His purpose, I could never reconcile this doctrine with either His purity or benevolence. But this is not the doctrine of the Scriptures; the doctrine of the Scriptures is that He suffers the wicked to pursue their way, gives them up to a hard heart and a reprobate mind, after having long resisted the strivings of His Spirit. And whatever may be said of Pharaoh, who, it is said, was raised up for the very purpose of affording opportunity for God to display His power, and whose heart the Lord hardened, it can be proved from the history that a permissive agency in relation to his sin was all that was intended. Therefore the case stands thus. Has God decreed an immortal to sin? He has not decreed to work or create it in him, but views him as one who has deserved to be given up to his hard heart and reprobate mind; and God has decreed not to make him sin, but to surrender him to his choice; and this execution of the Divine decree is accomplished every day, when He suffers miserable sinners to follow their choice to endless perdition.

6. The unblameableness of God in his decrees must appear from a *consideration of what he actually does in time*. From what He visibly does in time we may safely infer what He purposed from eternity. Whatever He

does now, He does from purpose and intention. If He acts righteously in time, (which we dare not question), His purposes from which those acts proceed and which correspond therewith, must be righteous also. If, then, it appears hard that God has purposed to save some and leave others to themselves, let us see whether this does not precisely correspond with His actions in time. Who can deny that God discriminates among mankind? Is any one saved—is it not by the regenerating act of God? Is any one damned—is it not by his own sin, God leaving him to his own impenitence? It is true all shall be saved that will, but there is none willing without the regenerating grace of God. The saved are, in themselves, equally unworthy with the damned, and all resist the grace of Jesus until they are regenerated, and God can, could as consistently with His grace, regenerate the one as the other; being equally unworthy, and equally disposed by nature to resist the mercy of God. After all, some sinners are wonderfully regenerated; and others, not worse by nature, pursue their impenitence. Who then maketh you to differ in time? Is here not temporal election? And if it be right in God thus to discriminate in time, was it not just in Him to purpose it beforehand?

When we thus speak of discrimination, we do not mean that God has denied to any one the powers or privileges of salvation, but only (and which is evidently the fact before our eyes) that some are made willing in the day of God's power, and others are left to themselves; for it is not from a want of power or privileges that any are damned, but from want of disposition to improve powers and privileges, which disposition God has it in his power to impart to all, but which, however, as fact itself demonstrates, is communicated only to some. Why then, O God, hast thou prepared some for glory by imparting the new nature, while others, no worse than they, are passed by? Were it not fact that stares me in the face, it would be hard to acquiesce; but now I must shut my mouth in silence and say, "Even so Father, for so it seemeth good in thy sight."

It is vain to object that the reason of this discrimination is, that some will and others won't; for though this is true, and the wicked are damned for nothing but their unwillingness, yet God could consistently have made the unwilling willing to be saved, even as he makes His elect willing—they being equally unwilling by nature. We trace this awful sovereignty of God in all His dealings. Why do some labor under the extreme disadvantage of being born and educated of parents whose examples are so fatal to their souls? Why are thousands left in the disadvantages of heathenism and thousands under the influence of Popery, thousands under the disadvantages of Mahomedanism and delusion? Why have not we been brought into existence under more advantageous circumstances like those who will be born under the millennium, who all shall know the Lord from the least to the greatest? It is true that all these disadvantages will be considered in the day of Judgment, and it is true that these disadvantages are not fatal to those who will improve their privileges under any dispensation; but the disadvantage lies in this, that there is so much less probability of salvation, because, under these dispensations, there are so few means to induce a willingness to improve their privileges. Accordingly the number of the saved in the millennium will be infinitely greater than at any other period, perhaps a thousand or a million to one. And if we say that there is upon the whole no such disadvantage to any, because all things shall be considered and proper allowances will be made in the day of Judgment ; then we must conclude that there is no advantage at all in written revelation, nor a preached gospel, nor in a revival of religion, nor in a millennial day. And why, O Benevolent Father, is this discrimination, whereby some of thy creatures are so highly favored with advantages tending to produce a willingness to be saved, while others live under such disadvantages tending to their ruin? Here then is the difficulty—the difficulty is not so much in the purpose of God from eternity, as in the discriminating work of God in time. I cannot deny His discriminating agency in time, for He could have made us all willing to be saved, and yet He leaves thousands in their unwillingness. And if the awful fact now stares me in the face, and I must believe that God is just notwithstanding, I am compelled to admit that He was just also in purposing so; if His work is right, His purpose is right. I dare not impeach his purity on account of His work. I therefore dare not impeach his purity on account of His purpose.

My only way is to learn the malignity of human corruption and the criminality of my unwillingness to be saved, on which account God is under obligations to none. The criminality of my unwillingness to be saved, is not the less because God doth not make me willing ; for I ought to have been willing without regenerating agency ; and this is my ruin, that I am so unwilling to be saved, inasmuch as God is willing to save, and shall save all that seek him.

My brethren, this is a subject so serious that our unwillingness to be happy makes us miserable, and that alone, and that effectually; that there is no hope for us but in Sovereign Mercy; and that we ought never to argue or meditate on it but in the Spirit of prayer and agony. I deny that we will ever acquiesce in the doctrine of Divine Sovereignty as we ought, until our souls are enlightened in regard to our baseness and demerit, and smitten with a conviction of our lost condition.

May God Almighty cause us to see that the fault lies not in Him but in ourselves who are ruined by sin, and who have no claim to favor, that we may seek earnestly and find Him an all-sufficient and willing Saviour.

In conclusion, permit me to urge again the necessity of discussing this doctrine in the spirit of *humility, candor and reverence.* Let it be far from us to proscribe those disciples, who think that the difficulties on the subject are insuperable; and yet let us not suppose that it has been recorded in the Scriptures for naught. If we cannot receive it with full acquiescence, let us seek nourishment from the milk of the word, the plain doctrines of grace. Leave it to others to feed on the strong meat. In making our opinion, however, let us not suffer ourselves to be influenced merely by purblind reason, or prejudice, or any notions we have attached to the doctrine contrary to its real import; but be resolved to submit to the infallible guidance of revelation, which cannot lie. At any rate, let us not condemn what we do not understand.

Let us not suppose the doctrine to be what thousands have represented it—let us not always dwell on the dark side of the picture, heedless of the excellencies which may be discovered and which are rendered more illustrious by a sense of our demerit. It is an easy thing to bring a doctrine into disrepute by misrepresentation and perversion. Let the most beautiful picture be soiled and blackened by ruthless hands and thus exposed to the world, and it will certainly create abhorrence. Were the doctrine of election precisely the same as has been represented by some Supralapsarian doctors—or were it what it has been often represented to be by its opposers, I would join in the popular cry in its opposition, and seek to expel it from the Sanctuary. But let me not raise my hand against my Sovereign, and cast contempt on the subject as revealed in the Scriptures of truth.

Let us practically improve the Doctrine for our own conviction and humiliation. It represents God Almighty as seated on the throne of the universe dispensing His favors in the Sovereignty of His pleasure, and dispensing His wrath on the workers of iniquity. It teaches us that we are all sinners and as such have no recommendation, or title, or claim to the mercies of Heaven. It teaches us that God was under no obligation to rescue any of our fallen race from ruin. It teaches us that if in the sovereignty of his favor he rescues some, he is under no obligation to save us all. It teaches us that while God is willing to save every soul that seeks him, yet he is under no obligation to regenerate the unwilling; and that as we are all unwilling by nature to love Him, so none shall be saved but those who are made willing by His preventing grace. It teaches us that there are thousands on whom God will inflict the terrible vengeance due to their sins and transgressions, from which they were unwilling to turn away; that we are absolutely in his Sovereign hand; and while in infinite mercy He is resolved to pluck some as brands from the burning, He can and will, in His just indignation, leave to themselves thousands who have despised the Cross. Must not this doctrine then, if it be believed, make each of us exclaim, God be merciful to me a sinner?

Let us improve this doctrine for our encouragement. God hath determined that Heaven shall not be destitute of inhabitants; and if we partake of the Spirit of Heaven, we may be assured of the purpose of God to carry us thither.

Do we deplore and hate iniquity, and are we filled with mourning in the consideration of our guilt and ruin? Let us be encouraged to seek His mercy, for the decree of election connects salvation with the penitence of the poor seeking soul. God has purposed the condemnation of none but those who live and die in impenitence and voluntary unbelief.

Is there no consolation in the idea that we live under the administration of a God who rules the world—not at random, not in subordination to our caprice—but with design and purpose and fixed resolution to make all things subservient to his glory and the good of his people? On the contrary, were his sovereignty destroyed, did we believe that there was such incontrollable obstinacy in sin that God could not soften and melt our hearts, O what gloom and discouragement would be the consequence!

If sinners puff themselves up with the idea that because God has extended regeneration to some, He is equally bound to impart the same blessing to all mankind; that he can no longer save as many sinners as he pleases, and send to destruction as many as he pleases of those who have a thousand times deserved it. If thus, in their own imagination, they can bring Deity to their feet, let them tremble for the consequence; for the result of their doctrine will be impenitence and presumption, and we fear eternal death. With regard to them we have no comfort but in Sovereign *Electing Grace;* they are so sinful and willful that we know they never will turn to God, except He regenerate them. As He is a sovereign God to accomplish his purposes by doing away the greatest opposition, we still hope that he will save many sinners ; we hope it, not because they will of their own accord seek him first, but because He can make them willing in the day of His power, " having predestinated them unto the adoption of children by Jesus Christ to Himself to the praise of the glory of His grace."

ADAM'S PROBATION.

Gen. 2: 16, 17. "OF EVERY TREE OF THE GARDEN THOU MAYEST FREELY EAT, BUT OF THE TREE OF KNOWLEDGE OF GOOD AND EVIL THOU SHALT NOT EAT OF IT, FOR IN THE DAY THAT THOU EATEST THEREOF THOU SHALT SURELY DIE."

This chapter is an appendix to the history of Creation and enlarges and explains more particularly on the creation of Man, for man was the special favorite of Heaven, the end of the inferior creation, the great centre and summary of creation's work.

Crowned with the blessed endowments of wisdom, righteousness and holiness which rendered him in the image of God, it was suitable farther that he should have a convenient and glorious residence.

Accordingly he was placed in Eden, the garden of pleasure. His residence was simple but glorious. The simplicity of nature, not the ornament of art, was best suited to his state of innocence and happiness. The roof of his habitation was the painted heavens, his floor the firm foundations of the earth, the shadows of the trees afforded places of retirement, and the rivers of Eden aided his devotion and delight. All around him creation shone with beauty in exhibiting its bloom.

Solomon in all his glory was not arrayed like the Parents of mankind. "Let his rest be as Eden," was a word of benediction among the Jews.

But this most accomplished place of pleasure and delight the Sun ever beheld, was but a *type and figure* of Heaven where angels dwell, and to which man was in due time to be translated. But how shall he reach this abode of superabundant bliss? Shall his Creator admit him into the third heaven *without any proof* of his integrity and worth? *In one point only* his happiness may be said to be incomplete—*there is* a remote possibility of failure—his happiness is not confirmed. However, he has power to *secure* the confirmation of it. God will not *impose* an intolerable burden. He will put him to a test, innocent in its nature, adapted to his condition, and easy to be borne. "Of every tree of the garden thou mayest freely eat ; but of the tree of the knowledge of good and evil, thou shalt not eat of it."

In order that the wisdom, justice and goodness of God may be evinced in placing mankind in this state of probation, we propose to consider—

I. *The general license* which the Almighty gave him.

II. The nature of the prohibition imposed on him.

III. The penalty annexed to disobedience.

I. The Almighty gave him a *general license* to eat of the trees of the garden. According to the description we have of Eden there were *many trees* growing in it, planted on every side, and all the trees were good for food. To these trees man became entitled by the *gratuitous grant* of Heaven. As man was the creature of God and consequently subject to His authority and control, *he had no natural right* to the use of any created thing ; *his right depended* on the grant of Heaven, for " the Earth is the Lord's and the fullness thereof." *But God was rich in goodness* and took pleasure in the creature of his hand, He therefore *permitted* him generally to eat of the trees, as created for his benefit, and to partake of these delicious fruits of Paradise as a *compensation* for his services in dressing and keeping it. Nay, He permitted him not only to eat of the common trees of the garden, but even of the *Tree of Life* which stood in the midst of the garden, and was pleasant to the eye. Probably this was a *single tree* the like of which God had not created, and exceeded all in the beauty of its form, and deliciousness of its fruits. It was called the *Tree of Life*, perhaps, on account of some wholesome virtue which made Paradise the abode of health where no sickness or infirmity could prevail. *No doubt the fruit* of this tree sustained life, invigorated the system, and rejoiced the heart of man. But principally it was called the Tree of Life because it was a sacrament of life, a symbol of heavenly glory, a sign and a seal which perpetually reminded man of the bliss which was reserved for him. *Of this tree* the Almighty *permitted, yea commanded* him to eat the fruit : "Of every tree of the garden thou mayest freely eat, not even the tree of life excepted. That tree I have planted for the *nourishment* of both thy body and thy soul. When this you see, and it is pleasant to the eye, think of me ; think of the goodness I bestow you ; of the promise of life which I have made you : think of the glory which is reserved for you and is hereby signified ; and on condition of obedience be assured of Immortality."

How easy must it have been for man to abstain from the fruit of the tree of knowledge, for there was *abundance* on every side to satisfy his hunger and please his taste. Indeed in all the garden there was none better than the tree of life. *God intended to make his trial easy*, and in order to reconcile the creature's mind thereto, he *first* told him how great his privileges were. "Surely then he will not murmur at one small piece of self-denial ! All the trees of the garden are his, therefore he will not fret at one solitary exception ! Having thus taught him My goodness, I will now teach him My *just demand. But of the tree of knowledge of good and evil, thou shalt not eat of it, for in the day thou eatest thereof thou shalt surely die.*"

II. The Tree of Knowledge which man was forbidden to touch, was probably also a *single tree*—it also stood in the midst of the garden and was pleasant to the sight. It was called the Tree of Knowledge with respect both to God and man. *With respect to God* it was called the Tree of Knowledge, because, humanly speaking, by that tree He would try and know whether man would continue good by persevering in obedience, or swerve to evil by the attractions of the world. In this sense God is said to have tried Hezekiah that He might know all that was in his heart (2 Chron. 32 : 31). *With respect to man* it was called the Tree of Knowledge, because if from love to God he should obey this law of probation, he was to attain experimental knowledge of unchangeable and perfect good. *But if disobedient*, he should know by sad experience the miserable nature of sin, and be acquainted with the horrors of death of which his ideas were hitherto confused and obscure.

Now, our position is that it was most *reasonable* and *right* that the obedience of innocent man should be tested by such a prohibition—a prohibition founded not in the nature of the fruit, but in the sovereign choice of Heaven. *For let it be well understood* that this was a positive peculiar discretionary precept, different from the moral law. Those moral precepts which are contained in the ten commandments are founded in the very nature of God and Man and the relation between them, and consequently are of absolute and unalterable necessity, for God could not have commanded us to despise His worship, profane His name, to murder, to steal or lie. But the reason of the precept now under consideration is fetched, not from the nature of God or Man nor from the relation between them ; but merely from the self-determining will, or choice of the Almighty. God could have prohibited Adam the use of any other tree, and allowed him the fruit of this ; for, to eat the fruit of this tree was in itself, or in the reason of things, an innocent affair, a matter of indifference, and became evil merely by its being forbidden.

1. By such a precept, *God displayed His proper authority* over man as He had done over the beasts of the field and trees of the garden. God had already displayed His holiness and goodness in the rational and moral faculties which crowned Adam, but had not so fully asserted His authority over him. Adam was indeed obligated to love God supremely ; but a sense of this obligation he derived from the moral nature and fitness of the duty inscribed on his heart, and his obedience to the moral law was dictated more by the holy inclinations of his heart, than by a sense of divine absolute authority. Was it not expedient then that there should

be a peculiar discretionary precept, founded, not in the law of nature, but merely on the will of God, and relating to a matter otherwise indifferent, to teach the human family more clearly their subjection to Divine authority?

2. By such a precept relating to such a *little affair* (a matter so contemptible in the eye of many) as the eating of an apple, mankind were taught their subjection to Divine authority in matters *apparently small*, so that they might become accustomed to obedience in every matter; and so trained to a more cordial submission in things both great and small.

3. By such a precept God gave him to understand that his privilege to eat of other trees of the garden was matter of mere favor and not of natural right. Thus it was calculated to inspire him with gratitude to God for His free and sovereign bounty in the garden.

4. By such a precept God informed him that not only his *soul*, but his *body* with his appetite, his tongue, his taste, with all his animal affections, all his sensitive faculties and organs must act in subordination to his Maker's will. The propensities of his soul already were in complete conformity to the moral law engraven on his heart, and the body too must be made to bow implicitly to God's authority.

5. By such a precept God put it into the power of man to *secure a glorious additional reward*. The probability is, had not God enjoined such a precept, that man during his obedience would only have experienced a natural reward, viz. present intrinsic comfort of obedience, without a promise of reaching unchangeable felicity; for it is difficult to see how Deity could consistently have bestowed the additional reward of confir-

mation in felicity for mere natural obedience to moral law to which unsullied nature necessarily prompted and impelled. What, a reward without labor! Without the least self-denial! A reward for that obedience which was merely the gratification of holy affections! A reward for that obedience which was so easy and almost unavoidable! By this precept then, which demanded self-denial, it was evidently put into the power of man to secure an additional reward, I mean, confirmation in glory. Here then the obedience of innocent man was properly tested. Here was a better trial of his obedience than if he had been bound merely by the law of nature which was inscribed on his heart. The sphere of his choice became enlarged, a slight difficulty was imposed to try him, and he had an opportunity of more honorably exerting the vigor of his mind to overcome it, than if such a prohibition had not been imposed.

Was it now more easy to sin, it was easy also to obey, and secure a ratification of honor and glory ; very easy for the image of God impressed on our nature, though it did not directly lead to obedience in this affair, yet indirectly had that tendency. Though Adam's wisdom did not perceive any intrinsic criminality in eating of the tree, yet it taught him that in all things, however originally indifferent, God ought to be obeyed.

III. If the precept was good, the penalty was just ; "in the day that thou eatest thereof thou shalt surely die."

By the Death here threatened, we understand all the evils to which sin exposes in the present and everlasting world ; all the sorrows of life ; the agonies of corporeal death and the corruption of the grave ; all the maladies of the soul ; the loss of the Divine image, of wisdom, righteousness and holiness ; all the storms and tempests produced by malignant passions ; all the remorse and anguish of a guilty conscience ; the forfeiture of Divine favor in this life—the anguish of despair in death and everlasting separation from God and glory beyond the grave. This threatening must appear fair and just from various considerations.

1. If man transgresses, it is rebellion against the rightful authority of Him who is Lord and proprietor of Heaven and earth, Who has the same right to interdict the use of the tree of knowledge as He has to grant to His creature the other trees of the garden. Had He not prohibited eating of that tree, its fruit might have been used with perfect innocence, but since it is forbidden by the authority of Heaven, that authority is insulted in disobedience ; and it becomes necessary that the Lord, the Proprietor of the world, act in defence of His authority and vindicate the rights of His throne.

2. Neither can the law of probation be violated without a violation of the *whole moral law* inscribed on the heart, for how can there be a spark of love in the heart that desires what infinite authority has forbidden ? Can there be a mite of true benevolence to men if Adam, regardless of the consequences to him and his posterity, willfully transgress ?

3. Had no threatening at all been annexed, the *natural course* and tendency of disobedience would have produced separation from God and glory. The positive law being violated, conscience alone would have created a hell within the bosom of the transgressor. The moral

law in the heart being violated, storms of malignant passion would destroy all peace of mind. The breach between God and man would become widened by the lapse of time, producing reciprocal alienation and hatred ; for there is no peace, saith my God, to the wicked.

4. Here is not only a threatening of death denounced, but a promise of life and immortality implied. *Only in case of disobedience* thou shalt die. If thou continue firm and steadfast thou shalt surely *not die*, as I have in the clearest manner signified to you when I appointed for your use the tree of life a pledge of immortality."

5. Nay, the kind benevolence of God is conspicuous in the whole affair. He did not act the part of an arbitrary tyrant who takes a malignant pleasure in the destruction of his creature, for we all see how a penalty was necessary to secure the authority of God to serve as a restraint on disobedience, and thus to promote the safety and unchangeable felicity of the creature. Had God concealed from our first parents the necessary consequence of transgression, it might have been suspected with more apparent reason that his intention was to ensnare them ; and that He could take delight in the execution of the curse. But such was his benevolence that he previously and kindly declared the necessary consequences of transgression. Without hesitation or disguise He sets before them the misery of sin. In the most positive tone incapable of perversion, He denounces the woe of guilt, saying, "the very day thou eatest thereof thou shalt surely die "—dying, thou shalt die—thou shalt most certainly and inevitably die. "Take this warning ! take this warning, my creature, take it to heart and dwell upon the thought that thou mayest resist

temptation and receive admission into my more immediate presence, and into that unchangeable glory which I have prepared for thee."

Here both the threatening and the promise are before them, life and death are fully in their view, both are intended to promote their obedience, their safety, their arrival at fixed glory. The glories of Heaven attract their attention and exhilarate their souls, and already they anticipate boundless enjoyment. The terrors of death shock them at the thought of disobedience, they resolve to persevere in duty and hope soon to be placed beyond the reach of possible woe.

By the threatening, a glorious inclosure is formed around the pit of destruction ; and by the promise, immortality is opened to receive them. The portals of Death seem to be fenced, and a ladder erected by which the parents of mankind shall ascend to glory.

I wait to see the issue of the contest. I can hardly doubt the blissful consequence. Soon will everlasting life and glory be the portion of Adam and all mankind. He has great advantages for the contest. He is a rational being. His talents are of the highest rank. He is possessed of the very image of his God. His moral character gives confidence to all our hopes. He has the noblest moral ability. He has the faithful warnings of his kind Creator. The angels of Heaven minister to his wants. Ere long, he shall come off more than conqueror from the contest. He shall come up to heaven with songs and everlasting joy upon his head, followed in slow succession by the innumerable myriads of his progeny !

O brethren, had we no further history of man, and did not observation teach a melancholy lesson, we would naturally conclude that Adam must have gained his point, had nobly overcome, had reached the unparalleled prize, and universal mankind are to be forever happy. But our delightful enthusiasm is interrupted. We tremble when we read the continuation of the story. The very commencement of the next chapter begets suspicion, indicates disaster. "The serpent was more subtle than any beast of the field," etc. Here the miserable, melancholy part of the story begins. We wish we had never been born! For even yet all "earth feels the wound, and Nature from her seat, sighing through all her works, gives signs of woe that all is lost." O that our heads were water, and our eyes fountains of tears, that we might weep day and night over that sad event, which has overturned the harmony of creation, covered our race with deep dishonor, stained our nature with foul pollutions, and makes all the children of Adam candidates for the grave, and legitimate heirs of hell.

Were it in my power, I would separate the children of Adam from the curse as well as the sin of their progenitor. The inclination to do so may easily be inferred, not only from our natural bias to defend our personal innocence and shield ourselves from wrath, but also from the multiplied and elaborate efforts of theologians to explain away the fact of original, total, universal depravity ; and the innumerable theories devised all the world over ; theories as rotten in their principles as they are dangerous in their tendency, proceeding upon the supposition of our native innocence. Almost all the errors and heresies which have distracted the Church of God relate, in some form or other, to the doctrine of imputed guilt and inborn depravity ; and many of them are urged and defended in the present day with so much cunning sophistry and metaphysical subtilty of investigation, that every soul is in danger in whom the spirit of implicit submission to the word of God is not carefully cherished and preserved. Let me then assert in the plainest, strongest, broadest style the doctrine that Adam's guilt is imputed to all his posterity. Though we did not personally commit that first transgression, we are treated exactly as though we ourselves had eaten of that forbidden tree which brought death into our world. "By one man sin entered into the world," etc. Nor is the Bible theory unsupported by the voice of Nature and the course of Providence. Who can deny the doctrine when he beholds the history of the apostasy of all our race, written in the most legible characters everywhere? We may not be able to comprehend all the reasons why our fate was thus connected with that of the parents of mankind, or what the grounds of this imputation; *but the fact*, the stubborn fact is before our eyes. It baffles every effort to explain the truth away. It is apparent in the very circumstances of our birth, our wicked dispositions, our continual troubles, the approach of inexorable death, and in our fears and apprehensions of approaching hell. And certainly that constitution of things which connected our fate with that of Adam, contemplated the richest, sublimest, immortal advantages to both. Merely by the abuse of it, it has gendered the inexpressible woes which have befallen our guilty race.

And now let us improve the history we have discussed to exonerate from blame the Benevolent Creator of the world. Wretches that we are, we are so disposed to exculpate ourselves that we dare to impeach the rectitude of the government of God. We have dared to utter a slander against the throne of God. Our wicked thoughts, how prone are they to imagine a want of righteousness, a want of benevolence, a want of necessary care on the part of God. That fact alone is dreadful evidence of a fallen nature. We are polluted indeed if we can resort to such an expedient to prove our innocence—O mortal! how darest thou let loose thy slanders against the good, the Almighty One! "Hast thou an arm like God, or canst thou thunder with a voice like His?" O how unreasonable, as well as wicked, to censure Jehovah's justice, or wisdom, or benevolence! Had He placed our race at once in a state of unchangeable felicity, our condition would not have been probationary at all—for that implies a *possibility of failure* —and had there been no possibility of failure, where could have been the excellence of obedience? Where the opportunity for such a reward? Where the use of such excellent endowments? Where such a sphere for the operation of reason? And is there any consolation in ascribing blame to our Maker? *Make it out*, if you can, that Deity was cruel! Then you prove that we are all under the dominion of an Almighty Tyrant who takes a malignant pleasure in our destruction, and feasts upon our sorrow. Is there consolation in this? Or can the heart that cherishes discontent be the seat of tranquillity or repose?

2. I annex importance to my subject, because a due conviction of our fallen state lies at the root of all our inquiries, all our efforts, all our energy with reference to salvation by the mediatorial system. If you are not fallen and thus wretched and miserable and blind and

naked, why concern yourself about the existence, or divinity, or qualifications of a Saviour? A want of conviction and sorrowful impression on the subject of your misery, your impotence and liability to eternal pain lies at the foundation of your impenitence, your insensibility, your unbelief, and the unmerciful cruelty which is cast upon the only Redeemer. Only be sensible of your corrupt and ruined nature and there is no room for rest or ease till you find the Desire of nations. "What was the Desire of nations to any of you before you found yourselves ruined and undone; and when the pearl of infinite price was presented to your view, did you not behold it with disgust and trample it under your feet? What made you look to the hills whence your salvation cometh, and ardently desire the sin-dispelling beams of the Sun of Righteousness? Was it not the deep, the dark, the dismal night of your fallen nature when you awoke from the sleep of sin, and found the dreams of life delusive?" And must not these sorrowful views of our ruined state be carefully cherished and habitually enlarged, and confirmed, and strengthened that you may entertain more regard and affection for your Divine Deliverer? And how shall we extend our views of our own moral wretchedness, except by meditating on the justice and benevolence of God which we have abused? It was an excellent constitution under which Adam was placed in Paradise, securing to him the most precious advantages. The contempt and abuse of these rendered his transgression so meritorious of the wrath of God. In the light of Divine goodness, learn the exceeding sinfulness of sin. And believe it, all the misery of earth and hell cannot overbalance the foul transgression of Adam and his race. If you did not participate personally in the transgression of Adam, you have practically justified it. You have *imitated* it. You have exhibited the same temper, the same unhallowed desire, the same spirit of ingratitude and pride and impious daring. Child of Adam, how can you exonerate yourselves from Adam's curse, while you voluntarily entertain the same spirit of transgression? *Your condemnation* is just and holy and righteous, and if the second Adam does not deliver us through our faith in his blood, nothing can be more righteous, more necessary, more equitable than our eternal ruin.

The sinfulness of sin, as justly meritorious of condemnation on account of the infinite benevolence of God abused, will endear to our affections the Son of His love. And if a new Covenant of Mercy has been ordained, and we live under its kind and happy ministrations, let us be careful that we fail not the second time, of gaining its rewards and reaching its promises. For never will another covenant more merciful in its conditions be proposed to our acceptance, for greater mercy cannot be revealed. All the resources of Divine wisdom and mercy are now exhausted in the appointment of the mediatorial system. Never again will God's dear Son pass through the fire and the pit to save thee. The counsels of Divine love are concluded. The condescension of Jesus Christ is the last effort of Divine Love to dying men. Surely there is but a step between us and perfect remediless ruin. If we cherish enmity to God until our present probation be over, it will be in vain to inquire "if there be no place for repentance, none for pardon left." For never will true reconcilement grow where wounds of deadly hate have pierced so deep.

3. And finally, let this subject teach the necessity of

trials and of self-denial in pursuit of glory. *Whoever* attained to honor and immortality without struggles and conflicts and dangers? Without these how would your humility and love, your fortitude and courage be tested, and improved, and confirmed? Could angels have reached that summit of excellence and honor which they occupy, without passing through scenes of peril and temptation? Peril and temptation, through the effect of which hosts of them fell like lightning from Heaven? Even under the covenant of grace, when salvation is not bestowed as the reward of merit, the crown is not to be attained without vigor and effort. Nay, the most splendid prizes are the result only of superior enterprise and surpassing diligence in the Christian race. And, under the Covenant of Mercy we have greater advantages in the Christian course than ever Adam and Eve enjoyed. *It is* a covenant so adapted to our infirmities that our partial failures, when repented of, will never rob us of hope. *Here Mercy* as a sovereign is seated on her throne, smiling with Divine benevolence, clothed with the magnificence of invincible power; her looks are sympathy, her heart is love, her language is balm to the bleeding heart, and her arm, salvation. If we survey the justice of the Deity we may well tremble in his presence, and were we ignorant of every other perfection of his nature we might well pray to be reduced to nothing. When we behold his goodness we may well admire and adore it, and envy the lot of angels who never sinned. But if we view our Maker enrobed in the sovereignty of Mercy, we glory in our lot as men, though we are sinners, and raise our eyes to immortality; believing that "as sin hath reigned unto death, even so grace will reign through righteousness unto eternal life by Jesus Christ our Lord."

THE FIRST SIN.

Gen. 3 : 6. "AND WHEN THE WOMAN SAW THAT THE TREE WAS GOOD FOR FOOD, AND THAT IT WAS PLEASANT TO THE EYES, AND A TREE TO BE DESIRED TO MAKE ONE WISE ; SHE TOOK OF THE FRUIT THEREOF, AND DID EAT, AND GAVE ALSO UNTO HER HUSBAND WITH HER ; AND HE DID EAT."

A variety of reasons may be urged why we should listen to the history of our original apostasy. Our object must not be to gratify a spirit of speculation, or amusement, or curiosity. Other considerations should govern us.

The original apostasy of Adam and Eve is the *Grand Parent* of all the crimes and transgressions which have since been committed by our race, and which will be committed by them through time and eternity, for that transgression was succeeded by the loss of the Divine image, and by a positive corruption which has contaminated all our race, and will continue to contaminate impenitent sinners forever.

The first apostasy was also the *grand exemplar or pattern* of which every subsequent transgression is a copy or resemblance. Not only the same principle of sin which reigned in our first parents dwells in us, but dwells in us subject to the same modifications, variations and combinations which originally accompanied it. So that in that history we have the best description we possibly can have of our own sinful character. And surely a discussion of this mournful history of man's original rebellion, if improved, must tend to impress our minds with a *conviction* of our guilt, our misery, our inability, condemnation, and danger. Let us consider the Prohibition and the Violation.

I. THE PROHIBITION.

The *Law* which they violated was the law prohibiting the fruit of the Tree of Knowledge of good and evil. It was called the Tree of Knowledge both with respect to God and man. With respect to God, who himself speaking by that tree would *try* and *know* whether man would continue good by persevering in obedience, or swerve to evil by the attractions of the world. With respect to man, it was called the tree of knowledge, for in consequence of obedience he should attain experimental knowledge of eternal happiness, the eternal sweets of innocence ; *and, in consequence* of disobedience he should have experimental knowledge of the bitterness and misery of sin.

Now, nothing could be more *reasonable* and *right* than that the obedience of innocent man should be tested by such a prohibition—a prohibition founded, not in the nature of the fruit, but in the sovereign choice of Heaven. For, let it be well understood, that this was a peculiar discretionary precept, different from the moral law. The moral precepts contained in the ten commandments are founded in the very nature of God and man and the relation between them, and are therefore of absolute and unalterable necessity ; for God could not command us to despise his worship, profane his name, or murder, or steal, or lie, but *this precept*, in relation to the tree of knowledge, flowed not from the nature of God and Man, but from divine choice and discretion. God could have prohibited Adam the fruit of any other tree and allowed him the use of this. To eat of this tree was not in itself criminal, but became so merely by the Divine will interdicting it.

1. By such a precept, God displayed his proper authority over man, as He had done over the beasts of the field and the trees of the garden. He had already displayed his holiness and goodness. Was it not expedient, therefore, that there should be a discretionary law founded merely in Divine choice, to teach man his subjection to absolute authority?

2. By such a precept, they were taught this subjection to Divine Authority in matters apparently *small*. It was but a little fruit that was forbidden which, in its own nature, was innocent. It was to teach us that in all things, great and small, we must be subject.

3. By such a precept, God gave them to understand, that their *privilege* of eating of the other trees of the garden was matter of mere favor and not of natural right; that they ought to be grateful for Divine bounty.

4. By such a precept, God informed them not only that their souls, but their *bodies* with all their sensitive powers, appetites, organs, the tongue, the taste, the sight, &c., must all be held in subordination to Divine Authority.

5. By such a precept, God put it in the power of man to secure a *glorious additional reward;* I mean the confirmation of felicity. The probability is that otherwise, man could merely have enjoyed a natural reward, viz. the comfort of obedience without the hope of being confirmed.

Here then the obedience of innocent man was properly tested. It was a better trial of his obedience than if he had been bound merely by the moral law. Some self-denial, a slight difficulty, was imposed on him to evince his sincerity. A better opportunity of more honorably exerting the vigor of his mind in pursuits of obedience. Was it easy now to transgress? It was as easy to obey and secure a confirmation of glory. He had every advantage in a contest with any tempter.

II. The Violation.

The first step in this delusion, the first introduction to this mournful transaction, appears to have been the condescension of the woman to listen to the insinuations of the serpent when he asked, "Hath God said ye shall not eat of every tree of the garden?" She ought not to have listened, because she was undoubtedly informed of the apostasy of evil spirits who might be prompted by envy and malice to beguile them. She ought not to have harkened, for though Satan very artfully personated an impartial inquirer of truth, yet he insinuated that it was strange, if this fruit was forbidden; strange, if such excellent fruit were created in vain; strange, if the appetites God had given them, craving it, should be unnecessarily denied. She ought not to have listened, for that exposed her to the necessity of replying. And her very replies might give occasion to the Tempter to renew and multiply his base insinuations. The next thing, we find she actually did reply ; and thus invited the discourse of the wicked one. We cannot precisely tell when the mischief of sin began to conceive in her heart ; but it is difficult to believe one altogether innocent when, in the spirit of friendship, he converses with another who insinuates blasphemy and falsehood. Next, we find she spoke contemptuously of the license God gave them. God had said in his overflowing kindness, "Of every tree of the garden thou mayst freely eat," but she in recounting this license said, "We may eat of the fruit of the trees of the garden," without noticing the freedom with which they might use that privilege. Then she told a lie, when she said that God had said, "Ye shall not touch the tree;" for though due caution would have dictated to them not to touch it, yet there was nothing said of *touching* in the original prohibition, yet she said that God said, "ye shall not touch it," and so insinuated severity and cruelty in God, in being so unnecessarily strict and rigid ; and instead of aiding her resistance to the tempter by saying that God said, " The day ye eat thereof ye shall *surely* die," she seemed to disregard that solemnity in the asseveration, and only said, "lest ye die."

No wonder therefore that Satan, who first approached her so distantly, so cautiously, so doubtingly, now assumed the tone of arrogance, boldness, and blasphemy ; and persuaded her to that horrible deed on account of which all nature mourns.

Again. She saw the tree was good for food. Let us ask this woman, (she was indeed our Mother), but let us ask how she *saw* so clearly that this tree was good for food, that it was not as an apple of Sodom or a grape of Gomorrah? Did she see that it was good for food because it was goodly to the sight? Must we favor her a little because she had no sufficient experience of the world to teach her, that a great evil may be concealed by a beautiful form, and that appearance is not reality? No, we cannot, for God had told her that the tree was pleasant to the sight, and yet that it was forbidden. What right then had she to think that the fruit was pleasant to the taste, because it was pleasant to the sight? Or shall we ask her whether she saw the fruit was good for food because she saw the Serpent eat it? Probably he pretended that in consequence of that, he was indued with the gift of speech, and reason, and wisdom. Could she indeed know that the Serpent's power to articulate and reason proceeded from that fruit? Or had we not better ask, whether it was not her own fancy, already deluded, that so affected her sight she saw that the tree was good for food? She spoke very positively, it seems. She saw it was good for food. Any person may deceive himself if he pleases. This work is in his own power. He makes his heart, not his understanding; his wishes, not his reason, the judge of truth. The woman stood gazing at the fruit while her eloquent adversary was delivering his eulogy on its superior excellence. She gazed, and admired; she looked and wished; she argued and desired. At length she was as certain, as if the matter was fully demonstrated. She saw the fruit was good for food. There is an old proverb in point, "We are inclined to whatever is forbidden." *And the circumstance* of its being forbidden, sharpens desire to grasp it. Stolen waters are sweet, fruit forbidden is therefore pleasant.

View then our unhappy Mother, aiming with steady eye at the forbidden tree. Why is this golden apple prohibited? The very prohibition gives it beauty, and inflames desire. "Because it is not in my power, it seems so excellent; it is forbidden, perhaps, because my Maker envies me the sweet enjoyment!" O, unhappy Mother! caught in the snare of thine own indiscretion, and deluded by fancy and by wishes.

And now she was equally confident that the fruit was much to be desired to make one wise.

It appears that Satan (for his art is extraordinary) availed himself of the name of the forbidden tree, as a foundation for the temptation. It was called the tree of *knowledge*. Now, says the serpent, " it is called the Tree of Knowledge because the fruit is to be desired to make one wise. It is the tree of knowledge, and therefore its fruit will give you more exalted understanding and enrapturing views of God and glory." It was right in her to thirst for knowledge attainable by lawful means, and if she thirsted, why not ask information from the partner of her life? But him, in all probability, she had indiscreetly deserted. *Why not* seek knowledge from her Divine Parent in supplication and prayer? Did she not know that he would impart to her the knowledge of what was useful to be known, and withhold it when it was better withheld? It is very probable that this desire of knowledge tormented her, when standing and gazing at the tree of knowledge, that she had reasoned herself into doubt and uncertainty as to the propriety of taking the fruit ; and, in this state of anxiety and pain, felt the necessity of further knowledge to direct her in her doubts ; that finally she concluded she must eat of the Tree of Knowledge to relieve her anxiety and uncertainty ; that in this affair the wicked one constantly addressed her by his vile suggestions. O, what folly ! to eat of the tree of knowledge, in order to know whether it be lawful and expedient or not, to eat thereof ; to try the tree of knowledge in order to know whether it might be tried ; to transgress the command of God to know more fully, whether it be expedient to transgress ! But she felt confident that its fruit would communicate wisdom ; for the tree was called the tree of knowledge. Satan had sworn that they should be as gods, knowing good and evil, if they ate, and now, her anxiety, greater than ever to attain wisdom, deluded her into the candid supposition that the fruit would make her wise.

Alas ! she finally took of the fruit and ate thereof, and gave to her husband, and he did eat.

What else is the *probable result* of temptation so long indulged ? Will not the ear having so long listened to Satan's lies, at length be too much polluted to resist ? Will not the eye, by gazing so long at a forbidden object, be so fascinated and charmed as at length to perceive an imaginary excellence to such a degree that resistance is improbable ? Will not lust, when it hath conceived, bring forth sin ? It is probable that at first, notwithstanding the extreme art of Satan in all his suggestions, she hesitated whether it was expedient to gaze on this forbidden fruit ; and after she gazed, hesitated whether it was expedient to desire it ; after desiring, hesitated whether she would dare touch it ; and after touching, hesitated whether she would taste ; and after tasting, whether she would eat. But O, the fascinating power of sin ! Gradually it urges us from one step to another until a black deed is perpetrated which creates lamentation and mourning. But the sad catastrophe is not yet completed ; Satan's object, for which he broke the vaults of his prison, was not yet accomplished. The *real representative of mankind*, from whom alone the ruin can be entailed on his posterity, is yet innocent ; and, were it not for a Covenant of Mercy, and could we have hoped that Eve, that moment dying, could have escaped the depths of hell, we could have wished that the arrows of certain death had laid her breathless at the feet of Adam, yet unseduced, for lo ! being herself seduced, she becomes a tempter, an engine, of her fell adversary. She gave to Adam also, and he did eat. Now, when he ate, when the representative of mankind ate ; he, in whose integrity the interests of countless millions were involved ; when *he* ate ; then all nature first felt the wound, and all creation groaned in agony. We have spoken disrespectfully of Eve, and she deserves it. But Adam, wicked Adam, perpetrates the cruel deed with circumstances of terrible aggravation. He listened to the voice of his wife, and not to the counsels of his God. He listened to the voice of his wife, and *surely* her eloquence could not have been so dangerous as the eloquence of the Serpent which deceived the woman. Did he sin through the weeping solicitations of his spouse? He, however, knew that the transgression was basely criminal, and his conduct evinced horrible presumption. Did he sin in hope of impunity, because his wife was not immediately struck dead on the spot? O, his conduct evinced horrible presumption ! Did he sin in despair, as though matters could not be aggravated even by his transgression? Even this evinced a presumption clouded with blackest horror. In the apostasy of Eve, more of deception, infirmity and ignorance are apparent ; but in the trangression of Adam, more of willful perseverance, presumption and cruelty ; for so the expression of Paul must be interpreted (1. Tim. 2, 14) : " And Adam was not deceived, but the woman, being deceived, was in the transgression." Truly, the first sin of Adam was the most complicated crime ever committed on earth, it being unbelief, ingratitude, rebellion, robbery, contempt of God, defiance of His wrath, enmity against Him, idolatry, pride, self-love, obstinacy, sensuality, discontent, envy, covetousness, murder; all these concentrated in this single transgression.

1. From this we learn what reasons we have for lamentation and mourning. No longer do we now read of the glory of that worthy progenitor whom the image of his Maker crowned, who was lord over this inferior world, and bid so fair to shine brighter than the morning star in the firmament of glory? No more do we read of the glory of that fair creature Eve, the pride of creation, the admiration of angels, the perfection of loveliness and elegance. No more do we find those fair creatures in the profuse enjoyment of innocence and bliss, amidst the shady bowers, the flowery plants, the delicious fruits of Eden; or on the banks of the River of Life regaling themselves amidst the beauties of creation. O, miserable world! It has become Aceldama, a field of blood; where the prince of darkness reigns: where fraud, oppression, slander, licentiousness, war and murder and death in shapes of horror reign! O, brethren, is such the world in which you are born? Is it your doom to have existence in such a world, the habitation of such cruelty, the region and shadow of death!

This moment we feel the effects of that bold transgression, that pollution of mind which makes us so averse from God and duty; of that anxiety and trouble which more or less pursues us while we live; of that infirmity of our frame which has become mortal by sin ; and the sad beginnings of that dissolution and death which will inevitably and quickly lodge us in the dark and gloomy grave. Weep, O my brethren, for all real comfort has forsaken the world, and the pleasures which remain are only imaginary phantoms which delude. Weep, O ye daughters of Eve, for ye are fallen, and the joys you anticipate in this life are mere delusions of fancy which will fail you. "Lean not on earth, its thorns will pierce you to the heart."

True, there is a Saviour, and a great one, whom you must embrace ; but we fear that sin, Satan and the world will carry on the fatal temptation which began in Paradise, and rob us of our only hope, the only Refuge of dying sinners.

2. Learn, we beseech you, the subtlety and art of Satan from whom you are in danger. The more we examine the history and the conduct of the Devil, the more we are convinced that nothing could have been devised more artful than the plan of the great Enemy to delude mankind. *How cunningly* did he avail himself of everything to forward the temptation ! He avails himself of the name of the tree of knowledge ; he avails himself of the serpent, who was known to be beautiful and playful and subtle, in order that he might not be suspected. He comes in the appearance of a friend who seeks the happiness of men. He only asks some questions like a fair and impartial inquirer. He comes to talk over matters which concern their happiness. He invites attention ; when he obtains it he appears to admire, to wonder, to doubt ; at length to insinuate ; and as surely as he gains attention he will by his astonishing powers

of reasoning pollute the fancy and imagination ; then the judgment ; then the conscience ; then the affections ; and make the unwary disputant his prey ! Can you cope with such an enemy of unparalleled craft ? According to the Scriptures, he is that enemy who made war in heaven, and then seduced legions of angels, holy spirits, from their allegiance ; having thus transformed them into his own likeness, he, with the whole apostate tribe, were banished from heaven into hell. God suffers him, however, to wander to and fro over the earth and in the air ; for he is denominated the "prince of the power of the air who worketh in the children of disobedience." He is still denominated the Serpent, the Deceiver of mankind, a liar from the beginning. As occasion suggests he acts the roaring lion, or transforms himself into an angel of light. Are you able to stand a contest with one who is so subtle and insidious ?

These spirits of darkness are possessed of uncommon capacities, of most subtle sagacity, of extensive knowledge and enormous power and influence ; and all this enormous power and craft they employ to effect the destruction of mankind. They despair of ever being delivered from torment, and therefore in their malice and enmity against God and all goodness, they aim at producing confusion and mischief in the world ; if possible, to subvert the throne of the Almighty. And no doubt his experience in the acts of fraud and subtlety for almost six thousand years must contribute to render him still more a successful and accomplished deceiver. Can you enter the lists with such an adversary ?

When or where, do you ask, does this enemy make havoc of wretched mankind ? In all the dark deeds which have cursed the world ; and perhaps even now, poor sinner, you are under his subtle influence, so soft and gentle, that you cannot discern him. He is not apt to use violence with you since you take sides with sin; he only wants you to persevere in sin till he may take you to himself. And you are very much corrupted, and your corruption is the stronghold of Satan, of which he avails himself; and under which he conceals himself that he may lead you gently down the broad path to ruin.

This enemy has even been so successful as to make it unfashionable with mankind to believe in his existence. So he persuades the infidel; so he cheats the philosopher; so he infuses security into the sinner. This is his own subtle device. So far, he has gained his point; and so he works in the dark and avoids suspicion. O, for such a warning voice as that on Horeb's top, when the trump of God waxed louder and louder to warn mankind of war, to warn the unwary against that base enemy who continueth to work with signs and lying wonders and all deceivableness of unrighteousness. "Our Father, lead us not into temptation!"

Finally, let us embrace the arm of our Deliverer to lead us safely through this evil world of trouble, temptation and danger—"the seed of the woman." He, the noblest descendant of Eve who has bruised the monster's head. Blessed woman! object of reproach, as having committed the first crime, introducing to all our woe—source of sin and misery, and yet the source of all our bliss. For this all generations shall call thee blessed. By thee "to us a son is born—a child is given, whose name shall be called Wonderful, the Mighty God, the Prince of Peace."

By the marvelous grace and strength of our Divine Deliverer let us take up arms against the destroyer. What a holy and lasting war is this, in which the whole seed of the woman are engaged against the serpent and all his seed. Where, brethren, is your breast-plate of righteousness? (you need it); your shield of faith? helmet of salvation? sword of the Spirit? This is the armor of God which alone is effectual.

Guard, we pray you, against all thoughts and insinuations of injustice in Deity in visiting you with the consequences of your parents' crimes. "Be still, and know that the Lord, He is God." "Shall not the Judge of all the earth do right?" Never controvert evident facts because they are mysterious; and never pretend to fathom the infinite depths of the Almighty's wisdom. Guard, we pray you, against imposing appearances of beauty and pleasantness, for it is golden fruit which is employed as the bait of temptation. Guard against the excursions of fancy, the extravagance of imagination and the violence of animal affection; for these are first polluted by the Serpent's breath, and hurry on to crime.

Let your taste, your appetite, your eyes, your ears be guarded, lest they become the inlet of iniquity. Touch not, taste not, handle not, lest you be tempted to eat forbidden fruit. Gaze not on unlawful objects, lest desire be inflamed and prompt you to criminal action. And especially plead the Covenant of Grace by supplication and prayer for defence against your adversary. O, how imminent our danger till we are guarded by covenant Mercy! Vain are all your efforts against the enemy, without an interest in that. But here no serpent can scale the walls of this Everlasting Covenant.

By this we stand on a foundation which is immovable, and gain a summit which is inaccessible to our foe! "Now to Him who is able to keep us from falling, and to present us spotless before the throne of His glory" be our prayers and adorations directed evermore.

Amen.

ANIMAL NATURE THE SEAT OF SIN.

Rom. 7 : 8. "For I know that in me (that is, in my flesh), dwelleth no good thing."

There is no fact more seriously to be regarded or more carefully to be impressed upon our minds than this, that there are very numerous and very powerful enemies who have conspired against our peace and happiness. There are millions of *fallen and malignant spirits* who occupy the airy regions, who have contracted the most bitter envy and jealousy against mankind, and who employ the most profound subtlety and art to seduce us into sin and ruin. They are denominated thrones and dominions, principalities and powers, and spiritual wickedness in high places ; spirits that work in the children of disobedience.

The means and instruments which they employ for our seduction are the world, and the things which are in the world. Here are objects which are calculated to beguile ; here are riches and honors and pleasures which attract the eye, which excite the appetite, and mislead the understanding ; and alas! our animal passions are already corrupted, and therefore are fit for the delusive operations of Satan and the world. Alas! they accord with the suggestions of Satan; they predispose the heart in favor of the world. I call your attention to explanatory matter, and to the dangers to which we are exposed from the corruption of animal nature.

I. Explanatory matter.

The word "flesh," has various significations; all founded, however, on the same original meaning. Sometimes it signifies the dispensation of the Old Testament, because it was attended with so much bodily service. (Gal. 3 : 3) : "Are ye so foolish, having begun in the Spirit, are ye now made perfect by the flesh?" Sometimes the *external* or *bodily appearance*, with regard to which the apostle observes (2 Cor. 5, 16) : "Henceforth know we no man after the flesh; yea, though we have known Christ after the flesh, yet now henceforth know we him no more." Sometimes figuratively, it denotes what is *soft and tender*, as (Ezekiel 11, 19) : "I will take the stony heart out of their flesh and will give them an heart of flesh." In this place it signifies the *animal nature* of man polluted by transgression, and includes all the animal affections, appetites and passions, which have diffused their malignant influence through the whole man, and operated as the sorest enemies to our peace and happiness.

Man is represented in Scripture as possessed of a *three-fold nature*, as to his natural character. First, an *intelligent spirit*, the seat of reason and memory, judgment and conscience. Secondly *a body* of curious texture, and most artful subtle organization. The union of these two is dependent upon an animal life. Various passions and propensities and appetites, not depending on either spirit or body separately considered, are founded in the vitative connection between them. This appears to have been the idea of the apostle in 1 Thes. 5 : 23 : "The very God of peace sanctify you wholly, and I pray God your whole spirit and soul and body be preserved blameless unto the coming of our Lord Jesus Christ." Here he speaks of a rational spirit, an animal soul, and a material body. Indeed this mode of considering the constituent parts of our nature, will enable us to give an easy, beautiful, and consistent interpretation of the apostle's doctrine in relation to the conflict between the flesh and the spirit.

This animal soul of man we are disposed to consider the *primary* and *principal* seat of our corruption. The body is indeed contaminated, but it arises from the diffused influence of the animal soul. The intelligent spirit is corrupted, but its reason, its judgment, its conscience, have become swayed and biased and perverted through the instrumentality and influence of the animal affections.

Without going farther into an attempt philosophically, to analyze the constituent parts of our nature, we would observe, that the animal passions or lusts of the flesh are exceedingly numerous and dangerous. (See Gal. 5 : 19.) " Now the works of the flesh are manifest, which are these ; adultery, fornication, uncleanliness, lasciviousness, idolatry, witchcraft, hatred, variance, emulations, wrath, strife, seditions, heresies, envyings, murders, drunkenness, revellings, and such like, of the which I tell you before, as I have also told you in time past, that they which do such things shall not inherit the kingdom of God. But the fruit of the Spirit is love, joy, peace, long-suffering, gentleness, goodness, faith, meekness, temperance. And they that are Christ's have crucified the flesh with the affections and lusts."

II. The dangers to which we are exposed from the corruption of animal nature.

It was through animal propensity our *first parents* sinned. It is hard to conceive how their minds could have been so deluded in any way but by the instrumentality and influence of appetite. It was this that perverted the judgment and induced our unhappy mother to imagine, that there would be extraordinary gratification in tasting of the forbidden tree; it was this that led to unbelief, discontent, and presumption; to rebellion, base and foul revolt. Thus lust, having conceived, brought forth sin; and sin, being finished, brought forth death. The iniquity which thus originated in animal nature, *diffused its pollution* over the rational mind; the understanding, memory, imagination and conscience being darkened and perverted thereby.

This animal corruption is *propagated* to all their posterity, and belongs to our nature at the first moment of our existence. *Our rational spirit* is not begotten like our animal frame, but is the immediate gift of God, who, it is said, "formeth the spirit of man within him;" and therefore receives its pollution through connection with the animal body. Our animal part, being begotten, we have the same corrupt affections with our parents. These corrupt affections, once begotten in our natures, are parts of our being; and thus born within us, are intimately incorporated with our native character, and nothing can be more difficult to eradicate. "Can the Ethiopian change his skin, or the leopard his spots? then may ye also do good that are accustomed to do evil."

Experience and observation prove, how easily corrupt affections will pervert the understanding and the conscience. Are we passionately fond of a forbidden object? how readily do we suspend the decision of our judgment, how vigorously do we go in quest of arguments to justify a criminal deed; how artfully do we explain away all the objections that lie in our way; how soon will judgment and conscience even come over to the side of our wishes and vindicate our lusts. *We find it too hard* to sin in direct opposition to the pointed decisions of our reason, and the severe remonstrances of conscience, and the dreadful authority of God; and therefore we must first pervert these decisions, and allay this remonstrance, and explain away this authority that we may sin more freely. And this is accomplished by enlisting our reason and our conscience on the side of error. Thus the ignorance that is in us comes, in a great degree, through the hardness of our hearts. Not liking to retain God in our knowledge, our foolish heart is darkened, and professing ourselves to be wise we become fools. Thus our passions operate, and thus our interests produce a prejudice. And it is dangerous even to rely on the oath of a man, in a case where his interests, passions, desires, and pleasures are concerned. How great our danger then, since even our judgments and our consciences are to be suspected of error in cases when animal lusts crave indulgence.

Certainly, reason and conscience require a Divine

illumination and renewal, before they can effectually aid us in a conflict with animal passions. No doubt they may for a season keep us back from gross transgressions, but if carnal nature plead strongly and constantly, they will at length yield to the Destroyer. No doubt, as reason and judgment belong to the intelligent spirit, and are therefore the superior faculties of our nature, they are worthy of cultivation and care ; and yet they can never be so cultivated as that, by their own vigor, they can counteract or subdue the animal affections. The philosopher, the moralist, the Pharisee, all will fall victims in some form or other to the force of passion and appetite except they become enlightened and renewed by the Spirit of God. Yea, persons of deep conviction and concern of mind, have returned to their former course of sensuality and vice, through force of unsanctified animal propensities. How severe then must the conflict be, in which we cannot hope to succeed, except we become created anew in Christ Jesus.

The force of animal nature in the pious even, is such that as long as life endures, they are in a state of moral imperfection and infirmity. Let no one inquire whence the necessity that dooms us to this sad predicament. The necessity arises not primarily from the condition of the intelligent spirit enlightened and sanctified by grace, for fain would that spirit soar above all animal corruptions and gratifications, and take its mansion near the holy throne of God. But that spirit which seeks to be disenthralled from sin, is yet connected with animal nature which holds it back, and thence results the mourning and lamentations of the children of God.

Yea, that animal frame, which is the body of sin,

has so much sinful appetite incorporated with it, that nothing short of death, (which is the dissolution of animal nature,) will effect the perfect deliverance of the spirit. Does any one ask how death can be our deliverer from sin? The answer is easy. The animal nature is the primary seat of corruption, and the one remains as long as the other. Does death dissolve the animal constitution? the stronghold of iniquity is then entirely overcome, and the sanctified spirit, which had panted for deliverance, is disengaged from its shackles; and passes unmolested to the perfect service and perfect enjoyment of its God. O then, our danger is in being driven away by animal propensities, since nothing but death itself can extinguish them! Indeed, our whole frame is so polluted that its entire structure must be dissolved in death, and reorganized in the resurrection in order to partake of the happiness of paradise.

Hence those strong expressions of Paul in relation to the conflict between his spiritual and animal nature, and which cannot be well understood upon any other principle. A sanctified spirit is in conflict with a corrupt animal soul. Rom. 7 : 15, 24. " For what I would that do I not, but what I hate that do I. Now then it is no more I that do it, but sin that dwelleth in me. For I know that in me, (that is, in my flesh,) dwelleth no good thing," &c. " For I delight in the law of God after the inward man : but I see another law in my members warring against the law of my mind and bringing me into captivity to the law of sin which is in my members. O wretched man that I am ! who shall deliver me from the body of this death?" And O ! if this holy apostle of the Gentiles, who so far exceeded the generality of

Christians in humility, holiness, disinterestedness and ardent desire of perfect holiness, was doomed to mourn over so many bad propensities of the animal soul, how great is our danger if we seek not the grace of God that we may succeed in the laborious conflict!

See finally with what earnestness, and zeal, and benevolence he has enjoined us to fight against animal nature, by attending to the superior faculties of judgment, understanding and conscience. Gal. 5: 16. "Walk in the Spirit and ye shall not fulfill the lusts of the flesh. For the flesh lusteth against the Spirit, and the Spirit against the flesh, and these are contrary the one to the other, so that ye cannot do the things that ye would," &c. (Rom. 8: 7.) "The carnal mind is enmity against God," &c. (Gal. 6: 7, 8.) "Be not deceived; God is not mocked, for whatsoever a man soweth, that shall he also reap. For he that soweth to the flesh, shall of the flesh reap corruption, but he that soweth to the Spirit shall of the Spirit reap life everlasting." (Rom. 8 : 13.) "If ye live after the flesh ye shall die, but if ye, through the Spirit, do mortify the deeds of the body, ye shall live." (2 Cor. 7 : 1.) "Having therefore these promises, dearly beloved, let us cleanse ourselves from all filthiness of the flesh and spirit," &c. (Rom. 8 : 1.) "There is therefore now no condemnation to them which are in Christ Jesus, who walk not after the flesh, but after the Spirit." (Rom. 8 : 9.) "They that are in the flesh cannot please God;" i. e., those who yield to the force of animal affections habitually and willingly, and thus make their reason, judgment and conscience subservient to the flesh must surely be miserable forever, for their rational spirit is thereby so polluted that they can never be prepared for the obedience and bliss of the heavenly world. It was undoubtedly a *sense* of the *danger* to which mankind were exposed of committing themselves entirely to the misrule of an animal nature, that drew forth such tender and affecting exhortations.

We conclude with a few directions.

1. Be not surprised at the doctrine of a rational spirit and an animal soul in man, which have a perpetual conflict with each other. This animal soul we possess in common with the brute, which is governed altogether by appetite, and finally dies. Accordingly Solomon says, Eccl. 3: 19. "That which befalleth the sons of men befalleth the beasts ; even one thing befalleth them: as the one dieth, so dieth the other ; yea, they have all one breath; so that a man hath no pre-eminence above a beast. All go unto one place ; all are of the dust, and all turn to dust again." And when he discriminates between the rational spirit of man and the animal soul of a beast, he says, "Who knoweth the spirit of man that goeth upward, and the spirit of the beast that goeth downward to the earth." And O, how lamentable if by suffering ourselves to be governed by our appetites, we *assimilate ourselves* to the beasts, and thereby pollute and debase the rational spirit which cannot, without Almighty power, be released from its influence in this life, and if not released in this life will not be released for ever.

2. Remember in all your actions your obligation to conform to the superior faculties of your nature, reason and conscience. Your animal nature is, indeed, very serviceable to your welfare ; but it was never intended by our Creator that its passions and appetites should be

our guide, or have dominion over us; but on the other hand that they should be regulated, restrained and ruled by reason and by conscience. If then we suffer the inferior faculties to usurp dominion over reason and conscience, they tyrannize over us to our destruction; reason and conscience will at length be so debased, degraded and weakened, as to fall in and side with appetite, and the whole soul will become a sink of disorder, confusion and turpitude.

3. Alas! this subjugation of reason and conscience to animal appetite and passion, has already taken place; and our natures are defiled by lusts.

We must pity and console the poor believer whose reason is become enlightened and sanctified, who mourns over the defilement of his heart, and consequently has taken up arms against sinful nature, and is resolved that reason and conscience shall control his flesh. O what resolution is required on your part! O what perseverance and watchfulness! O what a constant dependence is to be exercised on grace! We must pity the poor sinners too, who are constantly propelled by the force of appetite; who are driven by their carnal inclinations into almost every kind of criminal indulgence; whose reason is blindfolded; whose conscience is seared. Having resigned themselves to animal nature, to avarice, ambition, lust and revenge, they have thrown themselves into the middle of a torrent, against which they sometimes faintly struggle, but the impetuosity of the stream bears them along. Without Almighty grace, they will not strive nor subdue their enemies, and will not be undeceived until the light of eternity unfolds their destiny.

4. O, brethren, do you strive? Have you engaged in the conflict? Is your reason enlightened to perceive its necessity? Is your conscience so impressed that you are miserable, unless you obtain the victory over your hearts? Have you fled to Jesus for help against your foes, and do you do it daily? I can promise you no respite from this warfare while you are inhabitants of flesh ; but Jesus can help you, strengthen you, and comfort you amid all your toils. With God on your side, you shall overcome, though a thousand evil spirits avail themselves of your carnal appetites to seduce you ; and let Divine promise encourage you. You shall gain more and more ascendance and triumph until death (which you consider your enemy) will slay all your enemies by dissolving your animal nature, and so disenthrall your rational spirits, panting for immortality.

5. Be careful, however, that your religion do not consist in bare *animal emotion*. If Satan cannot decoy you into absolute indulgence, he may so operate on your animal nature, as to produce the semblance of religious affections. Your fears, hopes, sympathies and antipathies may be so excited as that you shall think you are governed by reason and religion, when all is nothing but animal commotion. Indeed, as we are possessed of such animal natures, we are exceedingly liable to deception in this respect. Be cautious, therefore, that your minds be properly enlightened ; that your piety may be rational, sober, uniform, as well as sincere and ardent ; that while you do not split upon the rock of a cold, heartless, lifeless profession, you may not advance to the gulf of fanaticism.

6. Finally, be not discouraged because you must die. If, by the grace of God, you can only maintain ascendancy over corrupt appetite, and keep your spirits pure from the overpowering influence of sordid passion, then your spirits will be prepared for perfect glory ; and the body of flesh which has so long maintained the conflict will gradually lose its vigor in the warfare, and at length drop into the dust, and there be purified from its contamination ; and the rational and immortal spirit, released from the body of sin, wing away its triumphal flight to that pure kingdom into which flesh and blood shall never enter.

Only watch and strive, and through the grace of God you will succeed ; for " Who shall lay anything to the charge of God's elect ? It is God that justifieth ; who is he that condemneth ? It is Christ that died, yea, rather, that is risen again, who is even at the right hand of God, who also maketh intercession for us." " For I am persuaded that neither death, nor life, nor angels, nor principalities, nor powers, nor things present, nor things to come, nor height, nor depth, nor any other creature shall be able to separate us from the love of God which is in Christ Jesus our Lord."   Amen.

NATURAL ABILITY.

Ezek. 18 : 30, 31. "Repent and turn yourselves from all your transgressions; so iniquity shall not be your ruin. Cast away from you all your transgressions; and make you a new heart and a new spirit; for why will ye die, O house of Israel?"

Long has the church been distracted by conflicting opinions on the subjects of man's natural ability, and of co-operation with God as to his own salvation. Some appear to think that such is our state of degeneracy, it is utterly impossible for us to act any effectual part in our own deliverance, and that Divine grace does everything; and in such a manner that we can do nothing at all; that the Spirit of God touches and moves the springs of action in so immediate and irresistible a manner, as violently or coercively to bear down all our agency, and to supersede all our exertion and the use of means.

On the other hand, some have asserted such an unrestricted and uninfluenced freedom of will, and such an amount of moral ability and independent power, as may be justly thought to derogate from the grace and sovereignty of God.

It makes little difference what men may think on any subject they know nothing about, without the light of Divine truth. When brought to this standard, both these opinions are wrong. On these subjects we should be exceedingly careful that we do not explain away the sovereignty of God, nor the free agency of man. Both are clearly revealed in the word of God, both are strongly illumined by the improved light of reason ; both are to be inculcated in their proper relation, and in their proper time and place, without nicely balancing forces according to our own ideas of the fitness of things. We are in danger of impairing the honor of God, when we advocate the one so as to intrench upon the other ; and this danger arises from our inacquaintance with ourselves and with the Scriptures, by which there is a mystery thrown over the whole subject ; and so long as it remains, we are liable both to be mistaken and to be misunderstood. There may be some who by advocating the free agency of man are led into error in regard to the sovereign agency of God, so that while they boast of the former, they may at the same time entertain opinions derogatory to Divine grace ; but we fear that there are some who, by insisting upon reliance on Divine sovereignty alone, are tempted to underrate the agency of man in the matter of his own salvation, thus relieving him in a measure from responsibility.

In our discussion of this point, we shall strive to present it in the light we have derived from the word of God, and then consider the subject of natural ability.

I. For the true understanding of the whole matter, we must not lose sight of the fact that man in his fallen estate is yet clothed with natural ability. He is not a stick, nor a stone, nor an irresponsible machine : but he is an intelligent, accountable, free moral agent who can rightfully be held to account by the Searcher of hearts for his thoughts, words, and deeds. Let it not be supposed that we intend, to contravene the doctrine commonly received in orthodox churches, that the Holy Spirit is the grand efficient cause of regeneration. He is the author of this work exclusively. No power but His is competent to effect it. The wretched sinner is morally impotent. The holy Scriptures have decided in the clearest manner this momentous point. Nay, we concede that when regeneration is considered, not in the complex sense as embracing all previous or concomitant exercises of the awakened sinner, but in the strict sense of a work divinely performed, the sinner is to be considered entirely as a passive recipient, without any holy active agency in the work which is performed upon him ; and as one destitute of all moral fitness for it. We concede further, that there are no moral means, no good efforts, no useful tendencies which the sinner will employ in the way of selfish action which are necessarily or invariably connected with salvation. For since he is under the continuous dominion of selfishness and sin, what tendency can there be in any of his actions to contribute to this work ? His means of grace, when employed, are always more or less misemployed ; and are thus more calculated to perpetuate his sinful habits than to effect any alteration for the better. I speak of them as used in separation from the blessing of God.

All this is conceded, but in consistency with it we contend that the sinner has an agency to exert, of infinite importance to himself. View him as a creature of God, possessed of the strong instinctive propensity of self-love, which does not mean selfishness, sighing for happiness and abhorring misery. That propensity may be, and often is, by the blessing of God, enlisted successfully in the prosecution of the means of grace. It is this which renders him susceptible of deep attention to his own case, and forces him to consider the import of guilt and condemnation, as they are proved to rest upon himself. View him now in the prosecution of means. A concurring agency he cannot employ in regeneration, since that great work is an act of God creating the heart anew. But means to the end he can, must, and does employ in reading, hearing, reflecting, praying ; in striving for perpetuating, increasing and deepening the conviction that he is a condemned sinner. At some period in such use of means, we believe, God puts forth His regenerating power. I know that means are in themselves inadequate, and the sinner's use of them may be sinful ; but then they have been prescribed by God, who can and does make them powerful. The clay used by Christ to open the eyes of the blind, was in itself utterly useless to that end ; but because He used it, the result was attained. We cannot employ means that we may judge good, and that God has not appointed, with any success ; and on the other hand, we may freely use what we might adjudge the most unseemly means, provided He has appointed them ; for it is His will we must consult, and not our own ; it is His direction by which we must abide, and by no invention of our own. The sinner's means are useless in themselves, but made useful by the blessing of God ; they may be, like the pool of Siloam to which Christ sent the blind man, utterly without virtue ; but *because* He sent him, the water becomes valuable to him alone. So the means of conversion are valuable for that end only because they are prescribed by God; and it comes within the province of natural ability to employ them.

The sinner's means may be sinfully used, but the sovereignty of grace comes in to comfort me. That sovereignty, by many denied and derided and explained away, comforts me : for grace is so infinite and free, so un-influenced and uncontrolled by the sinner's demerit and imperfection, that it can sanctify, bless, and make powerful even the polluted endeavor of a polluted sinner. Shall I then give up that sovereignty of grace, that which alone supports me in all my despondency, that which teaches me the way, and the only consistent principle on which God can hear the sinner's cry? If we give up this sovereignty in election and effectual calling, we also give up regeneration and justification ; we sacrifice the only remaining principle on which a holy God can consistently meet the unholy sinner in his unholy means, unless we admit that the unholy sinner under the unholy influence of his heart can do holy deeds. But this can never be. It is too unreasonable, unphilosophical, illogical for any one to admit. There must then be such sovereignty in God, which is the root of the distinguishing doctrines of our church ; and for which she is often assailed with foul reproach. There must be this sovereignty in grace, or the weeping sinner dies. Grace cannot save him, but in the exercise of its sovereignty blessing his poor means. Christ cannot save him, if the *holy* use of means be the indispensable pre-requisite to his acceptance. Means themselves can-not save him, for their natural tendency by themselves, is to end in delusion and death.

But I go further, and assert that man has an agency

in his own reformation besides what is generally understood to consist in the use of means. He has agency not only in the means of regeneration, but in regeneration itself complexly considered. I do not mean that in holy exercises he co-operates with God in the act of His regenerating grace, but I mean that as the convicted sinner had agency in the means upon which God was pleased to regenerate him, so he has agency in all that belongs to the process, the progress and the perfection of the work. All along, it must indeed be allowed, that co-operative grace is necessary to rescue the wicked heart from destruction, distracted as it is by sin and selfishness; therefore the strivings of the Holy Spirit are necessary to repress the influence of selfishness, to fix the mind intensely on divine things, so that the natural love of happiness may keep the mind so fixed, until it becomes wholly absorbed in the conviction of their infinite importance. While therefore an Almighty influence is required to renew the heart, this does not supersede, but requires the use of means on the part of the sinner; nor does it destroy the necessity of his acting in the whole process of regeneration.

II. The subject of natural ability is thus brought before us.

But what is natural ability? It is the power of mind which it naturally has to act freely upon whatever comes within its scope. We are not only responsible for the right use of this but we are equally responsible for the moral powers of heart which are lost by our own fault, by our own depravity. The agency then which God invokes, is that which our own natural powers must exert. "Repent and turn yourselves from all your transgressions, so iniquity shall not be your ruin." And then He commands that you perform that whole work which is implied in turning to the Lord. "Cast away from you all your transgressions; and make you a new heart, and a new spirit; for why will ye die, O house of Israel?" This indicates what we are bound to do, and for the non-performance of which what we are bound to suffer, because entirely to blame.

We have spoken of the means of regeneration, but we require more than means; even those actings of soul which, in regeneration, are as *strugglings* to the birth. The Almighty stands before you, and demands of you in earnest, not only the use of the means, but the performance of the work itself. What process is it then through which you are commanded instantly to pass, and which He enforces upon you by all the sanction of His awful authority, and by all the danger and penalties of eternal perdition?

He demands in earnest that you make Him the supreme object of your love. As you are His dependent creature, deriving all your advantages, pleasures, comforts from Him, you cannot be released from a perfect and perpetual compliance with His will. He appeals moreover to your self-love which naturally disposes you to seek the deliverance of a forfeited soul. Hitherto the world has held you in a willing bondage, you have chosen it in place of your Maker, as your chief good. To turn to the Lord is to change all this by choosing Him, His service and His glory, in preference to the world, though it glitter with ten thousand splendors. You have natural ability for this, and as it is infinitely right that you should exert it in this direction, every moment of failure augments your guilt. God stands

before you, and by His inspired truth, opens your eyes
to see the difference between heaven and earth, and the
result of choosing either as your portion. This poor
world on which you have doated is around you, and
puts on all its charms to beguile your unsuspecting soul ;
but He requires you to choose the good and refuse the
evil. Divine truth presses upon your mind with irresistible authority ; the scenes of judgment and eternity are
opened to your eyes ; and conviction sinks you under
the realized displeasure of Him whose wrath you feel
to be a consuming fire, whose frown is worse than death.
Now at such a period of conviction, when the sinner
feels that the only hope is in sovereign mercy, the spirit
of grace probably enables him to change his choice, to
cast himself upon the unmerited grace of a sin-pardon-
ing God, and to rejoice in the first gleam of hope. If
not, he either turns back to the full power of his own
corruptions, or in the agony of desperation becomes his
own executioner. At any rate, such is the period when,
if ever, the convicted becomes the converted sinner.

In demanding this at your hands, God only demands
a reasonable duty of pressing obligation. Your conscience recognizes it as such, and depend on it, God is
in earnest, and requires no more than your natural ability
can render, no more than what is your bounden duty.
But you plead that you are unable to perform it. You
certainly do not mean that you have not the natural
ability, for it is by that very ability exerted the world
and the things of the world are endeared to you. You
are simply required to embrace God, with that natural
ability you have for embracing ; and to let the world
and other objects go. But still you say you cannot.
Now God sees that your *cannot*, means your *will not;* that

your inability is nothing but your deep depravity; and base unwillingness to love supremely the Author of your being and your daily comforts ; on account of which, if He were to recede from His requirements, and relax His righteous law, He would countenance you in rebellion, and encourage you to press still further your unreasonable claims upon His forbearance.

Again you plead that grace and the Almighty Spirit alone can prevail to make this change in your affections, but this plea is an admission that you are so much opposed to God that you cannot love Him nor serve Him as you are bound. What is this but emphasizing your own guilt? Now God insists that it is your duty, as His creature, to employ your natural ability for love, in the service of loving Him supremely ; and that you must not wait until you are conscious of a divine operation, since you are bound to be holy without it. That is a fact which you must see and feel, for when divine grace operates, it will operate in such a way that seeing and feeling shall prompt into a voluntary change, and your choice shall be, to rebel no more. Again you plead that it is exceedingly hard to give up the world, to act contrary to your own taste and inclination, and to require you to wage a ceaseless war against all your instincts ; but God again rejoins and insists upon the work, as a work of supreme necessity and obligation ; and a work for the performance of which no *new* faculties are necessary, only the employment of the natural ability you already have ; and He threatens that if you dare to neglect it, the terrors of the law are fearful, and shall be fearfully executed upon the disobedient. Now if we do not rise up to our obvious and admitted duty under the monitions of His warning voice, we forfeit for the second time a soul of immortal worth ; and every additional act of rejection incurs another forfeiture, implies another insult, and diminishes the probabilities of salvation until the forfeiture be confirmed, and hope extinguished for ever. When He says therefore "make you a new heart," He does not mean that the *creature* must become a *creator* to itself in the formation of a new nature, but He means that you are to make your heart new as to the supreme object of its love ; to exercise your natural ability so as to love the Lord your God with all your heart, soul, mind, and strength, and your neighbor as yourself. For this duty you have the appropriate faculty, and the inherent natural ability. Use it therefore as God requires ; and if you say you cannot, you mean one of two things ; either that you have no natural ability to use your natural ability as you please (which is absurd) ; or that you have no inclination to use it as you ought, which is criminal.

Again, Almighty God, earnest to promote the salvation of our souls, demands an *immediate* compliance with all the duty we are bound to render. His wonderful mercy has accomplished wonderful things in our behalf, and justly does He require an *immediate* attention to and compliance with directions and duties in our interest and for His own glory.

"Let me wait a little," says the sinner, "until my affairs are so adjusted that I may with greater convenience and more advantage address myself to such a laborious and unwelcome task." But will God, after the display of unparalleled mercy, suffer the ungrateful sinner, through the whole intervening time, to sin on, and on ; to insult and abuse, and deride His friendly counsels? "Let me consider the thing," says the deprecating sinner. But is it necessary to defer the work for the sake of consideration, when the matter is so exceedingly plain, when your own reason and conscience have been made to understand, to feel, and to speak within you? Will you demand time to consider, in order to put off immediate compliance with known duty? Would you not require, if permitted, an eternity to consider? Will not consideration, carried on under the influence of lusts and wishes, only mislead and embarrass? *You* consider! as though it were a matter for *your* views and expedience to decide, and not for God's authority to determine. Consider you may, and must; but no consideration is allowed to interfere with immediate duty in itself so plain that it cannot be made plainer.

But then the sinner puts in another plea. "Let me use the means to prepare myself for such a choice, and such a momentous work of surrendering myself to God, and putting myself on the Lord's side." What means canst thou use, poor sinner, pleading for indulgence in rebellion—what means canst thou use which are not polluted all over by the loathsomeness of thy selfishness infusing its poison into your fancied or pretended observances, and carrying you back to a greater distance from the object you intend to seek at some future time? Is not death imminent? What correspondence is there between such polluted means and such a holy end? How can the sinful use of means prepare the heart for the principle of holiness? Means indeed you may and must adopt, but not such means as stand in the way of immediate compliance. Means you must pursue, but only such as comport with immediate duty, such means as are incorporated and identified with the very act of compliance.

"O let me, then," says the sinner, "let me wait God's time for his moving, overpowering grace; and run, as it seems I must, the hazard of my ruin." O no, says the Divine Redeemer, "*come unto me.*" That is the only way. He does not tell you to wait, but bids you "come." The remedy *you* propose is the worst of all. This is fatal, suicidal. It draws midnight darkness over every gleam of hope. Go rather immediately in all thy impotency, and try to make for yourself a new heart, and see what will come of it. Hear the words of inspiration: "Cleanse your hands, ye sinners, purify your hearts, ye double-minded." "Now is the accepted time, now is the day of salvation." "How long halt ye between two opinions; if the Lord be God, follow him; but if Baal, then follow him." "To-day, if ye hear his voice, harden not your hearts." To-morrow the curse of abandonment may overtake thee, and thou become insensible. There is no peculiar mercy in the morrow that bids thee wait, and therefore there is no precept, counsel, or warning applicable to any period but that of to-day. All the momentous cares that relate to eternity are crowded within the period of to-day. Wherefore repent and turn yourselves from all your trespasses, so iniquity shall not be your ruin.

But there is something more tremendous still. There is a fearful uncertainty as to the final result of all our imperfect efforts. And therefore the poor sinner, when attempting to renew his heart, to make himself better, is required in the whole process to do homage to sovereign mercy. No doubt, if the effort were a holy one, sovereign mercy would crown it with blessing. But what promise is there recorded furnishing any certainty of success to the doings of an unregenerate man making imperfect efforts for changing his own heart? It is indeed his duty to love God with all his heart, it is his duty to cease from indulging unholy thoughts, to change every unholy purpose, in short to be holy in all his ways ; and this duty grows out of his natural ability to love that which is lovely, to hate that which is hateful, to avoid what is wrong, and to do what is right. If he had not the natural ability for this, he would not be responsible for defection : nay, he would be innocent, and free from blame ; but because this natural ability is inlaid within him, and necessary to the integrity of his being, it cannot be taken away without destroying his responsibility and accountability. It is because he has the power to love God and hate evil, that he is bound to do so every moment of his existence ; and any condition of life at variance with this expenditure of that power, is a sinful condition in which the soul falls under the condemnation of death. Now, since I use my natural ability for an evil end, loving what I ought to hate, and hating what I ought to love, I am a ruined man, because I am by my own fault a moral outlaw ; I am a lost man, because I am out of the path of holiness, and am wandering in the wilderness of sin. I am a wretched man, because I have forsaken God and am without hope. My ruin and my wretchedness have sprung from my own inexcusable sin, and now what keeps me from despair? O, it is the sovereignty of God, who chose to show mercy to sinners of my race, which he withheld from sinners of another, whose rebellion in itself was no worse than mine. By the provisions of sovereign grace, I may be saved ; yet I have no claim ; I am encouraged, if I obey the call of Christ who is the Saviour of lost men that flee to him for deliverance; but if I neglect this mercy, I am doubly deserving of the ruin brought upon myself, and of abandonment as well. In the exercise of my natural ability, I can understand my wretchedness, I can use the means of grace which mercy has provided for me, I can see and know by my natural understanding, that my only hope is in Christ; and that I am bound to feel the wretchedness of my condition; and under a deep sense of my dependence that I must go to Christ just as I am, anxious, prayerful, pleading for mercy; and after all, that it depends upon sovereign grace whether my efforts, such as they may be, shall attract the favorable notice of God. But He has promised, He has provided; and I must rely on His promise, and act according to the directions of sovereign mercy. But be ye astonished, O heavens! we miserable sinners seem unwilling to do this; nay, we neglect; nay, we pursue the course of sin without regard to consequences; and pour contempt upon mercy as well as upon duty. Upon the whole, then, ours is a melancholy prospect. The probabilities are fearfully against us. We cannot deny that they should be so. Was there any promise that our imperfect attempts at religious duty would be successful whenever we might choose to make them, our anxiety, if we have any, might subside; we might then continue in our sinful neglect, with some hope that a prayer, or a cry for mercy at the prospect of the nearness of death, would accomplish the end, and so secure at last the interposition of mercy to the salvation of the soul. But there is no such promise, and there could be none, because it would be only an encouragement to sin. No matter then what may be our convictions, or feelings; until we are actually changed, our prospects are exceedingly dark and gloomy. And our present want of feeling, our present lack of anxiety doubles the darkness, and thickens the gloom. We may go on in this way for a few years longer, but then, inspiration by the mouth of Paul has said : " Unto them that are contentious and do not obey the truth, but obey unrighteousness, indignation and wrath, tribulation and anguish upon every soul of man that doth evil." And what evil is equal to that of despising the admonitions of the Lord, and of being contented in rebellion against both the law and the gospel? Do we not then see what ground there is for that awfully suggestive question, " How shall we escape, if we *neglect* so great salvation?" The first ray of hope for the sinner is in the conviction of sin, and even this may go out in darkness. So long as we are without conviction of sin, so long are we destitute of all hope excepting a false one ; and without this conviction, conversion will be impossible. We therefore are reduced to despair in ourselves, but the most alarming symptom of our condition is that we do not feel it. We are reduced to dependence upon the unmerited mercy of God, but the worst symptom of our case is the neglect of it. We are reduced to the necessity of a precipitous flight to Christ for salvation, but the sure sign of destruction is refusal to obey Him. Here is the end, and here comes in the thunder of an angry God : " Behold, ye despisers, and wonder, and perish !"

From this subject we learn some important lessons it is our duty to make use of for reflection, for deep consideration, and personal advantage.

1st. We have all natural ability to obey God, and to

perform duty to the utmost. When a lawyer said to
Christ : "Master, which is the great commandment in
the law," Jesus said to him. "Thou shalt love the Lord
thy God with all thy heart, and with all thy soul, and
with all thy mind. This is the first and great commandment, and the second is like unto it : Thou shalt
love thy neighbor as thyself." And when a young ruler
came to Him with the inquiry : "Good Master, what
good thing shall I do, that I may have eternal life ?" He
said unto him, " If thou wilt enter into life, keep the commandments." Now, it is readily seen that these words
of our Lord imply necessarily, that we have all natural
ability for this duty ; for if we had not, He would not
have spoken thus, and we should never manifest it in
any direction. But what is the fact ? We do actually
and continuously love the world, and the things of the
world " with all our soul, mind, and strength ;" we daily
put forth just that power of natural ability in pursueing
" the lust of the flesh, the lust of the eye, and the pride
of life ;" we love with all the strength and power that
man ever had ; we expend our entire natural ability,
in breaking instead of keeping the law of God, in pursueing the objects of earthly ambition, in yearning and
striving for the enjoyments of carnal things, and for the
satisfaction of possessing the pleasures of sin ; and we do
it willingly. We actually and daily *do, and prefer to do*
this ; and therefore we actually possess all natural
ability necessary to keep perfectly and perpetually the
entire moral law. It is the power of love which consti-
tutes natural ability, for in obedience to that, all the
activities of our nature are in constant motion. The
powers of understanding, perceiving, comparing, design-
ing, determining, laboring, are all in play under the

dominant power of love. This is natural ability. It is not taken away by sin; but it is captivated by sin, and that by our own consent. It is used in the service of moral evil, and therefore we are in ourselves naturally and morally, temporally and eternally ruined; and there is no hope of recovery. The old sinful nature must perish, because the *old* heart cannot be mended.

2. We learn another lesson. God has a right to command us to use all our natural ability that we may be perfect as He is perfect. It would not be so, if He had taken away or curtailed that ability; nor would it be so, if He had in any way weakened it. If our loss of strength were by His fault, then our disobedience would be measurably excusable. But it is clear that God's essential goodness is a surety to us He could never require what He took away, and His justice, an absolute surety that He would never demand what we had not the *natural* ability to render. Now should I say, " I have lost my power to obey," how just would be the reply : "your loss of power to obey God, does not create for Him a loss of right to command. If, for example, you hate God; is that a valid reason why He should release you from the duty of loving Him with all the ardor of your natural ability?" My mouth would be stopped ; what could I say? I am responsible for the perversion of a natural ability which He gave me to love Him with all my heart, mind, soul, and strength ; and if I do not, I must take the consequence. I cannot plead any advantage from my own wrong ; I cannot say to Him, " because I have lost, Thou hast lost ;" for this would be to make law the servant of sin. What an absurdity to think that wickedness frees a man from the law that forbids it ! This would be the destruction of all government, divine and human.

3. We learn, therefore, that we have no hope but in God's sovereignty. Explain it as we may, or excuse it as we may, the fact is fixed—"There is none righteous, no, not one; there is none that understandeth; there is none that seeketh after God; they are all gone out of the way; they are together become unprofitable; there is none that doeth good, no, not one." What then shall be done for this poor unfortunate race? Divine Sovereignty said : "Deliver from going down to the pit, for I have found a ransom." All heaven rang with joy at this announcement. Man's only hope is therefore anchored to Sovereign mercy. He is bound by the law, and yet he cannot keep the law. He is guilty, yet there is *one* way by which he may be cleared. He is a child of wrath, and an heir of hell; yet in one way he may become a child of love, and an inheritor of heaven. The atonement of Christ explains all, and we can fully understand how it is, that "he who believes shall be saved ; and he who believes not, shall be damned." The question therefore is reduced to a small compass, and of such easy comprehension that none need mistake. It is very evident that the man in the Synagogue, with the withered hand, whom Christ commanded to stand forth in the midst, had lost all natural ability over it ; but when he was commanded to stretch it out, he made the effort, and it was done. The same Saviour says to every sinner in this house : " Come unto me and be ye saved." Now, having lost your *moral* ability, all you have to do is to go to Him who can restore it ; and He will take care of the rest. This is your only hope. Go to Him, and cast yourselves at His feet, and in gratitude for His mercy, honor Him by loving His person and professing His name. This, O sinner, I repeat is your

only hope; and it is your necessary duty and your blessed privilege to-day. To-morrow, the duty will be impossible, if the privilege be withdrawn. Go then, with the agonizing cry upon your lips, " Lord, save, or I perish."

MORAL INABILITY.

Jerem. 13 : 23. "Can the Ethiopian change his skin, or the leopard his spots? Then may ye also do good who are accustomed to do evil."

Man is a creature whose endowments entitle him to the highest rank above all other beings inhabiting the earth. God made him in his own image, perfect, happy, and glorious. No matter what he has suffered by his deplorable fall, the rational powers of which he is possessed render him capable of discerning the existence and adoring the perfections of the Deity. They make him an accountable creature, and a fit subject of moral government. Capable of discerning the excellency of the moral law, and of the law-giver; formed for the influence of moral motives, and the exercise of a free moral agency, it would seem that he is formed for immortality; for vain would be his rational powers, and moral accountability, if his existence is not to be protracted beyond this life. Indeed it is that consideration only that will account for a judgment to come, for if there were for him no hereafter, the death of the body would also be the extinction of the soul.

Viewing man as he is, in his natural character he is

an exalted being, but in his moral character he is a
degraded being ; in his natural character he is a very
little lower than angels, but in his moral character
he is but a little above devils. In his natural character he is instinctive with life, but in his moral character
he is "dead in trespasses and sins." So desperate is his
condition, that the prophet in our text points to two
physical impossibilities to illustrate the moral weakness
of man, going to show that for all purpose of self-im-
provement in his moral nature it is total ; and he is
hopelessly ruined. "Can the Ethiopian change his skin,
or the leopard his spots? Then may ye also do good
who are accustomed to do evil."

Our purpose is to justify this representation of our
text, that we may see how true a picture the Scriptures
give of human depravity, and what should be our
exercises in view of the fact. The doctrine is that of
human inability to be or to do good. To set it forth,
so that you may see exactly what is the teaching of
Divine truth, and how it is borne out by history and
fact, requires me to present the subject by a negative
and a positive proposition.

I. The negative proposition is this. Man's inability
is not a physical want of power. This requires but a
few remarks. It may be proper, just here, to say that
physical inability consists in being deprived of faculties such as understanding, or bodily strength ; it is
want of means, of opportunity, or of whatever may
prevent our doing a thing which we are willing to do.
Moral inability consists in the want of disposition, or
of willingness to do a thing which we have physical
power to do ; it is a disinclination to expend our natural

ability in doing our known duty. The propriety of this distinction in many respects cannot be questioned, though in some instances it may have been abused. We repeat, that the inability we speak of, is not a want of physical power. For example : Joseph's brethren, it is said, *could not* speak peaceably to him, but no one supposes they lacked the power of tongue or language ; they only wanted the inclination to do so. Christ said : "How can ye, being evil, speak good things ?" It was not any defect in faculty of speech to which He referred, but to the want of a good disposition. If religion were above our physical capacity, God, in requiring our observance of it, would require a natural impossibility ; but He may rightfully impose it upon us as a duty fully within our natural power, though we find it morally impossible to exercise it for want of a proper disposition, or because we are strongly opposed to it in our hearts. In other words, He may require from us what is morally impossible to us, when that impossibility is simply unwillingness, aversion, or strong dislike ; but there is no proof of anything being required by God which is impossible, if we only have the disposition to do it. There seems to be no accountability at all, when there is physical incapacity. Infants and idiots are examples. The poor heathen are in a state of physical incapacity as to christianity, in proportion to their ignorance of Christ. Not knowing of Him, they are not guilty of rejecting Him. They are therefore accountable only for the misimprovement of the light of nature, the abuse of conscience, the neglect of moral intuitions, and of the duties within their reach. If natural incapacity be here understood as the difficulty in the way of sinners, it would contravene the certain doctrine that many of inferior abilities, and of the weakest capacity are saved ; for Paul says : " Not many wise men after the flesh, not many mighty, not many noble are called." And the Saviour says : " I thank thee, Father, Lord of heaven and earth, that thou hast hid these things from the wise and prudent, and revealed them unto babes." The want of natural talents and learned acquirements therefore is not the difficulty in the way of impenitent sinners. This further is evident from the fact that if natural incapacity were the difficulty, its removal would require the bestowment of new faculties, or the enlargement of power in those we have; but we never learn from Scripture that anything new in regeneration is imparted except a new heart, which simply gives a new direction to all our rational powers ; nor do we learn from observation, that religion strengthens a weak memory, or quickens a dull intellect, or enlarges the scope of any natural faculty of the soul.

That which creates and enhances guilt, is this consideration ; while sinners have physical faculties sufficient for every purpose of religion, and have no excuse for its neglect from natural inability, they turn away from it by reason of dislike ; they are opposed to it from the obstinacy of hate ; they cannot be reconciled to its requirements from malignity of heart. That states all the trouble. Salvation, under such circumstances, is a miracle of grace. The pardon of sin thus rendered utterly inexcusable, is the glory of Divine mercy. The Scriptures resolve the efficient cause of our condemnation, not into want of physical power to do our whole duty to God and man, but to unwillingness. Christ complained of His hearers : " Ye *will not* come unto me that ye might have life." He wept out the lamentation : "O Jerusalem! Jerusalem! thou that killest the prophets, and stonest them that are sent unto thee, how often would I have gathered thee, as a hen gathereth her chickens under her wings, but ye *would not.*" If then it be evident that it is not the want of physical ability that keeps us from duty and from glory, what can the inability be, but *moral;* that is, disinclination; obstinate unwillingness; determination not to be, and not to do, what we ought to be in religious principle, and what we ought to do in holy life?

II. The positive proposition is this. Man's inability is the want of a good heart. He *cannot* love God, because he hates Him; he *cannot* be inclined to holiness, because he is averse to it; and because God is infinitely good, and holiness infinitely right, this hate, this aversion is not only unreasonable wickedness, but an infinite sin. It is not simply a sinful act, but a sinful habit; not only a sinful habit, but a sinful condition; such is the nature of human depravity. An act of sin is finite, but the *quality* of it is infinite evil; the condition is temporal, but the nature of it is to become eternal. Say what we will, this is our melancholy state by the testimony of the Searcher of hearts, and by the evidence of a world of facts. Hear what the Scriptures say : "God saw that the wickedness of man was great upon the earth, and that every imagination of the thoughts of his heart was only evil continually." "The heart is deceitful above all things and desperately wicked." Peter speaks of them " that *cannot* cease from sin." Representations like these, in many places, exhibit *total* depravity as a doctrine clearly taught in the word of God. Then again see the iniquity of this age, and peruse the history of the past. Every page of it is blurred with crime ; every individual of every class, among the highest and the lowest in civilized or savage life, all over the world, from the day of the expulsion out of Eden to the present hour, without deviation and without exception, is a sinner. Total depravity is therefore proved true by the greatest induction of facts ever made. By this doctrine we do not mean any radical defect in the physical constitution of body or mind, but such a degeneracy of heart as is totally disinclined to true spiritual good. Whatever good you find, material, social, civil, or relative, in the best state of human society, it is destitute of that holiness necessary to make it good in the sight of God. Hence Christ said, "There is none good but God." If, then, our moral depravity be total, from the very nature of it a uniform steady opposition will issue against the divine law, for every precept of the law is equally holy, and equally requires a corresponding holy principle in the heart of man for its proper and perfect fulfillment; and it is for the want of such an inward fountain of pure motives that every precept is violated in some form of sin, either by omission or commission. If depravity be total, it wages war against every attribute of God, for every attribute corresponds with every part of the Moral Law. Hence the breach of one precept is the breach of all, because it strikes at the principle of holiness pervading the whole.

Furthermore, our moral impotence appears from the necessity held forth in the Bible for an Almighty influence to convert the human heart. This influence is therefore beyond our powers of exertion, unless we possess some of the resources of Omnipotence. Indeed there is no necessity at all for regenerating grace, if moral ability for this work exists within us to the smallest extent. Did the smallest part of it remain amid the ruins of our nature, it would have been found to have recovered some one in some age to a state of innocence, and would have kept him free from sin from the time of its exertion to the end of his life; but no such instance has ever occurred. We therefore say that no man can renew his own moral nature, because no one ever has. The representations of the Scriptures on this point are borne out by the history of mankind.

By regeneration we understand the infusion of a new principle of life in the soul of man; it is, according to the Scriptures, a "Being born again;" but if moral ability for such a change exists within us, then the absurdity would stand out in our faith, that a man may become his own spiritual father! Again, regeneration is declared to be, in so many words, *a new creation:* "For we are his workmanship created in Christ Jesus unto good works." Now, if it can be effected by an indwelling moral ability, then it is clear that the creature becomes his own creator!

The very terms used to designate this work are so suggestive as well as descriptive, as to make it plain that there is no moral power for such a work within the natural man who is "dead in trespasses and sins."

Was it worthy of God to form this marvellous system to which our world belongs, to send forth His Spirit to bring its rude chaos into order and beauty? Was it becoming the infinite Majesty to create the light, to form the sun, to ornament the out-growth of the earth with wondrous beauty? Surely then it was worthy of Him to send forth His Spirit to restore harmony in the moral world, to impart light to our darkened understandings, and life to our dead souls, so that this renewal of our nature should be a resurrection from death. "Son of man, can these dry bones live?" was a question to the prophet which he reverently referred back to Omniscience; and God showed him that Divine power could make bone come to his bone, and resuscitate the whole army of the slain. So the Apostle teaches us, "What is the exceeding greatness of his power in us who believe according to the working of his mighty power which he wrought in Christ, when he raised him from the dead." The inference is this: If we cannot do that which is intrinsically good without a new principle, and if that principle can be obtained only by regeneration, and that our regeneration can only be effected by an Omnipotent Agency, then we must prove ourselves to be omnipotent before we can demonstrate our moral ability to perform what is acceptable to God.

The principles of moral order bear us out in the idea of the sinner's moral inability, notwithstanding his unimpaired physical power. This power enables us to perform all that is natural in prayer, in devotion, in charity, in meditation and reading; but who does not perceive how necessary are the integrity, uprightness, and love of the heart, that these actions may be spiritually good? Were our physical powers properly directed by a good heart, how much more might they contribute to the glory of God and the good of our own souls! But here lies the difficulty. Will the heart, so corrupted, ever of itself become upright, sincere, and affectionate and zealous in the service of God? Can the heart, intoxicated with sinful pleasure, take delight in God?

Charmed with the honors of the world, can it seek the honor that cometh from God? Fascinated with the glitter of gold and silver, can it seek the true riches? Full of enmity, can it exercise itself in benevolence to all mankind? An enemy to Jesus Christ by wicked works, can it choose that holy, immaculate Saviour for its portion? Enmity itself against God, can it love Him, or even seek to be reconciled to Him as the source of true happiness and peace? Can the heart mourn for sin while it is in love with sin? Can it believe in Jesus while it hates his character and government? To all these questions we reply : Yes, if repentance consisted in an external humiliation, we might attain it ourselves, and like Ahab we might rend our clothes and put sackcloth on our loins, and go softly ; or if repentance implied no more than a temporary conviction, we might, like Felix, work ourselves up into trembling by the doctrines of righteousness, temperance, and a judgment to come ; but it implies much more, even a universal, generous, affectionate sorrow which is the gift of God. Yes, if faith consisted in a historical belief of the Bible, or in a bare assent to its doctrines ; then, without a special operation, like Agrippa, we might believe the prophets ; with Simon the sorcerer, we might confess the faith of Jesus ; and with devils, we might believe and tremble ; but it is something more : it is a faith of Divine operation, and consists in knowing, loving, and applying the truth to one's self for the purpose of doing the will of God, and living unto Christ. Yes, if piety consisted in external gifts of charity, in lengthy petitions, in biblical knowledge, or in suffering martyrdom, we might attain it without a special operation ; but it consists in much more, for though we had all faith, so that we could remove mountains, and understood all prophecy, and all mystery, and should give all our goods to feed the poor, and our bodies to be burned, the heart at the same time under the influence of corruption, we should be no more than sounding brass and a tinkling cymbal. How can the heart, willfully impenitent, delight in penitence? Can it willfully disbelieve, and yet seek a holy faith? Can it hate true piety and yet exercise it? No, the heart will not act contrary to itself. Our judgment and conscience may condemn it, but yet the heart obeys its own dictates, and no other faculty can control it. Will a man voluntarily choose what is contrary to his choice? This you see is inconsistent, for none can fail to know that it is impossible for the heart to hate what it loves, or to love what it hates. Alas! it is this wickedness of the heart and the will, which has a prevailing influence over our better faculties and powers. Instead of judgment, reason, and conscience controlling, they are controlled by the heart; nay, it seduces them into the service of iniquity. And would not the same wicked heart which refuses now to employ the physical powers we possess, in the same base manner prostitute the noblest natural gifts to the greater aggravation of our sin? Had we the physical powers of an angel, would not such wicked hearts inclining us to abuse them, only seem to give us more completely the character of a spirit of darkness? Had we even the omnipotence of Deity, enabling us to do anything, that omnipotence, being under the direction of the wicked heart, would never be employed for good purposes—for the wicked heart never wishes to be otherwise than it is—it cannot wish to be holy, or it would not be wicked; it cannot choose contrary to its own inclinations.

The Scriptures bear us out in this presentation of our moral inability to do that which is good in the sight of God; and it is remarkable how many passages clearly imply that it is not a want of physical power that can explain it. It is not a radical defect in the constitution of body or mind that creates this inability, but it is a disinclination of the heart and will towards good so strongly bent, that we cannot perform duty to the Divine acceptance. "Ye cannot serve the Lord, for He is a holy God; He is a jealous God." "Wicked men have shut their eyes that they cannot see, and their hearts that they cannot understand." Of the wicked man it is said, "A deceived heart hath turned him aside that he cannot deliver his soul, nor say, is there not a lie in my right hand?" God says: "To whom shall I speak, and give warning that they may hear? Behold, their ear is uncircumcised, and they cannot hearken; behold, the word of the Lord is unto them a reproach; they have no delight in it." Christ said: "A good tree cannot bring forth evil fruit, neither can a corrupt tree bring forth good fruit." And the Apostle James adds to the illustration, "Doth a fountain send forth at the same place sweet water and bitter? Can the fig-tree bear olive berries? either a vine, figs? So can no fountain yield salt water and fresh." "Why," said Christ, "do ye not understand my speech, because ye *cannot* hear my words?" "How can ye, being evil, speak good things, for out of the abundance of the heart the mouth speaketh." Peter speaks of certain wicked men as "having eyes full of adultery that they *cannot* cease from sin." These and many other passages confirm the doctrine of our text. "Can the Ethiopian change his skin, or the leopard his spots? Then may ye also do good, that are accustomed to do evil."

Common language certainly justifies us in saying that a man cannot do what his heart and inclination strongly forbid. Thus we say of a lazy man, that he cannot labor; not for want of bodily strength, but from disinclination. So of a deceitful man, he cannot be true; and of a drunkard, he cannot refrain from his cups. A thousand similar instances might be mentioned to show the truth for which we contend in a variety of aspects, all of which illustrate the deplorable fact, that the sinner's heart is so strongly averse to religious duty, that it may be said he *cannot* do it—not because it is above his physical capacity, but because the disinclination of his wicked heart is so strong, that he "loves darkness rather than light." Now if this wickedness be a valid excuse for this inability, then the greater the wickedness, the greater the excuse; and the devil himself would be the most excusable of all sinners in the universe! No; our moral inability is our great culpability, and our wickedness is our voluntary inclination to evil. We know that we disobey God, and are rebels to His law, and we are content that it should be so.

From this subject, we learn:

1. That the doctrine of man's moral impotence is consistent with his responsibility. It cannot be otherwise, without producing moral distraction in all our relations in life. If your impotence was a want of natural power, or opportunity, or means of doing your duty, there would be some plausibilty in the common objection made against this theory. But the fact is, that all this impotence is in your will, with its choice and inclination. In this, lies the depravity of human nature; by this, we

are rendered powerless and wretched. And is it at all admissible to make pleas, and apologies, and excuses founded on such inability of inclination? Is it a valid excuse to say, I cannot do my duty because I will not? And yet the only reason why you *cannot*, is because you *will not*. Are we to go free from blame because our hearts are so bad, our will so perverse, our choice so absurd, that we call evil good, and good evil? This amazing folly and madness which we acknowledge to be contrary to our own reason, is the very thing that piles our guilt mountain-high. We know the path of duty only to avoid it; we know that the claims of God are righteous; and cannot be relaxed because they are righteous, and yet we refuse to respect them, because we are unrighteous. We do just the reverse of what we know to be right with regard to God, "in whom we live and move and have our being," employing all our powers against the very end for which they were given us. Does not this course of conduct expound our hearts to be *enmity* itself? How can enmity be more clearly proven? O, that this subject might be regarded in the spirit of honest impartial consideration, that God might be justified by the penitential relentings of a deep and abiding conviction of sin! It must come to that, or there is no hope in our case. I am sure if palpable misapprehension did not prevail on this subject, if uncommon pains were not taken to darken and perplex it, there would not be any ground for controversy that men would not be ashamed to assume. If any subject of importance demand honest unprejudiced and prayerful consideration, it is the subject of our woeful apostasy. What question is equal to that which relates to the cause of our impotence? How is it that we *cannot* serve our Maker as we ought? We are self-condemned, self-ruined, and yet self-complacent in our perseverance according to the inclination of the evil heart of unbelief. God help us, miserable victims of wretchedness, and subjects of Divine indignation !

2. I am persuaded that a correct view of this matter is productive of that conviction of sin which enters the experience of the awakened sinner. Why does he ask "What shall I do to be saved?" Is he as ignorant as the Phillipian sailor? No, he is familiar with the gospel proclamation. Is it because there are many ways of salvation, and he is at a loss which to prefer? No, for he has all means of a correct knowledge on the subject. Is it because he is perplexed as to the requirements of the gospel? This cannot be, since he is made to understand that there is no salvation but by the atonement of Christ. Or does he ask this question because he is convinced of his moral competency to do all that is required? Surely the man who has any knowledge of his own heart will disclaim all pretentions to such ability. Or does he ask the question with regard only to the means which he must pursue for the gain of a Divine influence? But these also are made to him exceedingly plain and intelligible. There can be no difficulty on that account, for nothing can be clearer than that the duties of attention, reading, meditation, thoughtfulness, and prayer, are the necessary means of engaging the mind in work with this subject. But there *is* a difficulty of which the poor sinner is sensible, over which he agonizes, and for the removal of which he weeps. It is the conciousness of this difficulty that prompts him to exclaim, "What shall I do?" And the definition of it he works out by repeated reiterations of

the same question, as he goes farther and farther into the subject. What shall I do that I may obtain the pardon of my sins, while all the time I am sinning against a holy God whom I am unfit to serve? What shall I do to propitiate his anger so justly aroused against me? What shall I do, for an atonement for sin, when I am not in unison and love with Christ? What shall I do to overcome the rebellious feeling of my wicked heart following its worldly inclination? What shall I do to get the principle of holiness established in it, so closely shut against heavenly-mindedness, so faithless, so perverse? I know if I am truly penitent, God will save; but what shall I do to obtain a holy penitence any lodgment within this hard and deceitful heart? I know if I believe, He will save; but how shall I get this faith which works by love, while I do not feel the drawings of love within my soul? I know if I use the means which He has prescribed correctly, He will save me; but what shall I do for help to use them in such a manner? I know if I desire to be saved in reality, He will save me; but what shall I do when my wicked heart turns all desire upon forbidden things? O, my powerless soul, seeing thy ruin, yet unable to escape, what shall I do? What power less than Divine can inspire that love which I am bound to feel without it, and yet *cannot?*

Yes, my friends, put your awakened souls through such a catechism, you will find out what the difficulty is, in all its fearful magnitude. There is no other, or rather, all other difficulties are removed already. None other can exist in a mind enlightened by the Bible. But this difficulty is not easily overcome. The awakened sinner knows he cannot save himself, because he cannot renew himself. He knows to his sorrow that God Almighty is not to be controlled, and that He was not bound to offer mercy. He knows, too, that offered mercy, when rejected, may be withdrawn in righteous indignation ; and that a Sovereign God, if not bound to save under any circumstances, cannot be bound to save the sinner who insults his mercy, and does despite to the Spirit of grace. O what then shall he do to obtain an Almighty influence to subdue his wicked heart, a converting, sanctifying power to reclaim his soul? Thus you see that the subject we discuss, is the very subject that distresses him. It is the hinge on which his conviction turns. I cannot see why any sinner should be distressed at all, except for this. Every other difficulty is removed by Divine revelation, but Divine revelation does not tell the individual sinner that God will save him, or that his conviction will issue in conversion. Therefore knowing his natural ability by which he is held accountable for sin ; and knowing his moral inability by which he is so strongly disinclined to do his duty that he cannot change himself, and all the while inexcusable for not doing it, he mourns for his soul, as one that is in bitterness of a grief that cannot be assuaged. This is the condition of an awakened sinner, while he that is not awake is more hopeless still ; nay, altogether without hope, and without God in the world.

3. In the fulfillment of my duty, I must honestly tell you that there is a tremendous difficulty, O sinner, in the way of your salvation, a difficulty which I can make plain, but which I cannot obviate. God alone can do it. I can indeed say, if you believe, you shall be saved ; but I have said this for years without any effect upon

you. I can say truly, if you repent, if you pray, if you use the means of grace correctly, you shall be saved; but I have said this for years, and you have done none of these things. I cannot therefore settle the point in any other way than against you, because God does it, and Christ does it, and I dare not do otherwise. Perhaps you would have me remove every cloud that rests upon this subject, but I cannot by the book of revelation, much less by the book of nature. I never can, unless I might enter into the secret counsels of the Most High. And if I could remove all darkness from this subject in your individual case, then you would not do otherwise than you have done. Could I ascend to the throne of the Eternal, and thence bring the certain destiny of your soul before you, it would make no difference; for should I be able to say, you will be certainly lost; despair might settle upon you, but repent and believe you never would. Should I be able to say, you will be certainly saved, satisfaction might rest within you, and all concern be dismissed; but repent and believe you never would, in consequence of information thus brought from the very court of heaven. You never would be grateful for a salvation, which you did not learn to appreciate, through the agony of conviction and the joy of conversion. I say again, if you desire salvation you may have it freely, fully, gloriously; but I cannot say whether you shall ever have that desire, for I know not whether a Sovereign God will bestow it, after repeated offers on His part, and repeated rejection on yours. As to trusting to the efficacy of means without a divine operation, years of preaching have proved its fallacy. Your purposes, resolutions, all forgotten, you yourself ought to know by this time, are but as chaff before the wind, as withered leaves before the rising storm. I have preached to the utmost of my ability: God help me, I can do no more. You have heard and listened to my plea ; God help you, you have rejected it.

4. Poor encouragement, you perhaps will say, this affords for the careless sinner. Yes, so I mean it should be. Your prospect is a dismal one. Your case is a terrible one. I must say it is doubtful whether you will ever see the light of heaven. In great tenderness and sorrow of heart, I say this. I must be honest on this point, and would to God I could so picture the condition and wretchedness of a sinner rejecting the calls of mercy as to so discourage you, so dishearten you, so unhinge all your fallacious hopes, that you would cry out in agony, "What shall I do?" This is the very end of the discussion, to discourage, to unsettle, to put you out of humor with all presumptuous hopes. Indeed I know no subject, no doctrine but this, which will make the sinner tremble. What if I say, and prove, and illustrate that you are transgressors of the law? This difficulty you can easily meet, for you can say, the gospel of glad tidings of sovereign grace is revealed. What if I say, sin demands a satisfaction? You answer quickly and rightly, that Christ has died and set conscience free from pain. What if I demonstrate, that the gospel demands repentance as a condition of salvation, you retort upon me my own doctrine, that you have natural powers to repent whenever you feel inclined to do so. But if I tell you that you have no feeling to do so, and through years of opportunities have failed to do so, and never will have inclination to do so, till God give you repentance unto

eternal life; this, if you would realize and believe it, would thrust your very heart, and nothing could prevent your agonizing prayer, "God be merciful to me a sinner."

Perhaps you deprecate this kind of preaching. You say, "Do not preach the awful Sovereignty of God; do not preach about the purposes of God; do not preach the severe doctrines of the gospel. This may discourage the sinner. Yes, and for that very reason they must be preached. They are the truth that "is sharper than any two-edged sword, piercing even to the dividing asunder of soul and spirit, and of the joints and marrow, and is a discerner of the thoughts and intents of the heart." This truth of fearful import does discourage the sinner. Yes, it takes all the courage out of him, and is alone adapted to force the exclamation, "What shall I do?" I mean that it is this very subject which in some form or other, enters into the spiritual distress of an awakened sinner. And because he feels that this subject is calculated to mortify his mind, and convict him of his helplessness, he would rather turn his thoughts to a more encouraging topic, or hear an exposition more calculated to flatter and deceive him. This gives me anxiety. I fear misapprehension. I would not unnecessarily offend the sinner, but on this point, "the offence of the cross" will never cease. Our proud revolting hearts remonstrate and object, "This is a hard saying; who can hear it?" O beloved souls, consider honestly, prayerfully; humbly consider whether in the light of the past you have not a miserable prospect before you, by reason of this very impotency; I mean the unwillingness of your hearts, and the awful Sovereignty of God. Listen, that you may be discouraged and feel the misery of your natural condition ; for if you do not, one thing is certain ; go where you will, you will never go to Christ.

5. I said I had no consolation to minister to thoughtless minds. Whence can it come? Not from God, not from Christ, not from the Scriptures ; for he that will not think, cannot feel under any influence. Yet I have much encouragement to give to the anxious sinner, whose poor needy soul is crying out, "O that I knew where I might find him !" He who has lost the rebel's courage can alone be encouraged. He who finds his heart inclined to give up to Christ, and give over to Christ the interests of his soul, who is willing to hear, love and obey him, may be beset with doubts and fears ; but for such there is, blessed be God, large encouragement. Are you in earnest, yield not to anything that would allay the feeling. Are you serious indeed, indulge and increase that seriousness, that it may end in deepened conviction of your misery while out of Christ ; for at some point in the line of this feeling of serious conviction, it seems to be the purpose of infinite Sovereignty to grant the grace that regenerates, the grace that pardons, the grace that works faith and repentance in the soul. When thousands were distressed on the day of Pentecost, they obtained an unction from on high which occasioned unspeakable joy. It is your interest then to cultivate a deep sense of your impotence, looking to Christ who said to his disciples, "Without me, ye can do nothing." How much less can *you* hope to do anything without Him ? Totally dependent on gratuitous mercy, cast yourselves upon the infinite love of Christ, and despairing of all other sources of help, go to him just as you

are ; go to him by prayer, and if you cannot find words
to express your feeling, make to him the signs of the
dumb—He will understand. Be not content until you
feel that you do cast yourselves upon Him for all you
need. You must not go to Him for mere help, but for
the entire work ; He only can do it all—you cannot do
a thing beyond placing a loving trust upon the word of
His gracious invitation, "Come unto me." Be not content with bare possibilities and probabilities. Give him
your whole heart. Well, but you will say to me :
According to your own doctrine, I have no power. I
reply : See the man with the withered hand in the synagogue. He had no power to stretch it out, yet having the
disposition, he made the attempt ; and you know the
result. Christ, in like manner, has a word for you, a
blessed word of encouragement. He says : "Come
unto me"; "Follow me." You can make the attempt,
you can strive to obey. Like Matthew, you can rise
up, leave all, and follow Him ; and see where He will
bring you. Do it to-day. Surely you can go into no
secret place where His eye is not on you. In such a
place, with all your sense of weakness and inability,
surely you can look up to Him with tearful eyes and
say; "Draw me, and I will run after Thee." Remember
He does not ask you to do His work, but He asks you
to do your duty : compliance is salvation ; refusal is
death ! The poor dying thief simply asked for a far-off
blessing : "Lord, remember me when thou comest in
thy kingdom." He got more than he asked for : "To-
day, shalt thou be with me in paradise." When a leper
in all his uncleanliness came to Christ with the despairing cry, "Lord, if thou wilt, thou canst make me clean,"
Divine compassion said, "I will ; be thou clean." Go,

in like manner, and with the same plea; and Christ will
make your hearts rejoice by the power of a Divine infusion of spiritual life.   Do it to-day, for if you do not,
to-morrow may be a day too late. O, shall it be
necessary that another should plead with you for this
duty, while you are indifferent to it?   "Awake, thou
that sleepest, and arise from the dead, and Christ shall
give thee life."

NATHANIEL.

John 1 : 47. "Jesus saw Nathaniel coming to him, and saith of him, 'Behold an Israelite indeed in whom there is no guile!'"

No method of instruction is more pleasing and powerful than that which derives it from a true delineation of character, and a proper representation of facts. Facts are easily apprehended ; they make a lively and lasting impression on the mind ; they are easily retained in the memory, and the conclusions resulting from them naturally arise, and serve to influence our practice amid the various concerns of life. The soundest abstract reasoning, the most wholesome general rules are often disregarded, while examples of piety, which discover the amiable feelings of the heart, deeply interest our attention. They encourage imitation ; they operate upon our sympathy ; they represent to us, in a striking manner, the odious forms of vice, and the amiableness, simplicity, and integrity of the Christian spirit ; they impress us with a sense of our duties, and our frailties ; and, under the influence of the divine blessing, exalt and transform the soul.

It is true, Jesus Christ is the only perfect and fin-

ished character that ever appeared among mortals, to
the contemplation of whose example we should be
peculiarly devoted.   By it every generous feeling of
our nature should be roused, by it our hearts should
be made to glow with admiration and love ; but often
it is of unspeakable consequence to notice the history of
His poor and imperfect followers.   In them we see the
principle of piety in its earliest stages, in its first and
weakest efforts ; in its subsequent increase and enlargement.   In them we see it in its interesting struggles and
conflicts with a thousand infirmities, doubts, and prejudices ;   and from them we learn how the Father
Almighty is interested in behalf of his poor children,
and conducts them, by peculiar means, to strong faith,
and peace, and joy in believing.   Their example is not
above our imitation, they instruct us by their infirmities, their conflicts, and their prejudices ; they encourage us by their successes ; they console us exceedingly
by the history of their final triumphs, and of the
interposition of Christ in their behalf.   In view of these
things, let us attend to the case of NATHANIEL.   Christ
saw him coming to Him, and saith of him, " Behold an
Israelite indeed, in whom there is no guile !"

I. Our attention is at once arrested by the forcible
language of Christ, descriptive of his character.

When Nathaniel is denominated "an Israelite," no
doubt reference is had to his descent from the patriarch
Jacob, who wonderfully wrestled with the Angel of the
Covenant, striving in supplication all night till the dawn
of day, not willing to let him depart without a blessing.
So it seems Nathaniel wrestled in secret with God in

pursuit of that knowledge, wisdom, and grace necessary to the comfort and salvation of his soul.

He is denominated an "Israelite indeed," in contradistinction from those who gloried merely in their carnal descent from Jacob, while destitute of his spirit; for they were not all Israel who were so called; neither because they were Abraham's seed were they all children. Indeed the generality of the whole nation had so declined from the steps of their father Jacob, that every instance of honest piety among them was a remarkable exception, worthy of admiration and regard. Whatever others were, whatever the darkness in which the whole nation was involved; whatever the sad degeneracy in virtue and morals that marked the nation at that period, Nathaniel was a real Israelite, whom the Saviour Himself could not but notice and approve, and publicly applaud.

In him there was "no guile," no deception, no dissimulation; no profession nor appearance without reality; no ostentation, vanity, nor affectation; but in opposition to all this, honesty, simplicity, and modesty (which rather shrank from observation) characterized his piety. The meaning is, not that he was a perfect character, for he entertained unworthy doubts, prepossessions, and prejudices against Jesus Christ as the Messiah, shown in the objection: "Can there any good thing come out of Nazareth?" He had adopted the opinion which his nation entertained, that an earthly Messiah was to be expected for mere earthly purposes in their political renown. Notwithstanding this, he might be "an Israelite indeed, in whom there was no guile"; for Israel himself, Israel his father, whom he honorably resembled, on different occasions discovered inconsistency and dissimulation. Did he not circumvent his own brother and defraud him of his birthright and the paternal blessing attached to it? yet, as to his general character and prevailing spirit, Jacob was a plain man, artless, honest, and heavenly-minded; so was Nathaniel, notwithstanding the infirmities of his nature. He was sincere, and honest, and simple in his piety. There is a radical difference between occasional declension from duty and general perseverance in sin. No honest believer knowingly, habitually, and from preference will indulge in wickedness, for the seed of holiness is in him; and he cannot sin in this respect, since he is born of God. An apostle says of all such men: "Sin shall not have dominion over you, for ye are not under the law, but under grace." Nathaniel was of such a spirit that our Saviour passed upon him the highest encomium.

II. This character is set before us as a model, for such it surely must be, by the evidence of Him who knoweth what is in man. Let us examine the prominent points of it:

1. Humility. Because unobtrusive, the piety of Nathaniel was entirely unobserved, if we may judge from the efforts of the Pharisees to make theirs conspicuous. It is true, it had been his duty with becoming modesty on all proper occasions to discover to those around him the impressions he entertained, the convictions he cherished, and the reverence he felt on the subject of religion. He probably did this to some extent, but certainly he made no show of his religion; for the traits of his character were evidently

averse to it. This is always commendable, and yet it may be carried too far; for religion must appear in the religious, not as a matter of exhibition, but of manifestation. It is often the fault of believers that they court secrecy and silence, they affect indifference which too often seems like neutrality, in order to avoid the odious charge of hypocrisy; but surely they miscalculate; for such a course is likely to invite the very charge they are anxious to avoid. Whether Nathaniel erred in this particular or not, it is evident he could not be justly exposed to the charge of obtrusiveness or vanity, while his piety was not thrust forth for observation. No eye but that of Omniscience could see the emotions of his heart, and no other eye, as he thought, could witness the effect of them in the place and position he occupied, of which Christ, to his astonishment, spoke in the context. Whatever seed of regeneration had been planted in his heart, it had lain concealed there until its germination by the grace revealed to him in the presence of the Messiah. He was one of the Lord's hidden ones, whom the world and the church do not recognize, but whom the Lord alone notices and approves.

It is a consoling thought, that amidst the degeneracy of any particular age or nation, some exist who are upright and sincere in their desires and pursuits, though their precious characters be unrevealed to public view. Nathaniel was one of them. Whatever perplexity may have troubled him in regard to the agitation of his nation about the Messiah's coming, he remained a silent observer and seeker after truth. Nor did he seek in vain. The great Searcher of hearts knew and watched his exercises, and waited the best opportunity for his highest consolation.

2. Sincerity. This is made conspicuous even by his doubts and prejudices. No wonder that he had enough of them, since he was affected by the popular belief that the Messiah would appear in the form of a glorious earthly monarch, subjecting the nations under his control. The disciples, after their conversion and opportunities of gaining correct views on this matter, still seemed to entertain the hope that their Lord and Master would assume temporal dominion, in accordance with the popular belief to which they clung until after the Resurrection of the Redeemer. It was possible, therefore, that Nathaniel should be sincere, while under the influence of the same mistake. That his doubts and prejudices must have been honestly held, appears from the manner of his holding them. Most of the Jews, when they discovered that Christ was of a humble spirit, hated and persecuted Him. They demonstrated their insincerity by rage and bitterness; but Nathaniel discovered no malice because Christ came from Nazareth. He was indeed prejudiced against Him, and evidently on this account; but his prejudices were more properly those of the leaders of the people than begotten of his own heart. His doubts were derived, not from the Scriptures, but from the recognized doctors of the law; yet they were not cherished in the spirit of enmity against Christ. They did not precipitate him into virulent invective or outrageous madness. Calmly he heard of Christ, and considerately he spoke of Him. It appears, too, that he had bestowed some attention upon the study of the ancient Scriptures in regard to their prophetical declarations concerning Christ; for Philip appealed to them as familiar to the mind of Nathaniel, saying: "We have found Him of whom

Moses in the law, and the prophets, did write." And after his friend Philip had asserted the Messiahship of Christ, Nathaniel did not rail ; he did not contradict ; he did not positively deny ; but simply propounded a proverb common among the Jews, indicating their contempt for this little-village of Galilee. And though it had so often been declared that no good thing could come out of Nazareth ; yet he did not condemn Christ because of His disreputable home. Nor did he deny the truth of Philip's declaration, he only hesitated to believe, but did not make that hesitancy offensive ; nor was it, under the circumstances, unreasonable, and this plainly was the judgment of Christ himself.

3. Honesty was also conspicuous in this Israelite. His piety was not demonstrative, like that of the Pharisees, " to be seen of men," but it was unmistakably an abiding principle within him, for he was a secret worshipper of God. As such, Jesus Christ saw him under the fig-tree. What his meditations were, what were the particular subject of his devotion at that time, we are left to conjecture ; and we shall not perhaps be far amiss in our judgment, if we say that he prayed most earnestly to be enlightened with regard to the coming, and the intent of the coming of the promised Messiah. It is reasonable to suppose it, for this was the topic of the times that agitated the whole kingdom of Judea. With what earnestness then must he have sought the true interpretation of the prophecies ! With what interest must he have heard the various reports of the miracles and wonders wrought by Christ ! With what anxiety was he exercised, that he might be enlightened by the divine Spirit as to His character ! How he must have been agonized between two thoughts, that if

Christ should be an impostor, he himself would offend God by advocating his claims; and on the other hand, should Christ be the true Messiah, by rejecting Him, he would subject himself to the wrath of God, and the forfeiture of his own soul. This, indeed, was a matter well becoming his solicitude and secret devotion.

Under the sombrous shade of a solitary fig-tree, where he felt certain no human eye could observe him, there he poured out his doubts, fears, and perplexities in fervent supplication. Who, brethren, who would thus be engaged in secret, shunning the presence of others, that he might give vent to his conflicting emotions before God alone, but one whose honest heart was seeking light and consolation? Surely it was a momentous point upon which his soul was engaged, an absorbing question of which he sought solution. No man could solve it, no relief could come from any source but from God.

Secret devotion may possibly be practised for conscience sake, but then there will be no fervor, no agonizing, no wrestling, no soaring on wings of earnest aspiration. When therefore one, like Nathaniel, is thus engaged, his soul must be that of "an Israelite in whom there is no guile."

4. Candor in his conduct corresponded with the honesty of his heart. At the time spoken of, he was sought and found by a friend who had been relieved on the very point that engaged his own thoughts. Philip, rejoicing in his discovery, "findeth Nathaniel, and saith unto him : We have found him, of whom Moses in the law, and the prophets, did write, Jesus of Nazareth, the son of Joseph. And Nathaniel said unto him, Can there any good thing come out of Nazareth? Philip saith unto him : Come and see." No sooner said than com-

plied with; Nathaniel came, without interposing an objection. Candor dictated his conduct.

There is sometimes an obstinate spirit of bigotry met with, whose inclination is averse to such an experiment as that to which Nathaniel was invited; a spirit that will not condescend to examine anything encumbered with its own prejudice. Everything contrary to prevailing notions, and preconceived opinions, must be rejected without reason, and condemned without examination. Thus it was with the Jews. When they found that the character of Christ evidently did not accord with their notions of what the Messiah *must* be, they at once rejected Him; clamored against Him with enthusiastic madness, and demanded for Him the worst form of death. In like manner, infidels of the present day disdain the story of the crucified Saviour, and without any sober examination of prophecy, miracle, character, or any other evidence in its favor, condemn a religion which alarms their fears. So, too, conceited theologians reject indiscriminately every part of a system opposed to their own. So, too, nominal professors, pleased with the baseless hope they entertain of heaven, disdain to examine themselves or their opinions by the test of divine truth, lest their repose be disturbed. Not so, Nathaniel. He came to Christ. Humility, sincerity, honesty, and candor prepared him to "see" the dignity of His person, to hear and understand the import of His doctrines, to examine His miracles, and other evidence unfolded to his intelligence, and to come to a sure and reliable conclusion.

On a subject involving the salvation of his own soul, comprising everything dear to him and all mankind in the present and eternal world, he would bend all the energy of his mind; he would allow nothing to interfere with that perfect fairness such a subject demanded. No habits of thinking, no modes of reasoning, no prepossessions, nor partialities should warp his judgment in dealing with it. He would "come and see," unfettered, unrestrained, and with the help of God, examine for himself; and if Jesus be proved to his conviction, the Messiah and Saviour, he will sacrifice every opposing interest and place himself unreservedly within his arms. Could such a spirit be any other than one in which there was "no guile"? And when he came into the presence of Jesus, these qualities of a guileless soul irradiated his countenance, and placed him in the loveliest attitude before the Redeemer.

5. The approbation of Nathaniel's character upon the part of Christ, was expressed in surprising language. "Behold!" Nathaniel was aware of nothing in himself worthy of such a greeting. "Behold! an Israelite in whom there is no guile." Divine intuition gave utterance to divine approval, and thus Nathaniel hitherto ignorant of himself, came to understand his own condition and standing before God. What a happy discovery was his! Little did he think that his doubts, fears, solicitude and agonizing inquiry formed the evidence of his true character in the eye of Christ of whom he doubted, but who looked into his soul all the while he was under that fig-tree, far away from His bodily vision!

It is remarkable, too, what a train of measures was laid to make this miserable man a happy one. Has he been praying under the fig-tree in deep distress and yet concealed his feelings from others, the Father of mercies noticed him with tender compassion, and peculiar regard.

Philip is his companion and intimate friend, but Philip knows nothing of the trouble of his soul. Let Philip be called to the fellowship of Christ, and be first divinely enlightened, that he may carry the tidings of salvation to his friend. Such was the arrangement. Philip, made to rejoice in the glorious discovery, hastens to Nathaniel with the good news, whom he invites to "come and see." Nathaniel comes; he sees, he hears a voice which thrills his soul, and fills it with "joy unspeakable and full of glory."

But who could have thought of, or conjectured the method that Christ pursued to impart instantaneous and irresistible proof of His own divinity to the mind of this good man, who thought himself a stranger to the Nazarene? Nathaniel expected to reason and argue and study, and from certain premises to draw certain conclusions, carefully and slowly, so that, after a sufficient time for deliberation, he might satisfy himself as to the truth of what Philip had uttered: Jesus Christ took a shorter method. "Thou art an honest Israelite whom I saw under the fig-tree before Philip called thee." These words brought up a storm of emotion in the breast of Nathaniel. When he heard the encomium of Christ, what more natural than the question, "Whence knowest thou me?" And what more overwhelming than the unexpected answer, "Before that Philip called thee, when thou wast under the fig-tree, I saw thee." How rapidly did thought succeed thought in the production of an unshaken conviction: "Rabbi, thou art the Son of God; thou art the King of Israel." Nor was this too hasty a conclusion, although rapidly reached. Christ revealed to Nathaniel the possession by Himself of the incommunicable attributes of Deity. Omniscience and omnipresence must be ever associated with omnipotence; but, as none of them can pertain to any creature, the argument was no less strong than brief, by which this guileless Israelite reached and proclaimed his conclusion. How joyfully did he accept the privilege of being accorded a high place of honor in the little circle of the followers of the Lord!

The improvement that should be made out of this interesting narrative is quite obvious to every reflecting mind:

1. We see, my brethren, the importance of devotion, of secret devotion, when the heart, the soul, the desires, the affections, all are poured out in private prayer before God. Let it be followed up with the perseverance and sincerity of Nathaniel, and as in his case the Answerer of prayer will astonish us with unlooked-for responses that shall far outstrip our expectations. Let no one object that he must be previously enlightened, instructed, and impelled; for the inquiring sinner knows not how much he may be touched and enlightened already. The Lord imparts his Spirit in his own secret and peculiar way, and we must glorify his sovereignty. Duty is the consideration which should urge the sinner, a helpless creature of necessity, under the benign administration of free grace and wonderful mercy. What can he do, what ought he to do, but cast himself upon those precious promises that are as sure as the immutable God can make them?

Neither should we urge ignorance, or perplexity, or doubt on any subject as a reason for omitting our devotions. A worse reason cannot be imagined, because there is no connection between the premises and conclusion leading to such omission. The real encouragement which should animate us, irrespective of everything else, is the fact that God has not only allowed but commanded our prayers; and, when offered in the spirit of Nathaniel's piety, the Lord witnesses our cries, hears our groans, gathers our tears in his bottle, and answers our prayers according to his own wisdom and our necessities, of which we are not adequate judges.

Poor Nathaniel is but a poor Jew, of a degenerate nature, full of ignorance and prejudice and perplexities; yet, not only willing, but anxious to be brought into the light and truth and comfort that God alone can impart. He prayed, and the Lord answered him in a way of which he could not have dreamed, but which was infinitely a better way than he himself could have devised, if it had been left to his own decision. Thus it will be with all who put their trust in God humbly, honestly, sincerely, and candidly; referring all their troubles to His disposition of them, and resigning themselves to their duty and to His will, as the regulator of it, in all the details of life.

2. We see the necessity of sincerity to a freedom from guile. Insincerity is the result of a beguiling spirit, and, though it makes dupes of others, the greatest and most keenly suffering victim will be the soul in which guile has been a source of unholy motive. But nowhere is its operation so dreadful as in the matter of religion. O, what can it avail that you attend to the ceremony of worship while the heart is unemployed in the business itself, while you are unaffected with the burden of your sin, while you feel no need of pardon, no cause for fear, no anxiety to be saved from wrath? O, if salvation be

not your supreme concern; if it be not supremely sought; if it employ not all your heart and soul and mind and strength; if it be not an object of such paramount interest as to make every other matter inferior and subordinate, all your devotion is superficial, insincere, and unavailing. Yes, *unavailing;* for you are all the while in the midst of your seeming worship, treating God and Christ, death and eternity, with contempt; *unavailing,* for there is nothing in you that makes you susceptible of salvation, or that disposes the mind to receive it; *unavailing,* for God has determined never to bestow it except upon those who deeply regard it with heart-felt anxiety. Tell me how you will ever correctly and experimentally understand the Christian system without an honest and supreme desire to understand it? If there be no sincere concern with regard to your soul, will you examine your Bibles with proper motives? Will you not be swayed by prejudices, and vague impressions, in settling down upon any creed? Will you not then pervert the truth, and render the Christian system nugatory to your own souls? All your opinions and views of Christianity, will they not be such only as you yourselves fabricate by accommodating the Scriptures to your pride? To understand the Scriptures correctly, we must bring all our preconceived notions to be immolated on the altar of divine truth. We must be willing to resign our selfish views to the control of revelation. You ought to be willing to part with your favorite views, your modes of thinking, your habits of reasoning, for the sake of knowing that revealed truth, in its formative power, by which a ruined man may be saved from his own delusions, and may be redeemed. You must be willing to follow the Scriptures without hesitation and without reserve in every doctrine, every duty, every mystery they unfold. Then, indeed, and not otherwise, will truth divine enlighten, purify, and comfort your souls.

Would Nathaniel, think you, have found the Messiah and salvation in His name, had he not been humble, honest, sincere, and candid in his researches and devotions? If under the influence of guile and cunning quibbling he had come to Christ, would he not, like other Jews, have been more confirmed in error, more perverse in sentiment, more bitter in opposition to truth? Approaching the Saviour honestly and honorably, how kindly was he received; how marvelously enlightened and convinced! How beautifully is his conduct illustrative of the promises: "The meek will He guide in judgment; and the meek will he teach his way!" "If a man will do His will, he shall know of the doctrine, whether it be of God." "Then shall we know, if we follow on to know the Lord: His going forth is prepared as the morning; and he shall come unto us as the latter rain, as the latter and the former rain upon the earth."

Brethren, is it not possible that after all the opportunities of Christian knowledge we enjoy, and notwithstanding the flood of light which Christianity has poured upon the earth, we are more ignorant, more perverse in sentiment, more obstinate in error than otherwise we should have been, had we dealt honestly with sacred truth? The gospel, if not turned to a good account, becomes "the savor of death unto death." O, when Christianity does not enlighten you, it darkens your understanding, just as continuous gazing at the sun produces blindness. The longer men reject Christianity, the more exceptionable and offensive its doctrines and precepts become to them. Thus truth will either mercifully soften, or judicially harden the heart. Let this teach us all the necessity of obeying the truth with simplicity, sincerity, and honesty ; so that we too may be "Israelites indeed in whom there is no guile."

3. Some may say, "We will make no profession at all, that we may never incur the charge of hypocrisy or guile." But stop, are you sure that you will escape it, by refusing the most reasonable duty that you ought to recognize as pertaining to men blest with the light you enjoy ? "Certainly," you say ; "this crime is the crime of the church ; the sin of professors ; the disgrace of Christianity." We plead guilty to the charge, for it lies with fearful weight, not upon Christianity, or the church, but upon many who are avowedly Christians, but really so only in name. Would to God we could refute the allegation. We will not call it slander, for there is too much truth in it, so far as individual instances are concerned ; we cannot advance an unqualified denial. We lament the fact, and pray to be delivered from that lukewarmness, formality and inconsistency, which attach themselves to many, and so far, go to fix upon us the odious stain of hypocrisy and guile. Thus much we admit, as to the grain of truth in this charge. We desire, however, that you will be equally candid : Is there no guile, no insincerity in the practice of our accusers ? Because they have made no profession of Christ, they think that one good thing at least comes of their delinquency : they thus avoid the guilt of the hypocrite ! But are they not hypocritical when they profess a belief in Christianity, which is contradicted by their practice ? Christianity is every-

thing, or nothing; entire truth, or entire fiction. To the extent of their avowed belief in it, then, are they not hypocritical, so long as they prove indifferent to the thing believed? There can be no doubt of it, because real belief always produces sincere action in duty, so far as it goes. Are they not hypocritical when they say they cherish a good honest principle, and are unwilling to act it out before the world? Are they not hypocritical when they say they desire to be real Christians, no such desire being discoverable in a single effort to become such, and when a careless ease on the subject is plainly manifested all the while? And are they not hypocritical often, when they advance the charge against professors in broad, malicious, and unqualified terms, which their better judgment condemns at the very moment of its utterance? This defence therefore is like an overloaded canon, which does more execution among friends than enemies.

4. Let us carefully remember that there is a degree of hypocrisy to which a true Israelite never can advance. We know the infirmities of human nature exemplified in a thousand instances recorded in sacred history; and it is astonishing to what excesses even true Israelites have gone, through ignorance, weakness, inadvertancy, temptation, surprise. Yet we are authorized to assert that no pious person will knowingly cherish an abominable lust in his heart, nor habitually allow himself in a known neglect of any duty, nor advocate any known transgression. It is evident that if a professor can indulge himself in forbidden things, and knowingly, willfully, and habitually pursue any sin or course of conduct in conflict with the principles of divine teaching, he ought to relinquish his hope of heaven, and anticipate a full portion

with hypocrites and unbelievers. But let it be observed that infirmities of temper, and various weaknesses and imperfections, are not evidence of hypocrisy.

He who is conscious of honesty of purpose, and looks to God for guidance into the way of truth and righteousness, shall obtain the blessing. Christ came to save from *sin*, and the promise is infallibly sure: "He that cometh to the Father by Him shall in nowise be cast out." This is the sinner's only reliance, but it is ample; encouraging; and should be instantly adopted by all men, to whom "the glorious gospel of the blessed God" is announced, as the certain means of gaining admission into the kingdom of heaven.

O, sinner! If you are honestly concerned for your own immortal soul, the eye of heaven is upon you. If you are really candid in your doubts and prejudices and infirmities, desiring God Almighty to lead you into His truth, your errors shall be overlooked. If you are distressed in your doubts and perplexities, desiring Christ as your all and all, the bosom of the Almighty pities you. If you come sincerely to Christ for relief, light, and salvation, determined to submit to Him, the fullness of the everlasting covenant is yours.

O, can it be that such tender and abundant pity dwells in Him whom we have so grievously offended, and from whom we cannot justly expect anything but "fiery indignation which shall consume the adversary?" It is astonishing, but no less true, salvation is for the chief of sinners. We are warranted to expect extraordinary things from an extraordinary dispensation founded on atoning blood. O, Nathaniel! Happy Israelite; once poor and miserable, though honest and devoted: rescued by Jesus from "the horrible pit and miry

clay," and now crowned with applause, and numbered
with the princes of heaven! O, may we all, by the
same honest promptitude, when invited to "come and
see," obey the summons, and gain the approval of Him
who lovingly said to the honestly disposed sinner,
" Behold an Israelite indeed, in whom there is no guile."

NOT FAR FROM THE KINGDOM.

Mark 12: 34. "WHEN JESUS SAW THAT HE ANSWERED DISCREETLY, HE SAID UNTO HIM: THOU ART NOT FAR FROM THE KINGDOM OF HEAVEN."

Among the circumstances attending the ministry of Christ on earth there were some things peculiarly discouraging. The state of the Jewish mind was the state of error, perversion, and distraction, produced by false teaching and pride of ancestry, of opinion, and of fancied superiority. I refer, however, more particularly to the prejudices which existed in all the sects, parties, and denominations into which the Jewish nation was unhappily divided.

The Essenes was a sect entertaining the belief that, by austerity and bodily mortification, they should merit happiness, and so purchase the reward of heaven. They consequently retired into obscurity, and do not once appear in the New Testament history. They were like the monks of the dark ages.

The Herodians was a sect that distinguished themselves by their prejudices in favor of Herod the King as the legitimate ruler of the people, though he were a heathen. Their politics commingled with their religion.

The Pharisees was a sect, and the largest of them all,

whose immoderately inflated self-righteousness was their reliance as the meritorious favorites of heaven. Whoever might be lost, they felt that they should be surely saved, and, should they be deficient in anything, the merits of Father Abraham would supplement all.

The Sadducees was a sect of Deists, who violently contended against the immortality of the soul, denying the existence of angel and spirit, and ridiculing the doctrine of the resurrection.

Amid prejudices so diversified, so numerous and so deeply rooted, could it be supposed that the doctrine of Christ would prevail without opposition, or be accepted without keen debate? We are at no loss for an opinion made unanimous by our own experience "of the contradiction of sinners." Christ was opposed at every step by them all. Sometimes contrary sects who hated each other most heartily, would unite forces for the purpose of combating Him; they tortured their wits for the sake of entangling Him in His talk, and exposing Him to the obloquy and hatred of the common people. In the record of these things nothing is so remarkable as the wonderful addresses, the readiness of mind, and unexampled wisdom with which He instructed the people, and managed every controversy raised by His enemies. They saw and were made to feel something very extraordinary in His arguments, an admirable conclusiveness in His reasoning, and a singular adroitness in turning every objection to His own advantage, and putting them to silence the most mortifying, while He would take occasion from every circumstance to inculcate the sublimest virtue in the most captivating forms of speech; thus would He prepare the minds of His hearers for the reception of His gospel.

There were indeed a few honorable exceptions, such

as Nicodemus and Gamaliel. Among them was one (by profession an interpreter of the law, a man of erudition and ingenuity) who had been sent to try the skill of the Divine Prophet. He was disposed to be fair and honest in debate, and consequently experienced an effect somewhat different from those who had been forced to retire from contests to which they found themselves unequal. He seemed to be astonished and overwhelmed; his heart was evidently softened—he yielded, his conscience considerably moved and convicted, his judgment overborne, his sensibilities aroused: the best feelings of his nature prompted him to utter applause, evidently under a profound impression made by the conversation of this Heavenly Prophet. All this I would infer from his manner, from his candor, the cordiality with which he expressed his approbation of the doctrine of Christ; from the emphasis which he laid upon His words, repeating them with an amplification of expression and pertinent remark.

We feel an interest in the exercises that moved the heart of this honorable and amiable man. We do not certainly know what became of him afterwards, but we may hope he became a true disciple of the Master. He had already approached to Christian character, for Christ in parting, said to him : "Thou art not far from the kingdom of God." Let us consider the import of the Saviour's descriptive language, and the position of those to whom it may be applied.

I. The import of the Saviour's descriptive language. When he thus indicated the character of this scribe as one who had approached near to the kingdom of God, we cannot conceive Him to have meant that he was approaching merely to qualifications requisite to introduce him into external membership with the gospel church. The kingdom of heaven, or of God, means the social state of final happiness, in which the saints shall live under the government of Christ forever in heavenly glory; and specially does it mean, the Millennial reign of Christ in the latter day. For this He had taught His disciples to pray: "Thy kingdom come." It was not this sovereign reign of Christ over the world to which the scribe had drawn near, but it was to union with the King Himself, then on earth, by the establishment of those principles in his heart which would make him a subject of His kingdom. From such a position of citizenship therein, made sure to believers in Christ, he was not far. All men in whose hearts Christ reigns as their accepted prophet priest and King, are sure of places in His kingdom: therefore, not to be far from the kingdom, and not to be far from union with Christ the King, mean the same thing. It is being almost ready to submit to the dominion of Christ by faith in Him, allegiance to Him, and fellowship with Him as our Lord and Master. In this sense the convicted scribe was near the kingdom by being near to accepting the King as his sovereign and his Saviour.

Nor do we understand that one sinner, unregenerate, has a better moral meritorious fitness for a state of grace and salvation than another. If a man by his convictions and attainments and external exemplariness of deportment, seems to reach the highest summit of preparation for the kingdom without actually entering into union with Christ, he is, notwithstanding, in the eye of God, as far distant from the grand result as the most notorious transgressor on earth, or the vilest reprobate in hell; for God seeth the end from the beginning, and without regard to the probabilities and uncertainties which may throng our judgment, foresees infallibly the final result.

That total depravity also which attends the sinner as long as he is unregenerate, though he seems to possess the loftiest attainments, forbids the idea that in unregeneracy he has more fitness in himself than another who is the vilest of the race. Every unregenerate man, considered in himself, whatever his attainments, is as far from the Kingdom as he possibly can be in this world, because in himself there can be no native moral fitness for it. The same Almighty sovereign grace necessary for the salvation of the worst, is necessary for the deliverance of the best of sinners ; nay, in the best of unconverted sinners, whatever their progress, there is a predominant principle of rebellion, which makes resistance to God and to His mercy continually up to the moment when the kingdom of God is formed within them : and should God desert them in the very height of their natural preparation, they would as certainly and as justly sink into ruin as the most abandoned profligate ; nay, observation and scripture testify that publicans and harlots often go into the kingdom before them.

Yet the convicted scribe was not far from the kingdom in the views which he had already attained, for they defined his position, while no attribute of his own moral character could do it. Our Saviour seemed to regard his exercises as a point of commencement in the line of progress which usually and happily terminates in conversion to God. Now, in all human probability and hope the Scribe whose inmost soul was moved by the truths of religion, and was likely to cherish his views, would not be abandoned till the principles of the Kingdom of God were implanted in his heart. Probability and hope, however, are terms that cannot be applied to the judgment of God, whose attributes exalt Him far beyond all uncertainty and doubt. Of what use then are hope and probability, which perhaps are only the flights of lawless fancy, or partial dreams of wild imagination? We answer, that these hopes and probabilities have some foundation on which to rest. There is the ground of facts on which we believe that certain unconverted sinners will be converted and saved rather than others. It is not mere fancy or conjecture without reason, from which we hope for the salvation of some sinners, while we justly fear that thousands of others will be left in ruin. Our Saviour would never patronize chimerical conjectures. His object could not have been to encourage extravagant vagaries, or wild visions of the brain. It is an awful truth that the best attainments, without regeneration, are uncertain in their issue; but it does not appear that it was His primary intention, in the case of this Scribe, to establish this point. On the contrary, His intention was to declare that, notwithstanding the possibility of such an issue in failure, still there were grounds to say that the attentive scribe was nearer than others to salvation.

II. The position of those to whom His language may be applied. These grounds I will now explore in proof of the proposition that the Scribe was, and all others now similarly exercised, are near to the Kingdom of God.

1. I refer you to the temper of his mind, and the attention which he consequently showed, and the convictions he received. As to his temper, whether it was entirely constitutional and grew out of his mental or animal organization, or whether it was the result of careful education, it was a great advantage. His habits of

thinking and feeling were such that it would not be wrong, as he thought, to converse awhile with the obscure prophet of Galilee. He had the prejudices of a Pharisee, to be sure; and, at first thought, believed the interview would be unedifying and unprofitable. But what harm was it to examine Him, and try Him on difficult and perplexing points of literature and theology? No matter whether He has the cloak of a philosopher, or the dress of a peasant, or used the inaccurate language of a Galilean; he would see what wisdom He possessed, and whether His knowledge be equal to His reputation for wisdom. See how this temper of mind contributed to fairness of interview; how his natural moderation, and humility, and candor, and thoughtfulness, and prudence, and generosity induced him to listen to what a reputed impostor had to say.

The point which the Scribe would discuss was involved in the question which he proposed—"What is the first grand elementary principle of virtue?" Our Saviour, doubtless, was pleased with the subject propounded, for it might be employed successfully as the weapon to cut up the pride of his Pharisaical heart. His object was soon attained. The Scribe was so affected by the wisdom which Christ displayed not only, but by the awful truth which was made by tone and look to bear heavily upon himself, that he earnestly and pathetically enlarged on the point which settles human character forever.

Let any man whose soul is honest think of the nature of moral law, that law whose essence is perfect love to God and man, of plenary and perpetual exaction; let him ponder on its reasonableness, its comprehensiveness, its spirituality, its intrinsic excellence, its unbounded benevolence, its innate authority; let him then look into his own heart, the subject of that law, and see the disaffection, opposition, and repugnance to it existing there; let him only compare what he is with what he ought to be; let him think of the everlasting result of the foul pollution and depravity of his sinful heart under the administration of that God, who would rather see the universe dissolved than His own most holy law dishonored and unsustained; then see whether his mind will not groan in secret, his conscience ache in its approval of that law and in self-condemnation; his heart quake, and his very soul melt within him. Ah, the Pharisee felt the point of the sword! Conviction stole into his heart which it seems he wished neither to conceal nor control.

I am glad to find that he is so interested in this law, that instead of abusing he praises it; eulogizing it though it condemns him. He repeats that law with an explanatory epithet. He enlarges on its excellence by exalting it far above all burnt offerings and sacrifices, and all this with apparent sensibility, earnestness and sincerity. Were not his eyes thus shown to be open to the awfulness of human guilt? Can a man, if he be thoroughly convinced of this and does not sin away the convictions of his own mind, forbear to inquire whether there be any hope for repentance, any ground for expectancy of pardon? Would he not inquire what means, if any, Heaven has devised for human relief from the unavoidable condemnation? Would he not ask the Prophet of Galilee what he must do to be saved? When assured that he was not far from the kingdom, would not this be an invitation to prosecute the subject, that he might know what was his remedy? Ah, poor Scribe! In this he failed. What could his literature do for him in the solution of this question? But if he understood the code of his own nation, in which so many intimations were given of a Messiah, the Shiloh, the Prince of Peace, and so many ordinances adumbrating the wonders of redemption, he probably retired to reflect, and was in a fair way to embrace the religion of the wonderful Teacher.

2. Though we have no certainty of this, there was hope in his case; because it was a favorable period of the world when this Scribe was overtaken by solemn impressions, and where he least expected them. The day which Father Abraham wished to see, which the old prophets foretold, but were not permitted to see, had at length arrived. The hour was come when all the rites of the ceremonial law which referred to Christ were to be done away by the sacrifice of Himself for the removal of sin. We who are accustomed to the new dispensation, cannot appreciate the views and feelings of Jewish inquirers, who looked for "the consolation of Israel" at the time of its introduction. No wonder that Simeon took the child Jesus in his arms and blessed God for the gift, and the daughter of Phanuel lisped the song of exultation, and thousands in Israel sung hosannas in the highest. Christ was a light to lighten the Gentiles and the glory of His people Israel. The meaning of innumerable prophecies relating to redemption was now discovered, and when the incarnate son of God was personally present, would He fail to enlighten every inquiring spirit? Would this Scribe, convinced of his ruin, laboring under sad apprehensions of the misery which the holy law would inflict, fail to look to that glorious light which the gospel message revealed? It is difficult to believe that so much light as the Sun of Righteousness afforded when He rose upon the world, should all be poured forth in vain upon the mind of this attentive hearer. There is such a suitableness in this religion,

that the convinced sinner must behold it; such a fullness, such a freeness, such a sublimity, that all may embrace it, and all must wonder and adore. O! can it be
that any disconsolate sinner, in the consciousness of his
wretchedness, shall fail to see and admire the only star
of hope that lightens up the moral midnight of the
soul?

3. We are at least encouraged to hope that the convinced sinner will prosecute all the means of grace in
his power. Is he allowed to peruse the sacred Scriptures,
to direct his feet to the house of worship, to hear truths
dispensed by messengers appointed to expound, and to
bow the knee in earnest supplication, the state of his
mind will constrain him to prosecute these means until
Divine consolation blesses him, or the total darkness of
despair overwhelms him. We know there is a possibility that by some means or other his attention may be
turned away from the most useful and consolatory
truths, yet there is a natural tendency in his mind to
employ instrumentalities for relief; even self-denial, inconvenience and dissuasion will be encountered in the
pursuit of comfort; and if so, will all his researches,
and efforts, and prayers be unavailing and unprofitable?
I allow, that before his regeneration he does not prosecute the means with perfect accuracy, or unimpeachable
motives, much less holy purposes. Indeed, as yet, controlling depravity and error hold dominion over his
heart. But I ask, shall not his feeble but anxious efforts
waken no compassion in his behalf? They shall. Not
because of the inherent worth of his observances, for he
is as destitute of holiness as ever; but God, rich in mercy and full of compassion, we believe, will bless them ;
because the means He uses, as to the matter of them,
are of His own appointment, and He never allows them

to be used in vain: because if these means may be prosecuted in vain, their utility is annihilated, and their suitableness for the end ordained is blotted out forever; because, if the efforts of the awakened anxious unregenerate be useless by reason of total depravity, neither can the best observances of the regenerate be sanctified on account of remaining corruption; since the acceptance of total or partial disobedience is equally incompatible with the infinite purity of God and His perfect law; and because Divine Sovereignty acts impartially as to the efforts of saint and sinner alike. It is wonderful sovereign mercy that accepts the imperfect but sincere prayers of the former; but the same mercy can with equal consistency bless the poor exertions of the latter. Hence the promise, "Seek, and ye shall find; knock, and it shall be opened to you." "If ye, being evil, know how to give good gifts unto your children, how much more will your Father in Heaven give the Holy Spirit to them that ask Him." O, then, if the troubled sinner only persevere in the earnest prosecution of the appointed means for relief, then there is a blessed hope in his case, that in consequence of a regard to the order of means and ends established in respect to this matter, he shall be brought near to the Kingdom of God.

4. I have one more ground of encouragement which makes me hope favorably in the sinner's behalf, whose efforts thus instrumentally bring him near the gate of the Heavenly Kingdom. I mean the agency of the Almighty Spirit. Means and efforts, aspirations and pursuits of methods are equally feeble and fruitless in themselves, for they have no native tendency to implant true religion in the soul, nor to bring it out of trouble. They seem to draw the sinner near, but they fail to secure his entrance into the kingdom. His moral charac-

ter must be revolutionized, but they cannot do it; within him a new principle must be established, but they cannot do it; love for God Christ and Divine things must be a fountain opened in his soul, but they cannot do it; What then can? Not the thunders or lightnings that played around Horeb's top, for the thousands of Israel who saw and heard were impressed, but soon projected the molten calf; not the luminous cloud that passed before the Israelites, under the light of which they perpetrated foul abominations; not the earthquake, nor the tempest, nor the fire that visited Elijah; not the miracles of Jesus and his Apostles, for many—after the sight of them—were left to wonder and perish in their astonishment. What, then, but Thy Almighty Spirit, blessed Jesus, can regenerate an apostate soul? If there be no such agency for this work, then let the sinner sport away his convictions, and give his sorrows to the winds, for they are foolish exercises; let the light of revelation be withdrawn, for its rays are cold and comfortless; let the means of grace be given up, for there is no grace reachable by them. But if the Divine Spirit be the agent whose office it is to accomplish the work, then let convictions deepen; let sorrow become bitter, let the light of revelation blaze; let the means of grace be earnestly pursued; for they are like the mysterious star that led the wise men to the babe of Bethlehem.

Consider the case of this Scribe not far from the Kingdom of God. How did he obtain that nearness? Surely by the influence of the Holy Spirit. Why did He interpose? If the law alone, which he admired, could induce reflection and conviction, why was he not convinced and mightily moved before? Was it not by reason of the Spirit pouring light upon the law, and adapting thereto His mental vision? Was it not the

Spirit arresting his attention that made him susceptible
to extraordinary emotion? For what had the Spirit be-
got this emotion at all, if He were not willing to bring
it to a glorious issue? I know that He often seems to
conduct by strong excitements the sinner to the very
gate of Heaven and suffers him to recede again into
apathy and indolence. Why He does so to one and abandons another, both having forfeited His influence, none
can say. "Not Gabriel asks the reason why, nor God
the reason gives." The Almighty, if seen by the attributes by which He makes Himself known to sinners,
means to be viewed as on the throne of Sovereignty.
The plan of His grace involves the bestowment of the
Spirit to regenerate and sanctify the penitent soul.
Now, in the case of those "not far from the kingdom,"
His willingness to carry on His work till they have completely entered, appears from the nature of his office
in the economy of grace. This work is "to convince
the world of sin, of righteousness and of judgment;"
to take of the things of Christ, and show them unto
us ; to teach us all things whatsoever He has commanded. Must there not then be a willingness, a disposition on His part to carry on every good work He
begins to the day of redemption? When He moved on
the face of the waters, was it not to reduce chaos to
order? When He smote Saul of Tarsus to the earth
blind and impotent, was it not to raise him on his feet
again, a chosen instrument for good? When He came
like a mighty rushing wind on the day of Pentecost,
was it not to make the whole assembly cry out in
despair; and in the hour of their conversion to give
them entrance into the Kingdom of Jesus? Thus thousands and millions have been brought near to the kingdom unaware of their hopeful state, and finally brought

in by the regenerating Spirit. Those then who sensibly have convictions and desires on the subjects of sin and salvation, are nearest to the kingdom.

How can we better improve this subject than to fix our thoughts on the use, the advantages, the hopeful prospects of those who, though consciously apart from Christ, are yet as consciously awakened to the importance of seeking a personal interest in Christ, whom they feel to be the repository of hope? You feel a respectful regard to the character of Christ. You listen with an ear of attention, and feel a profound solemnity. Your heart is moved to sensibility, to anxiety, to admiration, in view of a suffering Mediator, whose death was the crowning evidence of unspeakable love. Your conscience is impressed with a sense of guilt by the study of that law which is the foundation of Divine government through all the universe. You see that something must be done, or you are hopelessly doomed to unspeakable ruin. Now, I ask are not these exercises of your minds, through the blessing of the Spirit, the means of renovation? Have not those that are already renewed come to that happy state through just such exercises? And in proportion as these means are pursued, and these exercises enlarged, are you not at least approaching the beginnings of spiritual life? We know that without a new creating agency, all is useless; but is it not the mind of the Divine Spirit to work by such mental processes as we have been speaking of? How much nearer to Heaven are you when solemn and earnest attention is exerted, than those who are heedless of truth and reckless of danger? How many thousands are there who cannot give attention to the subject in hand for want of a religious education, and by reason of bad habits, carnal affections, worldly attractions, infidel sentiments, insensibility, stupidity, and a disposition to indulge in profane ridicule of sacred things? Such a state of heart and mind strengthens that moral inability, by which they cannot attend to any exercise of religion, because they dislike it, and spurn it, and give up their whole being to the world, that they may bury themselves in forgetfulness of God. O, how far are these from the Kingdom of Heaven! Without excitement of mind, heart and conscience, how shall they ever attain the renovation of their nature, or the salvation of their souls? Would it not be better to give way to fanaticism, and associate with enthusiasts in their howlings and phrensy, than be utterly stupid and as unfeeling as a stone? Nay, the worshiper of a stone or block, in his blindness, is in a more promising condition than the despiser of religion; for there is some hope that those whose sensibilities are aroused may find deliverance from their errors of judgment, and be brought into the right way. But what probability is there for any hope in their case who despise all religion, and love darkness, and hate light? God only knows how far it may be consistent for the Spirit to infuse the beginnings of holiness in the hearts of the honestly superstitious, but I cannot see how the Divine Spirit can work at all in any man that has no respect for Christianity in whose light he lives, and whose God is not in all his thoughts, though Divine mercy pour upon him the bounties of His love. On this ground of sheer indifference, I say, it is better for us to unite with those whose irregularities and errors are deplorable, if they are but earnest, honest, zealous promoters, as they may think, of the Redeemer's cause, than to remain in the ice-bound condition of the indifferent. Whatever fanaticism may mingle with any religious service, whatever groanings, vociferations or yellings may attend the so-called religious meetings of excited zealots, it is more hopeful than the stolidness of the groveling sinner who burrows in the earth and remains in the torpidity of indifference. Blessed be the Holy Spirit, and the holy gospel, if we find it in our hearts to respond to the call of mercy. Let it ever be in our remembrance that " the Kingdom of Heaven suffereth violence, and the violent take it by force;" and let this Divine utterance lead us to see that the blackest pall of despair may well rest upon the indifferent and unfeeling soul.

But observe what an awful fact is implied in our text. It is nothing short of this, that a man may be brought to the very gate of the kingdom, and yet fail of admission. He may be a man of prayer, of sensibility, of charity, of decorum and consistency of life ; he may be in the judgment of others as in his own, a true disciple of Christ, and yet may fail because his convictions have only been the sorrow of the world which worketh death; his attention has been the mere effect of natural curiosity, his charity the result of constitutional feeling, his faith only a temporary excitement, his prayers the utterances of formality. And though he be very near to the kingdom, after all he may be resting on some fatal falsehood which spoils all his pretentions to religious character in the sight of God. Do we not read these words of our Saviour which seem to settle this point : " Many will say to me in that day Lord, Lord, have we not prophesied in Thy name? and in Thy name have cast out devils ? and in Thy name done many wonderful works ? And then will I profess unto them, I never knew you : depart from me, ye that work iniquity." The Apostle seems to suggest the possibility to understand all mysteries, and all knowledge, to have faith competent to remove mountains, to bestow all our goods to feed the poor, and to give our bodies to be burned, and yet to be nothing better than sounding brass or a tinkling cymbal, because destitute of that love which the convicted scribe had contemplated in the law. O how obligatory then to examine our hearts during every step of the progress we make until we have within ourselves the indubitable witness of the Spirit that we are born of God ! O may it never be the calamity of any of us, after attaining nearness to the kingdom, that we should be driven away in our wickedness, having partially improved our opportunities, and proceeded just so far that our neglect of doctrine and duty, and our want of the principle of Divine love, shall ensure the dreadful fall from the very gate of heaven into the pit of remediless woe ! " It is impossible for those who were once enlightened and have tasted the good word of God, and the powers of the world to come, if they shall fall away, to renew them again unto repentance, seeing they crucify to themselves the Son of God afresh, and put him to an open shame." This refers to those who have known and understood the way of salvation, and having been moved thereby to make some effort to reach the kingdom of God, have gotten very near but have turned aside, and become hardened in impenitency and unbelief.

Surely the neglect of opportunities and privileges so infinitely precious and valuable as those we enjoy, must be the cause of guilt peculiarly aggravated in the sight of God. O ye, who have advanced thus far on the way to the kingdom, give no place to the feeling of discouragement, nor to the habit of remissness, nor to the influence of unmanly fears. Whatever be the embarrassments of a sinful nature, the temptations of an apostate world, the consciousness of imbecility, the snares of the devil, the distress of unbelief, or any other trial, at this point you must not dare to stop : at this point you may not hesitate without encountering greater peril than that arising from anything we have mentioned ; you must not deliberate or parley with the world ; you must not lower sails and drop anchor in order to quell on board the mutiny of your passions ; but forgetting all the past, press on to the prize ; for O, there is danger, danger appalling and peculiar, surrounding here a " halting between two opinions." You are nearing the dividing line, between the grounds of condemnation and justification. Beyond that, there is for you the inheritance of an eternal weight of glory ; on this side, the dreadful inheritance of wrath, tribulation and anguish." O consider this, and press on to lay hold upon the hope set before you, for if you fail of this, all other hopes end in everlasting despair.

Are not the joys of salvation worth a lifetime of struggle to reach them ? Having come to a point so critical, so replete with unspeakable consequences of an all-controlling influence on your everlasting state, remember what will be the result of continuance a little longer. Perhaps the impressions, convictions, and anxieties you have already experienced are just issuing into a state of regeneration. We know not at what period of experience the Spirit of God produces this essential change ; perhaps it is in infancy, when unconscious of any thing, an implanted new life may account for seriousness, thoughtfulness, susceptibility of religious impressions from your youth, in which case would it be wrong to yield an early obedience to the faith, an early profession of Christ? Perhaps it is in mature life, when your attention was first called to religious subjects. You know not what has befallen you, though your soul be tossed amid conflicting emotions; the principle of grace may be the actual source of all your sensibilities awakened to great anxiety, and of those aspirations that take the form of prayer; in which case, being already brought into the kingdom, what have you to do, but to follow Jesus in the requirements of the gospel, "adding to your faith, virtue; and to virtue, knowledge; and to knowledge, temperance; and to temperance, patience; and to patience, godliness; and to godliness, brotherly kindness; and to brotherly kindness, charity." These things abounding, "they make you that ye shall neither be barren nor unfruitful in the knowledge of our Lord Jesus Christ."

Now suppose it to be to you a matter of doubt and uncertainty, whether your soul be really converted unto God, will not the very uncertainty be a mighty thing to induce perseverance to the attainment of assurance of faith in this particular? Brought nigh unto the Kingdom of God by opportunities, by efforts, by various exercises of mind, is there not the strongest encouragement that success shall crown your efforts? Yes, there is ample encouragement in the case. It is true you may be as dependent as ever, as unholy and unworthy as ever; nay, though you may be near to the kingdom, you have this moment more guilt and iniquity to answer for than ever before. But why has gracious heaven led you thus far? What means it that you feel in your heart this abiding impression of guilt and unworthiness; why these admiring views of God and Christ, as obtained by an appreciation of the gospel remedy? Why all this various interest that occupies the mind, and seems so acceptable to contemplation? Is not the very highest encouragement to be found in this state of things? Let these exercises be wanting, would not the greatest discouragement arise from indifference and unconcern? Cherish then these feelings, cease not treading onward in your discouraging way, until your feet find a resting-place upon the Rock of Ages. If you must wade through mud and mire, do so; for these difficulties are in the way, and must be encountered and overcome until you reach that Rock of Salvation where a new song will be put in your mouth, even praises to God forevermore. And if some have cast away their privileges by reason of discouragement, and have turned again to the world and vanity, let their ruin be a warning to you never to yield to the tempter. Go on, if you would go up to enjoy the blessings of that kingdom from which you are not far; go on, if you would go in to see the King in His beauty, and become enraptured in endless bliss; and may the God of all grace grant you speedily to realize the consolation of that "faith which works by love and purifies the heart."

OLD AGE.

Ps. 91 : 14—16. "Because he hath set his love upon me, therefore will I deliver him : I will set him on high, because he hath known my name. He shall call upon me, and I will answer him : I will be with him in trouble ; I will deliver him, and honor him. With long life will I satisfy him, and show him my salvation."

The introduction of sin into the world was an event which was followed with the most deplorable consequences to the soul and body of man. Both felt the shock in the fall, shattering his mental and physical constitution. The penalty of death must exhaust itself, in the case of the subjects of salvation even, by bringing down the body to the imprisonment of the grave, and finally reducing it to a small handful of dust. Say what we will, this is a melancholy subject. The contemplation of it always takes away the pleasant smile, and sobers us down to a gravity of expression that marks the countenance of the reflecting with an unmistakable solemnity. Were there no other evil to depress the mind, or to fill it with dark images of melancholy, the thought of inevitable dissolution is enough ; for life is the consciousness of being and enjoyment, to part with which we cannot be reconciled without enduring a pang. This is indeed quite natural, for we live not only in and for ourselves, but in and for others, who are bone of our bone and flesh of our flesh, and with whom we are intertwined by the very laws of our existence. The sad fact of compulsory dissolution has been the cause of many a gloomy proverb found in every language of a dying race. Even those who have enjoyed the greatest light and alleviation upon this subject have expressed themselves after this manner: "Man cometh forth as a flower, and is soon cut down; he fleeth also as a shadow and continueth not." "Man dieth, and giveth up the ghost, and where is he?" "What is your life? it is a vapor that appeareth for a little time and then vanisheth away."

There is no use, however, in magnifying the evils of our condition. If death be the wages of sin, there is more than an offset to the calamity in the fact that "the gift of God is eternal life through Jesus Christ our Lord." We therefore must not contemplate the dark side of the picture alone, or often; for it is well for us that there is hope in our case, and that the mercy of our Heavenly Father is not clean gone forever. We may recover from our fall and see a glory which, without the fall and recovery, might never have been revealed. Life forevermore, is joy everlasting; and the chief business of this life should be continuous effort to secure that which is to come. There are three periods of our earthly existence commonly designated youth, middle-life, and old age if we are permitted to attain it. Each of them have their peculiar advantages. We propose now to consider the advantages of old age.

This period however is usually looked upon as deficient in enjoyment, and a synonym for depression and pain and trouble. While such may be true of an old age alienated from God, it is not true in regard to the Christian, no matter what may be the bodily infirmities incident to his last days; and in proof of this I adduce my text. Here it is clearly announced that old age is a blessing to him. "With long life will I satisfy him, and show him my salvation." The previous clauses of it designate the character of the man to whom the promise is made and fulfilled.

So far as the vigor of life is concerned, it would be folly to magnify these advantages above those of the periods of youth and of mid-life. Considered in the aggregate, the advantages of early life must be regarded as superior in reference to their bearing on our everlasting happiness. If we have the good fortune to have been educated under the tuition and example of godly parents, the advantage is beyond estimation. If in our youth we have lived under the influence of church privileges and gospel training, we may not contemplate our condition without gratitude, in our old age; nor spend that period without praise to the Author of our destiny. Pious youth promises for them that attain it, a happy old age; for it was in that early period of life that the seeds were sown which produce the luxuriant harvest. Then how easily is the tender mind affected by the sad consideration which a dying world inspires, how tenderly moved by the history of Redemption and the narrative of a Saviour's sufferings to recover the soul from its ruin ; how tenacious the memory of histories and doctrines and discussions which relate to the immaterial world ; how lively is the fancy in the contemplation of such glorious objects as Christianity discloses. What sweet sensibilities are excited in early life by the study of those wondrous things which the Bible unfolds to the mind of a child; how soon may wholesome impressions be cherished, and wholesome habits established, and a broad foundation laid for future consolation and comparative moral excellence. Generally the whole course of future action is under the direction of habits formed in early life. The foundation for improvement we lay in our youth, is solid and permanent for the support of the most magnificent superstructural character that can be reared among men. Hence the admonitions and promises found in the Book of God to encourage diligence in the education of youth. "Train up a child in the way he should go, and when he is old he will not depart from it." This rule like all others has its exceptions in the results of its application, but these do not invalidate the general fact of human experience as illustrative of the sure principle it announces. "They that seek me early shall find me." "Remember thy Creator in the days of thy youth." And how greatly was Timothy commended because he had known the Scriptures from his youth. Without the protecting influence of early religion, how dangerous is the season of childhood and youth, when exposed to the poisonous influence of an ungodly world! Born in corruption and sin, how soon do children develop their depravity, and evince the predominance of a vicious nature? How presumptuous do they become, in seeking exemption from control, and setting up infantile judgment against the experience of riper years!

Salutary impressions are more readily made in childhood, but it cannot be denied that then, too, they are more easily lost, and perhaps may give way to deeper ones made by bad example; for where example does not illustrate and enforce precept, the discrepancy is sure to be detected even by a child whose first efforts at obedience is made by *imitation*. Young fancy, as indiscreet as it is lively, is ever ready to plunge head-long into a thousand irregularities congenial with native pride and arrogance. Temptations in a thousand forms meet the young every hour, and a little importunity is sufficient to seduce them into the paths of licentious-ness and forbidden pleasure. Bad examples, under the forms of fashion and familiar customs, entice their unwary minds, fascinate their uncurbed imaginations, and draw them into the miseries which are entailed by vice. The memory is more tenacious, but is liable to be unhappily employed in collecting and retaining the doctrines of a mistaken philosophy, and the arguments of corrupt and licentious infidelity. Judgment may at first be unbiased, but even this may be a circumstance exceedingly unfavorable, as it often renders youth the more liable to the easy reception of injurious senti-ments ; for the lack of a pious education will expose the young mind to follow its natural inclination, since "foolishness is bound up in the heart of a child." Thus growing up, the young grow into fondness for self-indulgence, and, alas! too often become the victims of the world, the flesh, and the devil.

How happy are they who have escaped the snares so dangerous to the inexperienced young heart, and have maintained a virtuous character, and whose religious opinions, sound sentiments and good habits through middle life, have come to beautify and dignify the period of old age! Their long experience in the world has confirmed their principles, fortified their faith, and convinced them of the importance of that religion which has led them along in "the path of the just, which shineth more and more unto the perfect day." If men have no heart-felt religion, they have no rational hope, no permanent happiness. But if they have sought their

comfort in Divine truth, how much will age contribute
to the stability of their sentiments, to the strength of
their faith, to the assurance of hope, and the enjoyment
of God! All their knowledge, experience, and observation tend to the great issue of heavenly-mindedness,
when disgust with the wickedness of the world shall
prove that they are not of the world, but are
chosen out of the world, and are the children of
God. They cling with a tenacious grasp to the
Lord Jesus, convinced that He " is formed within them
the hope of glory." The adversities of life are thus
shown to have been for them " blessings in disguise,"
and they can well understand Paul's declaration: " We
glory in tribulations also, knowing that tribulation worketh patience; and patience, experience; and experience,
hope; and hope maketh not ashamed; because the love
of God is shed abroad in our hearts by the Holy Ghost,
which is given unto us."

All that they have observed in relation to others, only
tends to enlarge their views of the wisdom of Providence, having seen Divine justice in the infliction of
punishment, and Divine clemency in the preservation of
God's people. They have seen so many changes and
revolutions, so many unexpected disasters, and so many
interpositions of God's mercy and favor, that their aged
hearts have settled immovably and forever in confidence,
trust, reverence and calm assurance that all things shall
work for good to them that love God. Nay, their own
infirmity shall not prove an exception, but pleasure shall
mitigate pain, while the heart draws freely from the wells
of salvation.

Again, how much is it to the advantage of the aged
that their passions have subsided, and sound judgment
is no longer under their control. It is true that pas-

sions long cherished and continually indulged, are some-times in old age tenacious of their objects. The old miser is an example. The leading passion of a man, when made the subject of cultivation, hardly ever leaves him. If the passion has been love to God and Divine things, this is a great advantage; but if it has been fixed on sinful objects and pursuits, it is as great a calamity. But, apart from extreme cases, we say that it is a great advantage that the passions cool with the advance of age; and in general reason and judgment have a better chance for reaching sound conclusions. Religion does not eradicate our passions, but it regulates them ; and when we grow old under its precious influence, no longer shall avarice seek for riches, honors or renown; no longer shall ambition encourage and excite itself by hopes of worldly attainments; no longer shall sensuality go in quest of pleasures which gratify no more; no longer shall impatience torment itself by sudden disappointments so often realized in younger years; no longer shall impetuosity precipitate its victim into inconvenience and painful experience; no longer shall anger, wrath or malevolence distract the heart.

You see, then, that quietness and repose contribute a large stock of comfort to old age. While you were young such was not the case, for youth cannot be happy except in the excitement of enterprise. Such is its love of novelty, its acuteness of sensation, its hope, its ardor, its best enjoyment is active employment; but to the imbecility of age, quietness and repose, calm reflection and sober thought are its positive gratification. This enjoyment, says Paley, renders age a condition of comfort, especially when riding at its anchor after a busy or tempestuous life. Because each period of life has resources of its own for enjoyment, we deny that youth is more happy than age. To the intelligent and virtuous, age presents a scene of comparative enjoyment; and this springs from obedient appetite, well-regulated affections, maturity in knowledge, and confident expectation. In this serene and dignified state the pious old man reviews his life with the humble contentment of an approving conscience. Feeling the sustaining power of faith, there is to him "no condemnation," no "fearful looking for of judgment and fiery indignation;" but he "rejoices in hope of the glory of God." Christ to him becomes more precious every day, and every day he feeds upon the manna of God's words with a thankful heart. Is not this the best happiness to be enjoyed? What if there be pain endured in the taking down of the old tabernacle, this will only produce a greater willingness to let go our hold on a mortal existence, that we may be ushered into the unspeakable bliss of life eternal.

But another thought comes in here. Much of the bodily afflictions of the aged consist in penalties due to early violation of the laws of their being. If we would have the pleasure of existence perpetuated to old age, habits of temperance and self-denial must be formed and adhered to all through the previous periods of life. Moderation in every indulgence is not only becoming, but salutary at all times; but in advanced life especially is the benefit realized. The powers of nature may be so unduly stimulated by excess that at length they lose that attribute we call "recuperative," and therefore they cannot so well sustain the burden of years laid upon them; but when they have not been prematurely exhausted, the constitution will retain much of its resisting force at the very time when infirmities may be expected to multiply. Now we have reason to be thankful for the opportunity to husband our stock of constitutional strength, so that in the event of reaching an advanced age, we may have the privilege of protracted comfort as to our bodily health; and should we not reach it, yet there is the advantage of exemption from irregularities that dishonor our manhood and disgrace our character. Decrepitude, stupefaction, impatience, dullness, morbid peevishness, irritating fretfulness, complaining discontent, childishness, and a thousand other evils are warded off, by long established habits of temperance, cheerfulness, and self-discipline. Sometimes indeed old men whose habits have been inimical to health have lived long by reason of vigorous constitutions, resisting and keeping at bay the maladies to which intemperance and other irregularities have exposed them; but such exceptions are comparatively rare; and when they occur other peculiarities besides constitutional vigor often account for them. We speak however of the general fact established by long observation, as well as by medical science. The old age of a temperate life is particularly distinguished for the retention of mental strength, clearness of thought and perception, soundness of judgment, correctness of reasoning, and capability of prolonging the exercise. This is a source of happiness to the aged that makes life enjoyable even beyond the four-score years set down as the utmost limit upon which the best preserved may calculate.

Nor is it a discount from their happiness, that the aged are compelled to contemplate the approach of death. We speak now of the aged Christian only. Who among this race of sinners is so miserable, or more contemptible than he who has spent a long life in the service of sin, a rebel against God, and an enemy of Christ? Standing on the border of the grave, yet making no provision to meet other realities of eternity than the gnawing worm and the fire unquenchable, how can he be happy? He may be lethargic, he may be stupid, but stupidity is not happiness. The most useless burden on God's earth, he dies unlamented and is soon forgotten. The hoary head with its crown of righteousness, on the other hand, is an object of veneration; and as the aged pilgrim nears the end, necessity forces upon him the contemplation of death; but he has learned to regard it with composure. Impersonated as a frightful skeleton, apostrophized as an unrelenting enemy, death becomes to the mind an object of horror. The "old disciple" has outlived that superstition. To him death is not an object of fear, but a subject of consideration. While familiarity with it does not breed contempt, it serves to rob death of those terrors with which it has been surrounded by a guilty imagination. The aged Christian therefore does not consider it a hardship, but a privilege to die; not that he can be in love with all nature's abhorrence, but because it is the dark tunnel through which he must reach eternal life. And O, how short the passage! "To be absent from the body is to be present with the Lord." It is, indeed, a solemn thing to die. To the wicked it is an awful thing to die; but to the Christian it is a joyful thing to die, whatever sorrow may be entailed upon survivors. In view of the condition of the departed, there is no personal experience and no standard of comparison by which sensation may realize it. "We know not what we shall be, but we know that when Christ shall appear, we shall be like Him, for we shall see Him as He is." Death alone stands between the present and this glorious future, the magnificence of which emboldens the Christian to encounter "the King of Terrors" without flinching. Think you, then, that the aged are taken by surprise, or seized with alarm, if by their age they have been induced to apprehend the common fate of men? Think you that their expectation is altogether a melancholy one? Far from it. Their preparation is in mercy made easy by the gradual process of bodily decay.

It is true, this is not always the case. The old may forget; often they become inconsiderate; and even in old age weak faith produces fearful feeling. But, on that account, it is still more their advantage that their age reminds them of approaching death, that a thousand circumstances combine in compelling them to think of dying; that their ghastly looks, their feeble steps, their stooping frames, their blinded vision, their conscious weakness, their faltering speech, their painful movements, should remind them of the grave. This, we say, is their advantage. This was the prompting of the Psalmist's prayer, "Lord, make me to know mine end, that I may apply mine heart unto wisdom." O! these infirmities pertaining to old age are advantages of a thousand fold more worth than all the pleasures of the world. By them God is warning us day by day to be ready for the mighty change. They point to it with steady finger, they announce it with signs and symbols, they magnify its importance by the deeply-felt progress of decay; and, blessed be God, He has appointed these warnings that we may watch and pray, and at last, unsurprised and unalarmed, yield to the fate which closes man's account with time.

And let us not forget that it is an advantage to become thus familiar with the fact that death is near. O! how wrong it is to indulge those alarming notions we often form of death. True, it is the gate of misery to every impenitent soul; and God forbid that we should explain away, with reference to such, its intrinsic horrors. But have we become old, and yet have never pacified the frowns of death, nor conciliated his favor? By humiliation, by confession, by faith in committing our all to God alarms shall die first; nay, by meditation, prayer, and communion with death, he assumes to our vision the form of a messenger of peace and glad tidings, a sweet angel of mercy to pious waiting souls. Consider his errand. He comes to take down "the earthly house of this tabernacle," intimating to us that a new tenement is ready for our occupancy. He comes to take apart this mechanism which, having subserved its purpose, is worn out, disordered, and unfit for further use. He comes to emancipate the redeemed soul, longing for a higher, holier, happier state from clogs of animal corruption. He comes not to extinguish existence, but simply to change the form of it, elevating and confirming it in a blissful immortality. He comes, not as the executioner of the penalty originally denounced in Paradise—"In dying, thou shalt die," but with the penalty so satisfied by the atoning death of Christ, that while the spirit and letter of the law are fulfilled, only a certain form of death appears as a vehicle sent to take us to our brilliant and eternal home. Therefore, it is not death to die. "He that believeth in me," saith Christ, "though he die, yet shall he live again. Verily, I say unto you he that believeth in me shall never die." The dissolution of the body then, by the declaration of Christ, is not death to the believer; so far from this, when he is brought down by the shaft that extinguishes the life of the body, he can utter these as his last words: "O death, where is thy sting? O grave, where is thy victory?" Is it then an evil, think you, to approach the period when we are

to lay aside the cumbrous load of sin, the burdens of
old age, and surmount the ills of mortality, and enter
upon an existence which shall realize to us all we ever
have read of respecting Christ and the glories of His
salvation?

> " Why should we mourn departed friends,
>   Or shake at death's alarms ?
> 'Tis but the voice that Jesus sends,
>   To call us to His arms."

Sacred history will furnish us many examples of the
happiness of old age amid the most vivid anticipation
of approaching death. The patriarchs and early fathers
had for many years endured their trials, bowed down
with toils and afflictions. Abraham was old, but
happy, for he saw from afar Him that was promised,
and he rejoiced. Isaac, though old, seems to have been
happy, very comfortable, while he sighed for a little
venison, and declared that he knew not the day of his
death. Jacob could prophesy glorious things, and
speak in the sublimest language concerning his sons,
and especially concerning "The Lion of the tribe of
Judah," when he was upon the verge of the grave.
Job was doubtless happy after all his unexampled afflictions, for he had seen the abundant mercies of the Lord
poured out upon him in his last days, and could say
" I know that my Redeemer liveth, and that he shall
stand at the latter day upon the earth ; and though
after my skin worms destroy this body yet in my flesh
shall I see God." Why should we mention all the
thousands who in their last days had discoveries of
things future, which not only reconciled them to death,
but made happy in their old age, in anticipation of
glory unseen by mortal eyes. They died in the faith,

not having received the promises, but having seen them afar off, were persuaded of them, and embraced them, realizing that while here below, they were but strangers and pilgrims in the earth.

The belief of a happy immortality so consoling to old age, seems to be conformable to the sentiments of mankind everywhere, and in every age.

Heathen poets, sages and philosophers spake of it as an undoubted truth. Homer represents many of his dying heroes as anticipating immortality. Virgil considers Æneas as having conversed with the spirit of his deceased father. Socrates expected a reward in the immortal world, and Cicero in old age consoled himself in the belief that soon he should see Appian and Claudius, Cato and Cæsar in a better world. What was only a conjecture or a tradition that had come down from the earliest age, and rode like a spark unextinguishable upon the dark tide of heathenism, is ascertained to us an infallible truth by infallible revelation. The way of reaching all the joys it unfolds by a glorious redemption unknown to Socrates and Cicero, is so plainly made clear to our perception, and so affectingly made acceptable to our hearts, that old age exults in the prospect of the "rest that remaineth for the people of God." And when they consider the descriptive terms used to make it impressive, "A far more exceeding and eternal weight of glory," "A house not made with hands, eternal in the heavens," why should discontent annoy them, or what apology could they give for being unhappy which in its utterance would not be choked?

Another advantage to old age is that dissolution is attended with little violence or pain. Sometimes, indeed, dying youth have expired with comparative ease and exemption from distress, and sometimes the aged have departed with paroxysms of agony ; but exceptions to general rules prove nothing against them. Ordinarily the loss of life in youth is occasioned by violent attacks of disease, terrible maladies that seem necessary to relax their strong hold on life ; and O how lamentable to hear their piteous moans and outcries, showing what severity is necessary to end their battle for life. Deeply penetrated with pain, the strong constitution will not yield until worn out with suffering ; but in old age we may hope for exemption from all this. Our frames are too weak to need a mighty shock for dissolution. Comparatively a breath of air blows us away. One little obstacle is enough to stop the wheels of life, already retarded in their motion. The strong young oak, having attained its size, is a monarch in the wood, braving storm and tempest. Nothing can bring him down but iron edged with steel, whose numerous strokes swung by muscular strength, must be repeated until the trunk is severed from the root ; but the tree of old age, decayed in every part, falls before a little breeze whirling through its withered branches. So the aged servant of God calmly falls into his grave. The language of inspiration is strikingly appropriate. "Thou shalt come to the grave in a full age, like as a shock of corn cometh in his season." Its leaves are withered, its roots decayed, its juices dried up ; and burdened with its precious fruit, it yields it all for food to man and beast, and then seeks its dissolution in the earth. So without violence or pain or tumult, the good old man leaves his fruits for the benefit of others, and quietly pillows his head to fall asleep in Jesus.

"Hail ! welcome tide of life where no tumultuous billows roll,
  How wondrous to myself appears this heavenly calm of soul;
  The wearied bird, blown o'er the deep, would sooner leave the
    shore,
  Than I would cross the gulf again that time has brought me
    o'er."

Finally. Having a thousand advantages attending us in the latter period of life, what responsibilities rest on the aged believer ? We expect nothing of the aged unbeliever. He is an object of pity, existing only to draw the tears and excite the pains of sympathy ; a warning ; a beacon ; a monument of the wrath of God; living and dying accursed. O how dreadful the fate of the old impenitent sinner, who has criminally linked in with it that of many others dragged down to perdition by his ungodly influence and accursed example. But this is a picture upon which we may not dwell. Let the aged believer, like the withered corn, yet standing, display his fruit matured by the Sun of Righteousness, and the early and the latter rains of refreshing grace. Let him not think that in old age he is irresponsible or useless. His example still speaks, his counsels are still regarded, his influence is still powerful. His gratitude should be unbounded, for divine grace has enabled him to make the most of the present and the future. He has lived to a good purpose, and he shall die for a good end. His comfort is now all borrowed from the future, to enable him to enjoy the present. His progress to the grave is easy, and why should it not be, since he realizes the fulfillment of the promise, " Even to your old age, I am he ; and even to hoar hairs will I carry you."

O, may youth be benefited and instructed by the pious examples of aged veterans in divine service.

May their uncertain lives be preserved that they may realize the advantages of a long life spent in that service, and in their turn as veterans exemplify the power of faith, bringing forth abundant fruit ; and may they in old age be living proofs of the faithfulness of God to the promise recorded in our text : " Because he hath set his love upon me, therefore will I deliver him. I will set him on high, because he hath known my name. He shall call upon me, and I will answer him. With long life will I satisfy him and show him my salvation."

RECEPTION OF CHRIST DEFECTIVE.

The place spoken of is probably Nazareth, where Christ had been brought up and lived during His minority in obedience to His parents. But when He entered upon His public ministry, because the people there had been familiar with the family of Joseph, His *reputed* father, they all the more readily rejected His claims. He performed some of His miracles there, and there taught the doctrines of grace; but no matter what evidences were unfolded in proof of His mission, it seems the intimate knowledge which the townsmen of Nazareth thought they possessed respecting Jesus led them to violence against Him; for on one occasion, when he taught by historical illustration the doctrine of Divine Sovereignty, "they were filled with wrath, and rose up and thrust Him out of the city, and led Him unto the brow of the hill whereon their city was built, that they might cast Him down headlong. But He, passing through the midst of them, went His way." We see therefore the reason for the declaration of the text, " He did not many mighty works there, because of their unbelief."

There are still circumstances in the world strongly impelling men thus to reject Christ. Long familiarity with truth resisted is often followed by malice against the truth itself, and in view of this amazing fact, well may it still be said by our Redeemer, "Blessed is he who is not offended in Me."

Not only then, when John the Baptist testified concerning Him and declared that no one comparatively received his testimony, but even now, when such multitudes have professedly embraced Him, there is something so defective in our reception of Him that there is great room for solicitude and inquiry ; I mean it is a question whether our exercises by which we professedly lay hold on "Christ and Him crucified" are appropriate and sufficient. It is possible for us to feel in some measure the truth of Christianity, *as a whole*, and so receive it; and at the same time fail of a personal interest therein by a misapplication of its benefits. We fear there are still but few who receive this testimony as they ought. And not many mighty works of conversion are done among us, *because of our unbelief*. This unreasonable thing is simply the rejection of testimony.

I. The reason stated in the text, that Christ "did not many mighty works there" was because of their rejection of Him, and of the ample testimony which His works bore to His claims. This reason substantially is true at this day, why conversion is a work the occurrence of which is comparatively rare, in consequence of men's rejection, or very inadequate reception, of the testimony respecting "Christ and Him crucified," that is, respecting the *atonement* as the only ground of a sinner's hope.

The testimony referred to is the gospel of Christ, containing the doctrines of salvation, and the expositions and injunctions of Christianity with all its awful sanctions, its overwhelming truths, and its tremendous delineation of rewards and punishments. The gospel is Christ's own account of the holy character and the inflexible justice and consuming wrath of God against our sinful race, salvation from which is the "glad tidings of great joy." This gospel embraces His own exposition of human misery resulting from total depravity, and the revelation of Himself, as the Saviour, whose atoning blood procures the remission of sin; His delineation of true virtue and piety, consisting in love to God, and love to all men, leading us to be good and to do good, by the impulse of a new life infused into the soul by regeneration; His self-denying injunctions requiring us to feel and acknowledge our depravity, to renounce our self-righteousness, to confide solely in the grace and righteousness He bestows, to resist our emotions of pride and anger, lust and ambition, to wrestle against sin and temptation of every form, to pursue prayerfully the narrow path of Christian obedience, to abandon the world and the things of the world as recipients of our love and energy, to endure adversity with a becoming submission to the allotments of Providence, and to confide implicitly in the promises, the plan and the provisions made for comfort, hope and peace.

The way by which Christ's testimony to His own gospel must be received is the exercise of faith, which consists in knowledge, assent, and embrace, thus commanding the co-operation of the intelligence, will and affections appropriating the thing believed as our own for the food of thought, for the growth of the soul upon the new principle of life imparted by the Spirit, and for the attainment of all the excellencies of the Christian character. We cannot comprehend the gospel until we understand the reason of it and the matter of it, as a thing essential to our deliverance from the condemnation of law; we cannot assent to the gospel until we become willing to be and to do all it requires for our deliverance; we cannot embrace the gospel until the feeling of love for its author becomes a controlling principle within us. Then the three-fold power of the soul must unite in the business of appropriating it to our spiritual want, just as the appetite for food uses it for bodily necessities of health and happiness. Thus the testimony of Jesus becomes the foundation of our precious hopes, and the fountain of our consolation.

It is not a very easy thing to receive this testimony in all its fullness, when we come to consider the requirements and humiliating import of the gospel; for it strips the moralist bare of everything which he naturally regards as the adornments of his personal character, as well as the wretch whose polluted garb of vice has made his very existence an offence. There is nothing in the testimony of Christ to flatter our views, to foster our carnality, to buoy the pride of our sentiments and opinions. It is not pleasant to admit that we are so ruined and undone, that our plea for justice from God could only be answered by eternal damnation; that we must be content to hang on Divine Sovereignty for favor unmerited, and that our escape from the misery of outer darkness will be a miracle of grace. It is not so easy to place our pleasures, our sins, our favorite objects of worldly cupidity, our besetting vices, and all our preconceived opinions upon the altar of " burnt offering " and swear allegiance to the law of Christ. And even when we feel somewhat the sweet energy of the Saviour's doctrine, how soon does the taste of it become faint by commingling it with something else ! Well might He say, in view of these things: "Strive to enter in at the strait gate, for many shall strive to enter in, and shall not be able."

In some respects indeed, "the offence of the cross" has ceased. Christianity has outwardly assumed a more acceptable form. Differently from the disciples do we contemplate the Saviour in His glory upon His Father's throne. We have seen the spread of the gospel, and the ameliorating influence it exerts wherever it goes, showing its own profitableness for this world, as well as for the next. We have imagined the church now as brilliant as the morning, as radiant as the sun in his strength; but we fear that while Christianity is becoming popular, and the profession of it fashionable and valuable chiefly as the supplement of respectability, the reception of Christ as required by the gospel is largely defective.

II. Let us particularly discuss this point—the reception of Christ defective. We refer particularly to feebleness of conviction, a want of submission, a partial surrender, a want of regard, an unwillingness to be known as Christians publicly recognizing Christ as our Lord and Master.

1. Is there not a failure in our faith with reference to that conviction of its paramount importance which it certainly implies ? I speak not of the unbelief of the Atheist who speculatively denies the Creator; nor of

the infidelity of the Deist who, while he acknowledges the Maker, hesitates not to blaspheme the doctrines of the cross; nor of the stupidity of the Jew who, while looking for the Messiah, cannot perceive any of all His characteristics in the Nazarene; nor of the credulity of non-professors who, while they admit the truths of the gospel, do not submit to them; but I refer to that kind of *mis*belief of many professing Christians, who hold their faith more as barren sentiment than as a living power within them. Are not our convictions too superficial, our impressions too fleeting, our affections too languid, our sensibilities too dull to be identified with the living energy of an emotional faith leading us to look at things eternal with constancy of gaze and fervor of desire that make heavenly-mindedness a daily habit? Perhaps some have founded their faith on hearsay evidence, some on educational bias, some on the influence of great names: perhaps we have not for ourselves examined the evidence of Christ's testimony, nor felt its forceful power on the heart and conscience; perhaps the question of Christianity has never been examined with much anxiety, nor consideration as to its dread import. In the meantime we may have yielded to the bias which the example or advice of others has produced. Surely, this is not for the confirmation of a reliable faith. O! every man should examine Christianity for himself, and with a view to his own salvation, as though he were the only sinner in the world. Our faith ought to have this for its foundation, as a sure and solid exercise. Let a heartfelt conviction of the truth be gained by a sober search for the testimony. Let the agency of the Spirit be sought to sink the weight of that testimony into the depths of conviction. This will enable us to give a reason for the hope within us and for the comfort and joy of our souls.

2. Possibly there is not only the want of an adequate conviction, but a want of complete submission in our faith to the doctrines of Christ. Every one who duly receives His testimony receives Himself as the only infallible Teacher of his soul. Shall we then modify and interpret His doctrines to suit ourselves, or shall we receive His own words in their obvious import as the matter of our faith? They are too holy to suit the carnal heart, too lofty to be tried by the purblind reason. To interpret them according to the standard of human inclination or desire, is to discard them as the touchstone of truth—an inconsistency too gross to be indulged in by any Christian. Yet sinners have been heard to say, should the Bible inculcate certain doctrines which they hate, they never could receive them as divine. Is not this setting up the standard of blind human reason as the infallible judge of what ought to be the truth? Can such persons cherish the Scriptures as the charter of their hopes? We do not say that every deviation from true doctrine consigns the errorist to ruin; but we say, if the indulgence of heresy involves contempt of the Bible testimony concerning Jesus as a Saviour, it is fatal to the soul. Indeed every error is dangerous in any degree in which it is in conflict with the word of Christ. We reject Christianity entirely if we raise exceptions to any of its doctrines. The whole of it, or none of it, is the inspiration of the Spirit. And we may not shield ourselves by the idea that errors may be innocently cherished since we are responsible for the integrity of our faith.

Generally there is iniquity at the root of all heresies.   If we embrace them, it is because we love them; and we love them because they excuse our sins, palliate our fears, and flatter false hopes.   No; we are not permitted to believe as we please.   We are as much responsible for our errors as for our sins.   Both proceed from principles and dispositions which corrupt the soul. We are as much obliged to give up vain thoughts that bewilder us, as vile vices that corrupt us.   The object of Christianity is to eradicate both.   Indeed, there is often such an intimate connection between opinions and practice, that they must share in the same approval, or partake of the same condemnation.   Most of the errors that have agitated churches and misled individuals have intimate connection with Christian practice and experience.   They often obstruct our progress in the path of duty, and hinder our advancement in the growth of grace.   How reasonable is it then to say : "Whithersoever the light of Revelation leads, thither will I go, however reason may remonstrate, or carnal nature gainsay."   The doctrines of Christ, as a whole, must entirely be the guide of our thoughts on the subject of religion, or we reject His testimony.   We must be careful that every high thought and proud imagination and loose opinion be subjected to the obedience of the gospel.   The servants of Christ dishonor Him by any reluctance to receive the whole of His truth, for it all belongs to the one great system of evangelical faith.

3. But if we cherish no material error in our notions, how often does our notional faith fail to secure the perfect surrender of the heart, which seems to be an essential act of the living principle.   If we receive Christ at all, we must receive Him as our Lord and Master in everything.   We should put our all under His control,

by a willing subjection of our all to His disposal, because we should prefer His wisdom to our own. However grievous our allotments, we should rather desire that His will, and not our own, should be done. Surely there is a willingness, a prevailing desire in the pious, that He should decide respecting them in His sovereign wisdom, without preference for their own carnal wishes; yes, a desire that their dearest sins should be sacrificed to His honor in a cordial submission to His purposes and precepts. Yet such is the faultiness, the guiltiness of our faith, that we dishonor our Lord by a very feeble, partial, reluctant submission. When we try to reform our habits, we are sensible of pain; if we propose to abandon our errors, our hearts are mortified; if we are solicited to yield our possessions and goods for the sake of His cause and at His command, we grumble, and shrewdly calculate how little we may give, and yet not forfeit our character for liberality. In part only do we seem to acquiesce in His claims, in part only are we obedient to His counsels, in part only do we consent to surrender to His authority. Now, what does all this mean but a defective reception of Christ? What does it amount to but a partial rejection of Him? Do you not see that opposition to one part of His code involves the principle of rebellion against the whole? With reference to the gospel no less than to the law may it be said, Whoso keepeth not the whole, but offendeth in one point, is guilty of all. What is demanded is a generous voluntary faith, a willing obedience, and an entire surrender of our hearts to God. Although it be true that failures and imperfections are not inconsistent with piety, yet where piety dwells there will be the principle of surrender, a beginning which is capable of glorious improvements; and until we reach the perfection of faith and entire submission to God, we dishonor the gospel. The testimony of Christ should ever be, in our estimation, the strongest and most compacted mass of historical and moral evidence that exists in the world, since there is nothing like it in the world's annals for clearness, variety, accumulation, perfection, naturalness, supernaturalness, and progressive enlargement with the lapse of time. There is, therefore, no excuse for our failure in utmost reliance of heart, and total surrender of will.

4. Our faith in this testimony comes short, unless it have the control of our affections in exciting them to honor Christ with supreme regard. The natural effect of it all, is to draw out of our hearts all the love of which we are capable. He who laid down His life to deliver us from eternal woe and bless us with eternal happiness, did not say too much when He said: " Whoso loveth father or mother more than me is not worthy of me; whoso loveth son or daughter more than me, is not worthy of me;" because there is nothing in these relationships that can compare with the wonderful union which the redeemed soul holds with the Author of its salvation.

We do not say that we have no love at all for Him unless we always feel it to be supreme, and are always conscious of a stronger tendency in our affection for Him than for any other object; for, as we are imperfect and mutable creatures, there will be conditions of our affections variable as the clouds; but we mean that our love for Christ is in its nature and essence a supreme love, capable of such improvements as will make it like an anchor to a buoy floating upon the tide, and so efficacious as to outrun every other tendency of inclination. But see what inferiority characterizes our regard for Christ. He does not, He ought not to tolerate a rival in our affections, or allow of compromise with any competitor. He is not only the greatest and best of beings, but the greatest and best of benefactors. Everything valuable to us in the continuance of our existence we have only in Him. If then He be regarded according to His own perfections, our love of adoration for Him should be supreme. If He be regarded according to our own interests in life temporal and eternal, our love of delight in Him should be supreme. But if He be permitted only to share the throne of our affections, if we love with an equal degree the idols to which He is opposed, if our thoughts cling to Him less lovingly and less tenderly than they do to worldly things, if the duties of religion are placed in a corner of our regard, or thrust aside to make room for the wider play of earthly attachments, what construction can this conduct bear but that of a guilty rejection of the testimony of the Lord Jesus, as proving Him "the chief among ten thousand," the compassionate Saviour of the world? O, what an insult to His memory, what an offence to His matchless love! What Christian can bear to think of it? Who of all His professed followers will be content to endure the disgrace? We all need to be humiliated into self-contempt when we think of our deficiencies in this matter. Let us hasten to correct our cruel fault, and pull down every rival for our love, whose wretched claims we may hitherto have been inclined to respect.

5. There is a great faultiness in our faith when it fails to recognize Him *publicly*, boldly, freely before the world. Many claim to believe in, to love, and to

hope in Christ, who at the same time refuse to express it as He requires. But does not the fact of his requiring a public profession of His name show that a reluctance to comply with His will, is a proof of the spuriousness of all such pretences? Do we ever act thus with our common friendships, preferences, or partialities? Are we not sure to make them known to the world? Do not the necessities of our position in life require that they should be known? Is it not then perfectly fair and reasonable, that Christ should still proclaim by the ministry of His word: "Whosoever shall confess me before men, him will I confess also before my Father which is in heaven. But whosoever denieth me before men, him will I also deny before my Father which is in heaven"? This duty is placed in a clear light by the Apostle with regard to our salvation: "If thou shalt confess with thy mouth the Lord Jesus, and shalt believe in thine heart that God raised him from the dead, thou shalt be saved. For with the heart man believeth unto righteousness, and with the mouth confession is made unto salvation." To both *joined together* is the promise of salvation attached, and no matter what we may say about confession saving nobody, there is the record, so plain that it requires an effort to misunderstand it. Our Lord has constituted our condition on earth a social one. We are united by a thousand ties of affection and interest. Intercommunion is the necessity of men in all relations of society.

Now this social position is advantageous to the progress of piety and the glory of Christ. Each one has an opportunity of promoting his Master's interest, by making the influence he possesses exert a bearing on His cause. This is doubtless one reason why a public profession of our faith, a public recognition of Christ is required ; nay, emphatically demanded, as necessary to His recognition of us before God. This profession is not one formal act in order to visible church-membership, but it is a continuous habit by which we are daily made known to the world as His disciples. But how many thousands fail to make a declaration of their faith boldly before the world? I refer not now to those who neglect membership in the Church of Christ, for as far as their hearts correspond with their practice, they seem to deny the Lord that bought them, and by their guilty omission are hazarding all upon an opinion in conflict with His decision. But I refer to a thousand others who *exist* in full communion with the Church, but *live* in full communion with the world. They have opportunities of saying something, devising something, doing something to aid the cause of Christ and His Church ; but if censures are to be incurred, if interests are to be imperiled, if popularity must be lost by embracing these opportunities, they choose to let them go by ; they will either shout "Hosanna to the Son of David," or join in the cry for crucifixion, according to the company they may be in, or the circumstances surrounding them. This is a melancholy fact, and calls for particular notice. How often have we failed to honor Christ before the multitude? How often have we shrunk from introducing a topic by which the Saviour might be honored? How often have we heard in silence the blasphemy of sinners? How often have we failed to vindicate the name of Jesus, when reviled and abused ; to speak when the Sabbath of the Lord was desecrated, to express abhorrence when the Holy Bible was insulted, and the name of the Lord Jesus profanely dishonored by the ungodly and the profligate? Do such omissions prove the loyalty of our love? Do they speak well for our fidelity? Is this failure to act, all the same as to act out faith in the testimony of Jesus? Do we not, for the time being, reject Him every moment when we do not adhere to our duty whenever it calls for our testimony in His behalf?

By our profession we say, "the love of Christ constraineth us." But when we fail to speak a word for Him that on a favorable opportunity might be spoken, and so conduce to the recovery of a soul dead in sin, which tells the truth, the profession or the failure? If we are the salt of the earth, why have we not diffused our savor? If we are a city set on a hill, why are we so inconspicuous? If we are lights of the world, why shine so dimly? If we have received the testimony of Jesus, why does not our faith gain victories over the world? Who of all our acquaintances take knowledge from our lives that we have been with Jesus? Other professors expected more from us, and we have disheartened them; worldlings expected more from us, and we have hardened them; the Master requires more from us, and we have robbed Him of His due.

For our own sakes, let us inquire how far the recognition of Christ before the world is an essential work of our faith, and whether our omissions in this respect do not declare its defective character. It is true, we may err in another extreme. We may place all our religion in public duty, public usefulness, public demonstrations of zeal, public vociferations in the praise of Christ, while the heart is unconscious of that humble penitence, brokenness of spirit, and loving lowly faith, by which privately our religion is purified from its dross; but ought not the inward acknowledgment of the soul prompt us to an open public recognition of Christ every day before the world, so that men shall know what we are, without being told?   Let it never be supposed that we have fully received Christ, if our reception of Him never impels us to seek His glory in the world.   Indifference to His cause and honor is quite enough to make the world believe that all our profession is a sham. Should we not ever avoid being the occasion of such an impression?   Believing with all our hearts, should be followed by acting with all our might in the way of Christian privilege and duty.   How can it be otherwise if we so believe?   What can we desire but that His attractions may draw all men unto Him ?   What should engross our zeal more than the prosperity of His Church ?   Thus is the reception of Christ connected in our hearts with a loving zealous regard to the interests of His Church.   And if it be otherwise, what do we mean when we sing :

> " For her my tears shall fall,
> For her my prayers ascend,
> To her my cares and toils be given
> Till toils and cares shall end."

Ah, the question needs no reply.   Such language attuned to any melody by the voice of a lukewarm professor, is the utterance of insult to God.

In the conclusion of our subject, we can say nothing more for the manifestation of its importance ; but we have something to say with regard to our own agency and responsibility.

Let sinners think of the pain of that disappointment we shall experience, if at last we should discover the sad mistake, that instead of having received the testimony of Jesus, we were despisers and rejecters of His person. Can there be a greater sin on earth? Provision is made by Him for all other sins, but who shall make an atonement for this? Let sinners remember that in the rejection of the gospel they put the greatest possible indignity upon Christ, for it is the rejection of a system in the device of which divine wisdom, equity love and mercy are conspicuous; a system extraordinary in its nature, and contrived for an extraordinary purpose; a system involving humiliation and shame, agony and death to the Son of God, that they might be delivered from hell, and taken to heaven; a system therefore requiring authentication by the most extraordinary evidence of miracle and prophecy with all other available testimony, so full and convincing, that none might be unfortunately mistaken in their reliance upon it. It is thus proved to be the only system adapted to recover them from their guilty and fallen state.

What, then, if after all, we should be found wanting in the matter of our reception of Christ? O, what imprecations are those which the self-deceived and the self-ruined in the world of woe heap upon themselves, when from the ease of self-indulgence and indifference, they wake up amid the torments of remorse! Should we not be cautious, lest hope itself indiscreetly and unwarrantably indulged, precipitate us more awfully into the condition of the almost saved, but finally lost?

And let Christians remember that when we reflect upon its contrivance, nothing short of omniscience can account for it; when we think of its comprehensiveness, nothing but omnipotence could make it so capable of universal adaptation to human woes; and when we see the method of its personal application throughout the world, nothing but omnipresence can explain it. O, what a precious hope is that which we build upon this foundation? It affords us a consolation unequalled by all the proffered comforts in the world, and a power of sustentation that bears up the soul on eagle's wings above the foul exhalations of this polluted earth. What would the poorest of God's people take in exchange for the privileges and the prospects it affords them? Human life is not to be thought of, when persecution demands the surrender of one or the other. Let the fires of martyrdom explain the priceless value that millions have put upon it, when "they counted their lives not dear to them" for its sake.

How interesting is the spirit of that Christian who receives the gospel, and the Saviour of whom it testifies, with unquestioning confidence. His faith is a living thing, a moving power of an inward spring never losing its elasticity. He receives the Christian doctrine with an understanding heart, in all its extent, no matter what difficulties he may encounter. He makes, not only willingly but thankfully, a total surrender of all he has to his Lord and Master, who is the supreme object of interest within the exercise of his affections, and it is his greatest regret that he can do no more.

O, what a sad thought that we ourselves, who are indebted to Christ for all our present comfort and our hopes, have dishonored Him before the world; that we have countenanced despisers in the contempt of Him; that we have shown any indifference to the glory of His name; that we have betrayed an ignoble shame in the espousal of His cause, afraid to encounter the stupid jeers of a scoffing world. And O, how admirable that spirit which serenely endures anything for the sake of Christ! How we stand with awe before the names of the martyrs of Jesus! O, such a faith as theirs shall receive an honorable reward, and they whom it has actuated shall be crowned with the greater glory when the angels of God shall point them out by saying: "These are they which came out of great tribulation, and have washed their robes, and made them white in the blood of the Lamb."

Wherefore, amid all our opportunities by the preaching of the gospel, let us endeavor to become enlightened, enlarged and confirmed in our faith. By what means can we more suitably honor, receive, appreciate, and profit by the testimony of Jesus? No longer let us insult His veracity by a faith so feeble faint and superficial. No longer let us revile the system of grace by a faith so inanimate, by ingratitude so ignoble. If our faith be suitable to the thing believed, it will be all-controlling: if it be weak, let it be nourished, strengthened and made more comprehensive by the prayerful study of divine truth; and thus shall we be led, in the spirit of obedience, to know of the doctrine and to rejoice in the liberty of the sons of God. This faith removes in part the veil that intercepts our views of the heavenly inheritance. It is true "We see through a glass darkly," yet we see enough to cheer us onward in our blessed path, which "shines more and more unto the perfect day." Faith on Christ is the soul's resting on an everlasting rock. It is "the substance of things hoped for, the evidence of things not seen." Believing, we rejoice in hope of the glory of God; and we have the divine testimony that this hope "maketh not ashamed."

Now, is it not true, that "He does not many mighty works here because of *our* unbelief?" Were we more united in our common faith—I mean, more earnest in unitedly expressing it before the world, would it not be followed by a more marked presence of the Holy Spirit? Them that honor God, He will honor; but if we dishonor Him in this matter, can we expect that He will do many mighty works of regenerating grace among us? Let us therefore repent of our inadequate reception of the testimony of Jesus, for this is failure in faith. Let us consider the infinite importance of the subjects of our faith, and the infinite reliableness of the testimony by which they are commended to our hearts, since upon this will depend the bestowment of the Spirit for the conversion of souls. God grant us that increase of faith we so much need, and then the mighty works we so much desire to see in the recovery of lost sinners to the enjoyment and comfort of His salvation, shall cause us to exult in the Divine remembrance of our low estate. O Lord, send prosperity, and glorify thine own name. Amen.

THE SECULAR AND POLITICAL REIGN OF CHRIST.

Luke 1 : 33. "HE SHALL REIGN OVER THE HOUSE OF JACOB FOREVER, AND OF HIS KINGDOM THERE SHALL BE NO END."

ALL who acknowledge Jesus Christ as their Master are ready to concede that He has a kingdom in the world. They receive him as the founder of an empire in which His subjects are intimately associated, instructed, and ruled, and trained for everlasting happiness. His religion was intended to be a social religion, uniting His people in the closest harmony, interest and co-operation. They form a combination of men, who are members of the body of Christ; living stones of one spiritual temple, edifying one another in the faith; and brethren of one holy spiritual family.

It is wrong to view Christianity merely as a revelation of certain truths to be believed, and certain general moral precepts to be obeyed. It is not a mere system of doctrine and rules, to be embraced by every one for individual interest, irrespective of the interests of others ; but it is a social system, binding every believer in the most sacred ties of amity to all his brethren, and consolidating the whole brotherhood into a most precious union with their Lord and Master.

As man is a social being whose propensities incline

him to associate with his fellows in all the common relations of life, so in the Kingdom of Christ, there is among its subjects holy communion of one with another. As the consolations of every day are derived from mutual sympathy and kindness, so Christ has ordained a bond of connection securing to His followers the love and help of their brethren, that the whole body may be thus edified together. As seclusion from all the endearments of social intercourse would be a most uncomfortable privation, if not an intolerable doom, our Lord and Master has appointed for us a social career which relieves us from such wretchedness and supplies to us sympathy and endearments of the most valuable kind, to smooth our passage through this woeful world, and sweeten the happiness of our everlasting state. This system of combination, securing to us these excellent provisions, we denominate the Kingdom of Jesus Christ. And while this view of the subject relates to ecclesiastical administration mainly, I think we do not do justice to it unless we take into this view the political form and visible operations of it in the world. We should therefore consider the Kingdom of Christ in a more enlarged sense as suggested by the text, and look at it as embracing the whole sovereignty of Christ. Its *comprehensiveness* is my theme, as yet to embrace spiritual, political and ecclesiastical forms in one civil administration over the world. In order to establish this view, we shall

1. Present two general observations as preliminary to the argument to be subsequently adduced:

1. That we are apt to narrow down our understanding of the Scriptures to the measure of some precon-

ceived opinion transmitted as the basis of an hereditary faith, is obviously true. Hence, because it is said in John 18: 37, "My kingdom is not of this world;" and in Luke 17: 20, "The kingdom of God cometh not with observation:" "The kingdom of God is within you;" many have inferred that it has nothing to do with secular governments, and will never interfere with political organizations; that there will always be distinct political and ecclesiastical administrations, co-ordinate but separate and independent; or two co-ordinate governments, an *imperium in imperio*. This would suit the spirit of certain men who seem to be afraid of any union in any particular between Church and State. Others there are, who are indignant at the idea, that when Christ shall rule upon the earth, all nations will be put under subjection to the Bible, as the standard of law, morals and popular virtue, by which human society must be governed, and all the interests of men regulated. They imagine that if there be but one government over the earth, and that kingdom be a theocracy, men would lose all their political rights, and all their dear-bought liberties, and be placed under a religious despotism, of all things the most intolerable: and therefore rejecting every other, they would defend the strict construction of the words: " My kingdom is not of this world." But this passage, I contend, does not mean that there will always be a political government among men, independent of the Mediator's Kingdom. It only signifies that the Empire of Christ does not derive its constitution or principles or maxims from the world. It never will authorize slavery, persecution, war, nor tyranny, as secular governments now do. It is a kingdom in the world, over the world, through the world; but it has not the spirit of this world. It was not formed after this world, or by this world, or under the influence of this world; otherwise his servants would fight, and persecute and tyrannize. Notwithstanding all this, it embraces the earth and was intended to absorb all other governments, secular, political, ecclesiastical, monarchial, republican, or whatever you please to call them. I mean their present forms will all be abolished and everything authoritative embraced within the holy government of Jesus Christ over mankind.

2. There are various forms, dispensations, and modifications, under which Christ's government has been already exercised in the world. Let it be first observed that the "Son of God" had the royal appointment from everlasting. He holds it by delegation from His Eternal Father. In "the counsel of peace between them both," it was ordained that in consequence of His Mediatorial humiliation as a sacrifice for sinners, He should be Ruler of the world, as far at least as the work of redemption should require it. Therefore He said to His disciples: "I appoint unto you a kingdom, as my Father hath appointed unto me." This was a matter of early revelation. Thus in Ps. 2 : 6, God says : "I have set my king upon my holy hill of Zion." 8th v. : "I shall give thee the heathen for thine inheritance, and the uttermost parts of the earth for thy possession. Thou shalt break them with a rod of iron; thou shalt dash them in pieces, like a potter's vessel." Is. 9: 6, 7 : "His name shall be called Wonderful, Counsellor, The Mighty God, The Everlasting Father, The Prince of Peace. Of the increase of His government and peace there shall be no end, upon the throne

of David, and upon his kingdom, to order it, and to establish it with judgment and with justice from henceforth even forever."   And in the later revelation, it is most distinctly declared : "God hath highly exalted him and given him a name which is above every name; that at the name of Jesus every knee should bow of those in Heaven, and things in earth, and things under the earth."   Christ said for the encouragement of His chosen witnesses : "All power is given unto me in heaven and in earth."   Thus from the beginning He was the *official* Governor of the whole world.   Though all mankind have not submitted to His sway, nor been subdued by His power, He is the rightful Proprietor, Ruler and Potentate of the whole world.

He intimated His right and designs at an early period when He declared, that "the seed of the woman should bruise the serpent's head;" when he appeared to Abraham on the plains of Sodom; when He constituted Moses His lawgiver, and chose Israel for His inheritance; when He redeemed Israel by power and signs, and mighty wonders; when in a fiery cloud he passed before the Hebrews in the wilderness; when He exercised temporal and spiritual sovereignty over the thousands of Israel; when He anointed Saul and David and Solomon and others as captains over His inheritance; when He ordained the whole ritual of Temple service, with all the oblations and sacrifices and incense, and whatever appertained to the Aaronic priesthood.

As King over all the earth, he inflicted punishments on the nations that persecuted His inheritance, as the Medes, Persians, Assyrians; the Canaanites, the Greeks and Romans.   He made them feel the power of His anger.

When He became incarnate, He commissioned His servants to preach, "the Kingdom of Heaven is at hand." When He was tried before Pilate, He acknowledged Himself a king. The learned Jews had been instructed by their religion to expect Him as Messiah, the Anointed King. The tradition had gone abroad into the pagan world, so that Herod and all Jerusalem not only had been moved, but heathen philosophers inquired: "Where is He that is called King of the Jews, for we have seen His star in the East, and have come to worship Him." Poets had learned to sing of His power :

> " Around thy cradle pageant flowers shall spring,
> And the old serpent lose his fatal sting ;
> Go, then, of race Divine, God's high-born Son,
> Now is the time to wear thy immortal crown.
> From us this day a glorious infant springs,
> Fated to rule the race—a King of kings."

His sufferings and crucifixion, His death and resurrection, His splendid ascension to heaven, to which He was escorted by thousands of angels, were but intended to procure that exalted throne on which He is yet to rule His vast domain. For a while His splendor was eclipsed, because He was not only a King, but a priest upon His throne. Hitherto His dominion has been but partial, as it is His plan by slow gradations and improvements to beautify His empire. Slow have His movements been, that the nations of the earth might learn their wretchedness and misery without the presence of their King; but enough has been done to convince us all that he is the official, the legitimate Monarch over all the world; and that in due time He will arise and assert His exclusive jurisdiction and proclaim Himself the Universal Sovereign of all the earth.

II. This political comprehensiveness involves the idea that all human governments, all carnal establishments, all imperfect institutions are to yield to His control. His kingdom will be civil and political, as well as spiritual.

1. The Scriptures represent His kingdom as *one and indivisible*, to the exclusion of all human institutions. This is plain from numerous prophecies. Zechariah, for example, says: "And the Lord shall be King over all the earth ; in that day shall there be one Lord." Nor are we left in doubt as to the nature of His coming, for in the previous context it is said : "His feet shall stand in that day upon the Mount of Olives, which is before Jerusalem, on the east." (Zech. 14: 4.) Timothy is thus exhorted : "Keep this commandment without spot, unrebukable, until the *appearing* of our Lord Jesus Christ, which, *in His times* He shall show, who is the blessed and only Potentate, the King of kings and Lord of lords." Not only so, but the nature and locality of the kingdom is clearly pointed out by Dan. 7: 27—"And the kingdom and dominion and the greatness of the kingdom under the whole heaven, shall be given to the people of the saints of the Most High, whose kingdom is an everlasting kingdom, and all dominions shall serve and obey Him." Many other passages might be quoted to show that no earthly kingdom shall be permitted to interfere with Messiah's reign, when He comes in the splendor of His power.

The inference we draw from this is, that all the kingdoms of this world must undergo such revolutions and changes, as shall give room for the Code of the Prince of Peace ; that His kingdom will at once supply all the enactments which shall be needed—ecclesiastical, political and spiritual ; that His empire, when fully established, shall comprise everything necessary to control us in the way to heaven, and at the same time regulate the social interests, peace, liberty and protection of men in all the world. Messiah's constitution will be so far ecclesiastical, as to provide for every interest in the Church; so far political, as to regulate human conduct in relation to society; and so far spiritual, as to advance the progress of men in holiness and happiness. Nor will there be more than one constitution or government, because there will be no need of divisions or separate classifications, for all these, as they now are, shall be blended into one, and under the same constitution. Church and State, religion and politics, the spiritual and civil code, shall be comprehended in the same organization which shall extend its benefits and obligations to all mankind.

2. In proof that all the departments of government throughout the world may be comprehended under one Empire, and that that empire will provide for all political and ecclesiastical regulations, we refer you to the commonwealth of ancient Israel. That government was a theocracy. God Himself originated and established it. We must refer your attention to it, because it contains a type, a figure, a general outline of Messiah's empire in the world. Was there ever a wiser or a better government? It was excellent as to their kings and judges, who were elected by the people, and afterwards divinely anointed, enlightened and qualified for duty; excellent, as a number of Prophets were Divinely anointed and endowed, who with the Levites everywhere instructed the people; excellent, as a company of priests were selected and commissioned to superintend the sacrifices and oblations, and all religious wor-

ship, that thus the whole nation might constantly be reminded of their interest in the atonement of Christ. The cities of refuge, to which the man-slayer might flee for justice was a most excellent institution to prevent murder, to protect the innocent, and to punish the guilty. The laws in relation to idolatry, slavery, marriage, jubilee, the day of atonement, and a thousand other things of importance in a good government, were all conceived with consummate wisdom, and promoted the spirit of brotherly love, and ensured security and peace.

In some cases the Jewish law referred to matters which may appear to us diminutive and insignificant, yet the results were exceedingly important. The very garments of the priests were prescribed by law. None might boil an animal in its mother's milk, slay the dam with her young, or muzzle the mouth of the laboring ox, or wear a garment not pertaining to the sex, or sow his field with a mixture of seeds, or plow with an ox and an ass yoked together, or treat a stranger unkindly, or force a slave to return to his master, or put out his money on usury to a brother. The object of all these regulations and enactments was to cultivate kindness, decency, compassion, decorum, benevolence, patriotism, and so make universal manners a means of universal social happiness.

O, when our Saviour shall come in the power of His Kingdom, what benevolence and wisdom and care and interest will He discover in all His institutions, statutes, and usages, by which He shall bind together every branch of His Kingdom, as the tribes of Israel were bound in cords of amity and peace! Then there will be a revolution in the governments of the nations. How many laws must be erased from their statute-books as irrelevant, inappropriate, useless and injurious! There was one commonwealth on earth, Divinely appointed, from which politicians in every age have received instructions; one commonwealth, which teaches us how happy is that people whose God is the Lord; one Theocracy, teaching us how careful the Messiah will be to abolish all useless legislation, and make all nations happy, when He comes to establish His blissful reign, with one wise, benevolent, comprehensive and religious constitution applicable and to be applied in all its particular provisions to the wants of our race.

3. The nature of the case seems to imply that all other governments must be merged into Messiah's universal empire. His dominion, of course, will be the most wise, benevolent and perfect the world ever saw. Shall it be introduced on earth, and must not all the imperfect and useless and hurtful legislation of human beings be abolished forever? Will He who is Supreme Monarch of the universe endure a rival legislator? Has He purchased His empire, and shall He not rule it without competition, opposition, or molestation from created power? Shall He not prevent all interference and collision between His own dominion and the governments that are founded in usurpation and fraud, ignorance and tyranny? How can He be supreme in the administration of affairs except He overturn the empires of the world or remodel them into conformity with His benignant spirit? If He choose, He can in a moment reduce the nations to willing and absolute obedience. If this be not His pleasure, He can destroy every rival dominion by an army of His chosen people, or by angels, or reduce them to a forced submission. All the world

in arms could not withstand the breath of His mouth. At any rate, He will in His own way place all the nations of the earth under a universal code of salutary laws, bestow the spirit of His grace on every upright subject, and put an end to the confusion and misery which distract the nations who know not how to govern themselves. "Be wise, therefore, O ye kings, be instructed, ye judges of the earth. Kiss the Son, lest He be angry, and ye perish from the way, when His wrath is kindled but a little."

4. What favors the idea still further that all secular human governments shall cease, and the dominion of Christ be a political as well as a spiritual empire, is the fact that His exclusive jurisdiction will best promote the true spirit of freedom, secure the precious liberties of mankind, and establish the peace and prosperity of the world. He alone can do it.

Now, there is great jealousy among the advocates of freedom, who dread, above all others, a spiritual despotism. There is a fear lest when Church and State be united, the hope of freedom will be blasted forever. The evils of the accursed Inquisition are dreaded, the exaction of tithes and taxes which oppress the people and strip them of the necessaries and comforts of life are dreaded; and that one denomination should be dominant over all others, monopolizing the patronage of government, and binding all citizens, on pain of death, to adopt a faith which they cannot receive, forcing them to forms of worship which they cannot relish, and demanding their money in support of an establishment they cannot approve. This fear is natural, since the sorrows of the Christian portion of the world have largely flown from this union of a corrupt church with a corrupt government. But no such consequences are to be apprehended from the reign of Messiah. Just the contrary will be sure to follow, and the happy period is anticipated with joy and gladness; for when the petition shall be answered, "Thy kingdom come," then shall also the correlative one be fulfilled, "Thy will be done in earth, as it is in Heaven." Rational liberty will be firmly established in every region; not, indeed, that liberty which implies a right to rebel and disorganize and destroy, not that licentiousness which contravenes law and order, and is an enemy to the best interests of society; but such liberty will be guaranteed as will permit a man to enjoy the fruit of all his labors, the possession of all his estate, and the freedom of worshiping God according to his conscience thoroughly enlightened by the instructions of the Prince of Peace.

Errors in judgment will then be corrected by the Lord's prophets, prejudices removed by kind exhortation, and the hearts of men will all be touched by the gentle persuasions of the Spirit of Grace. All shall be endowed with a teachable disposition, and all so taught of the Lord, as to love, approve and relish the Divine administration. A thousand subordinate governors, enlightened or inspired by Christ, may be the ministers of His blessed will. Many "saviors shall come up on Mount Zion—and the kingdom shall be the Lord's." Obad. 21. Why may not the people themselves, being enlightened by the Spirit to discern the requirements of duty, be invested with the elective franchise in the choice of their own governors, heads of thousands, of hundreds, of fifties, of tens, whom the Prince will especially qualify for office? Surely, in the Republic of Israel, which was the commonwealth of Heaven, a theocracy over which the Almighty Himself presided, there was the elective franchise; and the people themselves elevated to office and authority kings and princes, whom God anointed with the spirit of grace and wisdom?   What though the officers in Christ's dominion be denominated kings or princes, presidents or governors, emperors or judges, prime ministers or chancellors, if they be anointed by God, and thus qualified to rule, and worthy of all confidence?   What though we be bound by the strictest spiritual laws for the prevention of disorder, for the establishment of harmony, and the hindrance of social trouble?   What, if any should remain disobedient or rebellious, and they should experience the certain infliction of punishment, what reason will there be for complaint?   The rights of all will be regarded, and all things will be ordered and done for the promotion of universal prosperity and happiness.   Thousands, no doubt, in the present day would rather choose a government in which no obligations should bind them, no penalty restrain them, no punishment exasperate them; but such a government would be no government at all; instead, it would be a state of anarchy worse than despotism; a state of the world emblematic of the misery of hell.

Ah! let not wicked men suppose that they are now exempt from Messiah's jurisdiction.   They may imagine that if they obey externally the laws of their country, no more is required; that as to religious duty, it belongs to their choice either to obey or disobey; that they are no further responsible than obedience to human law requires.   They are mistaken, and the mistake is a dreadful one, because it leads to terrible consequences.   This moment they are under the dominion of Bible law, under the obligation of allegiance to Messiah, who has an all-controlling power in Heaven and earth.   They are under moral and evangelical obligation as much and as strongly as they ever can or shall be. Why, then, should they aim at greater privileges and greater exemption from the sovereign control of the Messiah? What are the secular laws of our country compared with His laws of universal adaptation to the moral, spiritual and social well-being of man? Human laws are changeable, sometimes injurious, oftener inefficient, the sport of wickedness. Every dominant faction in succession approves or condemns, modifies or repeals, according to its humor; but Messiah's laws are invariable, unrepealable, because infinitely just, authoritative and beneficent. In the millennial day they shall be delightfully obeyed, and insure peace and comfort in every portion of His empire. No; let none imagine that freedom in that day will consist in exemption from law. The glory of that day will be the universal prevalence of an obedient spirit bowing in joyful submission to His laws and in loving homage to the King of kings. Let no one imagine that when secular governments established by men have come to an end, there will be no authority to bind society; for Jesus Christ Himself will be the Supreme Governor, who will take all secular power into His own hands, and by His spirit create in the hearts of all men subordination, in the allotments of all men prosperity, in the social interests of all men happiness and peace.

5. Jesus Christ has already by His word introduced a secular code for the government of His empire. In that word we find His laws for civil government intermingled with those which regulate our moral and spiritual duties. He has ordained institutions and ordinances which in their proper observance shall fit us for citizenship in His Kingdom, and has prescribed political laws, which in their proper observance, shall make us better

subjects than human legislation can produce among the masses of any government on earth. He has promulged them in advance, to show us what shall be the nature of His Kingdom under an administration that shall bring all men under the sweet control of love to God and man, so that nothing shall hurt or destroy. In short, the moral law shall regulate civil and social rights. Is it not this which now underlies all human legislation relating to all sorts of crimes? Are we not already bound by this wonderful code, whose spirit is the civilizing element that elevates, improves, and advances every Christianized community? He has permitted human governments to carry out these laws in their own way, but the supreme authority is in His own hands. Men cannot administer them any farther than the regulation of outward human conduct is concerned. "The powers that be" are ordained of God to rule in His stead until the appointed time of His appearing. Their ministry, at the best, can only be partial, feeble, inconstant, inconsistent, and attended with confusion; but when He shall assume the control of the world, it will be the control of human hearts as well as human hands. His right is already established. He owns this world and the fullness thereof; and for all its present mismanagement, corrupt politicians shall be held to a strict account. Kings and princes, who reign by His indulgence, are at His disposal. He puts down one and sets up another, at His pleasure, for all circumstances and combinations of them are in His own hands. At last He will dethrone the rulers of the world of every kind, and establish a new dispensation, elevating to secular authority under Himself kings who shall be nursing fathers, and queens who shall be nursing mothers to His people.

6. His present spiritual reign, whereby he controls by

a sanctifying influence all His people, is introductory to the full establishment of His secular kingdom "under the whole heaven." The triumphs of the gospel, wherever it has gone, the barriers, now broken down, which have hitherto hindered its progress, the revolutions and commotions of empires and states, ending favorably to its publication to all people, are full of encouragement to the long indulged expectations that the whole earth shall soon be covered with the glory of His empire. Never before have such openings been made for the entrance of the gospel into the pagan world, and never before have such opportunities been afforded in Providence for the activity of the Church in her missionary work. Therefore, while the princes of the earth are tolerated for a while longer, let them be careful how they stretch forth their hands against the arm of the mighty Prince of Peace. They have not the supreme control; Messiah has not abandoned His rights. He asserts His own authority, and will infallibly show His power to maintain it.

7. Nor will Prince Messiah stop to assert His claims till He personally return to our earth in a glorious manifestation of His power, opening the dawn of the millennial day. We expect, indeed, that the usurpations of " the god of this world " will be sustained as long as the principalities of hell can resist. We expect that wars and devastations shall yet for awhile continue, and perhaps become more widely destructive, as this dispensation draws to its close; for the devil will rage with greater fury, knowing that his time is short : but christians will combine for resistance, and the conflict will be sharp and deadly, when at last He shall come and blow upon His enemies, and they shall be scattered like leaves in a whirlwind. Whether the manifestation of

Christ shall be personal and visible, or by an overpowering operation of His Spirit, we need not determine. The language of prophecy, however, is very strong.

"Thus saith the Lord God: Behold, I will take the children of Israel from among the heathen, whither they be gone, and will gather them on every side, and bring them into their own land; and I will make them one nation in the land upon the mountains of Israel; and one king shall be king to them all; and they shall no more be two nations, neither shall they be divided into two kingdoms any more at all. And David, my servant, shall be king over them; and they all shall have one shepherd; they shall also walk in my judgments, and observe my statutes, and do them. And they shall dwell in the land that I have given unto Jacob, my servant, wherein your fathers have dwelt; and they shall dwell therein, even they and their children, and their children's children forever; and my servant David shall be their prince forever. Moreover, I will make a covenant of peace with them: it shall be an everlasting covenant with them; and I will place them, and will multiply them, and will set my sanctuary in the midst of them forevermore. My tabernacle also shall be with them; yea, I will be their God; and they shall be my people. And the heathen shall know that I, the Lord, do sanctify Israel, when my sanctuary shall be in the midst of them forevermore." Ezek. 37: 21-28. "Behold, the day of the Lord cometh, and thy spoil shall be divided in the midst of thee. For I will gather all nations against Jerusalem to battle. Then shall the Lord go forth and fight against those nations, as when He fought in the day of battle. And his feet shall stand in that day upon the Mount of Olives, which is before Jerusalem, on the east. And the Lord my God shall come and all the saints with thee. And the Lord shall be king over all the earth. In that day shall there be one Lord, and His name one." Zech. 14. "And I saw thrones, and they sat upon them, and judgment was given unto them; and they lived, and reigned with Christ a thousand years. But the rest of the dead lived not again until the thousand years were finished. This is the first resurrection."

Though it may be difficult for us to interpret these passages upon any other principle than that of a personal manifestation, yet we do not hesitate to say that a spiritual coming by the sanctifying, overpowering operations of Messiah's grace is the most valuable, most advantageous, most to be desired. The spiritual purification of our world seems most necessary to make it the dwelling-place of the enthroned Messiah. It is enough for us to know that when He mounts His throne to exercise His spiritual and temporal sovereignty, the new Jerusalem comes down from Heaven prepared as a bride adorned for her husband. The walls of the city shall be garnished with all manner of precious stones, jasper, sapphire, chalcedony, emerald, sardonyx, sardius, chrysolite, beryl, topaz, chrysoprasus, jacinth, amethyst. There shall be no more death, nor sorrow, nor crying, nor pain. Jesus shall reign with His risen Saints on earth. The glorious company of the Prophets, the goodly number of the Apostles, the noble army of the martyrs, these shall be the Prime Ministers of His Kingdom; these shall be governors in the various provinces of it throughout the redeemed earth. For a thousand years shall they reign. "And the kingdom and dominion, and the greatness of the kingdom under the whole heaven, shall be given to the people of the saints of the Most High, whose kingdom is an everlasting kingdom, and all dominions shall serve and obey him."   With Him shall they reign after the first resurrection.   His Kingdom, thus established, shall be so perfected, purified and adorned, that it shall contain in itself all that is most beautiful and attractive, all that is most holy and glorious.   "Come," saith the Spirit to John in Patmos, "I will show thee the bride, the Lamb's wife;" and O, what transporting visions were opened to him!   "Behold, the tabernacle of God is with men."   Earth, once defiled and cursed, becomes the theatre of beauty and righteousness.   The Son of God dwells with men, and He is their God and their King.

All things are now in preparation for this grand event, for a period of glory and honor and immortality under the benignant reign of Prince Messiah, whose theocratic rule shall bless all the earth.   Every revolving year brings us nearer to the glorious era.   "The time is at hand."   Oh what an event in the history of earth! "The earnest expectation of the creature waiteth for the manifestation of the Son of God," but when the first resurrection takes place, this expectation shall be realized.   Then all the saints shall have risen from the dead; the wicked, banished from the earth, shall be sent to their doom, and the Kingdom of Christ shall rise to the zenith of its glory!   O God! how solemn, how sublime, how transporting the scene thus spread out before us!   "Blessed is he that hath part in the first resurrection."   "He which testifieth these things saith, Surely, I come quickly."   And let us unite with the enraptured apostle in saying, "Even so, come, Lord Jesus."